the
ghost box

FERREL D. MOORE

White Cat Publications, LLC.
2013

The Ghost Box is published by White Cat Publications, LLC.

Text is copyright © 2013 Ferrel D. Moore

Cover art copyright © 2012 Karen Koehler
http://www.khkoehler.com
Cover and Interior Design by
Stephen James Price
www.BookLooksDesign.com

Edited by Charles P. Zaglanis

ISBN: 978-0-9846920-6-4

Published by White Cat Publications, LLC.
33080 Industrial Road, Suite 101
Livonia, MI 48150
www.whitecatpublications.com

Acknowledgments
&
Dedications

The Ghost Box could not have been written without the hard work and patience of my editor, Charles P. Zaglanis. It would not have been written without the guidance and support of William Jones, who is the finest teacher a writer could have.

I dedicate it with love to my mother, my daughter Kate and my son James, my brother Thom and his wife Joyce, my niece Audra, my nephew Jason and to the wonderful, mysterious woman who has inspired me throughout the years.

Finally, I offer a special dedication to Nancy, whose tireless reading, editing and support for my writing gave her a special place in my heart forever.

Chapter One

They reached the bridge just before midnight.

Three vans, one truck pulling the RV and the twenty-six-foot long moving van. Their headlights tunneled through the heavy night air as the sky flared with heat lightning and rumbled like a Harley.

"You're sure it can hold our weight?" Ashley asked.

"Absolutely," Michael said. "But slow up and I'll check it out. Been a lot of rain lately and the water must be high. I can't tell from here. Don't want to get stuck at the bottom of this hill trying to find out. I've waited too long for this."

"Maybe we should call it off."

"No way. We can still do this. We can't let a little rain stop us."

When he had that look on his face, she knew nothing would stop him. She loved that look when they first met, but tonight, with the sky dark and tumbling with angry clouds, she hated it, too. The whole night was taking a turn for the worse.

"I'm serious, Michael. What if the bridge breaks? And you guys have got all this electrical equipment, what if we get hit by lightning? Maybe tonight's just not the right night. I've had a bad feeling about this ever since we got that letter from your Granny."

"She's just a superstitious old woman, Ashley. I love her, but she grew up in the hollers."

"The what?"

"The hills of Appalachia. I didn't even know she could write. Now I've got to get moving before it starts raining again."

Just like that. Anytime she brought up his family, he cut her off. It was the only thing he didn't discuss. The topic that had nearly ended their marriage only one week into their honeymoon.

"Do the others know?"

She meant the rest of the team. They were in the lead van, the rest of their nine-person crew spread out through the remaining vehicles.

"We don't have time for this now. We have to get moving," Michael said. "Aw shit. Too late—here it comes."

The surrounding woods lit in jagged white light as a fireworks display of spidery lightning zigzagged across the sky. Raindrops slapped the windshield seconds later and the roof made a sound like a slow drum roll. Ashley nervously twisted a loose strand of hair.

"This weather is all screwed up," she said. "It's October, for God's sake."

Michael flicked on the overhead light and rummaged behind his seat

4

for his raincoat. The van was packed full of "what ifs." Raincoats, flashlight, food bars and a case of energy drinks.

"Don't start with the global warming stuff, will you?" he said. "It's just Michigan weather."

She tried to backhand him, but he covered the side of his face.

"Knew it was coming," he said.

"Get out there and check that bridge. I'm not drowning before I write a bestseller."

He kissed her quickly on the cheek and hopped out into the rain. A second later he opened the door again and said, "Throw me the flashlight, will you?"

She was ready for him and tossed it. He caught it mid-air and vanished into the storm, slamming the door behind him. Three months since the wedding and they knew each other like they'd been married forever. Except he almost broke it off when she started poking around in his family history. Which is why she didn't even know he had a Granny Maudine until the letter arrived. Written in pencil, no return address.

Child, leave the dead be.

That was all it said.

Rain pelted the van roof so hard she almost didn't hear her cell phone ring. She was too focused on Michael's light circling and bobbing in the dark like a wobbly spotlight. They were maybe a hundred feet from the bridge, but even on high speed the wipers couldn't slap away the raindrops quick enough. She caught a glimpse of him slipping on the muddy ground. Twin rivulets of rain water flowed around his feet and disappeared into the dark beyond the headlights.

"Be careful," she yelled.

She flipped the headlights to bright which made it still harder to see. She swore and turned them back to normal. Another glimpse of him slipping and sliding in the wet mud and then he hit the ground hard.

Get up, get up, get up, she thought.

A flash of light in the tangled woods to her left and a startling crack as lightning exploded a tree. She covered her face and ducked instinctively. When she lifted her arm to see if he was on his feet again, he was already gone.

Michael was ten years older, but he sometimes acted ten years younger. He was the businessman, she was the writer. He should have been methodical, careful and predictable, but since the day they met, she'd been the careful one. Michael didn't know the meaning of the word careful. To Ashley, he was the most interesting man in the world. He had the three "R's" going for him—rich, reckless and really good looking.

Her cell phone rang again. She flipped it open, said, "Not now, damn it," and quickly snapped it shut.

She didn't want to think of Michael getting hurt. He was the best part of her life, even if he did spend his spare time looking for ghosts and researching life after death. What kind of businessman did that? But it was part of what made him so damned interesting.

Five minutes passed. Ten minutes.

Where was he? What if he slipped and slid all the way down to the river? Why didn't he ever think things through before he acted?

The phone rang again. She picked it up and flipped it open while craning her head from side to side to catch a glimpse of Michael.

"What is it?" she said irritably.

"Don't bite my head off," Shari said. "I'm calling to make sure you two are okay. Way this rain is coming down, if we don't get moving we're going to be on a mudslide headed straight into the river, and I don't know how to swim."

"Michael is outside."

"For God's sake, why?"

"He went down to make sure the bridge was safe. He knows what he's doing."

But Ashley was beginning to wonder.

"Calm down, calm down. Larry says it's too dangerous to stay, honey. We need to go back."

Like that settled it. Like what Larry said settled anything.
"I'm not moving until Michael gets back." Ashley didn't care what Larry said. Michael was the one financing this show.

"Can you see him? Wait … Larry wants to talk to you."

Before she could tell Shari *no*, Larry was on the phone.

"How long's he been gone?" he said in his scuffed-leather voice.

"Too long." She checked her watch. "It's been over ten minutes. I'm worried about him. Too dark and too much rain to see anything."

"Bill and I are going out to get him. We've got to move off this hill soon or we're all going to be in trouble."

Ashley bristled. Larry wanted to be in charge. Larry always wanted to be in charge. But this whole thing was Michael's idea and he was the one in charge.

"I'm going with you."

"You stay in the car in case we miss him. We're on our way."

Jackass. But maybe, for once, he was right.

"Take a rope, Larry, and run it down from the bumper so you can get back up."

"Good idea. Bye."

Ashley clicked the headlights between high and low again, but still couldn't see anything but rain. Water sluiced down the windshield like they were in for forty days and forty nights. She jumped when Larry's bearded face appeared at her window a minute later.

"Jesus," she said.

He held up a coiled rope, pointed to it then moved toward the front of the van. Bill lumbered behind him like a B-movie zombie. She watched them drop out of sight long enough to tie the rope, then get to their feet looking like they'd just come from a mud wrestling match. Larry gave her a thumbs up, took a step and fell, but Bill grabbed him by the back of his raincoat and kept him from landing face first in the mud.

The phone rang again as they held onto the rope and walked backwards on the muddy road like they were rappelling down the face of a mountain.

"What?"

"Did they find him yet?"

"They just tied the rope to the bumper and now they're going down after him."

"Men are such idiots."

"I'll call you when I know something."

"You want me to come up there with you?"

"Maybe you better. I'm getting really nervous."

Ashley thought about the letter Michael received from his Granny Maudine. Great grandma Maudine Hillis.

Child, leave the dead be.

It was signed Granny Maudine.

They should have stayed home. They should never have come. Ever since that letter she had a very bad feeling about investigating Sharkey's Park. She'd told Michael, but he wouldn't listen. Michael threw the note out, but Ashley went through the wastebasket, found it, and saved it. She flattened it out and read it a few times before she put it in her wallet.

Child, leave the dead be.

The passenger door swung open and Shari climbed in, wet wind slapping at her back.

"God, what a storm. It's like being underwater out there," she said.

She slid the rain hood back and shook her red hair free.

"Take this," Ashley said.

She handed her a wad of paper towels.

"Thanks."

"Did you see them?"

Shari reached over and placed a hand over Ashley's.

"Give Larry and Bill a chance. Larry was a Marine, you know. He'll find Michael."

Ashley didn't look at her. She didn't want to know if Shari believed it or not.

"I called Josh," Shari said. "Told him to tell everybody not to call. I said we'd give them a heads up when we knew something. You don't need any more stress."

"What if he's hurt?"

"If he twisted a knee or something, Bill can carry him back up. Got shoulders as big as you and me put together."

Ashley nodded but kept staring at the blurred cones of light, looking for her husband.

The rain hammered down. She didn't want to turn on the radio. Didn't want to hear about flash flooding. Drops hit the van with a sound like lead shot thrown into a bucket. Shades of deeper black crowded the night about them, moving blindly as lost spirits, drifting toward her headlights as though drawn without knowing why. Ashley knew it wasn't real. Just a trick her mind was playing on her because of the storm and stress. But it seemed real.

"Michael can swim," she said. "He's a good swimmer."

Shari patted her hand again.

"I'll bet he is."

A sudden blast of wind hit the van so hard it shuddered.

"Where the hell are they?" Shari leaned forward and peered through the windshield. "The bridge can't be that far away."

"Wait," Ashley said, "I can see somebody."

Yellow movement at the edge of the headlights beam.

Head down, burrowing into the wind as whomever it was pulled themselves forward hand over hand on the rope.

"Can't make out who it is," Shari said.

She leaned forward and peered through rain that came down like a waterfall.

"I think I saw a yellow slicker."

"There," Shari pointed into the darkness. "I saw something."

"A smoke," Ashley said. "I need a smoke. I wish I'd never quit."

A tree somewhere up ahead burst into crackly white light like a giant sparkler. The trunk fell forward as though knocked down by a giant.

"Oh, God!" Ashley screamed.

Before the rain quenched the sparks, she saw the yellow slicker again, pulling up the rope toward them, head still bent over, maybe twenty feet away.

"Michael, I see Michael. See there, right there. Michael, get your ass up here."

The hood lifted as though in recognition.

Ashley recoiled hard against the seat and Shari let out a low wail as the hood fell back.

It wasn't Michael.

Beneath the yellow slicker, something squirmed and twisted as it continued its way up the rope. Pulling hand over skeletal hand, coming toward them, coming for them. Eyes that pulsed scarlet red. A mouthful of squirming things.

Ashley pulled the shifter into reverse and slammed on the gas pedal. The transmission shrieked. The wheels spun before catching. They crashed straight back into Shari's truck.

"Go, go, go," screamed Shari. "Turn the wheel. Get us out of here."

No traction, just spinning tires and the smell of something burning.

A panicked grab for the shifter. Ashley yanked it back into drive and jammed her foot on the pedal again. The van shuddered as the wheels spun. Suddenly they caught and the van shot forward.

Another flash of lightning and they drove straight through an empty yellow rain slicker. It flattened on the windshield. Suddenly they were speeding forward blind.

"Stop!" Shari screamed.

Ashley stomped on the brake, pressing it down so hard she stood up in her seat. Her head slammed against the ceiling as the van began to turn sideways and over. She felt her back twist hard right before she smacked against the driver's side window. Her vision blinked in and out. A metal rod crashed through Shari's window, piercing one temple and pushing straight through the other before she could scream.

The van went up sideways and over. Water bottles tumbled and CD's flew from the visor rack. Ashley fell back hard against Shari's body as water rushed in through the broken window.

Chapter Two

Ashley blacked out, but the cold water immediately shocked her eyes open. Straight ahead she saw two long blurry cones of light disappearing into the river. Fear clamped her chest so tightly she could hardly breathe. The van was going under.

Going to drown, she thought. *Got to get out.*

The water surged up to her lap and kept moving higher.

Her coat was tangled in something. The water rose like a cold tide. She had to get loose. Had to get out of the van. She yanked and twisted, but couldn't pull free. She would die there, she just knew it. No room in her head for any other thought. Pushing on her, pushing on her. You're going to die. You're going to die. Like a crazy woman she reached up with her free hand and clawed at the door handle. The van lay on its side, but if she could get the driver's side door open maybe she had a chance. Finally, she realized that her coat sleeve was caught around the shift lever.

Despair flooded over her like the cold water.

The icy water rose as high as her heart and she started to shake. The weight of it pushed against her, pressing on her chest. It was cold, so cold it felt like she was immersed in an ice slurry. Michael and his friends were probably dead. She turned in a desperate panic to check on Shari, saw the rod sticking out of her temple like a dark spear. Ashley threw up on the steering wheel. Shari was dead. Shari was dead and if Ashley didn't get out of the van soon, she would be dead, too.

How did she get here? She was so cold she couldn't think. No time to think. Suddenly she remembered that face, that hideous face. The monstrosity she ran through and over. Her jaw tightened with fear. She had to find a way out before she drowned. The water continued to flow into the van. Steady. Relentless. Coming for her.

Wait. She could take the coat off. Just take it off. Just wiggle out of the coat. Then she could get the van door open.

Shari was dead. Ashley wanted to live. She couldn't get out of her coat.

Water to her chin. No room to look down.

Suddenly her coat was off and she was free.

As she groped for the door handle, something large and dark slithered through the head light beams. Suddenly, Ashley wished she had drowned.

Two loud thumps and the van slid. Her frantic fingers clawed to get hold of the armrest, or the door handle, or anything. She found the window control buttons and pressed them 'til her fingertips hurt. Nothing. She tried to punch the door window, but the water slowed her fist.

"Get away from the window." A muffled warning shout distorted by wild wind and rain.

She knew she heard it, didn't imagine it. She knew what it said. She pushed back as far as she could, but there was really nowhere to hide. The driver's side of the van was now on top. To get away from it she would have to take a big breath and plunge downward into the passenger side of the van where Shari's body was held in place by that metal thing sticking out of her head.

"Last warning. I've got a—"

She couldn't hear the last part of what whoever he was saying, so she took a breath and submerged, trying not to think how close she was to the body of her dead friend.

Something smashed through the window with a sound like breaking bottles underwater. Ashley recoiled but twisted her body to one side to avoid getting hit. The flat edge of the axe slid along her face as someone pulled it back. Panicked, she grabbed at it, hanging on, yanking it, pulling on it until it broke free and moved away.

She tucked her legs and pushed off after it. Her head hit a crooked edge of glass. The sharp warmth of a jagged cut. She was bleeding. Air. Had to have air. She had her lips up near the airspace two inches from the door and sucked in a lungful.

An arm hooked around under her shoulder, and she felt herself being pulled toward the broken window again and hauled upward into the storm.

"Hold on," the man's voice said.

He had a flashlight in his raincoat pocket that bobbed every time he moved. She saw his face briefly in its spastic movements. Hard to say who he was. Ashley knew she was cold and scared and maybe going into shock.

"Christ, you're bleeding," he said.

"Glass," she said and began to cough so hard she saw stars.

"Come on, give me your hand. Help me get you out of there."

Her hand was too slippery so the man grabbed her by the back of her shirt and finally got her through the window and on her feet. A gust of wind rocked the van suddenly and her feet went out from under her. Her back slammed against the van. Pinpoints of light flashed. She tried to scream, but the air had been knocked out of her.

"Easy, easy," the man said. "This thing ain't stable."

She gulped in air, and tried to sit up. A restraining hand pushed her back. A noise of metal scraping along rock came from beneath them and the van shifted again.

"Steady," the man said.

Josh. Lying on the ground looking up at his ridiculously thin face, she finally recognized him. Josh was their electrical man.

"Michael," she gasped. "Is he all right?"

Josh coiled a thick yellow rope around her waist and cinched it.

"Just in case. It's tied to the winch-cable on my monster truck up the hill. And I have that tied to a tree big as a telephone pole. You understand?"

Ashley nodded as best she could.

"Now I ain't going to lie to you. I don't know where Michael is or where this shitty-ass weather came from or what's going on here. I'm just going to try and get me and you back up the hill before we drown. You ready?"

Ashley looked around at the rising water, the sudden bursts of white fire in the air. She felt the slap of cold rain and wind trying to shove them in the water.

"I said are you ready? Because if you ain't I'm taking you back anyway."

She remembered the feel of Shari's hair tangling in her fingers when she'd ducked underwater to avoid Josh's axe. A sudden shudder convulsed her back muscles.

"Get me out of here," she yelled.

Josh pulled her back to a sitting position and then helped her to her feet. He put one arm around her waist and she leaned against him as they moved step by step to the edge of the van. Josh's flashlight bobbed unsteadily in front of them as they clambered over and into water that came only to their hips.

The van slid to the edge of the river, then a little further. If Josh hadn't gotten her out she would have drowned for sure.

"Hold the flashlight," he said.

As he pressed the button on his CB radio-phone, Ashley aimed the flashlight toward the other side of the river. The rain was deafening. She could see nothing beyond a few feet even with the flashlight. Somewhere past the swollen waters was the haunted park they had come to investigate. Ashley shuddered and closed her eyes.

"I said, turn on the damned winch," Josh yelled into his radio.

She opened her eyes and saw red fires rise up into the night over the far side of the river as though the abandoned park were burning. Flames danced and snapped. Ashley cowered and stepped back.

Not real, not real, she thought. *Can't burn when it's pouring rain like this.*

She felt a sudden tug on her waist.

"Hang on," Josh said.

They made it up the embankment and ten feet into the weeds, the water now to their ankles. Ashley slipped and dropped Josh's flashlight. It hit the water with a splash and its light extinguished in the liquid blackness.

"Wait," she yelled. "I have to find it."

Josh's hand fell on her shoulder. "No. We keep going. Look up there, look on the hill. See those headlights? That's where we're going, flashlight or no flashlight."

The darkness wrapped around them like a wet cape.

"I'm afraid."

"We just keep moving toward those lights up there and we'll be okay. Grab my coat if it helps."

Ashley kept one hand on the rope and the other clutched tightly to Josh's coat. Together, they took step after sopping step through weeds and rocks they couldn't see. Suddenly she stopped. She slid forward as the winch inexorably pulled the rope slowly upward.

"You all right?"

"I can't do it," she yelled. "I can't leave Michael."

Ashley felt Josh grab her arm hard and pull her towards him. A bright flash overhead and she saw him before the boom hit. Rivulets of water slid down his face while he blinked furiously. Blood on the side of his head, a crazy look in his eyes.

"Larry and Bill will take care of Michael," he yelled back. "My job is to get you back, now let me do my job."

He yanked on her arm and she slapped at him, felt her nails cut his cheek. The winch pulled them forward.

"You crazy bitch, I'm trying to save your life."

"I'm not going," she said but the boom hit and he didn't hear her.

She felt him yank again; this time so hard she felt a sharp pain in her shoulder. No matter how hard she struggled or how loud she screamed he kept pulling and yanking and even got behind her and started pushing. She kicked back at him and felt him stagger. Before she could turn and break for it, he shoved her so hard she fell face down in the muddy water. She swallowed a mouthful and spit it out as he hauled her up by her hair and got her walking again. The winch kept tugging, reeling the rope up slowly but steadily.

"Michael might be waiting up there," he yelled in her ear.

No way. She didn't believe him. But he kept pushing her, pulling her, telling her he was probably already there, waiting for her, needing her.

She gave up and quit fighting.

"We're going to make it," he yelled after five or ten minutes more of sloshing uphill in the dark.

A faint smell of roasted meat passed nearby and, for just a moment, she thought she heard screams coming from Sharkey's Park.

"Did you hear that?" she asked.

"Keeping walking. Don't look back. It wants you to look back."

"Did you smell that?"

"Don't think about it. It wants you to notice."

"*What* wants me to notice? What are you talking about?"

"Nothing. You don't want to know. Now keep up. Keep walking. Keep your eyes on the lights up the hill."

"What are you talking about?" she asked. "What's going on? Do you know something?"

He didn't answer. The steady pull from the rope around her waist kept her moving through the wet darkness like a sleep walker. She felt so tired she could barely stay on her feet.

"What is it?" she asked again.

"Just keep moving," said Josh.

More screams filled her head. Now she was sure they were from Sharkey's Park.

Child, leave the dead be.

Ashley closed her eyes and kept walking.

Chapter Three

Five hundred miles to the south, on a neglected property just north of the Tennessee border, the night was dry as cracked kindling. Two men with a vague family resemblance stood near a freshly dug grave in a flat space of hard ground ringed by twisted trees. The older wore a cashmere collared overcoat and a black felt fedora and peered intently at the gaping hole while the younger man stood away and illuminated it with a halogen flashlight. Four men formed a circle around them and stood guard with automatic weapons.

"Hold the light steady," said the older man.

"I am," said the younger man.

"No, you're not."

The old man's face was hollowed with shadows. Ian Hunter knew better than to talk back to his Uncle Bartok. But he didn't want to admit that his hand was shaking.

The old man's wire-rimmed glasses caught the lantern's light, flashing in the dark when he turned his head to review the guards. Ian felt relieved when he fixed on the tallest of them, a bulky man in a red flannelled shirt, roughed-up jeans and work boots big as buckets.

"Enid?"

"Yes, Dr. Bartok?"

"No one must follow us."

"None will, sir."

"Enid?"

"Yes, Dr. Bartok?"

"Do you love that weapon?"

Enid looked down at the compact rifle he carried as easily as city people carried netbooks. With a thoughtful glance, he held it before his face and studied the barrel, twisting it in the pale blue light of the electric lanterns. Enid Mozer was careful what he said to Dr. Bartok.

"It's been there for me when I needed it. We're kind of joined, if you know what I mean, Doctor."

"And the dogs?"

Enid understood immediately.

"I had to put them down, sir."

Bartok waited.

Enid did not look away. Ian felt the night crowd closer about them, but he kept quiet as the unspoken tension grew.

Bartok extended a bony finger toward the open grave.

"It is always better to lose our lives than something more precious. Do you understand that still, Enid?"

"I do, Doctor. I know what I signed up for."

"All the dogs, Enid?" pressed Bartok.

"Pardon?"

"I asked if you put down all the dogs."

Ian saw the man's eyes flash as though a tilt of his chin had caught a stray beam from the flashlight. A meteor raced across the dark arc of the otherwise bleak sky like a warning shot.

"Yes, sir," Enid said at last. "Had to."

The other three men looked away toward the woods.

Ian could feel their unease. They were Mozers and for generations these mountain men acted as both soldiers and caretakers for the ruined Hillis estates. When a Mozer returned from the military, they had a job waiting for them. In return for protecting and tending the grounds, they were allowed to live on the property in cabins built by their ancestors.

But no one except Bartok knew what they were really guarding.

The old man knelt, using his cane and the worn double-headstone for support. Ian watched his thin fingers probing the dry grass at its base. Brown leaves crinkled like wax paper as he pushed them aside. He perched at the edge of the dug-up grave, careful not to topple in.

The names on the marble were lined with moss dark as dried blood.

Here Lie the Earthly Remains of
Colonel Albert Magnus Hillis and Mrs. Emma Hillis
May They Rest in the Sweet Arms of their Savior
Albert Magnus Hillis 1836 – 1871
Emma Louise Hillis 1847 – 1871

Bartok coughed, pulled a handkerchief from inside a coat pocket and pressed it to his mouth. He was the only man Ian knew who still used a handkerchief. When he pulled it away from his face, Ian thought he saw bloodspots.

"Are you all right?"

An arrogant, brusque wind pushed through the old graveyard, sending scraps of paper rolling like tumbleweeds between the markers. Overhead, a thin, pale moon lit the cool night like a ghostly Japanese lantern pinned to the billowing black sky.

"Never mind that," said the old man. "I've found it. The mind waivers but the body remembers."

Ian changed the subject.

"Uncle Bartok, this place gives me the creeps."

Behind Bartok, on the far side of Townsend Mountain, moonlight silhouetted the ruined mansion against a pallid light. Generations of Ian's family had held this estate close as an unwanted disease and tonight, if what the old man had told him was true, Bartok was about to hand him that charge. The idea both thrilled and terrified Ian.

"You have no idea just how true that is," said his uncle.

Ian craned forward, trying to get a better look. Bartok changed position, his high-collared overcoat blocking Ian's view. Secrets, always secrets. He never knew what to expect from the old man. Nothing his uncle did could surprise him.

"Stand away from the grave," Bartok said.

"Why?"

But Ian stepped back quickly when, from beneath the hard soil, he felt the vibration of something mechanical coming painfully to life. He stopped when he ran up against the mound of freshly piled earth, reached his free hand into his pocket and wrapped it around the handle of his Colt. The sound of gears meshing together grew louder. He glanced nervously around from Mozer to Mozer; their faces gave nothing away. Ian suppressed the desire to run. The light from his flashlight jittered and bounced. Metal screeched against metal like birds spooked to screaming flight and then all was quiet.

The thick odor of rotted wood rushed suddenly from the grave and hung in the air like an unwelcome guest. Ian felt an odd tension squeezing at the back of his head until his neck muscles knotted hard and tight. *Why was he here?* he wondered. *Why was he really here?* But the answer was easy.

Bartok motioned to him urgently.

"Hurry. Don't just stand there like you're waiting for a bus. We don't have much time. Enid?"

"Doctor?"

"If we're not back within the hour, close the gateway and fill in the grave."

"Whoa. What's that about?" Ian asked. "What do you mean *if* we're not back?"

"Too late to back out now, Ian," Bartok said. "You're about to meet our family destiny."

Ian stepped forward nervously and shone the flashlight into the grave. Rock stairs descended down twenty feet or so then curved to the right and disappeared. The double grave gave room for two men to enter shoulder to shoulder, but through a trick of the thin light and perspective, Ian thought the tunnel narrowed as it plunged further underground. He didn't like this. No, he didn't like it at all.

"I have to go down there to meet my destiny?" he asked Bartok. "Just how far down are we going?"

"We are going to Hell itself, Ian. Does it matter how many steps it takes to get there?"

All four Mozer men lifted their weapons and closed around them as Ian put his foot down on the first step. He'd gone another five steps down before it occurred to him the Mozers were pointing their rifles down the hole.

The air grew denser as they descended. Halfway down, it felt heavy enough to hold in his hands. Ian gulped deeper breaths, as though he was struggling uphill instead of descending. He was thirty-five years old and in peak physical shape; this shouldn't be happening to him.

"The air's no good in here," he said abruptly.

"It's not the air," Bartok said.

"How do you know?"

"I know. I've been here before, remember? It will pass. Keep moving."

"Good."

"No. No good," Bartok said. "That's when the danger starts."

"Can you quit talking like that and just tell me what what's going on? Why are we doing this? What's down here?"

Bartok tapped him on the back with his cane.

"No time," he said. "Keep moving. And keep that pistol of yours in your pocket. The Mozers don't know any better, but you ought to."

Ian was about to ask another question when the old man hit him on the back again.

"Hurry. You're slower than me and I'm twice your age."

Ian swore under his breath and started moving again.

The stairway was still wide enough to allow them to walk side by side, but Ian led the way. The old man's cane tapped on the stairs behind him. If it were anyone other than Bartok, Ian would have offered to go back and help, but he knew the old man was too stubborn for that.

Last night Bartok summoned him by phone and told him it was time. *Meet him at the family estate after dark*, he said.

"Time for what?" Ian asked.

But he knew. Time to find the terrible truth he had run away from years ago. Time to discover the family secrets.

He put his phone back on the end table and rolled over to tell Mollie he had to go. In the garish pink light coming through a broken blind, he saw a pale glimpse of her flat stomach as she pulled her sweater over her head. She paused at the door, turned to look at him and left without either one of them saying a word.

Ian drove all night and part of the next day, arriving in the sparsely populated town of Lisbon, still four hours north of the barbed wire circling the family property. As he drove, he remembered the violent disagreement that caused Bartok to send him away and wondered if they could put it behind them. He didn't want to admit just how much he desired that.

After a few hours' sleep, a quick inspection of his pistol and a fast pot of coffee, he was on the road again, rubbing the sleep from his eyes and trying to find a radio station strong enough to make it through the hills of southern Kentucky. But the static and white noise only grew worse the closer he got to his destination.

Now, with dread pressing down on his shoulders like death and each breath harder to draw than the last, he wished he'd stayed in Detroit. He never dreamed the family secrets were buried beneath a Kentucky cemetery.

The walls were rough as pumice but glistened as though glazed in the glare of Ian's halogen flashlight. The stairs were so worn they troughed. His nervous footsteps whispered through the narrowing tunnel like the rustling of bat wings. Bartok seemed stronger now; carrying his cane in one hand and his ever present brown leather valise in the other. The recorded history of the family secrets in that one valise that looked the same age as the old man himself.

Bartok's breathing was erratic. What if the old man died during the descent? No, not possible. Men like Bartok didn't die until they were ready. Still, the thought unnerved him. He wanted to turn and shine his light back the way they had come to see if the Mozers still guarded the opening, but knew Bartok wouldn't stand for it. Bartok never turned back. Idly, Ian aimed the flashlight up at the rock arch ceiling.

Pain flared in his wrist and his hand went numb as Bartok's cane cracked into his forearm.

"Don't ever do that," snapped the old man. "Never, do you hear me?"

The flashlight clattered down the stairs and hit the floor at the end of the descent with a splintering crack and they were suddenly plunged into a writhing, purple-black darkness.

"I think you broke my arm," Ian yelled. "Are you crazy? How are we supposed to see?"

He felt the old man's face come to within inches of his. Bartok sparked anger so hot Ian felt his skin redden.

"Never look up at the writings," said the old man in a fearful hoarse whisper.

"What writings? How was I supposed to know there were writings on the ceiling?"

Bartok's fingertips bit into Ian's shoulder.

"Where do you think this evil light comes from, Ian? It's from them. From the petroglyphs. No, don't look up."

Ian was in too much pain to look up. His arm throbbed and it was hard to move his fingers. Bartok was squeezing his shoulder so hard it hurt as badly as his arm. But he heard the word petroglyphs through his pain like a distant warning. And he saw for the first time the pale, etheric glow that replaced the halogen lamp.

"The desire to look up at them can become quite powerful, I assure you," Bartok said. "But in that ancient script are the roots of madness. Your grandfather Edmund killed his own brother and left his body on these very stairs—right here where you are standing—after he fell under the influence of the blood glyphs. They glow and twist like evil snakes hoping to tangle their tentacles around our hearts, to squeeze out everything that is human. It was I who dragged his body out and buried him."

Bartok released Ian's shoulder and stepped back. He spun his cane and snapped its titanium tip hard against the rock floor.

"Pain can clear the mind," he added.

"Christ, you could have told me before we came down here, you know, instead of hitting me with your cane."

Anger welled up inside Ian, overwhelming the throbbing pain. But Bartok cut him short.

"Quit complaining, we have urgent business in this labyrinth. Get moving."

As the disturbing preternatural light slid across him, Ian's arm seemed to pulse faintly in rhythm with its ululations. It was then he heard it. An awful, high-pitched sound like nothing he had ever experienced. A wave of nausea passed through him. He pressed his palm against the injured arm and closed one eye as though that would quiet the keening sounds of the light.

"Can you hear that?" he gasped.

"Don't listen, Ian. It wants you to listen."

"It's like it's calling me."

Bartok moved past him to continue down the stairs.

"Hurry. Follow me now. Don't ask questions; just do what I tell you. We must keep moving if we want to keep our sanity."

《《—》》

"How much further?" Ian asked.

The passageway was quiet now, as though they had passed through Charybdis and Scylla and were safe for the moment. Bartok continued to lead. *Ascend to God like a child*, his uncle had once told him, *but face the darkness like an old man.*

"Not much," Bartok said.

Ian turned the corner at the bottom of the stairs just behind the old man and came to a complete stop. For the first time in his life, he felt his blood chill. They were at the entrance to a hewn chamber nearly twenty feet high and more than fifty feet in diameter. On the far side of the man-made cave was a segmented metal aperture that roiled with movement as the wriggling purple light slid through the room.

"Now, you see it for yourself."

Ian couldn't believe his eyes.

"What is it?"

"It's the doorway to Hell, Ian," Bartok said gruffly. "That's what I call it. Your great grandmother called it Aeyrik. None of us knew why and she did not pass down her reasons."

Ian looked at the gigantic door, tilting his head back until his neck hurt. It seemed to ripple purple-black in the semi-darkness. Fifteen foot tall and perhaps ten feet wide. Formed from what seemed to be a segmented metal with interlocking reflective metal pieces that looked more like scales.

"It's like a snake's skin," Ian said.

"Never mind that. Do you feel the air move and press on your face?"

Bartok said. "What can it mean? What does it mean?"

In the shifting, uneasy semi-darkness, Ian sniffed the air, then held his breath and felt the pressure change in the room, as though the chamber itself were breathing. His eyes grew wide and he turned to stare at his uncle.

"Is that thing alive?"

"Take your pistol and shoot it."

"What?"

"Now," snapped the old man.

Ian thumbed the safety to the "OFF" position on the Colt. The door pulsed and flashed with colors he could not identify. He felt slightly disoriented, as he had in the earlier passage. The door seemed eerily alive, as though it were an oval organism covered with transparent skin. Again, Ian became uncomfortably aware of the low, urgent sound that rose and fell in pitch as the purple blackness squirmed inside the door. He felt the soft pressure waves press against his face. In and out. In and out.

Alive, impossibly alive.

Ian jerked his hand up and aimed straight at it, altered the angle once, and then altered it again. His sense of purpose blurred and he lowered his weapon without firing.

"What about the ricochet?" he asked.

"Do as I tell you."

Ian raised the gun and fired.

He flinched in anticipation, but didn't hear it impact the door. Where the bullet should have hit there was only a disorienting spider-web of electric light. Ian felt suddenly clearheaded, as though, since the moment they took their first step below ground, his thinking had been clouded.

"Your first lesson in this unforgiving hell," Bartok said. "Disrupting the patterns around us weakens their control. This thing, this doorway or portal, does not, I think, actually exist in our world. We see it, but I don't believe it's really here. Yet it exerts power as though it were. Do you understand? *They* created it, and because of that, this doorway has power."

"Who are you talking about? Who built this?"

"No time for that, Ian. We have to go through it."

Ian couldn't believe what he was hearing. "What the hell are you talking about? There's no knob. No handle. No way to get it in. My bullet didn't even dent it. Hell, I don't even know if I hit it. So how exactly are we supposed to go through it?"

"There's this," Bartok said, and from inside his coat the old man pulled out a knife with a long scalloped blade that flashed pale silver violet in the chamber's peculiar illumination. The handle was black as a charcoal briquette, but at the hilt's top was mounted a red jewel that pulsed rhythmically in bursts of muted light the color of crude oil.

Ian felt a sudden apprehension grip his spine and lock it straight. He felt as though he could not twist or turn away from the sight of the artifact.

"What do you do with it?" he asked.

"Me? Nothing. My time is past. I no longer have the strength. Your time is upon you this very moment."

Bartok extended the dagger, hilt first.

After a moment's hesitation Ian grabbed hold and took it. He turned it over and over, feeling its energy touch his own. There were symbols carved into the hilt. But in the serpentine twisting of purple-black illumination that slithered through the under-ground air, they were impossible to read.

"What do I do with it?"

The old man stared at Ian for a few moments, and pointed an elegantly long finger toward the door.

"Hack through it," he said. "Cut away its muscle and sinews and let its evil blood drain on the floor until you have cleared a way through which we can walk."

Bartok's eyes were locked on his own with a frightening intensity.

"Is it alive?" Ian asked.

"Oh, yes," Bartok said. "It is indeed."

Ian stepped to within a foot of the door, the knife held point forward in his hand. Suddenly he lifted his new weapon over his head so hard he felt his back pop, and then swung its bladed edge forward and down. When it sliced into the first metallicine skin-plate, a rush of angry bees swarmed through his thoughts.

"Don't stop," shouted his uncle. "Cut, cut, cut. Kill it if you can but for God's sake at least cut us a way though."

A caustic heat flowed over Ian's hands and shot up his arms. It spread up his shoulder and he knew it was coming for his mind. He screamed and hacked away like a battle-crazed berserker.

Chapter Four

Ashley lay on a gurney, rolling toward Intensive Care.

Her face pale, her hair dull and plastered to the side of her head pushed back from the four inch swath where they'd shaved and stitched her scalp.

Part of her blanket fell away, showing a pale, bare foot.

"She going to be okay?" Josh asked nervously as she rolled past.

He knew he was in big trouble. Knew it was going to get worse before it got better. His hands started to shake again so he thrust them hard into his coat pockets.

"Sir, you'll have to wait in the ICU lobby," sthe nurse said. "Someone will be out to see you."

And that was that.

He wasn't family. Couldn't follow her back. But he didn't care. No time to follow her back. He had to get away before the police showed up. He didn't even know why'd he'd helped her. Didn't owe her anything. And he was never going back to jail again for anyone.

"You're sure you're feeling okay?" the nurse asked.

"I'm okay."

They'd tried to check him over when he first got there with Ashley. He told them he was fine. A few scrapes and bruises. He'd been worse. He'd live. Mostly, Josh didn't want to get stuck in the hospital in case the police showed up.

The rest of the team was probably still at the top of the hill. His truck was the only vehicle they could pull out of the mud and he only had two seats, so Josh drove Ashley to the hospital while the others waited for help to arrive. He called it in to 911 when he got a few bars worth of signal. Fifteen minutes on the road before he got that. The storm played hell with the cell towers. Twice he'd had to pull over because the rain was coming down so hard he could hardly see.

Josh fidgeted, wanting to run full speed through the emergency room doors, jump in his truck and get gone. But that wouldn't do. He had to act natural. Worried about Ashley. Stressed out. Then walk out like any other law abiding citizen.

There was going to be a lot of explaining to do. No one would believe what he saw. No one would ever believe what really happened. He would never pass a lie detector if he made something up.

Michael was dead. He knew that sure as he stood there caked with mud. Bill and Larry, too. Shari drowned. Four dead. The police would want answers. Josh couldn't stay around for that.

Because it was all his fault.

"I got to go to the hotel room and wash up," he told the nurse. "I'll be back in a bit."

"You could change clothes, too," said the nurse.

"Yeah, I guess I could do that."

Halfway down the hall she called after him, "Do you have a number I can reach you at if we need to?"

He gave her Michael's number instead of his own. Thought he had it right. It was getting hard to think clearly. He felt warm. Worried maybe the stress was going to give him a heart attack.

"Do I have that right?" she said after repeating the number.

That was Michael's number, all right, and he was clean, cold dead and no coming back. No chance anyone would be answering that number tonight.

At least he hoped not.

The nurse disappeared behind a set of double doors that whispered shut. Air whooshed softly through the overhead vents, but other than that, an eerie silence settled over the empty hallway. Like a dead zone. He'd done a lot of late-night emergency room vigils when his mother was ill. Half the time he thought he was the only one in the building. The night she'd died he'd gone down for a smoke and hadn't seen but two people between him and the hospital exit. Time he got back, she was dead.

Like Michael.

But Michael had it coming.

We all got it coming, he thought. *I just don't want to be around for mine.*

He was about to turn and walk away when he felt a sharp pain slice into his ankles and his feet were yanked out from under him. Panic shot through him as his elbows smacked the floor and then he was in the air, flying backward, picking up speed. Terrified out of his mind. Mouth and eyes wide open.

Before the glass doors could open, he smashed through them, felt the shards rip at him as his chin bounced off the metal door frame. His head snapped back and then he was through, rising up, face down, seeing the ground rush away in a dizzying blur of slick wet color. Something had him, taking him way up high into the rainy night. He couldn't catch his breath to scream. Rain soaked him as he flew upside down, but his insides burned with fear and cold air rushed by him like he was flying through a wind tunnel.

No. God, no. Down, please down.

Two stories, three stories, then up above the gray bricked hospital with its rows of bright windows. Cones of light from the parking lots. Surrounded by a whirling darkness as he spun faster and higher with his arms swinging in desperate circles. Acid rushed from his stomach to his throat. Blood rushed to his head as he hung like an upside down marionette suspended on strings clutched by the Devil.

And then he was falling, falling. Rushing toward the asphalt as the flashing red and white lights of an ambulance screeched to a stop just below him.

«« — »»

The police cordoned off the hill as best they could in the downpour. Headlights from four police cruisers on high beams lit the area while two officers and a paramedic worked to set up a small generator and a ring of halogen lights. The rain was still a steady drizzle and orange Emergency Responder raincoats moved around with grim purpose. Bright yellow crime-scene tape marked off the restricted areas where techs collected samples, took photographs, and probed parts of the soft, wet ground.

And the smell of burned flesh floated through the air like evil memories.

Detective Alvarez stalked the perimeter like an expectant father, waiting to hear something from the medical examiner. She was having trouble with washed out roads, but she'd make it. She was a pro.

Alvarez was tense for another reason. One he kept to himself. One that went back a long time ago and happened in the same place.

Sharkey's Park was past the edge of town in the long abandoned area that used to be called Corktown. All the houses were torn down long ago, leaving nothing but splinters and rumors. Corktown was where the unschooled, sometimes illiterate, hillbillies and illegal immigrants lived in houses built like barns. Sharkey's Park was all that was left. But it should have been torn down first.

Sharkey's Park was where Alvarez's grandfather died. Dismembered and burned to death fifty four years ago along with a bunch of his neighbors. Murderer never found. Case abandoned. No real leads, no real interest except to get it off the front pages. Nobody wanted to hear about problems in Corktown. Riff-raff like his grandfather lived there.

Tonight was a repeat. Only this time Alvarez was the detective on the scene. This time, he was going to make sure it didn't go unsolved.

Alvarez knew that if he told the Captain right away about his grandfather's murder, he might have to let the case go. Conflict of interest was what they called it; but if the Captain didn't know, the Captain couldn't object. And Alvarez didn't want to let it go. Not when he had a chance to solve both cases. They were tied together, he just knew it.

The night his grandfather and his neighbors were murdered there was one man whose body was never found. One that got away and was never seen again or murdered and no one could find his body. That man was Becker Hillis. No clues as to what happened to him. Becker Hillis was Michael Hillis's grandfather. Now, it was the grandson who disappeared, leaving behind another slew of bodies.

It was, like that baseball player said, déjà vu all over again.

Alvarez didn't like it. There would be so much media attention it would get in the way of finding the killer. Or if the Captain found out the connection between Alvarez's family and Sharky's park.

But the Captain would throw his ass right off of the case if he told him about it. So Alvarez was going to keep his mouth shut for a while, at least until he found out more. He was willing to take the chance. If he solved it before they took him off the case, he was a hero. If he got busted for conflict of interest, he would be the goat. It was always better to be the hero than the goat.

He walked past his men, sometimes watching, always listening. They looked down at the ground, trying to ignore the rain, trying not to show how they felt. Trying to pretend they were immune to the horror. Talking about what needed to be done. They focused on the process to ignore the hideous reality of the details like mutilated corpses and bodies burned to a crisp.

Jesus, what a night.

"Got to cut that one down sooner or later," said an officer named Leonard, pointing up into the branches of a ponderous old tree with bark like furrowed asphalt. "Fuck, I hate this rain."

"It's too wet," said Platt. "You're too old to be climbing trees in this kind of weather."

"I don't mean you should climb the tree, dumbass. I mean get the ladder."

Six policemen. Four paramedics. All nervous. None had ever seen anything like this. With all her experience, Alvarez didn't think the Medical Examiner had seen anything like it either. None of them were going to sleep tonight unless they raided the pill bottles. Most of the cops Alvarez knew ran on auto-pilot or pills.

Three bodies ripped up and then burned by serious crack-heads or whoever. Just like thirty years ago. Alvarez took two more antacids to keep from throwing up.

"You leave it where it is," he told the two officers. "Wait until the ME gets here and she can call the shot. We screw something like this up and we're going to get our asses kicked. Media's going to be all over it."

Two EMS vans were parked twenty feet away, their engines idling so low Detective Alvarez couldn't hear them. White tailpipe puffs floated up and dissipated into the darkness like spirits cut loose from their earthly bonds. Alvarez rubbed the back of his neck again. It itched.

Fucking Hillis family, he thought.

Sharkey's Park gave him the creeps. He couldn't get over the feeling that they were being watched. Not likely the killer would stay behind at the crime scene, but sometimes they did.

And the night was quiet. Way too quiet. The rain wasn't so noisy he couldn't hear something, anything. It was like a predator came through the woods and the birds and frogs and crickets were too scared to make any noise. So somewhere in the darkness beyond the car headlights, Alvarez knew there was something watching them. Something that even scared the crickets. He felt the knowledge crawling around the back of his neck like a tick looking for somewhere to fasten its little teeth.

"Hey, Sarge," called an evidence tech.

"Yeah?"

"Take a look at this shit they were hauling."

"What do you got? I was having a good night until this shit hit."

"Yes, sir. Anyway, you ever watch those ghost hunting shows on TV?"

"I have a life. What about it?"

The tech had glasses like Clark Kent and black hair he kept wiping out of his eyes.

"Yeah, well, the stuff these citizens were carrying looks like ghost hunting equipment."

"And you know that how?"

"Take a look. They've got thermal imaging cameras, micro-phones, tape recorders, infrasonic detectors and a few portable generators for power."

"So that tells you they're ghost hunters?"

Hank grinned.

"And a copy of *How to Conduct a Paranormal Investigation* lying on the front seat of this Jeep."

"Huh," Alvarez said.

The halogen lamps suddenly switched on as the generator coughed to light. Suddenly the night was lit up like a sporting event. Everyone covered their faces to shield their eyes.

"What jackass did that?" Alvarez shouted. "Tell somebody for fuck's sake before you turn on those damned things. You could blind people."

"Sorry, Detective," someone called back.

Jackass.

Gradually, he lowered his arm, blinking fast like it would wipe away the spots flaring inside his eyes.

"Hey, Detective," called Officer Leonard.

"Hey, Leonard."

"I got something for you."

"Yeah, well yell it out, why don't you? I'm tied up being blind right now."

"Sure. They admitted Ashley Hillis into Seacrest Hospital. The guy that called the scene in took her there."

"I know all that," Alvarez said.

"Yeah, well did you know that he just jumped off the top of the hospital and landed on an ambulance?"

Chapter Five

Frantic screams from down the hall brought Nurse Lincoln Jones to his feet so quickly he knocked over his chair and fell down so hard his teeth clacked. He shook his head, remembered why he fell, and then scrambled to his feet and ran down the hall. The call went out through the overhead intercom for assistance in room 422. Others were probably closer, but Lincoln felt compelled to respond. It was the raw terror of the screams that got him moving.

As he rounded the corner, he saw Nurse Nancy Wilson hustle into the room. Patients anxiously poked their heads out of their rooms to see what was happening.

"Back inside, everyone," he said. "Everything's under control."

But the patients knew that something wasn't "under control."

Lincoln made it to the door, his breath coming in and out so hard he felt like he was going to be the next emergency.

The patient was thrashing wildly on her bed, eyes wide open and terrified. She hit the IV pole and it crashed back against the window then clattered to the floor. Lincoln stared at her from the doorway, almost afraid to enter. The woman looked demon possessed.

"Grab her other arm before she hurts herself," Nurse Wilson said. "Security's on the way." She held one of the patient's arms down against the bed, using her two hundred and forty pounds to keep it pinned to the mattress.

Lincoln approached warily, trying to avoid her other hand. The patient bared her teeth at him like an attack dog.

"Hurry," said Nurse Wilson.

"I'm trying," said Lincoln.

As he circled in closer and leaned forward, the patient screamed, "Don't touch me, don't touch me," then swung her leg around viciously and kicked him in the head.

Lincoln fell back into the curtain, flailed his arms like broken windmills and took the entire thing down—ripping the rings off the railing and wrapping him in the cloth as he spun like a mummy. He hit the floor like he'd been dropped from the ceiling. The bunched material cushioned his head, but the air burst out of his lungs from the impact like someone had slammed him in the back. The curtain covered his mouth and he panicked. He grabbed the cloth and tried desperately to rip it while the patient continued screaming like a fire alarm in Hell.

"Lincoln, get over here," Nurse Wilson yelled.

He got enough of the curtain pulled away from his face that he could

27

breathe. Got to his knees and unwrapped the curtain from his head so he could see. Nurse Wilson was locked in a struggle with the patient, who grabbed handfuls of hair on both sides of the larger nurse's head and started banging foreheads with her.

Lincoln got to his feet as quickly as he could, but before he could rush to his co-worker's assistance, two bulked-up security guards shoved him aside and took over. They pried the patient's hands from Nurse Wilson's head and began strapping the woman to her bed.

"Watch her feet," Lincoln warned.

Too late.

The patient kicked one of the security guards in the head and tried to do the same to the other. The second man ducked, snatched her ankle and in less than a minute and a half she was completely strapped in.

"Damn, am I glad you got here," Nurse Wilson said, looking at the blood on her hands. She reached down, grabbed the IV pole and righted it.

"Hook her up again." she said to Lincoln, "Give her a ten milligram Xanax push while I get cleaned up."

"Where—"

"On the window sill, Lincoln."

"Got it," he said.

The patient chomped at him like a starved vampire. Her eyes were red-rimmed and wild.

"You guys okay, now?" one of the security guards asked.

"I think so," said Lincoln, "unless she bites through the straps."

"We're fine," said Nurse Wilson.

"You know," said the security guard, "looks like she was kicking the shit out of you, Lincoln."

"Yeah," said Lincoln.

"Any little girls try to take your lunch money, you let us know and we'll come save your ass."

"Out," Nurse Wilson snapped.

"Yes, ma'am," said the guard and the uniformed men were gone.

"Lincoln, you got that done?"

"I did," he said. "Ten milligrams, like you said."

"You okay?"

"I'm good."

"You better wash the blood off your face, too. And put an ice pack on your cheek or your face is going to swell up and you'll bruise."

She walked toward the patient and Lincoln went to the sink. She was right. He was going to be bruised and swollen unless he used an ice pack.

In the mirror, he saw Nurse Wilson bend over to pick up things that had fallen on the floor. The patient was quiet now, muttering low words that he couldn't quite understand.

Hope the guards keep their mouths shut, he thought.

But he knew it would be all over the hospital before the night was out. Between Nurse Wilson and the security guards, even the lab techs attendants would know.

He was about to ask Nurse Wilson for mercy, when he saw a swirling black and red mist rise from the patient's head. He blinked. He blinked again. Still there. He felt a blast of hot air and the room filled with an awful sulfur smell.

Lincoln stepped back and held up his hands.

Inside the twisted apparition he saw a terrifying face glaring at him. Marking him. Remembering him.

Its mouth opened and he saw a deeper blackness widening to swallow him whole.

"Lincoln?"

Nurse Wilson was still crouched on the floor, staring up at him like he was crazy.

"What's the matter with you?"

He looked back at the apparition, just in time to see it seep into the ceiling and disappear.

«« — »»

Detective Alvarez pulled into the hospital parking lot with a bad feeling riding his shoulders. It was already a long night and getting longer. He logged in his arrival on his computer—it wasn't officially a police car anymore without a computer—and took a swig of lukewarm coffee.

Ghost hunters. Freak show was what they were.

The ambulance was cordoned off. The patient had been taken to the emergency room. Couple of paramedics and a few off duty nurses were hanging around, waiting for something exciting to happen.

A single plain-clothes officer was standing near the perimeter, going over his notes. His name was Matt something or other, Alvarez thought. Been around the force forever, keeping low, trying not to make mistakes and hoping to stay alive long enough to see retirement.

"Hey, Detective."

"Any of these civilians know anything?"

"Not as far as I can tell, Detective."

"Then get rid of them. Clear the area. Only people I want here are us, any witnesses and anybody was in the ambulance when our friend here hit ground zero. Got that?"

"Yes, sir."

Alvarez looked up.

Problems. Big problems.

Alvarez already knew he had a goat rodeo on his hands.

There were two points from where the stiff could have leapt out into space. The first was the roof. The other place was the edge of the canopy roof that covered most of the emergency entrance area. That was a three-foot jump and that didn't work either because it was too close. No way could the impact-damage on Josh's body look like it did from a three-foot jump. So Alvarez was going to go with the roof. Problem with that was no one had seen him going up there. Big problem number one. And there was the matter of the shattered glass door. Fragments lay scattered about it, as though something had been thrown through it. But there was nothing on the sidewalk except glass.

He walked over to it and saw that some of the fragments were coated with what looked like blood. Great. Don't think about it, he told himself. File it away with the rest of the facts. Can't figure it out? Just keep collecting evidence, Emilio, and sooner or later the evidence will tell you what happened.

But one thing he already knew. It wasn't a suicide. It was what he thought it was the moment he arrived—a goat rodeo.

"Detective?"

Officer Matt was back.

"Yeah?"

"Do you want to talk to Nurse Oldman? She was the last one to see him alive."

"Damned right I want to talk to her."

"Okay."

"And you want to bet me whether or not the blood on this glass on the sidewalk is from the dead guy?"

«« — »»

The Kentucky night sky was sequined with tiny points of white glitter. From where she sat rocking, Maudine Hillis thought there wasn't anything prettier to look upon except bluebells in season. A faint breeze tickled her cheek and she closed her eyes to enjoy its touch. Tomorrow Kenneth would drive her north to Michigan, and she knew the only way she was coming back was in a box with the lid nailed shut.

She lived by herself at the top of the big hill in the middle of the family's property. Her nephew Kenneth lived at the bottom, where the land was flatter and the rolling grass stretched to the limestone cliffs. Kenneth's wife and son died in a car accident when they'd lived in Lexington, so he moved back to the family homestead and lived down there by himself, which Maudine didn't think was good for a grown man.

Neither one of them saw more than one or two of their neighbors during the course of any given month. Maudine didn't think that was good, either. Oh, people would still find their way to her door when they needed advice or when trouble or sickness found them, but she liked to think of herself as retired. And they had to get past Kenneth and his double barreled before they could come calling.

Her little house was modern enough for her tastes. She had a tin roof good for another ten years, screen windows, a root cellar, and an indoor toilet. On a small desk in the eastern corner of what she called her parlor she had a black rotary phone heavy enough to hold the whole place down if an angry wind came blasting through the pines. Maudine had her health to boot, and for a 96-year-old woman that was something to crow about.

God had a reason to keep me around so long, she thought. *Had to be something big or he would have let an old granny woman like me go a ways back. And now God is calling in his marker.*

She pulled her pipe from a shirt pocket, tapped the bowl against the side of her chair and then filled it with Prince Albert tobacco. A while back her sister Izorah had given her a pipe that you could slide filters into the stem to suck up the tars and nicotine. Said it would be safer to smoke and maybe keep her around a while longer.

Maudine smiled at the thought. Keep her around a while longer? Poor Izorah died a year later. Choked to death on a granola yogurt bar with a bottle of purified water sitting on the table in front of her. And here Maudine was still puffing on Old Glory.

It's a cruel world, she thought.

With a flick against her thick, yellowed fingernail, a match head flared. She lit the bowl and puffed it to life. The sweet, acrid odor diffused into the night but a tiny bit of its aroma lingered on her porch. The smell reminded her of nights when she and her brothers had burned trash back on the barren patch between the house and the barn. Memories rose up and drifted away like the smoke coming from her pipe.

The Hillis family had kin scattered throughout the country. Most went west. A few went north. For the most part, she never heard from them, save when they were trying to track down family history. Only one she'd paid much attention to was that young man from Michigan. Wrote her a letter first before coming to visit. No asking around for her email—she didn't have electricity, much less a computer. No use anyone trying to get her on the phone.

No, at first he seemed a proper young man, even though he descended from bad seed. He'd written her a letter on good quality writing paper—with a fountain pen, no less.

So after a while of thinking about it, she'd had Kenneth write him back saying she'd be most pleased to have him come visit. She'd had to browbeat the stubborn cuss into writing that letter since he didn't like company and he had no use at all for strangers. But she'd whipped him into place.

So the boy came down a year or so ago.

He was real polite and a good looking young man to boot.

Michael Hillis was his name, and it pained her to know that he was the grandson of Becker Hillis. Becker was her older brother, second in line only to Johnny. Johnny was as a good a man as she had ever known to walk the earth. Becker was just plain bad seed like most of the other Hillis men. Nothing good ever came of Becker Hillis, but that was no fault of the grandchild. The boy was second generation removed, but Becker's evil shadow was to darken his life one day. She knew this before she ever met the boy, just as she knew there was nothing she could do to stop it.

But she'd made one mistake. She'd told him about the madstone.

Too old to be making mistakes.

She'd tried to warn the boy. But he was a Hillis, and that was the same as being born mule-headed. His ears perked right up about the madstone. Wouldn't let it go. Pestering her about what it was, where it came from, how to use it and where was it. She'd told him it was buried where it should be. That was the worst of it all. Now, if her sense of it was right, they were all going to pay for her mistake and she knew her sense of it was right.

It was the curse of being a granny woman. You plain knew too much.

Maudine saved Becker once, a long time ago. And now, she was going to regret it. But he was her brother, and that was that, no matter how bad he was.

Now, she fingered the little straw figure she made when she first felt the evil coming. Pipe in one hand, twisted straw in the other.

Time to go North and make things right. Hard things to do. She would have to be tough. People got in their way, Kenneth would handle them. People were afraid of Kenneth, and sometimes that could be put to good use.

"Well, little man," she said to her handiwork, "tomorrow you and me gots to get to work."

She closed her eyes to feel the breeze on her cheeks again, but it, like her hopes of dying a quiet death, had already faded away.

Chapter Six

Ian kept his eyes clamped shut as Uncle Bartok led him through the monstrosity of the door. His mind was assaulted with terrifying images, his nose filled with the smell of mechanical charnel and it was almost more than he could bear. And he could hear nothing, nothing at all. Viscous fluid flowed over his skin and his stomach lurched. Bartok's strong grip on his wrist was all that kept him sane.

And then it was over.

"Keep your eyes closed," he heard Bartok say. His voice echoed as though they were in an auditorium. A low hum filled the air, like the sound of a power substation processing huge voltages.

Ian, still trembling, could only nod.

"When you open them, you will see things such as few men on this earth have ever seen. You must be strong and not fearful. Steel yourself. The Hunters have always been strong people. Their blood flows through your veins. But when good people go astray, the results can be catastrophic. Always remember that. Now open your eyes and behold the truth of your heritage, the very place where it all began."

Whatever Ian expected, he was not prepared for what he saw when he opened his eyes. They were in an immense cavern. The air glowed softly as though ionized and threw liquid shadows around the room as it was blown about by invisible currents. And lit by that occult light he saw an army of giant mechanical men interconnected by luminescent tubes radiating from a dark something suspended in the air far back in the subterranean hell.

"Uncle Bartok, what is this place?"

The old man waved his valise at the mechanical men as though to introduce them. Ian saw that at the top of each metal head was a glass dome of glowing iridescent light like that which flowed through the connecting tubes. Their bodies were constructed of a green-gold metal and their joints were complex geared mechanisms like those that drove the wheels of steam locomotives.

"Don't be concerned with them. They are dormant mon-strosities, waiting for their master's command."

They were no more than twenty feet from the nearest mechanical soldier, and Ian could see that they were at least twelve feet tall. Their metal hands were segmented gears and tubes that reflected the caverns ethereal light in tiny glints.

"What are they?"

Bartok took a deep breath and looked toward the suspended monstrosity at the far end of the cavern, then spoke in a troubled voice racked with a strange blend of anger and awe.

"Children of a madman. Twisted obsessions transformed into aberrance by something both alien and repellent to our world."

A honeycomb of pulsing purple-green light at the far wall caught Ian's attention. The thing from which all the filament-thin fluorescing tubes originated came into focus. Ian took a step back. The mechanical spider at the web's center looked almost human.

Bartok stepped in to break Ian's view. Bartok glowered at him, his dark eyes fixed on Ian's.

"Does what you see disturb you? Have you learned so little? I have come to show you what dark secrets our family has been guarding for generations. You will now do the same. So do not be distracted by what you see, but focus on what all this means. Your great grandmother wrote that each of us can come here only twice, and she had good reason to tell us that. "

But Ian was not listening. When Bartok blocked his view, he turned in a slow circle, his eyes taking in giant purple-gold gears and glassine orbs the size of tangerines that turned and tumbled through the air. The side walls of the cavern were pillared with a mother-of-pearl marble as though someone tried to build a Greek Temple underneath the hills of Southern Kentucky. He thought about all the times he had wandered about the ruined mansion standing guard over this underground maze of occult technology without realizing what lay beneath his feet.

Bartok's voice brought him back to the moment.

"Come, Ian. It's time to meet the patriarch of the Hillis family."

«« — »»

The old man led him down the long center aisle between rows of gleaming metal automatons. An army of towering mechanized men hidden below ground for generations, their armor plates glistening as though oiled only hours before. Ian suppressed the desire to turn and run back to the hideous skin-door.

"Did you see that?" Ian asked abruptly. "There are faces in those domes. I saw them, I swear. They press against the crystal and then fade away."

"There are indeed," Bartok said without stopping. "Each mechanical automaton houses the essence of at least one poor soul. The spirits of dead men are trapped in these aberrations."

Ian caught up to his uncle, and saw that they were only thirty feet away from a nightmare image. He gripped Bartok's arm, and the old man stopped to allow the scene to sink in. Suspended ten feet in the air was a dead man. His arms were cut off at the elbows and his legs at the knees. From each appendage, grafted onto the joint, extended a glassine tube through which liquid light pulsed as though moved by a heartbeat. The tubes tentacled throughout the complex, connected in some obscene way that Ian could not see to the army of silent mechanical soldiers.

The man hung, transfixed in the pulsing light tubes and filaments like a spider stuck in its own web. His hair was long, black and wild and matched by a full beard at least a foot long. Mercifully, his eyes and mouth were closed.

"Say hello," Bartok said severely, "to Albert Magnus Hillis."

The dead man's eyes popped open and he stared directly down at Ian.

"It's alive," Ian screamed.

He wanted to run but couldn't move. Magnus Hillis's eyes were glints of pure silver. Crescents of metal were implanted into his eyes like insectile mirrors.

"Even after a hundred and fifty years," Bartok said, "this monstrous man lives on."

Ian's fingers gripped his Uncle's upper arm as though hanging on to a lifeline. The old man's presence was all that kept him from running.

"You mean that creature really is alive?"

Gently but firmly, the old man peeled Ian's fingers from his arm.

"I believe that he is both dead and alive. Don't ask me to explain it—I can't. But now, you have seen it for yourself. Here is the secret our family has so desperately hidden from the rest of the world. Here is what we protect humanity from."

"But why us? Are we cursed? Why are we the ones guarding this terrible secret? At least tell me that."

The suspended creature opened its mouth and shrieked so loudly that Ian took a step back and pulled out his pistol.

"Put that away," snapped Bartok.

"It is, it's alive," Ian said. His voice trembled so badly he could barely understand his own words.

"And you think killing it will solve our problem? It is the one thing that your great grandmother wrote must never be done. If this pathetic creature dies, his army of mechanical automatons will wreak such destruction on our world as neither you nor I can contemplate. So I tell you again, put that gun away."

The silver eyes stared at him. Ian's finger tightened on the trigger.

Bartok stepped between him and the monstrosity.

"The eyes, they hold you, don't they, Ian? Your great uncle called them Mesmer's Eyes. They project a controlling power that is too real to deny. That's why none of us come here alone. There must be two. Never forget that. And put the gun back in your coat pocket. Please."

Slowly, Ian did as his uncle instructed.

"What has all this to do with us, Uncle Bartok? How is our family mixed up in this?"

A current of lightly ionized air floated past his uncle's face, and splashes of purple-green color lit his skin. It gave his face an eerie look, as though it were made from molded, colored wax.

"It was your great grandfather who learned of this calamity, Ian. The story is in his journals and those of his descendants, which I carry in this valise. At the time of his death, his last wish was for his descendants to somehow destroy this cavern without causing a disaster, without sentencing the poor souls trapped in these machines to Hell. We—you and I—are the last of his line. We're all that's left of the secret lineage. No one else knows of our relationship to this place except the Mozers."

"So what is it you want me to do?"

Bartok's face hardened. "You must find what our ancestor called 'the ghost box.'"

"The what? I don't understand."

From ten feet overhead came another piercing shriek, and fear coursed through Ian like a sudden fever. The back wall began to pulse erratically. A blast of static energy like particles of sand hurled against him and prickled his skin. The air resonated with pressure waves as though he was standing too close to a gigantic speaker.

"No time for questions," Bartok said. "It's waking."

"What's waking?"

"We have to get out right now."

Ian heard fear in his uncle's voice.

«« — »»

Bartok turned and began to hurry back the way they had come in. Ian followed him. He had lots of questions, but he felt suddenly more afraid than he had all night.

They'd only gone a short distance when Ian heard the sharp crack of breaking glass. Fear-fueled adrenaline shot through his body. He broke into a full out run, dragging his uncle behind him.

"Drop the valise," Ian shouted.

Bartok ignored him.

Ian was about to yank it from the old man's hand and throw it away, when a luminescent blur caught the corner of his eye and a cable shot into the side of Bartok's neck. Blood spurted from the wound as the sharp tip of a clawed metallic tentacle made a noise like an electric drill as it burrowed into his uncle's flesh. The old man's scream pierced the phosphorescent air while eerie silver-blue light lit his neck as though the energy flowing through Magnus Hillis pumped into his body.

Before he knew what he was doing, Ian's right hand grabbed the cold cable just behind the claw and his left hand slammed into the back of his uncle's head. Bartok screamed again and flew forward as the claw came free and blood and blue light spurted from the back of his neck and the cabled claw. Ian pulled out his pistol and turned to shoot the cable but it moved too quickly. He switched tactics and hammered it with the butt of his gun to keep the thing away from his face.

Solemn rows of giant automatons watched like sinister spec-tators as Ian ducked and weaved to evade the metal lash. He got a slippery grip again with one hand, put the barrel of his pistol to the metal and pulled the trigger. The tip slid off as the shot fired and Ian panicked as the bullet punched a hole through the tip of his boot. He tried to use his bodyweight to control the snake but it yanked and pulled and soon he felt it coil around him and tighten.

Bartok lay bleeding on the floor, his hand pressed to his neck. Ian saw him pulling off his scarf with his free hand, but lost sight of him when he was whipped away by a hard yank. The pistol clattered along the floor. Another coil looped around his waist and began to tighten. He saw the gun disappear into the army of automatons and realized he was going to die if he didn't do something.

As the coil tightened around his waist he tried to pull it loose, but his hands were covered with sweat. He looked desperately around for something he could use to pry it free, but he couldn't see anything. In the background, the monstrosity kept up a shrieking Samurai chatter. Twinkles of light popped and exploded in front of Ian's eyes like a fireworks display. He thought he saw Bartok rise from his knees and prayed the old man could get away.

Pressure built up in his ears. He closed his eyes for a minute to clear his thoughts. When he opened them again he was staring into the clawed tentacles. They were six inches in front of his face. As they spread apart as though to grasp prey, he saw the brilliant tip of a drill slide out from beneath a metal sheath and begin to spin so fast it turned into a thin blur. He felt the coils band tighter against his midsection and he vomited.

The bit was coming slowly toward him, as though the creature controlling it were tormenting him. Ian's breath came in huge, gasping gulps but he screamed when he realized that in a few seconds the bit would bore right into his forehead.

Two inches away and it stopped the exact second the thing behind him screeched loud enough to fracture bulletproof glass. The coils around his waist loosened and he would have fallen to the floor had not someone caught his arm and held him up.

"You're going to have to take it from here," whispered Bartok in a thick voice. "I'm losing too much blood."

The old man had wrapped the bloodied scarf tight as he dared around his neck to staunch the bleeding. In his right hand he clutched Ian's knife. In the other he still clasped the weathered valise. Ian took the knife back and put it in its sheath.

"Thanks," he said.

"Never mind that. Get me out of here."

Ian took the valise, shouldered his uncle and tried to ignore both the sharp pain in his ribs and the maniacal sounds coming from the back of the cavern. They moved as quickly as they could past the mechanical soldiers. He looked up once and saw spectral faces look down on them from their domed crystal fluorescent heads. He shuddered and moved faster. Bartok's breathing wasn't good and he was still leaking blood, but Ian was just glad he was alive.

"How are we going to explain your neck wound at the hospital?" Ian asked.

"Don't talk," Bartok rasped. "Keep moving."

Chapter Seven

"I want to caution you again, Detective, that although she's more stable now, she's not recovered fully from the trauma of the other night."

Alvarez had heard it all before. Doctors talked like warnings on the side of a prescription bottle—*Although this medication is supposed to help you, it may cause headaches, nausea, dizziness, a severe drop in blood pressure, a four-hour erection or death, etc., etc.*—usually delivered by a silver-haired white guy in a lab coat. Like Dr. Geitner.

"I'll do my best to keep that in mind, Doctor."

Dr. Geitner, tall and thin like an expensive cane, looked doubtful.

"I mean it, Detective."

"I know you do."

"Yes. Well. Just remember, she's a patient first and a witness second. Are we clear on that?"

Detective Alvarez didn't like looking up to meet the doctor's stare. He didn't like his pompous, officious attitude. Alvarez had at least three murders, one suicide, three unexplainable deaths and one missing person on his hand. No clue as to what happened yet. No leads. No ideas.

"I understand," Alvarez said.

"Can I count on that?"

Alvarez wondered how well the doctor would hold up in prison. Wondered how his bullshit attitude would play out there. *Love to find out*, he thought, *if I could just come up with a legitimate reason to send you there.*

"Cross my heart," Alvarez said.

He swallowed six sleeping pills before he finally crashed last night. Bad dreams haunted him off and on until dawn. Bodies shredded and hung from trees in a deserted, dark park past the edge of town made his heart pump so fast he woke up screaming two or three times.

Lucky he lived alone.

His wife left him six months to the day after they'd been married. Three months after they'd done the for-better-or-worse thing. She wouldn't have understood him sitting straight up in bed screaming *No, please no*. He was a policeman, after all.

He'd woken up wet as if he'd slept in the tub. And this woman, this Ashley Hillis, was in each of his nightmares. Burning. Lying in a hospital bed engulfed in angry flames. And pulsating red eyes that seemed to be looking for him floating above her bed.

He'd studied the woman's picture the day after the accident, when he was preparing to question her. Her photo was easy to look at. She appeared too decent to be tied up with Michael Hillis. But he knew that nice pictures sometimes hid ugly secrets. The more he thought about it, the more guilty she looked. That was probably what started the dreams. Suspects often found their way into his dreams when he was working on a case, but never before had one made it into his nightmares.

Then again, he had never seen anything like the Sharkey's Park murders. Read about it, but never seen it. And now the papers had brought up the murders from fifty seven years ago.

"Still Not Safe to Go Into the Water," was the headline in the Detroit East End Press. Had to happen sooner or later. It meant that Alvarez was now on a shorter leash.

But his mind was filled with the images of the horror that wouldn't leave him, terrifying images of the young woman who was the only witness to what happened. He tried to put them away and think of the woman as a witness. Only as a witness.

Ashley Hillis.

She took a good photograph, he'd give her that. Pretty. Dark brown hair. Twenty-six years old. White and rich. The kind of girl you'd dream about if you didn't have cable.

Her unaccounted for but presumed dead husband was Michael Hillis, owner and CEO of Quantum MW Technologies, now on the missing bodies list. Sole stockholder in the company. Worth somewhere in the range of fifteen million dollars. And he was the grandson of Becker Hillis. If they found his body, she was the new owner. He'd have to be careful how he treated her. She'd have lawyers. Lots of them. She could afford them.

But Alvarez would wear them down. She was tied up in this mess somehow. The survivors always were. And she was married to Michael Hillis, so she *had* to know something.

He followed Dr. Geitner into the darkened room. Private, of course. She had the room to herself. People with money always did.

"Ashley," said the doctor, "this is the policeman I told you would be coming to visit."

Alvarez blanched when he saw her.

"What is this?" he asked.

"We don't know," the doctor said.

Her hair was completely gray.

She had the face of a twenty-six year old, but both her eyebrows and her hair were the color of faded steel wool.

"Did you find Michael's … body?" she asked.

Her legs dangled over the edge of the bed. An IV was taped into place on the back of her hands. Tired eyes. Slack face. Poster child of a woman in mourning. A gray-haired young woman in mourning.

"No. I'm sorry, Mrs. Hillis."

Before she could ask anything else, Alvarez turned to Dr. Geitner and thanked him.

"Well, yes," the doctor said. "Ashley, I've told Detective Alvarez that although you were much better, I wouldn't tolerate you being subjected to stress. He's agreed to that, haven't you, Detective?"

"I have. For purposes of this interview."

Dr. Geitner studied him as though he were about to start another lecture. But after a moment's silence, he left the room without so much as a goodbye. A second later, the door opened again and he reminded Ashley that if she felt the interview was too much, all she had to do was push the nurse's button. He didn't look at Alvarez before closing the door for the last time.

"Do you mind if I pull up a chair?" Alvarez asked.

"Please," she said.

He grabbed a chair from near the foot of the bed and pulled it over toward the side with the food tray. A pitcher of ice and a short stack of cups were placed there and when she saw him look at it, she offered him a drink.

"No, no thank you," he said, handing her a card.

"Detective Elvio Alvarez. Did I say that right?"

"Close enough."

"I'm sorry no one told you about my hair. I looked it up on the internet," she said, pointing to the television at the far end of the bed. "It's not supposed to be possible. Stress can't turn your hair white. I Googled it. All the doctors say fear can't turn your hair gray. It's a myth."

She seemed ashamed to say it.

He noticed the wireless keyboard balanced on the edge of her nightstand and understood. This might be bad. It hadn't occurred to him that she could be up on the case. But if she had access to the Internet, then she had access to the news.

"Well, something did," Alvarez said.

She smoothed her hospital gown. Grief took hold of her face and wouldn't let go. But she kept her eyes on him. Not ashamed of the tears.

"You want a tissue?" he asked, looking around.

"No. Sorry. It just comes over me. I'm feeling okay and then it hits me that he's gone. Can you tell me anything, anything at all?"

She wiped her eyes with the back of her hand and shook her head as though to shake off the bad thoughts.

"We don't really know much yet, Mrs. Hillis."

"Ashley," she said, "Call me Ashley."

"You've probably been following the news," he began.

"No. I quit. Couldn't listen to it. They're awful. Reporters are awful."

There will be a lot more of them when you get out, Alvarez thought. *You're going to be a media event. Good-looking victims play well on the tube. And that gray hair will get you the sympathy vote.*

"Have they been bothering you?"

"The hospital staff keeps them away. But every time an orderly or a nurse comes in, I wonder if they're undercover reporters. You know, trying to get the big scoop. But I don't have a big scoop. I don't know anything."

Alvarez had interviewed a lot of people over the years and he knew the moment had come to set the pace.

"I'm sorry to intrude on you, Mrs. Hillis," he said, "and I appreciate you talking to me."

He withdrew a pad and paper from his pocket and began writing. With the ease of years of habit, he started with her name and particulars, writing while he listened.

"I didn't know anyone still did that," Ashley said.

"Did what?"

"Took notes. I thought you used digital recorders or something."

"Well, I'm kind of old-fashioned. Now, what I'd like for you to do is to tell me what happened that night. Anything you remember. You're the only witness we have right now."

Ashley folded her hands together in her lap and began to rub the back of one with the palm of the other. She looked down at the pale brown floor tiles as though looking for a teleprompter.

"Take your time. Anything at all will be helpful."

"It was awful," Ashley said. "We should have never gone."

Alvarez waited a beat before he continued.

"Why is that?" he asked.

"What do you mean, why?" she said, suddenly angry. "My husband might be dead or he might be alive but nobody knows for sure. Josh brought me to the hospital and then committed suicide by jumping from the roof. And the rest of my friends that went are already dead. I heard that much on the news. So what do you think, Detective? Was it a good idea to go? Is that what a good idea is like?"

Alvarez leaned back casually to reduce the tension, nodding his head like he completely understood. She was torqued, that was for sure. Wound tight. Already didn't like him. And in addition to being rich, she had a temper. He'd keep that in mind.

"I'm sorry, Ashley. That was thoughtless. Would you like me to go now and come back another day?"

She glared at him for a moment, then her face softened.

"No. I'm okay. Okay as I can be, I guess. It's not you, it's just I don't want to go back to that night. I want to forget it ever happened."

"I'm sorry. But I can't investigate without something to go on. Can you tell me anything that happened that night? Anything?"

The fight seemed to drain from her and he saw her shoulders slump.

"I can try," she said.

For the next fifteen minutes, she told him everything she remembered, no matter how crazy she thought it sounded.

And to Alvarez, it sounded *very* crazy.

《《—》》

"Do you think I'm crazy?"

"I'm not a psychiatrist, Mrs. Hillis. But I've heard a lot of strange stories."

And Alvarez had heard his share of weird things. Like the lady who kept calling the police because aliens were keeping her up at night with their noisy landings on her roof. Like the man who wouldn't use his toilet because he was afraid rats would come up through the sewer and bite him on the ass.

"And?"

"And I've given up trying to figure out what's true and what's not. I just follow the facts."

"What kind of facts, Detective?"

Time to get into it.

"How long have you and your husband owned Sharkey's Park and the area surrounding it?"

No sign of recognition whatsoever in her beautiful face. She just stared at him, as though wondering if he were crazier than her.

"Where in the world did you get that idea?"

"Public records," he said, without looking up from his notepad.

"That's crazy."

"It's a fact, Mrs. Hillis. I don't know what to do with it yet, but it's a matter of public record."

"Well, you'd better check again," she said, lifting her chin defiantly, "because as far as I know, we do *not* own that property. That is the last piece of real estate I'd ever want to own."

She stared hard at him, daring him to call her a liar.

"I'll do that. Was the other night your first trip to Sharkey's Park?"

"Yes, absolutely yes. But Michael had been there before to check the place out. Even after the letter came, he still wanted to go ahead with his investigation."

Now Alvarez was off balance.

"What letter?" he asked.

"It was a warning."

"What did it say?"

"It said to leave the dead be. I saved it," she said. "It was in my wallet. My wallet is in my purse. It's probably still in the van. Probably soaked."

"Leave the dead be? Is that exactly what it said?"

Alvarez wrote the information down, pressing hard with his pen, barely aware that his hand was moving.

"Yes. Exactly."

"And do you know who sent you this warning?"

"Michael's great grandmother from Kentucky. She's like a hundred years old or something. I wish we'd listened to her."

She was starting to tear up again. Time to go for the kill.

"We found a grave in Sharkey's Park," he said.

"A grave?"

"Yes, a grave. Someone dug it up recently and then covered it over again. Do you know anything about that?"

"Why would I know anything about it? I didn't even know there was a grave until you told me. Do you mean there was a cemetery on the property?"

Alvarez flipped through his notebook as though looking for information.

"No, just a single grave. Inside we found the remains of a girl that we estimate to have been roughly ten years old at the time of her death."

Ashley looked bewildered.

"I don't know what you're talking about."

Alvarez heard the door open behind him and knew his time was almost up. He turned to tell Dr. Geitner that he was nearly through, but the man in the doorway wasn't Dr. Geitner. He was twice Dr. Geitner's girth and dressed in a suit that probably cost more than Alvarez's entire wardrobe. His black hair was slicked back and hung almost down to his shoulders.

"You'll have to come back later," Alvarez said sternly, "We're having a private discussion."

The fat man smiled broadly and pointed his finger at Alvarez.

"I think not, Detective," he said. "My name is Henry Wendland, and I am legal counsel for the Hillis family."

Ashley started to object, but a glance from Wendland silenced her.

"From this moment forward I will need to be present each and every time you interview my client."

Suddenly Ashley stood up, yanking a cable free. Her monitor started beeping frantically. She pointed an accusing finger at Alvarez and screamed at him.

"Why aren't you trying to find my husband instead of asking all these stupid questions? He's out there somewhere. He could be hurt. Maybe he's got amnesia. Why aren't you looking for him instead of trying to make us look guilty of something? You're worse than one of those reporters."

"Calm down, Ashley," Wendland said. "The policeman is just doing his job. It doesn't help to get upset."

Ashley whirled to face her lawyer.

"Upset? You haven't even seen upset. I've never met you before in my entire life, so how do I even know you're my lawyer?"

Wendland pulled out an envelope from his inner jacket pocket as smoothly as a magician producing a hidden scarf.

"This should explain everything," he said. "My apologies for taking so long to get here, Ashley, but I was out of the country when Michael went missing. And Detective, are you quite through here so my client and I can talk in private?"

An abrupt voice from behind him told Alvarez he was indeed through.

"I warned you, Detective."

Dr. Geitner had returned to defend his patient. Alvarez wondered how long it would have taken to show up if Ashley Hillis was unattractive, overweight and poor.

"Just doing my job, Doctor," he said, putting his notebook away.

He left the room without saying good-bye.

Chapter Eight

Alvarez rang the buzzer for the third time.

Still no answer.

The address was right. 11155 Wilmot Avenue. Lincoln Jones's residence. The nurse who quit the hospital three nights ago. A blond-brick ranch with blue shutters. Well-kept lawn with a winding sidewalk. Curtains drawn, Ford Focus in the driveway with the correct license plates.

The neighborhood was middle-class suburban. Everything neat and organized. All the lawns cut the same length. Every yard the same length. No cracks in the sidewalks. But the sun was headed toward the safety of the horizon and the dark shadows of night would soon take over the neighborhood. Alvarez knew what kind of things happened in nice neighborhoods when the sun went down. He'd been a cop a long time.

He knocked.

"Mr. Jones, it's Detective Alvarez with the Milford police. I just need to ask you a few questions."

Alvarez hated standing outside while Jones huddled behind the door, pretending he wasn't home. If he wanted to pretend that he wasn't there, the least he could have done was park the car somewhere else.

"Mr. Jones, if you don't answer the door, I'll call in a warrant. Then we'll have to bust open your door and that is so unnecessary. You have a nice looking door here; think what it will look like if we have to use a battering ram."

Of course, that wouldn't happen, but the average civilian didn't know any better unless they spent every night watching cop shows.

"I don't want to talk to anybody," came a muffled voice behind the door.

"I'm not anybody," Alvarez said, "I'm the police."

"I didn't do anything."

"I know that, Mr. Jones. I just want to talk to you for a minute. You're not a suspect."

"Then why do I have to talk to you?"

"Because if you don't, I'm going to get a warrant citing you as a material witness in a homicide investigation, then we'll bust down your door and drag you away in front of your neighbors."

Alvarez started counting in his head. One second, two seconds, three seconds. He knew Jones was going to open the door, Jones knew he was going to open the door. Now if the man would just do it.

He'd made it to twenty seconds when he heard the deadbolt being pulled back and saw the door swing open.

Jones was six foot tall, built like a former athlete with an inner tube around his gut, and the hooded brown eyes of a man who suspected everyone was out to get him. He opened the door all the way and stepped back.

"Let's get this over with," he said.

"Next time I knock," Alvarez said, "just open the door, will you?"

Jones's living room was clean and neat. Like he had a maid on call. Light blue carpet, a couch the size of a small car, and a big screen television. Football game on mute. Alvarez didn't pay any attention to football. Two cats, one white and one black, milled around the floor as though Alvarez had come to visit them.

"These are my cats," Jones said. "Minx and Eve. Say hello to the policeman, girls."

"Nice," Alvarez said.

"You want to sit?"

"Sure."

Alvarez went to a recliner on the far side of the room, directly underneath a Thomas Kincaid print, and sat on the edge. Jones remained standing for a moment, as though hoping Alvarez would change his mind and leave. When that didn't happen, he walked to the couch and fell back on it.

"You got any ID?" he asked suddenly.

"Should have asked that at the door."

But Alvarez flashed his creds anyway and then gave Jones his card.

"Detective Elvio Alvarez? Elvio? What's that, like Spanish for Elvis?"

Everybody is a comedian, Alvarez thought.

"Close enough. But let's get to it, okay? Only reason I'm here is to find out why you quit your job at the hospital."

"Got nothing to say about that," said Jones.

Alvarez pulled out his notebook and propped it on his knee.

"We going to start this crap again? Just tell me why you quit. I'll ask you a few questions, then I'll leave and you can go back to pretending you're not home. Only you might start by putting your car in the garage so it will look more convincing."

"I didn't do anything."

"I didn't say you did. Just tell me why you quit."

"What did she tell you? She say I'm crazy?"

"Who?"

"Don't give me that. Nurse Wilson. She told you what I saw, didn't she?"

"Somebody tells me something, it's confidential."

"Well, I'm not crazy."

"Good, I'm glad to hear it. So why did you quit? What happened?"

Jones's two cats wandered over and rubbed against his legs. He reached down and petted them. Alvarez didn't particularly like cats, but if it kept Jones talking, he was willing to act like he did.

When Jones didn't say anything, Alvarez kept quiet. Waiting him out. The trick was, you had to keep looking at the person. Alvarez hated staring at Jones. Just once, he'd like someone to answer a question without all the cagey bullshit. But he kept looking at him, fighting back the urge to look around the room and see if he could find anything incriminating. Or just get up and choke him until he talked.

Finally, Jones spoke.

"I got a better job offer, that's all."

Jesus, this guy was a terrible liar. He looked down at the floor when he said it, like he was ashamed to be doing it.

"Name?" asked Alvarez.

"What?"

"Who offered you the job? And I need their phone number so I can verify what you're telling me is the truth so I don't have to charge you with obstructing justice."

"What's that mean?"

"That means I'd get to drag you downtown, grill you under hot lights, and then throw you in a cell with a bunch of smelly bikers until you were ready to tell me what I want to know."

Jones stood up slowly, stretched and said, "Well you might just go ahead and do it. That's all I'm going to tell you."

He said it defiant-like. Tough guy taking a stand. Alvarez didn't bother to get out of the chair. First, because Jones was a lot taller than him, so it would kind of ruin the authority dynamics, and second, because he was comfortable where he was.

"Okay, Mr. Jones."

Jones looked at him suspiciously.

"What do you mean, 'okay'?"

"I mean, if you don't want to help. Okay. We'll just leave Nurse Wilson's statement as the only record of what you said you saw. I was trying to get your side of this, since you may be called in as a material witness."

Jones started backing up toward the kitchen. There was a thin sheen of sweat trickling down from his bald head. His right hand started slapping against his hip.

"Material witness to what? Why don't you just leave me alone?"

Drugs, maybe? It crossed Alvarez's mind. Nurse. Worked in a hospital. Easy access. Sure. Or maybe just a normal guy really scared of something.

"Calm down, Mr. Jones," Alvarez said. "In fact, sit down and quit freaking out on me. I'm trying to help you, for God's sake."

"Help me? How's that?"

Alvarez had enough.

"Sit your big ass back down. Now."

Maybe he'd called it wrong. Jones suddenly looked like he was going to cry.

"I didn't do anything wrong. I just went in there to help her. She was freaking out so I went running to see what was going on. You should have heard the way she was screaming her insides out. So I left my desk and went to help. Was that wrong?"

"You did the right thing," Alvarez said.

Jones laughed. A high, uncomfortable laugh laced with pain.

"The right thing? Oh, man, no, I did the wrong thing. If I'd have stayed right where I was and let the floor nurses take care of it, you wouldn't be here. The only reason I saw it was I went to help."

Alvarez leaned forward on the edge of the chair. He tried to look genuinely encouraging.

"Go on, Mr. Jones, you're doing fine. What did you see?"

Lincoln Jones seemed to drift off, turning his eyes inward. His face contorted with fear. His pale white skin seemed to mottle and his breathing grew hard and loud.

"What I saw? I don't know what I saw."

He held both hands in front of his face, as though to shield himself from something.

Alvarez waited for an answer.

"I saw a demon, that's what I saw."

"A demon?"

Hard to act like he believed that one, so Alvarez tried to keep a neutral game face.

"And where did this demon come from?"

"What?" Jones asked.

He lowered his hands and looked at Alvarez as though *he* were crazy.

"I mean," Alvarez said, "how did this demon get into the room? Through the window? Through the door?"

Jones looked thoughtful for a moment. Thoughtful. How the hell somebody as whacked as Jones could look thoughtful was beyond Alvarez.

"It was hugging her, I think. Scared the shit right out of me. And that bitch was wild. Kicked me in the head and tried to claw my eyes right out."

Alvarez pretended to be taking accurate notes.

"So it didn't come out of her body, it was just clinging to her body, is that it?"

Jones nodded his head enthusiastically.

"Absolutely. That's it. Like it was trying to get in, but couldn't. Then we show up. I think that's why that woman Ashley was acting so wild. Because that thing was trying to get inside her head and she was fighting it off."

Where is that video cam when you need it? Alvarez wondered.

"And what did this demon look like?"

Damned if Jones didn't seem to think about that, too.

"It was like angry smoke. That's what it looked like to me. With these red eyes looking out at me."

"Angry smoke?"

"And it was like it saw me, and it was like it saw me, and it was thinking, 'I'm going to get you.' Like it cursed me. Like it was going to come back for me. That's why I quit. I can't go in that place—ever. It's going to come back for me."

The worst part was, this big, overweight professional medical man believed every bit of what he was saying. Either a druggie or a genuine whack job. Alvarez folded up his notebook, put it back in his pocket and stood up.

"Thank you, Mr. Jones," he said. "Thank you very much for your help."

Alvarez started moving toward the door. The cats huddled beneath the coffee table as though embarrassed by their owner.

"You believe me, don't you?"

"Have a good day, Mr. Jones."

"Can't you give me some kind of police protection?"

There was a desperate, too eager sound to the man's voice. No wonder the guy kept his door locked and the windows closed. He wasn't hiding from the police; he thought he was hiding from a demon.

"I'll look into it, Mr. Jones."

Alvarez was glad to pull the front door closed behind him.

Chapter Nine

Ian looked into the barrel of Enid Mozer's automatic rifle.

"He's hurt. We've got to get him to a hospital," he said, looking over at Bartok.

"Don't take another step," Enid told him.

There was cold fear in the man's voice that caused Ian to panic.

"What the hell is wrong with you? I said he's hurt. He needs a doctor."

Bartok was slumped against his shoulder. They were three steps from the grave's lip. Ian sucked in air in painful gasps. His uncle's blood smeared his hands and face and adrenaline had his body on overdrive.

"Drop him back down the stairs. Come up alone. If you don't, I'll shoot you both and we'll fill up the entrance."

The four Mozers stood silhouetted against the night by the thin illumination of a hooded lantern. They rimmed the hole, Enid at the mouth of the grave's maw standing tall and dark as Death itself.

"Listen to him," Bartok choked.

Ian's arm circled the old man's waist to keep him from falling. As tall as his uncle was, he felt no more substantial that a stick man wrapped in wet clothes.

"Look at his neck," Enid said.

Beneath his Uncle's skin, Ian saw wisps of eerie light swarming like phantom parasites. The sight of it almost caused him to drop the old man and bolt up the remaining steps.

"He can't come out," Enid said.

Bartok raised his head.

"Like the dogs, eh, Enid?"

"Yeah, like the dogs."

Ian loosened his grip on Bartok, shrinking back from him.

The old man turned his head and fixed his dark eyes on his nephew, and as he did Ian saw twisting rods of light blurt across them.

"I'm sorry, but Enid's right. Leave me behind, Ian. There's nothing else to be done."

"I can't do that," Ian said.

"Step aside," Enid said.

The ground suddenly began to tremble and Ian fought to maintain his balance. He saw a look of sheer horror transform Enid's face as a garish light emanated from down below them.

"It's getting stronger," Bartok gasped.

And then a violent blast of burning wind threw them into the air and hurtled them full on into Enid, the force of it knocking him backward as though he had been crashed into by a battering ram. The impact twisted Ian's body and he landed on his back so hard it knocked the breath out of his lungs. He lay on the hard ground gasping for air. Wild winds shrieked around him like tortured spirits. Dark rainbows of forbidden colors erupted around him. He crawled backwards, dragging himself along by his elbows and the force of his sheer terrified will. A strong hand grabbed the collar of his coat and yanked him to his feet.

Bartok's face came into view just inches from his own.

"Hurry!" the old man shouted. "Grab a shovel!"

Bartok released him and hurried away, skirting the open grave, striding purposefully through the madness. Ian saw him drop to his knees on the far side of the headstone and fumble with something near its base. The earth shook again and the sound of giants gears turning cut through the howling winds.

But the underground door closed slowly and Ian shook with the urgent knowledge that whatever alien presence was wakening had to be contained. The awful purple-green light and the violent tourbillion of scorching air still blasting from the open grave seemed to be alive with rage. And from within the madness, Ian could hear whisperings, the urgings of Albert Magnus Hillis's diseased mind.

"Are you deaf? Grab a shovel," Bartok snapped.

The underground slab finally rolled completely shut, instantly cutting off the wind and light as though a switch had been thrown. Ian's nerves still jumped and twitched with fear. Too close. Whatever it was trying to follow them came too close to escaping.

Mozers lay fallen about the grave opening like scattered bowling pins. He stared at them, unable to understand what had happened. But when Bartok grabbed a shovel and began tossing dirt into the hole, Ian shook off his confusion and did the same. Fear drove him; the consuming desire to bury the terrors below ground and seal them away forever stoked his efforts.

He stole occasional glances at his uncle and couldn't believe what he saw. Bartok's wound was gone. He seemed filled with angry vitality, shoveling like a tireless machine. Ian could barely keep pace. Pain flared in his back, shoulders and arms. Then one and then another of the Mozers was beside him, digging into the pile of dirt and frantically flinging it into the grave. No one spoke. Each was driven by the need to close the gateway.

They shoveled like madmen until Bartok said it was enough.

《《—》》

Enid was on his feet again.

The old man had bent down, grabbed the lapels of his coat and picked him up with one hand and stood him upright.

At the sight of Bartok's strength, Enid's eyes narrowed with purpose. He swung his head toward the other Mozers who stood together near the edge of the freshly filled grave.

"Guns," he said.

As he said it, he twisted and turned to get some distance from Bartok, but the old man, to Ian's amazement, effortlessly yanked Enid close.

"Don't be a fool," he said.

"Shoot him," Enid shouted.

Ian went for his gun, and then realized he'd dropped it somewhere underground. He scanned the grass, saw Enid's automatic weapon and went for it. A single shot knocked it away.

"Stop right there," one of the other Mozers said. "Another step and the next one's in your back."

Glancing toward Bartok, Ian saw that the old man held Enid in front of him like a shield. Ian saw a thin glint of silver and knew that his uncle held a blade to the eldest Mozer's neck.

"I'll cut his throat if you don't listen to what I have to say."

The other Mozers began to drift apart, their weapons held loose. They were angling for a clean shot.

"Give me five minutes to explain," Bartok said.

Ian searched the ground for another weapon, found none and simply stood where he was so as not to complicate the situation. The Mozers stopped moving, waiting for Enid's cue. The chill night air seemed to thin, and Ian's nerves were on overload. From somewhere near the mansion, he heard a low, muted howl that made the skin on his neck pimple with fear.

Enid flinched.

"Take us to the dog," Bartok said.

Enid kept quiet. The other Mozers stood still. In the pallid light, their skin was the white-washed gray of park statues.

"How long did it take to turn?" Bartok asked.

"Week, maybe two."

"Give me what time you can," Bartok said, pressing the knife edge against the man's Adam's apple. "Things have gone very wrong down below. Ian saw it. Tell him, Ian."

"Tell him what?" Ian asked. "He saw what just happened."

"Don't help him," Enid said. "He ain't human anymore."

Without thinking, Ian took a step toward his uncle and his prisoner.

"Stay back," Enid said.

"Why?"

"Line of fire."

Ian got the point and stayed where he was. He could think of nothing else to do. Bartok took a step back with Enid. His eyes flared like tarnished silver, and then dimmed.

What has happened to him? Ian wondered. He remembered the cable squirming into the old man's neck, pumping him full of strange, fluid light and shuddered. It affected the old man somehow, changed him.

"You're wondering if I'm the same," Bartok said. "All of you. You fear that I'm contaminated by what's below, and you're right to be afraid."

Enid opened his mouth to say something, but hesitated when the old man slid the point of the blade underneath his chin.

"Don't move, friend."

"I ain't your friend anymore."

"How long do I have?" Bartok asked. "How long before I am no longer who I am?"

"You're already gone."

"Tell me."

"Couple of days. Maybe a week," Enid said. "You're bigger than the dogs."

"What are you talking about?" Ian demanded.

"The dogs took a few days to start turning. I figure you got a week."

"He doesn't know about the madstone," Bartok said, jerking his head toward Ian. "He doesn't know the history, doesn't know what we're up against. Neither do you. You'll need my help. You need my knowledge."

"Let me think a minute," Enid said to his brothers.

"Can someone please tell me what's going on here?" Ian asked.

"Shut up," Enid said.

Ian looked at the man in disbelief. But when Enid Mozer fixed his eyes on him, Ian kept still.

"I can't trust you," Enid said.

"Then handcuff me. Do what you have to, but keep me alive to tell Ian and you what you need to know. It's coming alive down below. Something's happening and we have to move quickly. You know what will happen if we don't. You need my help. Use me while you can, kill me when you must, old friend."

With that, Bartok removed the knife from Enid's neck, stepped away and dropped the blade. Three rifles followed him, locked on his chest with laser dots. Ian held his breath. The Kentucky night was cold, quiet and uneasy. He was miles from anywhere with four armed rednecks and a crazy old man whose eyes flickered with alien light. No one knew where he was. No one knew where to look for him.

"Rake, get me the chains from the back of my pickup."

Rake, the youngest Mozer, hesitated, afraid to take his weapon away from Bartok.

"I said do it," Enid snapped.

"There's no need to chain him," Ian said. "He's an old man. He's not dangerous."

Bartok stared hard at him.

"When the time comes," the old man said, "if Enid is not able, you will have to kill me."

"I can't do that."

"Remember the ground on which you stand, Ian. Think of what you saw below. Yes, you remember, I see that. When the time comes, if your hand falters, remember what you saw and you will be glad to pull the trigger."

«« — »»

Michael was burning.

Ashley screamed and ran toward him. The acrid, awful stench of burning skin was so strong that it hurt to breathe.

Michael was screaming.

It was night. They were in Sharkey's Park. Michael stood between the dance hall and the concession stand like a human torch. Ashley ran up the hill toward him screaming and choking and slipping on the wet grass. Her feet flew out from under her and she landed hard on her elbows and knees. Up again, running toward him, hearing him scream her name.

"I'm coming," she cried.

Wind tossed the trees. Empty drink cartons sprang up and flew past her.

"Coming, I'm coming."

Michael was dying. He burned impossibly bright as she crested the hill.

She looked frantically for a faucet, a bucket of water. A blanket. Nothing. Nothing to put out the fire.

Blackened skin fell from his face. He held out his arms toward her as he started to fold over.

The sight of him made her stop and cringe.

He fell apart. He crumbled and folded in on himself like a burning mound of grayed charcoal.

Ashley began to sob and beat her fists on the ground, calling his name over and over. Rain pelted her but she didn't notice, didn't care, wasn't aware of anything but her deep and overwhelming grief.

"You got to get up, Ashley," a familiar voice said.

Shari.

"He burned and I couldn't save him," Ashley sobbed.

She felt the reassuring pressure of her friend's hand on her shoulder and turned her head to look up.

Shari, steel rod still sticking out the side of her head, grinned down at her.

Ashley screamed and screamed and screamed.

Chapter Ten

Despite her violent nightmares, Ashley was released the next day with a purse full of medications and under the supervision of her lawyer, Henry Wendland. The hospital staff, under the strict instructions of Dr. Geitner, cooperated with the plan to have her released quietly through a side entrance. But the press was tipped off and they were waiting for the attorney and his client. Henry Wendland, however, had arranged a trick of his own. The young woman he escorted out the side entrance in a wheelchair was not Ashley Hillis, but a secretary from his office.

«« — »»

Ashley Hillis, wearing a jogging outfit, baseball cap and wide sunglasses provided for her by Wendland, checked into an inexpensive motel two towns away. Her driver, too, was an employee of Wendland Associates. The lawyer provided her a key in advance, and there was no need for registration as a suite of rooms was registered under the name of a shell company which paid a week in advance. A team of bodyguards discreetly kept watch over her room.

You won't even know they are there, Wendland assured her.

He also provided her with cash, a company credit card, a laptop, reading materials and a prepaid cell phone.

"I'll be there later this evening," he said. "There are company details I have to attend to on your behalf. When that's taken care of, we can talk. I'll fill you in then on what you may not know."

Ashley pressed hard for the lawyer to tell her right then, but he assured her that he needed time to get the details straight. She swallowed a Xanax and chased it with a long drink of water. The schedule, Dr. Geitner had told her, had to be adhered to. Recovery took time, so she sank back into a chair next to the reading lamp and waited for the pill to take effect.

Numb my brain, she thought. *I can't take this.*

Something in the way Wendland said things was disturbing, as though she wouldn't like at all what she was about to hear. And she wondered if there were things he wasn't telling her.

"Seven o'clock tonight," he said.

So Ashley waited, flipping through magazines, waiting, finding movies on cable and waiting some more. The waiting was the hardest part. She felt lethargic, empty and alone. She couldn't believe that Michael was gone and most likely dead. She kept thinking back to the day they met when she interviewed him for an online magazine.

Dead. He was probably dead. The thought drained her of emotion.

Memories of what happened that night draped over her like a lead blanket. The storm. Her last look at Michael. The water. The cold, dark water. The feel of Shari's dead body when she'd ducked underwater to avoid Josh's axe. The long walk up the muddy hill while the wind whipped around her and rain lashed her face.

The police still hadn't found Michael's body.

This ambiguity tormented her. Was there any chance that he was still alive? Logic said no, but she could not overcome the need for it. But if he had survived, then where was he?

If he was dead, sooner or later she would have to identify his body. She didn't think she could do it. Maybe if she told them his identifying marks, that might be enough. He had four scars. One on the bottom of his left foot where he stepped on a nail a few years back. One on the top of that foot where the nail came out the other side. One nail, two scars. Another scar ran across his jaw where he'd fallen and cracked his chin open in the fifth grade while running to catch a baseball. But those were all old scars, faint, but still there. Then there was the newest scar he got right after they were married. The deep cut on his thumb that he'd sliced with a box cutter at the office.

She unpacked the clothes Wendland had provided for her, arranging them on a shiny steel rack in the room's only closet. She organized the remainder in drawers. Her toothbrush and the rest she left on the bathroom counter. The room came with a small kitchenette, which Wendland, ever thoughtful, had stocked with food and coffee.

Her lawyer was an enigma. Michael had never mentioned him. Oh, she knew his company retained attorneys, but it bothered her that this man, whom Michael apparently trusted to run his business in the event of an emergency, just appeared out of the blue with all the appropriate legal documents. She felt angry that Michael had never as much as mentioned Wendland to her. The way he hadn't mentioned Granny Hillis until the letter arrived.

The hours ticked by. Ashley felt as though her life was now totally in the hands of people she didn't know. Her lawyer and that devious Detective Alvarez. Both of them apparently knew more about Michael's affairs than she did. Why had Michael shut her out? Why hadn't she asked more questions?

Twenty minutes of restless pacing and she stopped in front of the mirror on the wall above the long dresser. She looked like Morticia Adams. Her face was drawn, and what little eye makeup she'd applied wasn't getting the job done. And the gray hair and eyebrows didn't help. At the hospital, they'd try to get her to color it back to her normal brunette, but she refused to do that. It would make Dr. Geitner happy because he kept telling everyone how it was simply not medically possible. She wanted to believe that, but looking in the mirror made it hard to do. Scientifically, a woman's hair could not turn gray overnight because of stress.

So much for science.

She grew tired of movies and magazines and eyed her laptop. It occurred to her that she was a writer, that she researched things for her stories. What if she treated this situation as a piece she was investigating? Writing was the only thing she really did well, and at that moment it seemed the only way to regain some sense of control.

Feeling a sense of purpose for the first time since the whole thing started, Ashley put the laptop on the room's only desk, plugged it in, opened it, and pushed the power button. Time to organize what she knew, what she wanted to learn and how to go about learning it. For the first time since that horrible night, she allowed herself a small smile. She was a good researcher.

The sudden intrusion of the hotel phone ringing startled her so badly she almost tipped the chair over. The only people that knew where she was worked for Wendland, so after a moment's hesitation she picked up the receiver and said a tentative hello.

"Ashley? It's me, Henry. How are you holding up? Wait. Stupid question. Listen, I can't meet you until tomorrow morning around nine. Too many loose ends to tie up. But did you know that Michael's great grandmother was coming to see you?"

"How could I? I've been in the hospital."

"I mean, was this planned? Her nephew, somebody named Kenneth who talks like Jed Clampett, keeps calling around trying to find you."

"Granny Hillis is here? No, I had no idea she was coming."

"Her nephew says it's important. He says she has to talk to you."

"Why?"

"Ashley, I'm just the messenger here. I'd advise you let me speak to her on your behalf. You don't need this now."

Ashley fingered the phone cord like it was a rosary. There was an odd tension in his voice that Wendland was doing his best to disguise. Something was very wrong.

Child, let the dead be.

"No, I want to see her."

"I advise against it."

Again, that slight edge to his voice.

"Set it up, Henry. She knows something and I want to hear it. It's about Michael, I just know it."

Silence on the other end of the line for a few seconds, then a heavy sigh.

"I'll take care of it."

"Thank you, Henry."

After hanging up the phone, Ashley typed in the name Granny Hillis as a resource. She was going to get to the bottom of this and find Michael, no matter what. And she'd talk to anyone who could help her.

The Xanax finally numbed her anxiety. She turned out the lights, laid down on the bed and drifted away.

«« — »»

Michael's face in a dark, foggy mist. His hands desperately reaching out for her, pleading.

"Not dead, Ashley. Not dead. Help me. Please help me."

His words tore at her heart.

Not dead. Michael was still alive.

"Trapped. Can't get back. Help me. Save me."

Ghostly vaporous arms, reaching through the mist, wrapping around him, pulling him back, back into the darkness.

She reached out for him; saw her hands grasping at him as he vanished into nothing. A hard wrench at the back of her head, and she was suddenly staring at a black wall. Where was she? Another hard pull and she fell down, landing on the bed in her motel room. The room around was dark and terror jolted her fully awake.

Michael wasn't dead. He was trapped somewhere in a dark place in terrible danger, but he was alive. Or she was losing her mind.

«« — »»

Lincoln Jones divided his time between searching the internet and shopping. Looking for wards and talismans against demons and then scouring New Age shops until he found them.

He arrived home from the last trip just before dusk, breaking the speed limit all the way home. With his arms full of shopping bags, he fumbled at the front door keyhole and made it inside just as the last light of day disappeared. He double-bolted the door behind him, then took his armload into the kitchen and deposited everything on the glass and chrome table.

His research had been very helpful.

He took out six red candles and put three on the floor in front of the front door and three in front of the back door. They were long burning candles and he'd bought replacements. He just needed to get through the night. Tomorrow he was leaving town and heading for Chicago. Nurses with his qualifications were in demand everywhere and Lincoln was glad of it. He couldn't bear the thought of spending another night alone in his house.

Things had scratched at his windows for the last two nights. He didn't have the nerve to pull back the drapes and see what was there. Maybe it was cats. But his own two cats had stayed under his bed and refused to come out. Lincoln took that as a bad sign.

His hands shook as he nailed everything from pentacles to crucifixes to the wall. In the act of pouring rosewater into cereal bowls, he spilled half of it on his kitchen counter.

"Rosewater can suck the life out of a demon," he kept telling himself while positioning bowls underneath each window in his house.

The top of the line electromagnetic field detector he'd purchased was just like the one they used on the TV show "Ghost Hunters." Same with the FLIR he'd bought so he could look for cold spots. And stacked on his microwave were the twenty-four high-octane energy drinks he'd purchased to keep him awake.

A person is more vulnerable to a demon's attacks if they are asleep, he'd read online.

He looked at the digital numbers on the cable box. Eight thirty. Darkness controlled the neighborhood. No more going outside. No going to sleep. One more night. That's all he needed. Just one more night and he was out of this town.

He wished he'd never gone to help Ashley Hillis.

Around his neck, in a glass tube suspended from a silver chain, were the ashes of a burnt chicken. The clerk had taken him into the backroom to explain that they weren't from just any chicken, but a sacrificial chicken used in a voodoo rite to ward off evil. Lincoln didn't believe in voodoo, but he wasn't taking any chances.

He fell to his knees and began praying. Asking for God to protect him. Asking the angels to protect him. Asking Allah and Buddha to protect him.

By eleven o'clock his nerves were so bad he sat on the couch with his head between his knees, crying.

That detective may have thought he was crazy, but he hadn't seen what Lincoln had. He hadn't witnessed those red eyes surrounded by orange and black flames. He hadn't felt them measuring who he was, remembering him, marking him. Jesus, that thing was going to come for him. He just needed one more night and then he was gone; long gone.

He stood straight up and screamed.

"Why do you want me? I haven't done anything wrong. I was just trying to help a poor sick lady. Leave me the fuck alone."

There. He'd said it. He'd said it out loud. He'd told the demon to leave him alone. Maybe that was the best magic of all.

Then he felt a chill rise from the bottom of his spine to the back of his neck. The EMF detector in the other room started making a crazy beeping noise and then started to squeal like an air raid alert.

Lincoln ran to the kitchen and took out every sharp knife he owned and carried them into the living room. He arranged them in a haphazard row in front of him on the coffee table, points away from him. Somewhere he'd read that demons were terrified of knives. About time something other than him was terrified.

"I've got knives," he shouted to the empty room. "Don't you dare come near me. I've got a table full of knives.

The EMF detector continued wailing. Lincoln took a knife with him and ran to get the ghost detector and the FLIR imager so he could look for cold spots. Demons come from flames, but they draw the energy from everything around them to hide their coldness. He'd read that somewhere, too.

Lincoln Jones didn't know what to believe.

Back on the couch, he tried to make sense of the EMF meter. The numbers kept climbing, but what did they really mean? Maybe there was a storm building outside and it was driving the thing haywire. There was a manual in the box it came in, but Lincoln wasn't leaving the couch to get. No, sir. He liked being next to his table of knives.

He looked over at the phone.

Maybe he should call that detective. And tell him what? That his ghost detector was going off? Yeah, right. He could call his neighbors. Maybe they would come over and do the nightly vigil thing with him.

He looked around the room, at his bizarre collection of talismans fixed to the walls, the bowls of rosewater beneath every window, and the burning candles. Maybe he was crazy. Maybe if he called anyone else, they'd know he was crazy. He had no relatives to speak of, damned few friends and the neighbors weren't all that sociable. Lincoln had always been a loner, and now he really, really regretted that.

When I get to Chicago, I'm going to round me up some friends, he thought.

At twenty minutes past midnight, the lights in his house began to flicker on and off.

"Oh Jesus," he moaned. "Don't let there be a power failure. Just get me through tonight and I swear I'll be living the life of the righteous. I swear it."

The lights went out and Lincoln screamed. He began rocking back and forth on the edge of the couch like a frightened child. The smell of his own sweat filled his nose and he felt his heart pounding in his chest the way it did that night in the hospital when he ran to help the crazy woman.

"I'm a good person," he cried out. "Leave me alone."

The candle flames before his front door disappeared as though snuffed. The EMF detector started to smoke and Lincoln threw it against the wall in disgust. It stopped squealing as soon as it hit. Lincoln wondered for an insane moment if he'd killed it.

He wanted to run but was afraid to leave the house. His over-wired body began to shake.

"Please, don't be happening," he whimpered.

A spectral light began filling the room, an angry blend of orange and black, pulsating like a living thing. With a sudden rush the light came together and twisted in a horrifying spiral dance. Lincoln pressed back against the couch, too terrified to move. The spirit fire made popping and hissing noises like lard in a frying pan. Lincoln smelled, absolutely believed he could smell, sulfur.

He edged away toward the kitchen. Tears ran down his cheeks and he tried to speak, but nothing came out. It was as though something had tied a knot in his vocal chords.

When he saw the face forming within the flames, Lincoln froze. The red eyes had found him.

A blast of burning air picked him up and threw him against the far wall, slamming him in place with a loud *thunk*. He hung there, barely alive, his shoes two feet off the floor. The pain was unbearable.

His eyelids were pulled up and he knew at some level that this was so he would be forced to look at the demon. It came closer and he saw to his horror that the face within the fire was the half melted visage of a little girl. He could not move his head to look away. He couldn't close his eyes. When the knives lifted off the coffee table and turned their points toward him, what little was left of his mind shut down. If he were still conscious, he would have felt the blades drive straight through his body, fixing him to the drywall like a trophy.

While blood ran over his shoes and pooled on the beige carpeting, Lincoln Jones began to smolder and then burst into flames.

Chapter Eleven

Wendland knocked on her door the next morning at precisely nine o'clock.

After a quick look through the keyhole, Ashley let him in, then hung the "Do Not Disturb" sign on the outside knob and locked and chained the door shut.

"Have you been comfortable?" he asked, glancing around the room. His eyes settled on the laptop.

"I've been organizing my thoughts."

Wendland looked at her and said, "Did you sleep at all? You look…"

"Nightmares. I had nightmares. I'm handling it."

She didn't want to tell him about her dream that Michael was still alive. Not yet. He wouldn't believe her. And she didn't completely trust him yet.

"Good. You've suffered too much stress already. By the way, you are hungry, aren't you? Breakfast is right behind me."

Avoiding her eyes, he walked past her and dropped a huge, two handled briefcase on the floor next to the round table near the window that all motels seemed to consider part of their essential furniture.

A polite knock at the door.

"I'll get it," he said. "You stay out of sight."

When Ashley came out of the bathroom, she saw a large, round tray on her bed.

"No sense letting anyone see you who doesn't need to," he explained.

"How long do I have to live like this?" she asked with a hint of irritation in her voice.

"Not long. Just until we've put together a battle plan. Meantime, let's eat. Enjoy the moment."

"What exactly do we need a battle plan for?" she asked, arms folded across her chest.

Wendland settled himself at the table, uncovered a plate of scrambled eggs, bacon and toast then picked up a fork. He looked up at her in surprise.

"Because there's a war going on out there and you're at the center of it."

《《—》》

"Do you have the heat turned up?" asked Wendland as he mopped his forehead with a handful of napkins.

"No. Now tell me what is going on."

"There's a lot you don't know," he said after he'd stacked the plates back on the tray and placed all but the coffee pot and their cups near the door.

Ashley leaned back in her chair, staring directly at Wendland.

"Have they found Michael yet?"

Wendland frowned.

"No. The police have not found either him or his remains. You see the problem?"

"A five year old would see the problem. Why can't they find him? They have the entire police force looking for him."

Wendland folded his hands over his ample stomach.

"You've hit the nail straight on the head, Ashley. All of your companions are dead, but Michael is still missing and you're still alive. You see how that looks?"

Ashley's eyes widened with bewilderment. "How it looks? What are you talking about?"

"Think what you're asking. All those people dead. Someone killed them, and Michael is missing. His wife was spared."

"And?" she demanded, her eyes narrowing into angry slits. "Go ahead, say it. I'm not afraid. Just tell me."

Wendland idly straightened his jacket collar. He seemed to be thinking, trying to find a polite way to discuss the issue. Finally, he gave up and told her straight.

"Some people think that Michael's disappearance is too convenient. They wonder if he might in some way be guilty. Of course, you and I know that isn't true. I've known Michael since he was a teenager. He could never have been involved in those deaths."

"But?"

"*But* there are circumstances relating to that night that might seem incriminating to people that didn't know him. People like Detective Alvarez."

"What circumstances?"

"That, unfortunately, is the least of our problems."

It hung in the air between them like an unpleasant odor. More secrets, more things Michael had kept from her.

"Well?"

"There's no need to be difficult about this, Ashley. I'm here to help."

"Then tell me. What is the worst of our problems?"

Wendland looked down at his briefcase nervously. A fine sheen of sweat covered his face as though the more he thought about it, the more uncomfortable he felt. After wiping his forehead a second and still a third time, Ashley saw that he was *still* sweating.

"I was going to suggest that you allow me to handle the situation. There's really no need for you to get involved."

But Wendland did not seem anxious to tackle the problem, whatever it was, by himself.

"Don't."

"Don't what?"

"Don't patronize me," she said.

"I certainly was *not* patronizing you."

"You most certainly were. Now what are you so afraid of?"

The lawyer was about to object. Raised a hand and extended his fore-finger as though to lecture her on the matter, but then, after thinking it through, he lowered his hand and closed his eyes. He sat like that for a few moments, not moving, not saying a word.

"Mr. Wendland?"

He opened his eyes at length and looked straight at her.

"I am recommending again that you—"

"Tell me."

"For your own safety—"

"Tell me!" she yelled.

Defeated, he shook his head in agreement, but when he spoke, his voice was a horse whisper.

"Did Michael ever … mention something called the 'ghost box'?"

«« — »»

"The ghost box? No. What are you talking about?"

Wendland pulled his briefcase up and onto his lap, rummaged through it for a moment, then extracted a single manila folder and laid it on the table. After returning his bulky briefcase to the floor, he pushed the folder across the table to her with the tip of his index finger.

"Open it," he said.

Ashley hesitated, then picked it up and did as he asked.

Inside, she found a single color photo of what looked like a combination antique miniature phone booth and radio. It was made of brass and highly polished dark wood. Dials and knobs and what looked like a gramophone speaker on one side and a tall box on the other that was gated with dull iron bars and a medieval key lock.

"It looks like something Michael would have in his collection," she said carefully. "But I've never seen it before."

"He hoped it would be the crown jewel of his collection," Wendland said.

Hearing the tremor in his voice, she looked up quickly.

"But what is it? And is this the problem you were talking about?"

"Yes, it is the problem. Well, not it, but the man Michael bargained with."

"Just lay it out, will you?"

"I'd rather not."

"I don't care whether or not you want to tell me. You're my lawyer and I want to know now, right now."

Wendland turned his bulk toward the door, as though considering making a run for it. Then he gave up and faced her again.

"I've met everything from white-collar criminals to murderers during the course of my career, Ashley, but when I went with Michael to make the deal for this device, I have to tell you, I begged him to back away. To void the contract. Something about this individual frightened me, truly frightened me."

"Did he threaten Michael?"

"Well, no. Michael was eager to make the deal. But he was blind to the person he was making the deal with, if you understand what I mean. He was so anxious, almost obsessed with acquiring the device that he thought of nothing else but coming to an arrangement."

Ashley felt a sinking feeling in the pit of her stomach. Michael was like that. When he saw something he really wanted, he thought of nothing else but getting it. But, like that horrible night at Sharkey's Park, he didn't always think about the consequences.

"Who is this man and why is he such a terrible problem for us?"

"His name—please don't attempt to make contact with him in any way, can we agree on that?"

"Tell me."

She knew she'd won by the way his jowls sagged. Henry Wendland looked more miserable than any human being she'd ever seen.

"Emile Chirac," he said finally. "Don't ever ask me to repeat that name."

"Who is he?"

"He's ... a collector of sorts. He has the most amazing artifacts. Occasionally, he makes one or two available for sale if the buyer will agree to his terms."

A sense of both disbelief and alarm flooded Ashley's emotions.

"And why is he a problem?"

"Because, my dear, Michael did not keep his end of their bargain."

Ashley slapped her hand on the table.

"Don't lead me on like this. Tell me what's going on without me having to prompt you all the time. You're driving me crazy. I just got out of the hospital, I want to go home instead of hiding out from the media in this stupid hotel room, my husband is missing and everyone thinks he's dead and I don't have a lot patience. What was Michael's end of the bargain?"

The unexpected rebuke reddened Wendland's puffy cheeks and he compressed his lips together in an effort to hold back his own anger.

"The problem is, Ashley, you married Michael without knowing very much about him. And I feel very awkward about being the person to explain this to you. I fear there is a great deal about Michael that you don't know. But you asked what his end of the bargain was, didn't you? His end of the bargain was to provide Mr. Chirac with something called the madstone in return for this ghost box. Before you ask what a madstone is, it is a legendary stone used by Appalachian women to cure disease and ward off evil. Yes, I know how it sounds, but that was the deal. There was a certain madstone—one that Mr. Chirac had been seeking for many years—and Michael was to find and give him that madstone. At that time, Mr. Chirac would give him the device you've seen in that picture known as the ghost box."

It was a hard thing to hear that she didn't know her own husband as well as she thought she did. They had only known each other for three weeks before they married. But that's what a whirlwind romance was all about, wasn't it? They were swept away in a gust of mad passion. Michael was a high profile businessman. She wrote dark fiction. Michael was also obsessed with finding out about the afterlife. She wrote about ghosts and vampires, werewolves and other things that went bump in the dark. Paranormal romance was big business. And what better could happen to a writer of dark fiction than getting married to a rich paranormal investigator? She would never run out of stories with Michael for a husband.

But now her husband was gone, her friends dead in what was supposed to be a serious paranormal investigation they could maybe turn into a documentary. How had everything gone so wrong?

Harry Wendland was about the only man in town who seemed to have the answers and the contacts she needed. He was the kind of resource a writer could use to get started and Ashley decided she was going to keep asking him questions until she knew everything that he did.

"How much am I paying you?" she asked abruptly.

"I beg your pardon?" replied the portly lawyer.

"I asked you how much I'm paying you."

Wendland seemed confused for a moment, and scratched the side of his head more with annoyance than irritation.

"You're paying me five hundred dollars an hour."

"If you want to keep that hourly billing rate of yours," she said, "you're going to have to work faster. I want to talk to this Chirac and Michael's Granny Hillis."

"Please just let me handle this. You most definitely don't want to discuss anything—and I mean *anything* with Mr. Chirac. And this Granny Hillis character is so old she must be senile. She—"

"I'm not paying you five hundred dollars an hour to argue with me. I didn't grow up rich like Michael and I don't believe in wasting money, so give me Chirac's number. And the number for Granny Hillis. I want to talk to them both right now. And after that I want you to take me home so I can investigate what's happened to my husband. I'll work better from my own desk. The police don't seem to be getting anywhere—they're too busy prying into our affairs. And I'm not going to hide out here in this motel room when Michael needs me. "

Because Ashley was more certain than ever that Michael was alive and in desperate need of her help.

«« — »»

"So that's what I've got, Captain," Alvarez said. "There was a little girl gone missing a couple of weeks before the first murders. Name of Bonnie Mazatiks. She may have been the remains in the grave. Nothing definite yet, but we're working on it. Been digging into Quantum MW Technologies, the Hillis company, too."

"But nothing on Hillis himself?"

"No."

"So what are you looking for?"

Alvarez shrugged and said, "I don't know yet. Following a hunch. Might be something there."

Captain Hendricks looked up at the ceiling and said, "You know I've just got nine months to retirement, right Elvio?"

"Sure, Captain. The way I see it, though—"

"So this shit has to happen nine months before I retire. I wake up every morning after getting up five times to piss, and I come here and find out I can have nightmares while I'm awake. The Sharkey's Park murders, episode two, is playing on every television in town."

"The media is running with it, sir."

"And now there's this expert who goes on TV and says the people in the park were probably hit by freak bolts of lightning, which would explain why they were all fried to a crisp. He says it's happened before. Media's running with that, too. Other experts agree, some disagree, but this keeps up and there's no murder investigation. Would make our lives a lot easier."

"Lightning? That's bullshit, Captain. How come they were up in trees?"

"You tell me."

"I say it's bullshit."

Captain Hendricks steepled his fingers and propped his chin on them. He was too irritable to look like he was praying or meditating. Alvarez knew he was prepping for the killing point.

"So you know what else I hear on today's episode, Elvio?"

After what he considered to be an appropriate pause, Alvarez answered. "What's that, Captain?"

"I hear that my lead detective on this case has a grandfather who died in the last Sharkey's Park slaughter. What do you think of that?"

"I've been kind of busy. And he died a long time ago. I didn't see a connection."

The Captain's face reddened and he leaned forward on the desk. Alvarez saw his mouth working and knew the old man was getting ready to go ballistic. But he was saved by a sharp knock on the door.

"I'm in a meeting!"

The door cracked and a thin faced detective named Garrison stuck his head in the door.

"Just came in, Captain. I thought you two might want to know. Patrolman called it in. The Carrier got worried when the mail was stacking up in the mail box and he smelled something."

"What the hell are you talking about, Detective?"

Garrison opened the door wide and stepped in.

"That guy Alvarez interviewed, that nurse named Jones. Patrolmen forced their way in and found a body—probably his—pinned to the wall with knives."

"How long ago?" Alvarez asked.

"Just called it in. And they think it's his body, but it's burned so bad they're going to have to make sure it's him. Like he was in a fire, but he's the only thing was burned. The rest of the house is clean."

"Say again," Alvarez said.

"I'm just the messenger."

"I got to go, Captain," Alvarez said.

"You and me aren't done with this yet," the Captain said.

"Yes, sir," Alvarez said. "Soon as I get back from the scene."

Chapter Twelve

Same house, same neighborhood with a few added cop cars, an EMS vehicle and a whole bunch of people wearing badges and looking serious. Alvarez was getting too old for this. He got out of the car and headed toward the front door. A few nods. A few looks. A few questions he ignored.

Neighbors were gawking from adjacent lawns. The usual scene. Two teenagers on their smart phones, maybe trying to catch a text as to what was going on, oblivious to the fact it was going down right in front of them. An older couple, the man leaning on his cane, his eyes fixed on Alvarez, waiting for an answer. His white hair so thin Alvarez could see his red blotched scalp showing through even from where he was. The woman was staring at the house, shaking her head back and forth, mulling over that secret knowledge of violent death that old women seemed to understand and accept as part of the human landscape.

Alvarez saw a young girl in a blue and white checked dress standing next to them, her gaze wide-eyed and attentive. Her hair was like twisted gold threads wound into cascading curls. Clutching a cloth doll. She looked vaguely familiar. Staring right at him.

Cute kid, Alvarez thought and turned away.

But from the corner of his eyes he saw one of the teenagers turn and start to leave. Alvarez looked back. The teen was texting as he walked and was going to walk straight into the little girl. The little girl's eyes began to burn. Her hair started to smolder and smoke. The detective opened his mouth, but could think of nothing to say when the boy walked straight through her and the girl disappeared.

Suddenly a shocked Alvarez remembered who she was. She was the girl in the picture. The girl's remains they'd found buried in Sharkey's Park. And she'd looked right at him like she knew him before she disappeared.

«« — »»

"You okay, Detective?" the officer stationed at the front door asked.

"I'm fine. Thought I saw something is all. You going to get out of the way or what?"

Alvarez wondered if he was losing his mind. He'd seen a dead girl in broad daylight.

"Smell's pretty bad."

Alvarez pushed two odor plugs up his nostrils. He didn't like using them. They never fit right and they made him want to sneeze. He slipped

69

the shoe covers on that the door officer handed him. They made him feel like a cable technician.

"What did you see?" the officer asked.

"Nothing. Nobody. You been here long?"

"Too long. Inside it's—you'll see. Too many sick fucks running the streets, Elvio. Too many."

Alvarez didn't reply, he was still thinking about the little girl with the burning eyes who was there, and then not. Stress, that was it. Too much stress. Or lack of sleep. Maybe he just needed sleep. Too many hours sticking his nose into Hillis family business. Or maybe not enough. Too many hours going through files and staring at the computer. He'd Googled and Yahooed everything he could about Michael Hillis and Sharkey's Park. Nothing was making sense. As soon as this was over, he was going to sleep for a whole weekend.

The smell rolled over him like an invisible, greasy wave as he stepped into the living room.

"Close the door," somebody said.

It was hard to see what she looked like behind the face mask and with her hair stuffed up in a net.

"You in charge?" asked Alvarez. "I never seen you before."

"That'd be me. And we're about to peel him off the wall now, so do what you have to do and give us some space."

Alvarez followed her eyes and what he saw nearly caused him to throw up. Burnt meat in the vague shape of a human body. What looked like an open mouth. The eye sockets. The blackened steel blade through what must have been his throat. Others through arms no more than burnt blood on melted bones.

"Jesus," he said. "Is that him?"

"That's him, Detective."

"What the hell happened to him?"

"We're going to try and find out. I'd say somebody roasted him over a spit somewhere else, and then staked him to the wall here, but that's not how it happened. It's more like he was set on fire right where you see him. But the wall's not burned enough. More like he was microwaved in place, but there's no radiation source around to make that happen."

It was hard for him to follow what she was saying, because he was remembering Lincoln Jones, the person. No way the burnt flesh pinned to the wall was him. No way. But it was. And the way his mouth was open he was screaming in agony as he died. A halo of black surrounded the body, like a hideous burned blood outline.

"You okay, Detective?"

"Just thinking."

"Not much we can tell you now except what you see. We'll know more when we scrape him down."

"Maybe the neighbors saw something."

"They don't know nothing about nothing."

"You see a little girl outside when you came in?" Alvarez asked.

"No. Why?"

"Never mind. Let me know what you find out soon as you got anything."

"Just like on television," the evidence tech said.

Alvarez decided to leave before they started scraping Jones down.

«« —»»

The dirt road ahead was lit by an up and down swinging of the truck's headlights.

A deer shot across the road ahead of them so quickly that, before Ian could shout a warning, it disappeared into the trees on the other side of the road. Bartok's valise lay on the floorboards next to his feet.

Enid was at the wheel, avoiding the ruts and bumps with a practiced hand. His face was ascetically grim in the occasional shafts of moonlight that penetrated the cloud cover. Ian had spent the last ten minutes telling him what had happened below ground.

"Jesus, I should have shot him soon as I saw the light in his eyes."

"But you didn't," Ian said. "He's a human being."

"For now," Enid said. "Whatever that thing put in him is changing all that. But we can't do this without him. He's the only one knows the whole story about what's going on down there. I thought you knew, too. Since you don't, we're going to have to keep him alive."

That was the problem. Ian was almost as clueless as Enid. After the dispute that sent Ian away, he and Bartok had hardly communicated.

"Did we have to chain him like wild animal?" Ian asked for the third time since they'd left the cemetery.

"You ain't seen the dog," Ian said.

"They're dead, right?"

Enid looked straight ahead, his eyes on the road, his rifle in what looked to Ian like a hand carved gun rack behind the seats.

"Are you going to answer me?"

Ian risked a glance behind him. Through the back window he saw Bartok sitting tall and straight, chained to a metal rail that ran around the sides of the bed.

"See for yourself," Enid said.

Ian grabbed the armrest for balance as the truck came to an abrupt stop after doing a sliding spin. He let go, took a deep breath and saw a concrete building whitewashed in the headlights. No windows. Just a metal blast door. It reminded Ian of an above ground bomb shelter from the fifties.

"Why are we stopping here?" Ian asked.

"Dr. Bartok wanted to see the dog—the one I didn't kill."

"You mean you kept one alive?"

"Shut up and get out of the truck."

Enid turned off the engine and stepped out into the dry night air. Ian considered going for the rifle, but decided against it.

"You can take it if you want to. You know how to fire it?"

"You'd shoot me with that handgun in your pocket before I got it un-hooked," Ian said.

"Maybe," Enid said. "but most likely not. The way Bartok is, you're about the only hope I got."

From the back of the truck, the old man called out, "Hurry. More than my life is at stake here."

Ian got out, heard the gravel crunch beneath his feet and stretched.

"You want me to help?" he asked Enid.

Enid came around the front of the truck with the rifle held in one hand and handed him the key with the other. As Ian went to pull his hand back, the eldest Mozer caught his sleeve and pulled him close, so that their faces were less than a foot apart.

"He ain't just your uncle anymore. Don't forget that. He's contaminated. He's going to change, hear me? You unchain him from the rail first. Then help him to roll over and out."

"Why don't I just unchain his ankles, too, so he can get down by himself?"

"Boy you are as stupid as a pig showing up for work at a slaughterhouse. We got to keep him under control or it will be all over with before we even get going."

Ian would have called him crazy a day ago, but considering what he'd seen underground, he kept his mouth shut.

His uncle sat rigidly upright. His face stern, his eyes fixed on Ian. Nothing moved within them. Had he just been seeing things earlier? Had the stress caused his mind to play tricks on him?

"Enid's worried you're going to go nuts on us," Ian said. "Try not to make any sudden moves or he'll shoot you. I'm going to unlock the chain looped through the railing and then help you get down off the truck."

"Quit talking and get it done," Bartok snapped.

The key opened the lock with a soft click. It came apart smoothly, as though it was well oiled and used often. Ian shuddered at the thought.

Enid had already gotten the gate down and stood back a few feet with his gun pointed at the old man. Ian was about to climb over the railing to help his uncle get to his feet, when his 72-year-old uncle leaned forward and then straightened himself to his full height. There was no sign of the arthritis, no sign of straining to maintain his balance. It was like watching a well-trained athlete in action. Before Ian could recover from the sight, Bartok was walking short steps to the end of the truck bed, his chains clanking behind him.

"Wait, I'll help," Ian said.

But before he took his first step, Bartok flexed his knees, and then sprang off the gate. He landed like a gymnast finishing a dismount, without faltering, without swaying. He was a fearsome figure standing between the two men, just under a foot taller than both of them, his posture straight, his chin tilted slightly up, his terrible eyes surveying them both; a "contaminated" man as Enid had said. Yet he was the only one among them who seemed unafraid.

"That seem like the way your Uncle Bartok used to get around?" Enid asked.

Ian didn't know what to say.

"Get moving," Enid told Bartok.

A shivering light slithered across Bartok's eyes.

"Can I have a gun, too?" Ian asked.

He was more afraid of Bartok than he was of Enid.

"Now you're talking. It's in my right hand pocket, but don't walk between me and your uncle."

Ian felt Bartok's eyes on him as he walked over and got the gun. Enid stayed focused on the old man, his rifle pointed straight at him.

"You know how to use that?"

"I do."

"Then let's move on over to the shed."

They were so far into the mountains that Ian wondered if anyone was close enough to hear a gunshot other than the other three Mozers he and Enid had left back at the cemetery. The air was cool and thin, the smell of pine was overpowering.

"It's so quiet out here," he said.

"What'd you expect?" Enid asked.

"It drives them away," Bartok said.

"God's truth," Enid said. "Gradual at first. We—me and my family—grew up in these mountains. We started noticing little things. Bird population dwindled down. Thought it might be a new disease or something but we never saw any dead birds. They just quit coming around. Frogs. Squirrels. Same thing happened with them. The black beetles, though, we got a lot more of them. Whatever it is underground, they like it."

They stopped ten feet from the concrete building.

"There's air holes you can't see," Enid said. "Filtered, of course, in case of emergency. When the other dogs started acting funny, I should have figured it out right then. Animals get influenced by it first. Smaller they are, faster it seems to get to them. I'm just guessing that, but I think I'm right."

"You are," Bartok said.

"So you killed them?" Ian asked.

Enid hesitated, and then looked straight at Bartok.

"All but one," he said. "My own dog. Just couldn't do it."

Ian looked at the concrete bunker, apprehension building as he tried to imagine how the dog had changed. The truck was still running, its headlights trained on the blast door, and the three men cast long, dark shadows over it.

With his rifle still trained on Bartok, Enid reached into another pocket and produced a key.

"You take this, unlock the door and then get back here quick. Don't open it. I'll take care of that. You keep your pistol trained on your uncle there. He makes a move, shoot him."

Ian took the key and did as he was told. The locking mechanism pulled back smoothly, as had the other. Enid Mozer was a careful man when it came to locks. As he stepped back from the door and took up a position three feet away from his uncle and trained the pistol on him, Ian heard a high, keening sound.

After a last look at Bartok, Enid went to the door and, with the rifle in his right hand, he grabbed the handle, turned it and pulled back the door. He stepped back and swung the rifle up, holding it now with both hands. He was off to the side as the headlights shone directly on a squirming mass of tentacles and teeth. Scales and claws lit by a hideous, mind-jarring purple black light that radiated from its malformed body like a halo of evil. It leapt toward them, but caught on a mass of chains and dropped back to the floor with a sickening flop.

Eyes, it was covered with red eyes and it began to shriek. The sound ricocheted through Ian's brain like a bullet.

Then Enid pulled the trigger and the sound of automatic weapons fire filled the night as Ian screamed and backed away. He was three steps back when Bartok's body slammed into him.

Chapter Thirteen

Emile Chirac adjusted his straight-backed chair to the optimal distance from his marble inlaid desk. It was late into the night and a large journal with precise script lay open before him. Lily sprawled on a richly colored Persian rug a short distance from the rock wall of the fireplace. In the flickering firelight thrown by fading flames, she glistened like thick black velvet.

"You are a magnificent animal," he mused.

An angry yellow eye opened and fixed on him.

"Yes, I understand your anguish, Lily," he said softly. "Such power in your sinewy frame. Such fearsome incisors and terrible jaws. With but a single bite you could snap my neck and tear out my throat."

Chirac reached for his enameled fountain pen. He only used fountain pens. A ball point pen, no matter its price or craftsmanship, was the mark of a man more familiar with Formica than marble.

"But you must admit you want for nothing since I took you as my own. You dine well on such succulence as I select for you, you roam freely where and when I allow you, and you nurse the undiminished, desperate hope that one day I will set you free. Of course, if something should happen to me, our bargain would be void and you would remain here forever."

A low growl escaped the panther. She extended the claws of one paw before her as though examining their lethal points.

Three knocks at the study's double doors resonated throughout the room.

"It's late, Ricci, and I was about to indulge my occasional need for the written word."

There was no response.

Chirac extended one hand before him and studied his pale, blood-red ring the way the panther studied her claws.

"If you must, if it is dire that you speak to me, you may enter."

The doors opened and a man whose shoulders would have stuck in a single-door frame entered. Ricci was six feet four inches of muscled slabs joined by powerful sinews. His weightlifter's neck was topped by a scarred, round face and bald head.

His hands were large as baseball mitts and pocked with ugly, puckered burns that healed badly after the torture.

"I got a call from somebody you might want to talk to," he said.

Chirac scowled.

"You neglect Lily."

"She doesn't like me much since I introduced her to you."

Although the big cat lay only five feet away from Ricci, she was at the limit of the chrome chain and collar. The other end was fixed to a rose colored granite obelisk bolted to the floor joists.

"So, just so," agreed Chirac.

Ricci ignored the books and manuscripts that lay on long wooden tables. He ignored the giant magnifying glass perched above a priceless manuscript held in a thin double layer of argon filled glass. He ignored the magnificent marble balustrade that circled the second floor and its ornate cherry wood and gold spiral staircase. So many years had he lived in this house that his memories of prison sometimes confused him. Chirac was a very different type of warden than his last.

"And who was this person that called?"

"Mrs. Ashley Hillis."

Chirac's countenance darkened immediately.

"Wonderful."

"She wants to come see you."

"Lovely. Our client's wife comes calling minus her husband. Tell her I'm quite busy and don't have dealings with spouses. My arrangement was with her husband."

Lily growled again, a low, throaty sound filled with menace.

"That's the thing—her husband's gone missing and probably dead. It's been all over the television."

Mr. Chirac, Ricci knew, never, ever watched television.

Chirac steepled his fingers thoughtfully, considered the matter carefully, and then told him, "Tell her that I would welcome her presence two nights hence at exactly midnight. Neither a minute before nor a minute after will suffice. In the meantime, Ricci, we must prepare for the arrival of Mr. Jester. He would like to purchase something from my collection."

«« — »»

"I called from the road. I'm Detective Alvarez here to see Dr. Knight."

The receptionist, a middle aged man with hair like Elvis, looked him over carefully.

"May I see some identification?" he asked.

Alvarez pulled his identification from his inside pocket.

"She's expecting me."

The receptionist returned his ID.

"Yes, she is. Have a chair over there, please."

"I think I'll stand," Alvarez said. "I got too many hours behind a desk this week."

"Suit yourself."

Five minutes later, a doorway to the man's left opened and Dr. Olivia Knight said, "Come in, come in Detective. I have a very tight schedule today."

White lab coat, tortoise shelled glasses and thick luxurious hair. Perfect posture, perfect body and a face like a nineteen forties screen leading lady. Russian accent to boot. Alvarez wanted to stay where he was and just enjoy the view.

"Detective?"

"Sorry. You look familiar."

"Yes. Of course. Follow me, if you please."

The receptionist gave him a bored look as he dutifully followed Dr. Knight through the door.

Down one hall of offices, turn right to the elevators. She stopped in front of a mirror and waited.

"Don't you have to push the button?" he asked.

The doors hissed open.

"Facial recognition," she said.

"Figured. That's why there's no buttons in here for the floors, right?"

"Floor fifteen," she said.

The elevator began to move.

"Can't hardly hear it," he said.

"No."

Alvarez was starting to feel like he was in over his head.

«« — »»

Her office was the size of Alvarez's apartment. Lustrous black desk. Furniture that cost more than his retirement fund was worth. Hidden lighting and classical music coming from somewhere but could have been anywhere. Fish tanks built into walls, where brightly colored tropical fish swam in lazy circles like they were lost but didn't care. Paintings of cities from all over the world gave her office a classy look.

"You should name those," Alvarez said as he settled into plush leather guest chair.

"Excuse me?"

"Well, like from where you're sitting, you see these paintings all the time. It's a nice place. You got the big window behind you looking out over the Detroit River and all this art stuff. But me, when I come in here, it's my first time seeing them and I don't know which cities they are? So if you had a name plate that said Paris and Moscow and whatever, I'd know."

"Most of my visitors, Detective, have actually been to those cities."

"I should have figured that out, shouldn't I?"

She'd unbuttoned her lab coat and Alvarez caught a look of red silk and smooth skin. He kept his eyes on her face, but she was so good looking it was still hard to concentrate.

"Now what can I do for you, Detective?"

No coffee, no glass of water. No small talk. A woman on a schedule. Okay, he could handle that. He took out his notebook and his pen, crossed his legs and leaned back in the chair.

"I'll be quick, Dr. Knight. I'm just looking for some information and seeing as how you're the chief doc here at Quantum Fusion, I figured you'd be the one to ask."

"Then ask."

What struck Alvarez as odd was that there was not a single book to be seen anywhere in the room.

"You got a computer?" he asked.

"Of course. I have many computers. Why?"

"I just figured I'd see a lot of books, you being a scientist and all."

Dr. Knight smiled.

"Books are like artifacts still in use. They are as outdated as horse-drawn buggies. Why would I have books when I can read on my computer? Now, please ask me what you came here to ask."

"You mind if I get up and walk around while I talk? I get tired of sitting so much."

"Then why did you sit down?"

Alvarez stood and began to talk as he walked around the room inspecting the fish tanks and the art.

"Give me the poor man's version of what this new technology Quantum Fusion has been working on is all about. No technical stuff, just what is it supposed to do? I've been reading up on the company since your boss disappeared and it seems like it's the biggest thing since they found the atom. I read online that this new energy technology he was working on will be worth a fortune."

Even with his back to her, Alvarez could feel her assessing him. *Take your time*, he thought. *I've been through this before.*

He turned to face her.

"Doctor?" he chided.

A few seconds slipped by before she answered. Behind her smokey brown eyes, her mental wheels were turning.

"What is this all about? What does our company's technology have to do with finding Michael?"

"Lot of money at stake, doc. Big money means big motives."

She sat straight up in her chair and looked up at him with more anger than irritation.

"That's ridiculous. This is an important breakthrough in energy technology. The world needs what we're developing here. Why would anyone want to harm the president of a company that is developing solutions to the world's energy problems?"

"I don't have any answers yet. Just a lot of questions. So tell me about the technology."

Dr. Knight looked at the door to Alvarez's left as though considering leaving. Her lips compressed as though to hold back a tongue lashing. After a few seconds of that, she breathed out carefully, controlling her temper, and then began to talk in a neutral lecture-the-classroom voice.

"I have time constraints, Detective, as you might imagine with Mr. Hillis missing and his wife, a writer of *paranormal romance* novels, in nominal control of our extremely technical company."

The way she said paranormal romance writer sounded like "janitor in hell." No bad blood there. Alvarez filed it away for future thought.

"So who's actually running the day-to-day operations of the company?" he asked.

"Well, I am, of course. Mr. Hillis and I are very close and although the vision and inspiration for the Quantum Technology is his, the theoretical and practical applications of the technology are solely mine. We are at a critical time for our company, as you intimated, and someone who understood Mr. Hillis's vision had to take control."

"And you were the logical choice?"

"Certainly."

"Mrs. Hillis must have a great deal of confidence in you."

That did it. Her cheeks actually reddened. Definitely something going on other than business between her and Hillis. An unexpected bonus.

"I communicate through Mr. Hillis's lawyer, Henry Wendland."

"I've met him. Swell guy. Now about the technology?"

"The technology? Our great project is splitting water into hydrogen and oxygen."

"Can't they already do that?"

She seemed disappointed.

"Of course. Electrolysis is one very old method, of course. Very expensive. We use an entirely different approach. Do you remember some time ago the man who was able to break water into hydrogen and oxygen simply by using microwaves?"

"No."

But Alvarez did. He'd done his due diligence.

"It was on television."

"I don't watch much television."

"Well, it was an interesting phenomena, but also not feasible economically. It simply cost too much. Too energy intensive. The goal, of course, was to produce hydrogen as a fuel. A good idea, but too expensive. But we have changed all that. Mr. Hillis thought that we could reduce the energy requirements by weakening the bonds of the water with a catalyst. I was able to achieve it. That alone made the approach feasible, but when I improved on existing microwave technology to make it both more powerful and less expensive to generate, we knew we were on the verge of an energy revolution."

And now the hard part, thought Alvarez. *Time to put on the clueless mask.*

"But it must still be a huge microwave device. I mean how big is your prototype? The size of a fire truck?"

Dr. Knight went into full blown prideful contempt mode.

"Hardly, Detective. My prototype is not much larger than a briefcase. It's quite portable. Surprised? I have dual doctorates. You didn't know that, I see. It strikes me that, for a detective, you know very little."

"I'm a good learner," he said with an embarrassed grin.

"I'll believe that when you find Michael."

"You mean, Mr. Hillis, don't you?"

The red face again.

As he walked to his car, he remembered the *expert's* lightning theory about the burn victims in Sharkey's Park. Bullshit. Time to go through the equipment they'd found in the vans at the scene again. This time he knew what to have the techs look for, and it sure as hell wasn't lightning.

Chapter Fourteen

Their headlights tunneled through a mountain fog that rolled across the night, covering the road like thick, white smoke. In the spectral reflected light of the car's fog lights, Enid's face was a sallow, sharply angled sculpture.

"That stupid, stupid son of a bitch," Ian said. "All these years hid it from me—the underground cave, the mechanical army and that hideous monstrosity hanging in mid-air. Why couldn't he have just told me instead being such a secretive old bastard?"

"He said you two don't get along too well."

"He knocked me down and tried to bite me. Wasn't for you he would have."

"I mean before that. How long since you seen him last?" Enid asked.

"Before tonight? Twenty years. He threw me out twenty years ago and that was the last I heard from him until two nights ago when he told me about this Hillis guy in Detroit and how it was time to learn the family secrets."

Enid kept his eyes on the foggy road and said nothing.

"You want to know why we didn't get along? I'll tell you. My parents died when I was a kid and he raised me. Can you imagine living with him? It's bad enough half my ancestors were occultists and ghost hunters. Living with him was like being reminded of it every day. I couldn't have a normal life with him around. You know what it was like trying to get a date? No chance I was bringing a girl home with all the occult books and paintings all over the place. It was like living with the Addams family."

"So you had enough one day and told him off?"

Ian looked into the backseat to see if his Uncle was awake.

"No. Not like that. He wanted me to join the Society, as he called it. Go through the ritual. It's the twentieth century, you know, and he wants me to join a group of crazies like him. He was obsessed by what he called esoteric knowledge. Like anybody cares about that anymore. He was born before television was invented. They had less to do back then. Secret knowledge my ass."

"So what happened?"

Ian thought a bit before answering.

81

"It was like this. I was going to join. I was actually going to do it to keep him happy. He kept telling me that he couldn't confide the family's secret charge, that was what he called it, unless I went along with the ritual. But I couldn't do it."

"Why not?"

"Because I didn't believe in God, that's why. I told him straight out. I was an atheist. I didn't and don't believe in an afterlife. We argued and he threw me out. Said he couldn't confide the family secrets and treasures to a young man who didn't believe in God. Occult secrets and family treasures, by the way, went out of business before they invented toilet paper. Son of a bitch. He wanted to live in a fantasy world, that was fine with me. Believe in magic? His problem, not mine. So I hit the road. I got an engineering degree and started writing books scientifically debunking every bullshit paranormal idea he'd ever told me. I proved conclusively there were no such things as ghosts and spirits. I make a good living at it, too. It's my way of totally pissing him off. "

Enid jerked the wheel to the left and then back again.

"Don't run us off over the edge," Ian said nervously.

"I been driving these roads since I was fourteen. We'll make it. Freeway's no more than an hour away."

Ian glanced at the backseat again. They'd left the truck behind, picked up enough guns and ammunition to take over Detroit and put them in the trunk of one of Enid's barn full of cars. The other Mozers were supposed to take care of getting Ian's car back to Detroit while Enid and Ian drove to Detroit to find Michael Hillis. Bartok was wrapped in twisted steel cables in the back seat. The cables were hooked to a ring bolted through the car's floorboards and the whole arrangement was covered with a blanket that came up to Bartok's chin.

"You think he's okay?" Ian asked.

"He'll be fine."

"Hope he wakes up with a massive fucking headache."

"Uh-huh."

"You hit him pretty hard with your rifle stock."

"Better than him taking a bite out of your throat."

After knocking him to the ground outside of the bunker, Bartok had inched toward him like a snake, snapping his teeth, heading for his neck. The memory sent shivers through Ian.

"Thanks for stepping in. I should have said it earlier."

"Had to be done," Enid said. "And I've cracked more than a few people in my time. He'll come out of it sooner or later. And in case you didn't notice, he ain't exactly helpless since what happened down below. Whatever got into him, turned him into a handful."

"Stop the car," Ian said. "The son of a bitch is coming to."

From the backseat came a low moan.

"No reason to stop. We got to keep driving."

"The hell we do. Pull over so I can get in the back seat with him and talk to him."

"For what? He won't have nothing to say."

"Just pull over, will you?"

Enid pushed on the brakes and the car slowly came to a halt.

"Hurry up and do it," he said. "No good stopping here. Not much traffic, especially this time of night, but if some fool does come barreling along, we won't do too well."

But Ian was already out of the car before Enid completed his sentence. He opened the back door, slid inside and slammed it after him. Enid eased the car forward again.

Bartok looked at him, trying to remember who he was.

"It's me, you son of a bitch. Ian, you remember? What the hell did you think you were doing keeping this secret? Why didn't you call in the National Guard or something to handle that underground mess? Answer me? And what the hell was that mutated dog all about? Did you know about that?"

"Head hurts," Bartok said.

"Too fucking bad. Now tell me, what the hell was behind that wall? Why didn't you just blow the whole damned place up and bury it? You're a crazy fuck, you know that? I've been waiting twenty years to tell you that."

Bartok stared blankly at him.

"Try one question at a time," suggested Enid.

"Okay, okay. Uncle Bartok, pay attention. Listen to me. What the hell was behind the back wall of that cave?"

Filaments of light began to slide across his uncle's eyes again and his face hardened.

"Oh shit," Ian said.

"Behind the wall?" Bartok said. "Something to fear."

Ian felt his stomach tighten.

"What? Exactly what?"

"A ship, Ian. From another world."

"You're out of your mind."

Bartok's eyes filled with the squirming lights until his eyes actually glowed purple white. He grinned, lips pulled back to expose his dentures.

"The mechanical men will march, Ian. Destroy everything in their path. And then … "

"And then what?"

"And then we will consume the living and the dead."

Ian pulled away, pressing his back against the car door, fighting to breathe.

"Stop the car, will you," he said to Enid. "I think I'd like to ride up front again."

《《—》》

Bartok lay with his head lolled to one side, his eyes closed and his breathing slow.

"Well, that was good news," Ian said. "For twenty years I've been debunking ghosts to get even with him, and all this time I should have been writing about UFO's."

"You believe him?" Enid asked.

"I have no idea what to believe except there's a nightmare in that cave. You didn't see it. It's un-fucking believable. And what the hell is happening to him? And don't say he's changing, I already figured that out. Is he going to wind up like that hound from Hell?"

"Buddy," Enid said.

"What?"

"His name was Buddy. He was my dog. I loved that animal."

"Look, I'm sorry about your dog, but is my uncle going to end up like him?"

"You know what I love most about dogs? They never lie. People lie, people can deceive you. Dogs always are what they are."

"Enid, let me ask you this—how exactly do you and your brothers fit into this? I know you work for my uncle, but was all this shit in your job description?"

"You could say that."

"You're kidding me, right? What, are you like a member of his secret society or something?"

Up ahead, a sign for I-75 showed through the fog. The windshield wipers snapped up and wiped the glass clear of water droplets. The car shuddered as Enid ran over something invisible in the mist.

"You don't hardly know your uncle," Enid said finally.

"Considering what I've seen tonight, I'm going to have to agree with you. I should have had him locked up a long time ago."

"You should have listened to him a long time ago. Then we wouldn't be in this mess. Man who don't believe in God isn't no use to nobody in this kind of a fight."

"So how'd your family get involved in this?"

"My great granddaddy had to kill your great granddaddy because your great granddaddy didn't have no fingers left to pull the trigger."

"Christ on a pony," Ian said. "Am I the only normal person in this car?"

Chapter Fifteen

The big door closed behind them.

"If I didn't have an attached garage," Ian said, "I don't know how we'd get him into the house without one of the neighbors noticing."

Bartok was still asleep in the back seat, his head lolled to one side like he was unconscious.

"Let's quit talking and get it done," Enid said.

"What if he wakes up?"

"I'll knock him out again."

"He doesn't frighten you?"

"Not yet. Ask me later and I might have a different opinion."

Enid got out of the car and Ian did the same. Enid opened he backseat door and stared at Bartok while Ian walked around to join him.

"How exactly do we do this?" Ian asked.

Enid reached inside his coat and pulled out a rectangular box with two metal points.

"I'm going to do the lifting. The way I've trussed him up, he won't be able to move too much. If he gets wild, Taser his ass with this."

«« — »»

Enid followed Ian in through the kitchen, then down a hallway to the guest bedroom and dropped Bartok on a double bed.

"I'd swear he looks younger," Ian said. "Stronger. More vital."

"Yep. That's the way it starts."

"So what do we do now?"

"I'm going to get our gear, and bring that briefcase of his in. Then you read through his stuff while I get everything ready. Then you come up with a plan."

"You're going to leave me here with him?"

"He's your uncle."

"He used to be my uncle. I don't know what he is now."

"You'll be fine. But if he opens his eyes, don't look at them."

"Why not?"

"It ain't good." Enid turned abruptly and left the room.

«« — »»

They'd driven through the night to get to Detroit, and it was now early afternoon. The energy-saving film transformed the light coming through the bedroom window to the color of the shadows that hid between the city's somber gray buildings. Against the soft color of the light green bedspread, the cables binding his uncle Bartok's wrists, knees and ankles matched the color of a lead sinker. The old man's hands looked gray-green.

The buzzed-brain feeling of exhaustion and lack of sleep made him want to sink down in the corner armchair and zone out for a few hours, but one look at his uncle told Ian that sleep would be harder to come by over the next few days.

"Why didn't you trust me? Look at you now, old man. This is crazy. You should have trusted me."

Behind him he heard Enid hauling things into the house.

"I'm closing all the blinds," he called out. "Can't have nobody seeing inside."

Ian saw the eldest Mozer walk past the bedroom door, a sleek black pump shotgun hung over his shoulder.

"You can't shoot my neighbors," Ian said.

Enid quit walking, turned around, and stood in front of the guest room door.

"I'll shoot anybody tries to stop us," he said. "We got things to do what needs to get done."

"I'm just saying we should keep the body count down," Ian said.

Calmly, smoothly, Enid slid the shotgun off his shoulder and racked a round. "Any questions?"

"Not right now."

"Good. Get reading and come up with a decent plan before it's too late. I'll secure this place then come back to guard him while you look for answers." Reaching behind him, he brought out the weathered brown valise they'd brought with them from Kentucky and handed it to Ian.

"Your uncle kept some papers in there he wanted you to have. Told me so himself. So start reading."

"Enid, I'm tired. I didn't sleep much in the car. Aren't you exhausted?"

"No time to be tired. You seen what happened to your uncle. You been down below. You're the only chance Bartok's got. He's already changing. You can't find a way to stop it, and then he's no better off than my dog. And if that thing down below is getting stronger, the rest of us are in some serious trouble."

It was the most sentences Ian had ever heard come from Enid's mouth.

"If I can get some sleep, I'll understand what I'm reading."

Enid stared him down.

"You look at that old man I trussed up on the bed. Go on, take a good look."

Although he didn't want to look, Ian followed the line of Enid's tan, weathered finger to where Bartok lay bound on the bed. He started with the scuffed soles of his uncle's black boots, the dirty black pants and shirt. They'd all spent some time in the dirt and it showed. Even his uncle's face, stern even in sleep, looked grimy.

"He said you're the smartest one ever been in the family. Don't let him down. Now I'm going around to secure this place. Be back."

And Enid was gone.

The temptation to sit in the corner chair grew with every second Enid was gone, but Ian knew it was a bad idea. He'd be asleep before he opened the valise. If he kept standing, he could at least keep awake. But he felt like he wanted to just collapse on a soft bed and sleep 'til his nerves quit jumping. Too much had happened too fast. Too intense, too quick and too much over the edge. His mind was on cruise control until he could sort it all out.

The creature hanging in the cavern. Silver metal eyes and those clear tubes filled with living light pumping that thing and the mechanical men. Automatons lined up and ready to go to war. The clawed metal snake burrowing into Bartok's neck and pumping him full of viscous light. That hideous alien dog.

"Uncle Bartok, why didn't you tell me about all this? Why? What made you think you could hide things like that from the world?"

Bartok's eyes popped open, filled with twisting filaments of purple-black light. Ian felt an electric jolt light up his brain.

"You're still in there, aren't you Bartok? Tell me what I have to do to save you."

The filaments began to swirl and the room began to darken. Ian stepped toward the bed, hoping that his uncle would say something to him, that his uncle would be … his uncle again. That Bartok would tell him what to do. The old man's lips moved and he said something. Ian leaned forward to hear what it was.

Pain in his shoulder and he was flying backward. The back of his head hit the wall and he slid down, landing hard on his ass. The room wavered in and out and he had a hard time catching his breath.

"What'd I tell you? Something not clear about it when I said not to look at his eyes?"

"Shit that hurt. What the hell did you do that for?" Ian pulled himself up using the chair and straightened his back. "I think I pulled a muscle."

Enid moved at him, slapping him on the chest with an open palm and knocking him up against the wall again.

"I don't care about your back. You don't do what I tell you, you might get us both killed. That man lying on the bed is dangerous. Don't you get that yet?"

"Would you quit knocking me around? I made a mistake. I'm sorry, okay?"

Enid shook his head in disgust.

He was about to say something when Ian leaned to one side and looked at Bartok.

"I told you not to—"

"I'm not looking at his eyes. I'm looking at his skin. Look at his hands. He's turning green. I thought it was the window film, but it's not. He's turning *green.*"

"It's going to get worse," Enid said. "This is just the start. Stage one. You don't want to see stage three. So get to work. Bartok said you was the smartest in the family. Show me some smarts before it's too late. Find yourself someplace to read and get to those papers while I blindfold Bartok so it don't happen again."

"What about you? Aren't you tired?"

The mountain man's eyes narrowed.

"I can handle it. Spent three days once half-buried in mud waiting to nail a courier. Stayed awake reciting the Bible in my head. Besides, I got things to do. So get to it. That old man's life is at stake and a whole lot more, too."

«« — »»

Ian made a cup of coffee and took it and the valise full of his uncle's papers into his home office. He laid the valise on a small walnut table next to his desk, pushed the keyboard back and set down his coffee cup. His body ached and his eyelids drooped. He looked around at bookshelves that lined the wall, filled with books on ghosts and the paranormal. He smiled when he saw the top shelf where his own books were arranged.

Writing about the paranormal made him a good living. Ghost stories and legends, paranormal investigations and the like were hotter than ever. His editor was always on him for the next book. Even his favorite topic— debunking claims of hauntings—sold well. He always ended each book by leaving the door open to the possibility of life after death. It kept people coming back. People needed hope.

Half a cup later, he was feeling a little more awake.

He thought about Bartok and Enid. He thought about the thing underground. He wondered if in his uncle's papers he would find a way to save the old man.

When his mother and father died, Bartok took over and raised him. For most of his life, he thought the old man was the smartest, most interesting person in the world. He seemed to know everything about everything. And there were the secrets that Bartok hinted at. He talked and taught Ian about secret societies, about the history of magic. He taught Ian about the mysteries of life. Other parents took their children to school events, to sports and band. Bartok took Ian to sacred burial grounds, to haunted houses and taught him the art of Alchemy. But eventually Ian grew up.

"Old man," he said aloud, "what have you gotten us into?"

Then he opened the valise, pulled out a thick stack of handwritten bound journals, and laid them on the desk. Skimming through them he saw that they were written by a variety of people at different times. There were diagrams and symbols. Old newspaper columns taped carefully into place.

But when he saw the volume labeled "The Diary of Albert Magnus Hillis," he knew where to begin. It was written in a tight, perfectly drawn script and divided into sections. The first was titled Incident on Track 13. Intrigued, he began to read. By the tenth page, Ian no longer felt tired. What he began to feel instead was an indefinable mixture of awe and terror.

Chapter Sixteen

Mr. Chirac was a dangerous man, but at least he had been civilized. Alvin Jester had worn his best writing jacket to the meeting. It was the kind of jacket that Papa Hemingway would have appreciated. Manly. Thick tweed. Twisted threads the color of scuffed bark.

They discussed Proust, Dostoyevsky, Goethe, and Norman Mailer. Alvin attempted to bring up Truman Capote, but Mr. Chirac fixed him with a grim stare and told him that he would rather sweeten his tea with lye soap than discuss an undisciplined writer. Embarrassed, Alvin had taken a quick sip of bitter but expensive wine and returned to the topic of the chair. Hemingway's actual writing chair.

"You are obsessed," Chirac observed and ran the tip of his left index finger across the edges of his moustache. "But I understand obsession. I respect obsession. You wish to sit on the same chair that Papa did. You dream of closing your eyes and imagine that you share thoughts with the great writer himself the way a lover breathes in the aroma of his beloved. Yes, I understand obsession, my friend, but it is always an expensive habit."

"I have the money," Alvin said, taking another sip of wine. Perhaps he shouldn't have had so much to drink. Alcohol affected his judgment, making him prone to blurt things out without thinking, as though he were desperate.

"But are you sure that you have enough?" asked Mr. Chirac smiled, revealing only the edges of his tiny white teeth.

Alvin stepped back and bit the inside of his lip.

"How much?" he asked. "You haven't told me how much."

"Ah, then you must not have too little. But I understand your concern."

"What? I don't know what you mean."

With a single stride, Chirac closed the distance between them. He straightened to his full height and looked down at Alvin. Like a father speaking to a son who has disappointed him, Chirac placed his hands on Alvin's shoulders.

«« — »»

"You doubt. That's it, isn't it? Will it work? You would do it if you knew for certain when you sit in Papa's chair his spirit would inspire you, even for only the briefest of moments. If you believed that to be true, if you knew for certain that you, too, could write the words that could make a man feel like a man, then you would not even consider the cost. If your belief burned

90

as bright as your obsession, you would reach into your pocket and give me your entire billfold this very moment."

Alvin's left hand moved to his jacket pocket to do just that.

"To tell stories the way that Papa did," continued Chirac, ignoring his guest's intention. "Think of it—how would it feel to know that when a woman read your stories she truly felt the earth itself move beneath her feet?

"To be strong like Papa. How much do you desire that? How much do you need that? How much would you pay for that?"

"I—" Alvin began.

"Be careful, you've spilled wine on my carpet," Chirac said.

"I'm so sorry," Alvin said. His hands were shaking. He looked down. "No, it's all right. It's only on my shoe."

"You poor man," Chirac said. "Look at yourself. Go ahead. Walk to the mirror over there. Tell me what you see. Tell me if you see a man of obsession, his eyes on fire, his heart pumping strength and confidence through his veins. Is that what you see, my friend? Or do you see an accountant, his hands shaking because he has forgotten to bring his calculator?"

Alvin walked over to the mirror and did not like what he saw.

Over his left shoulder, he could see Chirac appraising him. Chirac with his tailored gray suit and light pink shirt and a tie that could have been designed by Matisse. Chirac, with his perfectly trimmed hair black and lustrous as shoe cream. Sideburns tapered to a wicked point matched by the slight sharpness at the apex of his ears. His moustache was tightly trimmed, his eyebrows arched as though he were always amused. He had a forehead wide and tall enough to write on, but angled back like a tilted white-board. His skin was pale, but his eyes were dark-colored and disturbing. He was a slender, formidable, polished man.

Alvin looked at his reflection, at his ill-defined chin and the fold of flesh that ringed it. A double chin. Perhaps a triple chin.

My posture makes me seem shorter than I am, he thought.

"The chair," Chirac said, "will be the bridge to bring his spirit back from the other side. It will allow him to step out from the shadows of death and into your mind. Not many have the courage to give over their own body to a departed spirit. I know something of spirits and I speak from a lifetime of experience. I will understand, Alvin, if the man you see reflected before you pales before the task."

Alvin Jester reached for his checkbook.

«« — »»

"Come in, Ricci. Our new client has left to prepare himself for the delivery of Hemingway's chair. The very chair on which, legend says, that he wrote *For Whom the Bell Tolls*. A magnificent piece."

"Lilly's downstairs now, locked up. I fed her like you said."

"So, just so. And now, I require you and your abhorrent associate Larry to deliver our part of Mr. Jester's contract."

"I don't need Larry."

Chirac's eyebrows arched.

"But I require you to take your associate."

"I'll do it."

"Yes, indeed. Later in the evening, precisely at midnight, you will meet me at the very same place where you and I made our own agreement. Do you remember the place?"

Ricci's jaw tightened. "I'll never forget it."

"So, just so. Mr. Jester has arranged a room in his home, a study I believe, that is a replica of Hemingway's own. The same pictures, a typewriter of the make and model that the great man himself used. Replicas of the pictures that adorned Papa's own writing area. A desk procured from one of the Hemingway heirs. Even a shotgun in the corner of the room of the identical type which the tormented writer used to kill himself. Mr. Jester's attention to detail is commendable. You will place the chair in front of the desk that he has arranged, and stay with him as he attempts to invoke the great man's spirit. Mr. Jester will then attempt to type the manuscript many believe Hemingway was working on. You will return that to me along with the chair."

"I thought he bought it."

"Really? We shall see. And Ricci…"

"What?"

Chirac toured his study, his hands crossed behind his back.

"I would like very much to acquire, shall we say, a white panther."

Ricci's jaw tightened and he closed his eyes.

"I enjoy so the company of dear Lily. Yet we must find another woman to be my pet as well. A man with only one female companion has too few options in his life."

Ricci left the room to get the chair. His huge hands, Mr. Chirac noticed, were balled into fists.

《《——》》

At midnight, Ricci descended the chipped concrete steps to the landing where Mr. Chirac waited. In the darkness, he saw a brief flame and the tip of a cigarette glow with both life and death. The streetlight provided enough light for Ricci to make it down the steps without falling and breaking his neck. Mr. Chirac stayed in the shadows.

"There were, perhaps, complications?" Mr. Chirac asked.

Ricci made it to the landing and stopped at the edge of the light. Mr. Chirac stayed in the shadows.

"It went pretty much the way you laid it out," said Ricci.

"And our dear friend Larry?" Chirac asked.

"He died in the fire. Burned the place to the ground. I had to get rid of the evidence, and he didn't wake up in time. I took the chair back like you said to, though."

"And where is it?"

"In the van."

"Excellent."

"Don't I always do like you say?"

"Do I detect a slight sadness in your voice? Amazing, a killer such as yourself, who spent twelve long years in prison, and yet you still have your sensitivities. I think that I will never understand people."

"I think you got us down pretty pat, Mr. Chirac," Ricci said.

Even in the darkness, Ricci could see a momentary glint of teeth.

"So. Just so. But aren't you forgetting something, my faithful friend? Was there not something else you were to return to me?"

"Yes, sir," said Ricci. He took a piece of paper from his jacket and handed it to his master.

After a few minutes of silence, Mr. Chirac chuckled, and Ricci's stomach turned sour.

"How perfectly appropriate. A suicide note. Of all the things that the great Papa should feel compelled to write for us and the insignificant Mr. Jester to record moments before his death, he decides on this."

Ricci shrugged.

"Ah, well," Mr. Chirac said.

A second later, Mr. Chirac flicked a flame once again from his lighter, and the page caught fire. Mr. Chirac held it for an impossibly long time—even past the moment that Ricci himself could have held it. When the flame disappeared, Mr. Chirac blew into his hands to dissipate the ashes.

Sometimes, on nights like this when Alvin Jester shot himself, Ricci missed his prison cell very much.

Chapter Seventeen

"Madstone," Ashley said. "Here it is. Google knows everything."

Wendland looked up at the clock in the Hillis library. "She'll be here soon. Why did you have to see her? She sounds like she probably has dementia. Anything she says should be considered suspect."

Ashley ignored him and kept reading.

"You've been at this for hours now. It's dark outside."

Ashley ran a hand through her hair to hide her irritation. Henry Wendland was keeping things from her, she was fairly certain of that. Possibly to protect her feelings. Possibly because he was a sleaze bucket. But she'd get it out of him. Either way. She had to find out what he knew so that she could find Michael. And God help him if he was holding out anything that caused her husband to get hurt.

"Sometimes called a bezoar stone," she read from a website. "Used to draw out poison, to heal, to ward off spirits. Okay Henry. Show me why you're worth five-hundred-dollars an hour. What is so different about the madstone that Chirac wanted from my husband than from every other madstone? You said he called it the madstone, not a madstone."

After driving Ashley home, Henry Wendland stayed with her to answer whatever questions she had and to be with her when Granny Hillis arrived. She and her nephew Kenneth were at a motel only an hour or so away and they would be the first of Michael's relatives that she had ever met. Ashley asked them to come in a few hours, so that she could get settled in and make sure they weren't harassed by reporters determined to follow up on Michael's disappearance. They'd gotten in without incident—there were no reporters hiding in the bushes—and Ashley had spent the rest of the afternoon grilling Wendland and surfing for answers on the internet.

"This one was different," Wendland said tentatively.

"I just asked you in what way and you ignored my question," Ashley said, sounding every bit like a frustrated schoolteacher.

Wendland showed her his palms.

"I don't know, just different. The peculiar thing is that Michael seemed to know which madstone Chirac was asking for. He seemed to think it might be in the family like an heirloom or something. But it was still very odd, you know? I've known Michael since he was a child. His bizarre obsession with this kind of New Age mumbo jumbo has always been most distressing to me. His father was a spiritualist, did you know that? His gift to Michael for the lad's sixteenth birthday was a miniature psychomanteum."

"A what?"

"A psychomanteum is a mirrored room which some claim facilitate contact with the dead. The term is actually relatively recent; the technique has been around since the Oracles in ancient Greece. Michael's father had a tabletop version of the device constructed. Fine gift for a red-blooded sixteen year old, wouldn't you say?"

A knock at the front door interrupted Ashley's response.

"I'll get it," she said and stood up.

Wendland straightened his ponderous bulk.

"I know you're not afraid of running into reporters, but you have no idea what the ramifications of that could be. Therefore, I'll answer the door. You stay here and keep a low profile."

"What if it's Michael's granny?"

"Then I'll bring her straight in and hopefully we can get rid of her quickly."

Ashley went back to her computer. She typed in the name "Emile Chirac." Nothing came up. What were the odds of that? Everyone came up when you typed their name on the internet. Obviously a phony name. Possibly to cover a criminal background. Like a relic dealer. Fences stolen relics. Tried to con Michael. But Michael wouldn't fall for it.

No, Michael did go for the deal. He'd get the ghost box if he could find the madstone for Chirac. She made a note in her note-to-self program. "How did Michael know about the special madstone?" Another note. "Why didn't Michael ever tell me about any of this?" And yet another. "What exactly is the ghost box?"

Frustrated, she typed in the search term "the ghost box" and got everything from an independent label in the UK to an electronic box programmed to interpret electromagnetic field radiation as speech from the other side. The latter was a favorite of amateur paranormal investigators.

She went back to researching the term madstone. It was the same thing on every site she went to—"stony concretion," "calcified hairball" from the stomach or intestines of a deer, goat or cow. Supposed to neutralize poison, heal the sick, and ward off evil when worn as an amulet.

"What would Chirac want with a madstone?" she asked herself. "There are a ton of magical amulets out there already. Why would he want one from the guts of a deer?"

This was getting too frustrating. Madstones were of various sizes, but most were about the diameter of a quarter. They were different colors but supposed to have similar powers. Still no mention of the madstone that Chirac wanted. In fact, there was nothing at all about a special madstone. Perhaps Chirac was ill and was looking for a miracle cure.

"What is the difference between a madstone and *the* madstone?" she asked out loud again. The frustration was getting to be too much. So many questions and no answers.

Then came a rough old voice.

"Young Missy, if you'll pay attention to this old granny woman and tell me no lies, I believe I can explain that to you. God help you if you lie."

«« — »»

A little bird of a woman in a red and black flannel shirt and roughed-up jeans stood in the doorway to the library. She wore a felt red felt cap with two earflaps pulled up and snapped into place. All total she couldn't have been more than four foot ten and a hundred pounds. Her hiking boots could have added another five pounds, but that would be it. The gray-white hair that sprang out from beneath her hat as she took it off was just a shade whiter than Ashley's was after the incident in Sharkey's Park. Over her shoulder she carried a quilted purse big as a grocery bag.

Directly behind her stood a man tall as skinny as Henry Wendland was short and wide. He was dressed a little less country in a white shirt open at the collar with tufts of curly black hair showing around the neckline. His forehead was covered by a wild shock of hair. Sideburns thick and tapered to a point. Eyes dark as bore holes, staring straight at Ashley, then Wendland, then back again. Like a sniper's spotter, clicking off the range to each target. His arms were long and loose. Right hand hanging by his side, his left hidden in the pocket of fleece-lined jean jacket.

Henry Wendland stood behind the two, halfway between the front door and the archway leading to the library. He looked distinctly unhappy.

"You're the one who wrote us the note," Ashley said simply.

The old woman stared back at her with a peculiar intensity.

"You read it? I wrote that to my great grandnephew. Did you pry into what was his or did he read it to you? Answer me quick. You kept me waiting on you when I done come up all the way to see you, and I ain't happy about that. Ain't going to live forever and every day is mighty precious to me. You hear that and remember it, little girl."

Ashley was so shocked that she almost burst into tears. "I didn't mean to pry into your letters," she said. "Michael threw it away and I got it out of the trash and read it because I had to know why it upset him so."

She was on her feet in her own defense without realizing she knocked the desk chair backward and over onto the floor. Her arms were shaking and she felt crazy.

"Mrs. Hillis, please," began Wendland.

"Kenneth, shut that man up," Granny Hillis said.

"I will not be quiet. This is my client's home and she is under tremendous stress."

The jowls beneath Wendland's chin trembled. His finger wagged at Granny Hillis while his hand shook.

"Oh, my God," Ashley said.

Her corpulent attorney was suddenly up in the air and over and lying flat on his back looking up at the ceiling with the air knocked out of him. The impact of him hitting the floor knocked over her desk lamp. And Kenneth was on him like a wrestler, pinning his arms to the floor, leaning his face over to within inches of Wendland, grinning wildly. Ashley watched in horror as Wendland pressed his head back hard against the floor, his face a mask of horror.

"You take listen to Granny and you can sit or stand any which way you want. But her time is serious important and you lay waste to any of it and I'll take you out back, truss you up like a hog, toss your big ass in the trunk and ain't nobody in this town going to ever know 'bout it till they find what's left of your body spread 'tween three states. What you got to say, lawyer man?"

"Leave him alone," shouted Ashley.

She was in motion toward Wendland and Kenneth when the look in Granny Hillis's eyes stopped her.

"Are you people crazy?" Ashley asked.

"Kenneth was a hog wrestler," Granny Hillis said. "You know what that is? Ever seen a man could wrestle a hog? Not a pig, child, but a fully growed hog. Man's got to be long with long arms. Tough. Got to take the pain. Got to be ready to die when the time's right. Your fat lawyer ready to die if I say it's his time?"

Ashley didn't know what she was expecting Granny Hillis to be like, but it wasn't this. Maybe she'd expected a kindly old hill woman who'd come to give comfort and wisdom. Maybe an old woman with a bad memory confined to a wheelchair. But nothing like this. Nothing like Kenneth. This was crazy. Granny Hillis was completely out of her mind.

"Don't hurt him. Why are you doing this? Nobody has to be hurt. What is it that you want?"

"Hold him down, Kenneth," Granny Hillis said.

She crooked a crack-nailed finger in Ashley's direction and motioned her to lean forward. Ashley stepped back. Granny chuckled and Ashley saw her lower dentures slide back and forth as she did.

"Child, are you afraid of Granny?"

"No," Ashley said.

"Tell the truth, child. Don't tell Granny no lies."

Ashley's eyed darted around the room, looking for a letter opener to defend herself with.

"Well why wouldn't I be? You're a total stranger who comes into my house; your friend over there knocks my lawyer down and threatens him. I'm married to your grandson, doesn't that count for anything?"

"Great grandson, and it does count for something. It means your husband done stole away the one thing protected that little girl's soul and kept the haint at peace. Don't even know her name, do you? Now either you give me back my madstone or I'm going to let that worthless husband of yours pay the price."

"But I don't have your madstone."

Wendland tried to say something, but Kenneth Hillis slapped him so hard he immediately shut up.

This can't be happening, thought Ashley. *This is* my *house*.

"You're married to the line of Becker Hillis, you little fool," Granny said, "and you and that man of yours didn't heed my warnings. He had to dig her up. Just had to. Worse than Becker. Had to steal the madstone and look at what's become of you all since. I been watching the TV in my room while you kept me waiting. I heard all about it. God help you both."

Then the lights began to flicker. They heard a crackle like someone stepping on packing popcorn.

"You see that Granny?" Kenneth called.

"I do."

"What's going on?" Ashley asked.

The room filled with the unmistakable odor of burned hair.

Granny's eyes darted around the room and she reached into her bag.

"The haint has come calling," she hissed.

Kenneth leaped off Henry Wendland and was at the old lady's side in an instant. She took something from her bag and gave it to him. He closed his big hands around it before Ashley could see what it was. Wendland scrambled to his feet and looked around wildly then headed for the front door.

"Get him," Granny Hillis said.

Ashley felt the terror building inside her.

"What is it?" she demanded.

The curtains on the window behind her desk burst into flames as the lights went out and darkness rushed in only to be pushed back by the fire. Ashley leapt back and covered her mouth with her hands to keep from screaming.

But Granny Hillis walked straight toward the flames as the curtains melted away to reveal the window that looked out onto the backyard of the estate. Beyond the window, a burning apparition flared an angry red and everyone but her brought their hands up to protect their eyes. It seethed and sparked like a live wire and the old woman shouted something that no one else could hear over the roaring winds that sprang up outside. She jabbed the air with something clutched in her right hand and continued shouting.

The glass seemed to glow red and then exploded inward as the apparition disappeared and the night returned to silence. The lights flashed on again and Ashley saw Granny Hillis crumple forward and drop to the floor in a mess of blood.

«« — »»

Alvarez stuffed the remains of his drive-through fried chicken dinner in the waste basket, washed his hands in the kitchen sink to get rid of the grease, and set his coffee cup in the middle of the table. It was surrounded by a small mountain range of news-papers, notepads and internet printouts.

The evidence techs hadn't found anything remotely resembling a microwave device in the collected effects from Sharkey's Park. That was the first piece of bad news for the day. Then, he'd been dressed down by the Captain. The department was going along with the lightning experts opinion that the deaths in Sharkey's Park were caused by a freak storm event with the "…exact details unknown." The prominent businessman Michael Hillis was missing but presumed dead. No body yet. No trace. A terrible tragedy.

Alvarez hadn't liked that.

But if there was something more sinister involved, Alvarez couldn't come up with a motive or a method to link Hillis to the deaths. Hillis's disappearance hurt his company's credibility. Since the company's finances were sound and they had a great new technology Hillis had been personally spearheading, there was no motive for him to go missing. None that Alvarez could come up with, at least. The Sharkey's Park investigation was therefore considered "closed."

When he told the Captain about his microwave idea, the Captain told him it was unsubstantiated speculation, plain and simple. He had no evidence whatsoever to support that conjecture. That nailed the lid shut.

And Lincoln Jones was a separate case. No linkage to Sharkey's Park. That was the verdict. Nothing to tie the two together.

If Alvarez was a drinking man, he would have been drunk out of his mind.

Instead, he nursed the cup his cup of black coffee and thought back on years of being a cop. He was a good cop, methodical and persistent, but in all his years he'd never really solved a big case. Nothing really came his way that gave him the opportunity. He had a good enough arrest record. Had a few commendations for his police work. But it wasn't enough.

His wife had been dead for eight years and nothing had ever filled her absence. She'd died of a heart attack while he was working midnights. Doctors said she was young for it, but it wasn't unheard of, which didn't do much to wipe away the guilt. He stayed to himself, mostly. Dated some, hung out with other cops some. Quit going to church, took up chess and tried to read more. Tried golf and gave it up.

He sold the house a month after his wife died, moved into a small apartment and lived a small life. Waiting out his days for something big enough to come along that would give some meaning to his life. In the beginning, he thought Sharkey's Park was it. Now that it had reached a dead end, he felt the beginnings of depression coming back. The mystery of his grandfather's death would never be solved.

Alvarez had no use for amateur ghost hunters like Michael Hillis. He really couldn't understand why a rich guy like him would waste his time looking for ghosts anyway. There was no such thing. People died and that was it. You thought anything else and you were just leading yourself on.

No matter how much he'd wanted his wife's ghost to appear and talk to him, no matter how many times he'd thought he felt her presence, he'd never seen her. He'd prayed and prayed just to see her one last time, but it never happened. If there was life after death, Maria would have contacted him. He believed that.

People who thought they saw ghosts were just seeing memories. Or maybe they were just seeing what they wanted to see or were afraid to see.

He thought about the little girl he'd seen today. That was a good example of stress and work. No one else saw her but him. Therefore, she was only there in his imagination.

Another sip of coffee. He drummed his fingers on the table and looked at the ceiling. Another thing that bothered him was that there was no connection that he could find between the deaths all those years ago and those that just occurred. There were things in common, of course, but not enough to make a productive linkage. They both happened in the same place. A Hillis disappeared both times. An Alvarez dead in the first case, no Alvarez dead in the second case. A little girl's grave. That was there for the first incident and still there in the second. No idea how it fit in.

"Sorry, Grandpa. I don't know what to do. I've got nothing."

Alvarez thought at first that the chief scientist he'd interviewed was tied with the second incident, but couldn't figure out how.

He pulled out an old newspaper from one of the stacks and re-read the first report on the original case. Written by a reporter named Kilburn, now deceased.

What the hell happened that night? he wondered.

His grandfather's name was there. Burned to death just like the others. Probably lightning, the Captain would say. Sharkey's Park and freak thunderstorms. He'd probably assign a team of weathermen to investigate.

And then Alvarez saw something that made him sit up so quickly he almost spilled his coffee. He was looking at another name on the reporter's list of victims. Something rang a bell. He knew that name.

Richard Wendland.

Ashley Hillis's attorney's last name was Wendland.

Chapter Eighteen

Major Albert Magnus Hillis. Mechanical genius and deranged Confederate officer known as "The Butcher of Lexington." Filled with rage and headed into his home state of Kentucky on an armored train filled with gold, war-hardened soldiers, equipment, raw materials and a plan that bordered on insanity. By order of General Robert E. Lee, who failed in his campaign to take Washington, DC, the Major was to undertake a secret mission to build the greatest weapon in military history—a mechanical war machine that would succeed where General Lee had failed.

It would be impervious to rifle fire and would lead the charge against Washington, D.C. for the Confederacy. With its incredible firepower it would destroy anyone or anything that stood in its way. It would be the greatest military campaign of the war, and when it was over, the South would be victorious.

The plan was conceived by Major Hillis, and a desperate General Lee authorized him to "take any and all measures Major Hillis deems necessary without fear of either censure or penalty." Plumes of fiery smoke puffed from the stack as they roared their way north. The tracks rattled and sang as the massive black beast code named "Iron Spear" sped along toward its destination deep within the Kentucky hills.

Rows of gun ports lined the cars. Two cannons were specially mounted on top of one car near the front, the other near the rear. Iron rails and plates were bolted along the sides as armor. They traveled without discovery or incident until the bright blue morning when they came to a section of track known as Track 13, where all of Major Hillis's plans were radically changed.

A spotter noticed it first. A great multi-colored disc shot into position above the train and hovered a hundred feet above them matching their speed. So terrified was the man that for a full minute he stared at it with his neck craned back far enough to hurt. It was like nothing he or anyone else in the whole wide world had ever seen.

Finally, he called down below to the other soldiers in a voice so shaky he had to shout his message three times before he was heard and understood.

Word was passed to Major Hillis. By the time the Major climbed the iron ladder to the spotter's position, every soldier on the train knew of the mystery and felt the twin thrills of wonder and terror.

Major Hillis had no eye for the passing scenery. The rolling green hills, the cloudless, bright blue sky or the riotous wind blowing his hair back. Forgotten was the most important commission of his career. The Confederacy itself was no longer of significance to him. All that mattered to this mad genius was the giant spinning array of colors hovering above the speeding train. He knew instantly that he was witnessing the most important event of his life. The most important event of any life.

The hovering disc, he knew, was no natural phenomena. It seemed to be constructed of a light emitting metallic material. *Absolutely marvelous*, he thought. How it hovered in the air was a mystery. But he knew instantly the power it represented. He knew that with technology such as this, he could bring the Union army crashing down onto its knees.

Who is operating this magical mechanism? he wondered. *Why is it here? I must have it, I must.*

And as he considered this last point, the strange ship began to pulse and grow brighter as its spinning colors whirled faster and faster until they were a nearly homogenous blur. At that moment, a beam of blinding blue-white energy radiated from the underside of the craft and lifted the six-foot-four bearded madman straight up into the air.

«« — »»

The sound of drilling startled Ian. He got up from his desk and walked down the hallway to the guest bedroom. At the doorway, he stopped and stared in horrified amazement.

"What are you doing?" Ian asked.

Although Bartok still lay on the bed blindfolded, his uncle was wrapped in a mesh of thin wire cable held in place by eight more cables that spread out to the side of the old man like insect legs. Seven of these were screwed into the floor. Enid was bent over, anchoring the last one into place with an electric screwdriver. His uncle's skin was now a faint yellow green.

"Making sure he don't move."

It was like a horrible scene from a movie.

"You could ask before you start drilling into my floor, you know. What if my neighbors came in and saw this?"

"You really going to open the door for your neighbors to come on in? You read all them papers yet?"

"You really think all this is necessary?"

Enid picked up his tools and stared at Ian as though he were mentally incompetent.

"You remember my dog?"

He did. The thought of it made him ill.

"What if we have to take him to the bathroom or feed him or something?"

"They quit eating or drinking when they're infected. Don't ask me why, I don't know. They just do. They don't piss or crap or eat or drink anymore. Maybe they're living on something we can't see."

The thought of that disturbed Ian in a way that he either couldn't or didn't want to understand. Everything that happened to him since the night

Magnus looked back at the instrument, studying the gauges and knobs, seeing his image multiplied a thousand times in the tiny mirrors within.

What strange magic, that this device would allow him to communicate with and exercise power over the dead. In time, he would learn to bring their energy through to power his army. But first, he would listen to the spirits and glean what could be learned. With that knowledge, he would let loose upon the world the terror that he had brought forth in secret.

But in a jagged crevice halfway up to the distant ceiling of the cavern, a ragged man watched him carefully through a pair of field binoculars. He kept a journal beside him and wrote down everything he saw and heard.

«« — »»

From the journal of Bradley Hunter
I write this down over and again so that I do not forget.

Although I do not stay long during any foray, I feel the curse of this strange underground world has descended upon me. My appetite has left me and I know that this is a terrible judgment. Whatever evil dwells behind the back wall of this vast rock sepulcher casts its spell over all who enter. A saint might walk here with impunity, but not a traitor such as me. I was damned the minute I deserted my commission and this is my hell.

This man, this Magnus, is surely the Devil.

I was on the run for two weeks when I first saw the train. I was most of the way up a walnut tree making sure that I'd outdistanced anybody on my trail, so I had a good post. With my binoculars, I was able to see the armor plating and gun turrets. It was not, I knew, one of ours, although as a deserter from the Union army both sides were now my enemy. I had seen the brutality of man no matter what color uniform he wore, be it blue or gray, and I was done with it.

There is no such thing as civilized war. I saw the remains of women and children burned to death in schoolhouses by Union soldiers. I saw the bodies of women bayoneted by the Rebs. And in Kentucky, which is my home, I saw with my own eyes families killing one another for the color of their uniforms. We no longer abhor death and dishonor, we have become both.

So it was that when I first saw the train, I put aside the desire to in some way communicate the information to my former regiment. It was their war, let them fight it. I was about to climb down from my tree and ride away when the giant spinning light appeared like a burning chariot descending from Heaven. I raised my binoculars and held my breath.

The thrill and terror of what I saw will be with me as long as I live and am human.

A blast of wind hit the tree like the slap of a giant hand. If my arms and legs weren't wrapped around the thick branch I would have been thrown to the ground. I heard the tree creak and groan as it was pressed backward by this invisible force. A mighty roaring filled the air. Lighting crackled around the disc and even as I clung to the tree for dear life, I wondered at that moment if Judgment Day had arrived to rebuke our country for mur-dering our own citizens in this war.

But when I looked up, I saw a man lifted from the train, drawn up into the air and taken into the giant spinning disc itself by an invisible power. It seemed to consume him. I pressed my face back against the rough tree bark and willed myself invisible.

My horse reared in terror and I wondered if it would break free from the walnut tree I had roped it to. In moments of great duress such thoughts fly through the brain like leaves tossed about in a windstorm. What I knew for certain was that if I lived at all it would be because I stayed where I was and hung on.

But when I was either courageous or desperate enough to raise my head again, I saw the train slow to a halt as though all its motive power had been drained away. It was as though time came to a halt. Nothing moved on the landscape below. No soldiers came running out. It was a ghost train. In spite of the cool air, I felt my scalp moist with perspiration; I was afraid to move. The wind still pushed at the tree, keeping it bent backward with my body fixed to its side like a bearded tic.

The fantastic disc flashed angry, disquieting colors that filled me with an unaccountable dread. I had to look away. Ugly memories rose within me when I looked at it. Things I had seen and done that I had buried deep within me. The brutality of war provides a writhing, ugly mess of images to stain a man's soul. These were the remembrances this evil thing evoked. I clung to the tree like it was a moral lifeline.

Time passed. The wind continued to blast and I tried to tie myself to the branch but dropped the rope. My arms ached. My joints screamed with pain. My muscles began to cramp. But just when I thought I could not stay in my tree blind even a second longer, I heard an awful sound like a rush of evil winds. I opened my eyes and saw the man descend back again from the underside of the spinning light to the train as though falling in slow motion. His arms were outstretched as though he was coming down from the sky like a fantastic antichrist come to claim the world as his own.

And as he descended, I raised my binoculars and tried to see his face, but could not get a clear enough resolution. But I have come to know his face well enough over the passing weeks. At that moment, as he disappeared into the train, fear like I have never known came over me.

There was no understanding the impossibility of what I had just seen. I'd cried out to God for salvation in these last days. The wind ceased, but the nightmare moved on.

When the thunderous winds quit and the giant disc whipped away, I should have ridden the other direction for my life and soul, brother. Instead I stayed to the ridge and followed the train, my heart beating in my chest like the hooves of my horse over the hard ground.

Perhaps as you read this, Taylor, you will ask yourself why. Why did I do this? Why did I ride after this train?

You may give no credence to anything I answer when you reflect that I am a deserter and a coward. That is what they will tell you, I know, when they come to you inquiring as to my whereabouts. They will call me a traitor and a coward and tell you how I deserted my post. I am a traitor to their war, Taylor, but I am not a coward. I am not particularly brave, yet I have always stayed the course until these last few weeks. My word has been my bond. I swore an oath to the government of the United States. For my own reasons, I broke that oath. There may be no reason you can countenance for my desertion, and therefore you may reject what I tell you now about why I rode after that train.

But it is the truth.

I felt the presence of evil that day. Evil that transcended even what I had seen in this war that rips asunder our great country. The memories that ship had evoked in me were too wrong. A danger to us all had descended from the heavens that day, and I had to find out what that danger was. So I pursued it.

Why did I not leave and communicate what I saw? That is a good question, bother. But remember, if you will, I am a deserter. And no one, not even you, would believe my testimony. I would be court martialed. No one believes the word of a deserter. So I followed the train to gather proof that could not be disputed.

I followed it to this God-forsaken hole in the earth.

But tonight I must remind myself who I am and why I am here. I have devised a plan, you see, and these journals are that plan.

Perhaps you wonder now why I do not sneak down and shoot this Magnus. You will no doubt think again that I am a coward. There is no defense for me. I do have one round left in my pistol, it is true, but I am saving that for myself. I am changing, Taylor. Very slowly, but I doubt I can ever be fully human again.

I see now that he has turned on his new device. His army of giant mechanical soldiers was not enough. Until now they are the most frightening thing I have seen. But this new device, though only as tall as a powder keg, is somehow more frightening still. Through its front glass panel I see a spectral blue-white light forming within.

God help me, I must get closer.

Chapter Nineteen

Alvarez went for the gun in his nightstand.

Ghostly moonlight filtered through the curtains and lit his skin a pallid hue.

Disoriented, sweaty.

Locked in a shooter's stance moving the gun slowly around the room. What had he heard? What had jolted him from sleep?

He remembered the little girl's scream.

Help me. That was it. Bloodcurdling.

Please help me.

Arms stretched out toward him. Tears. Her head shaking violently from side to side. Someone on top of her. Oh God, no. Forcing her down into the dirt. Pushing against her. Grinding against her.

Help me. Please help me.

Arms stretched toward him.

He lowered his gun. Reluctant to put it away, he slid on his shoulder holster, tightened it up and slid the gun into place. Something didn't feel right.

The case, what was left of it, was really getting to him.

He pulled on a pair of pants, buckled his belt and put on a pair of loafers. There would be no going back to sleep now. It was three o'clock in the morning. Time for coffee.

As he microwaved a cup of water, he kept going back to the dream. It was the same little girl he'd seen outside the Jones house. He was sure of that. Too much looking at her picture trying to figure out how she fit in and what had happened to her. After a few minutes digging around in the cabinets for where he'd place the instant coffee, he found it and dosed the hot water.

There was a stove in his kitchen, but he used it to stack dirty dishes. No sense using a stove when you could microwave.

The weight of his pistol felt good, somehow grounding. It pulled him back to reality.

Help me.

A young girl being raped.

Could it really be the way it happened? Were dreams or nightmares ever really true? He remembered this murder case twenty three years ago. Wife killed her husband with one shot to the head while he slept. Last name was… Brooks. She claimed self-defense. He was going to cut her throat while she was napping. It came to her in a dream. Night after night she dreamed the same dream. She could feel the knife slicing through her throat. She could feel the warmth of her blood as it poured over her skin. So she killed him. She couldn't believe it when she was convicted.

The memory of that case nagged at him. Something...

He took his coffee to his work table. Shuffled through the papers.

Edwina Brooks.

Something about her. And then it hit him. Maybe, just maybe...

Moving through the stacks. Quicker now, almost frantic. He was on to something. More coffee, more re-arranging of paper. Screw it. He opened his laptop and kicked it out of sleep mode. Brought up the search engine and typed in "Sharkey's Park" and "Josh."

"Come on, come on."

Damned thing was too slow.

And then the links appeared to the news accounts. He clicked on one, swore to himself next time he would buy the fastest damned laptop he could get instead of the cheapest.

Joshua Brooks.

Alvarez sat back in his chair and whistled.

No relation to Edwina Brooks, he was sure of that. It was just the last name that triggered his memory. Joshua Brooks, supposed suicide. Leapt from the top floor of the hospital and flew straight down to the pavement. Joshua Brooks died right after leaving Sharkey's Park. Decades before, one of the men who died in Sharkey's Park had the last name of Brooks. Michael Hillis, dead or missing just like his ancestor Becker Hillis. Then there was the earlier Wendland. Henry Wendland was, to Alvarez's knowledge, still alive. Add his own family member, Sergio Alvarez, to the mix and the coincidences were piling up. Then there was Jones, Lincoln Jones. Fried and pinned to his living room wall with kitchen knives. Could he fit in? Nope. No one named Jones in the earlier murders. And how about the others in the ghost hunting team? Collateral damage maybe?

Alvarez logged into the online databases and plugged in the name and information he had on Lincoln Jones. Nothing useful. Nothing that came together.

His eyes felt dry. A wave of tiredness came over him. Hints and clues that led nowhere. Threads that should tie together but didn't. The letters on the laptop screen began to blur. He rubbed his eyes and drank more coffee. Got to keep rolling. He wasn't getting anything but he couldn't give it up.

Forty-five minutes later he found it.

A name change.

Lincoln Jones had changed his last name ten years ago. Lincoln Jones, formerly Lincoln Winken. *Yeah, I'd change that*, thought Alvarez. And sure enough, a Claude Winken had died in the earlier murders. Well, well.

Hillis, Brooks, Winken, a.k.a. Jones and Alvarez. Five names that matched. Others that didn't. The others were collateral damage, he was sure about it. Not sure how he knew, but it felt right. The key names were Hillis, Brooks, Wendland, Winken and Alvarez. Three dead so far. Two alive.

For now.

He didn't know where the thought came from, but it felt right, too. It hit him like a fist to the gut. His name was on the murderer's list. For the first time he considered the idea that Michael Hillis was dead, murdered along with the others. Was that possible? They didn't find a body. Vanished into thin air, just like Becker Hillis had decades before.

But if Michael Hillis wasn't the present-day Sharkey's Park murderer, then who was? Whoever it was would be coming for him, he was sure of it. He and Ashley Hillis's lawyer. But who was it?

Help me, said the little girl in his nightmare.

«« — »»

"Don't touch that phone," Kenneth said. "Mrs. Hillis, you bring me her bag. Haint won't be back tonight. Granny seen to that. You—fat man. Stay right where you are or you'll be walking on stumps."

Ashley stared at the phone on her desk. They'd put out the curtain fire and smokey haze.

"We have to call nine-one-one. Open a window and get some air in here."

"Granny don't need doctors. And you really want to open a window and let that thing was out there in? Just you get me her bag. You heard me. Nobody leaves this house."

"But she's bleeding."

"I can see that. Hurry it up."

Kenneth took off his flannel shirt, and then his undershirt. Lean muscles tensed beneath his dark skin.

"Fat man," he said. "Chair."

He was pointing a long, gnarly finger at an upholstered burgundy chair off to the side of Ashley's desk.

"My name isn't fat man," Wendland said.

But he walked over and sat down.

Ashley handed him his Granny's bag. She glanced over at the old woman and winced at the sight of so much blood.

"Go close the doors that swing close over where the sliding glass door was," he told Ashley. "Make it quick. It ain't likely to come back, but that ain't all that comforting. Close them up and lock them down if you can."

She didn't argue. The idea of whatever had exploded the window returning was reason enough to close the security doors over the opening.

"Help me roll her over and hold my shirts up against the wounds when I tell you."

He thrust the bundle of clothing at her.

"Easy, easy, woman. She's ornery as hell, but she's old, too."

When they rolled her over on her back, Ashley saw the extent of the old woman's wounds. Blood, so much blood. Sharp-edged fragments of glass stuck in her chest and arms. A piece the size and shape of a quarter protruded from her cheek. The dark scarlet bloodstain looked like a flower opening to the moonlight.

"She's going to bleed to death," Ashley said. "We've got to take her to the emergency room."

Kenneth's hand disappeared into the old woman's quilted bag and pulled out a small black velvet pouch and what looked like a small sewing kit. He opened the velvet bag by loosening the drawstring and dumped the contents into his calloused hands. It was a gray-brown stone the size of a shelled almond. He clasped his hands together, whispered something, then reached down and placed it on Granny Hillis's blood-stained neck.

"What are you doing?" Ashley asked.

"What she told me to," Kenneth said.

"What is that thing?"

"It be a madstone, lady. It will stay fixed to her skin like a leech until the healing's done."

He took a pair tweezers from the sewing kit and began to pull glass from each wound in turn.

"I can see you, fool. Sit your fat ass back down in that chair and keep it there or I'm going to hurt you good. You, woman, put pressure here."

The Hillis woman wanted to say something, he could see it.

"Out with it. Get it out now. You got thoughts I need to hear?"

When Ashley looked at up him, he could see the trembling anger in her face. He saw her look down at the blood covering the old woman's chest and then back at him again.

"How can you see what you're doing? There's so much blood. We need to get her to the emergency room."

"No."

"At least open her blouse so you can make sure you're getting everything. And she may need stitches."

"No."

"Well then I'll do it. She's bleeding to death you ignorant hillbilly."

"Lady, can't you see she's stopped bleeding? Look there at the madstone and tell me who's the ignorant hillbilly."

She did not look right away. Her face was flush with anger. But when she did, he saw the shock and disbelief on her face.

"That's right," he said. "It's changed, can't you see?"

And it had.

The madstone was now the color of blood.

"This isn't possible," stammered Ashley.

"What in the name of God?" Wendland said.

Kenneth deftly plucked the remaining glass shard from Granny Hillis's cheek. Fresh blood did not pour out. The wounds were beginning to clot. The old woman's eyes were still closed and her breathing was shallow as if she were drifting in a deep and troubled sleep.

"Now, Mrs. Hillis, I need you to fetch me some facecloths and a bowl of warm water so's I can clean Granny up. You might think about finding another phone and calling out. I can understand that need. But this ignorant hillbilly wants you to think about something. That haint'll be back to kill you, and when it does, the only thing between it and you is me and Granny. And this old woman will be fine and shining before too long. She just needs to sleep. We're Hillis folk just like you. You going to trust your own kin or this lawyer of yours?"

It was the most talking he'd done in a long time, but it needed to be said. She was spooked, he could see that plain. But he needed her help and he needed her to understand who was on her side and who wasn't. She was thinking. Crinkled up forehead beneath hair the same color as Granny's. Good looking woman even with that. Strong face. Eyes the color of mystery. Better than that snake Michael deserved, sure enough.

"Please."

He said it straight out. Hard to do.

She scrunched her hands in front of her into little fists like she was going to take him on, then turned and stomped out the door.

"I'll be back," she said, just like what's his name in the movies.

"Are you just going to leave your grandmother lying there on the floor? Can't you at least put her on the couch or something?" Wendland asked. "You really are an ignorant hillbilly."

Kenneth looked down at Granny Hillis, and began to methodically unmess her hair the best he could, pulling apart strands stuck together with congealed blood. He didn't say anything for what seemed a long time.

"Old woman," he said. "You got a few miles yet to go."

"Answer me," Wendland said.

Kenneth stood up and stretched to his full height. He held his hands up so that Wendland would look at the blood. Ashley Hillis came back into the room with a stack of towels, a big black garbage bag and a bowl of water.

"Only reason that old woman is lying over there with blood on her is because you're here."

Ashley set the bowl of water on the floor next to Granny and began wetting the towels and wiping away the blood from her skin.

"Forget what I said," Wendland said. "I was distraught."

Without looking up, Ashley asked, "Tell me that again. What you said about Henry."

Kenneth grinned.

"You hear that? She's a quick one, ain't she?"

"Please. I'm sorry," Wendland said.

"Shut up, Henry," Ashley said.

Kenneth walked over and slapped a hand on the lawyer's meaty shoulder.

"This man here, Mrs. Hillis, is the reason the haint done come to your home. Ain't that right, lawyer?"

Kenneth's hand strayed to a spot halfway between Wendland's shoulder and his neck. After a casual smile, he squeezed his finger and thumb together, pinching hard.

"Jesus," Wendland said. "Please don't do that again."

"Then why don't you tell young Mrs. Hillis what this is all about?"

"I don't know what you're talking about," Wendland said nervously.

Ashley shoved a handful of bloody towels into the garbage bag.

"Sure you do. Why don't you tell Mrs. Hillis how we met last year? Why don't you tell her how you and Michael came down to see Granny? Why don't you tell her what you two was looking to find out?"

The dynamic tension in the room changed at that instant.

"Michael?" Ashley said. "You and Michael did that and neither of you told me?"

"He did," Kenneth said.

Wendland looked down at his shoes as though the answer to his dilemma were written on the glossy toes.

"You don't understand," he said finally. "He's taking it all out of context. It was that man started it all. That ex-convict Joshua Brooks. He started this all. Michael asked me to travel south with him to see the old woman there. It wasn't my idea. Joshua put it all in his head. He had a diary and was trying to blackmail Michael. I warned him against the man."

"You're fired," Ashley said.

"Ever wonder why he ain't asking you about the haint, Mrs. Hillis?"

"Please," Wendland begged.

"Shut up, Henry."

"See, it's because he already knew about it. Been knowing about it all along. Knows what it is. What it wants. What it will do."

"Stop it," Wendland shouted.

Kenneth squatted down until he and the lawyer were eye to eye. Studied the man. Looked at him square, let him see what he was about.

He was about to say something when Ashley Hillis made a run at them and hit the lawyer in the head with her balled up fist.

Chapter Twenty

From the journal of Bradley Hunter

Dear Brother,

I am still a human being, though for how long I can't say. For days and nights I have, at great risk to my own life and soul, made my way in secret to stand among the mechanical soldiers unnoticed by Magnus Hillis so that I could hear the conversations between him and what I have come to know as the ghost box. My time in battle has repaid me well as I have been able to move undetected, even in this awful world where the air itself is lit with unnatural light.

Forgive me if my writings wander tonight, brother, for I am wrought with fever and my hand trembles. I am changing still. My skin feels like thin leather stretched tight. My mouth is dry, always dry and I have begun to hear strange whisperings in my head. You may wonder where I gather the courage to do what I have done, to risk discovery to hear the voices from the ghost box. It is not courage, brother; it is fear that drives me. Fear for the continued existence of the human race.

Magnus is every inch a bedlamite. He talks to himself always, shouting out his settings as he twists the knobs of the strange device, calling out to the dead, waiting for them to answer. Like a hungry reporter, I scribbled as many of his words as I can remember.

It was on the third night, I think, that he had his first success. It was that night we heard strange, indistinct voices coming from the machine. For the next day, he listened to the mindless dead, trying to make sense of them. Dead souls lost within the aethyr between Heaven and Earth, crying out for release, howling sometimes, crying at others. He grew quite agitated, brother, and called out several times for the spirit of his dead wife. His cries echoed throughout the cavern, sounding oddly metallic from where I hid concealed by his mechanical soldiers.

On the fifth night, when I returned from resting on my ledge, I heard Magnus speaking to the box again. This time, however, I heard a voice answer clearly. A man's voice, strong and resonant.

What, I wondered, did I miss while I slept?

"Is my name so important?" asked the spirit.

The voice was like the purring of a sleek and deadly cat.

My desire to inch forward and snatch a furtive view of Magnus and the

116

disincarnate entity who spoke to him surprised me. To be caught would be certain death. And yet the ghost's voice had such a seductive quality that I had to will myself immobile.

"You must tell me the secret of power," said Magnus. His voice was desperate with imperial anger.

"I can do that and more," said the voice.

It was the answer the madman wanted to hear.

I hear Magnus pacing, his heavy boot heels scuffing over the stone floor.

"The masters," Magnus said, "have told me to unite the two worlds of the living and the dead so that my army may march."

How this must sound to you, my brother. In earlier letters I have written you about a strange array of thoughts. From the sanctity of our United States in the face of secession, to the moral depravity of slavery, the unthinkable brutality of war and the deep troubled waters of my soul stirred by my own willingness to fight and kill my own neighbors. And now this. I am biographer to the mad genius of Albert Magnus Hillis, his astonishing mechanical soldiers and his mystifying device that allows him to speak to the dead.

Do you realize that I am now crouched between rows of the strangest creations the world has ever known? Automatonic soldiers made of a strange metal I have never before seen. Red-green in color, gleaming in the phosphoresced air like the iridescent swords of raging angels. These mechanical monsters tower above me. They are perhaps ten feet in height. Gears and hollow cables made of a clear material are integrated into their mechanisms like muscles and tendons. They are all connected to a central web of glassine tubing that hangs before the back wall of the cave.

The soldiers, before they cocooned, built stone steps leading up the axis of this network, which connected all the tubes of this system together into four tubes each the thickness of a man's arm. These four main tubes stopped open-ended at an empty circular space six to eight feet in diameter at the central point of the hub. It was as if the final piece were still missing, waiting to be installed.

On my first foray to get closer so that I might hear, I was terrified that these mechanical soldiers would awaken and I would be torn limb from limb. Yet it became clear that they are not yet vitalized, as Magnus says. His Masters, as he calls them, instructed him how to build the ghost box, but not how make the connection that would allow him to bring through the vital energy from the astral plane. The thing behind the wall, the living ship as he called it, had died before communicating to him the name of the disincarnate entity he was to contact through his spirit device. So Magnus had called out through the void, explaining his need, pleading his savior to step forth from among the dead and speak to him, to tell him how to complete his mission.

"I can do that and more," said the spirit.

"Tell me how."

"The living always ask much from the dead."

"I am Magnus, and I ask in the name of the invisible masters."

"A name of great power," said the spirit.

May I tell you, brother, my worst terror, my brother? It is not that these mechanical men will come alive and go marching across our country as Albert Magnus Hillis wants, it is instead the possibility that I sit here alone in this cave, quite mad, believing that I am recording the most frightening events in human history. Perhaps I am near death and have only rabid bats for company. How strange that would be. Perhaps I am delirious with yellow fever and have crawled into this cave on my hands and knees not only to escape the wrath of my regiment, but to escape the dreadful heat of the mid-day sun as well.

No, I lie to myself and to you.

My greatest fear is that I am not hallucinating and that this is all happening.

"Power from the other side," said Magnus. "How do I bring it through?"

His voice echoes throughout the cave as he shouts this.

There is a strange smell in the air. Perhaps it has been here all along and I am imagining it now. It is the smell of potatoes gone bad. It may be my own odor. I have not bathed or performed personal hygiene in so long I must be rank. In fact, it amazes me that Hillis has not located me already, if only because of my pungent odor.

"What great fortune that we have found each other in this way," said the spirit voice. "How long I have waited for you to come seeking my occult knowledge. How wise of the masters to choose one such as you."

"I am Magnus."

"A name fit for a Caesar," said the voice.

"Who are you?"

"Those passed over have no name. What use have the dead for names?"

There was silence as the madman digested this. After all this time of living with only the sound of Magnus talking to himself, I should have been grateful for the sound of another voice. But something in the sound of this spirit's voice caused me deep uneasiness.

"Tell me."

Another silence, followed by a deep sigh.

"So, just so. I walked the earth as a Frenchman, and I was both born and murdered in Paris."

"Murdered?"

"Tell me again how you met the masters," said the spirit voice.

And as I listened, hidden behind Magnus's metal men, I began to realize that it was no longer clear who was commanding who. Once again I listened to the story of Magnus's abduction into the spinning disc and his story about the transparent masters. I heard a faint slurring to his voice that grew more pronounced, as though he were overwhelmed by the reality of what was occurring.

"And your name?" repeated Magnus when he finished re-telling the story. "Tell me so that I know you are the one the masters spoke of."

"Can you see where all of the connecting tubes join together near the wall? I can see them clearly my friend, for it is a curious fact that the living can rarely glimpse the world of the dead but that we are forced to see every detail of your world. That empty space is where the missing element must be placed, the element that allows power to flow through the system initiated by the device we speak through. The device cannot channel the occult power of this side of the membrane unless that missing piece is inserted."

"You must be the one, if you know this," said Magnus.

I heard him clap his hands in gleeful satisfaction.

"Tell me, what is the missing element?"

I got to my knees and inched around the metal kneecap of one of the soldiers. My curiosity got the better of me, but all I could see was an agitated Magnus Hillis striding back and forth in front of his ghost box. His hands were clasped behind his back in a futile attempt to control his furious anticipation.

"A sacrifice, dear Magnus. A living human being must be connected to the web of crystal tubules that unites your army."

"Yes," said the madman. "It is completely clear now. But I am the only man here."

My breath hitched in my throat.

Albert Hillis was wrong.

I could be connected to that machine. It was time to leave, but I could not risk the chance of making noise and being detected. Before now I only worried about being shot. But it would be worse to be connected to the mechanical soldiers on Hillis's stone altar.

"You would make that sacrifice, I know," said the spirit voice, "but the masters have made provisions for you. You will bring me through the device, and I can be the sacrifice in your place. After all, you are Magnus and I am but a poor Frenchman murdered by a jealous rival."

I breathed a sigh of relief.

What have I become, brother, that I write of such things as though taking receipt of a new pair of boots?

This spirit, this ghost was persuading Magnus to bring him through this portal device, so that, once restored to life, Magnus could use him as a living sacrifice to both activate his army and restore power to the buried ship. Once restored to life. Could this device, this ghost box, return the dead to life? Such a thing should be the province of God alone. Who then were these devils, these masters who would usurp the authority of the divine by the use of a device coupled with a human sacrifice? By using this ghost box, was Magnus really about to open the door to Hell itself?

"Yes, yes," said the future emperor enthusiastically, "you will be my propitiation and die in my place. How can I bring you through to this world?"

"You must adjust the dials to these settings and invoke my name."

And the spirit told him the settings.

Terror began to shake me like a rattle. Something profane was about to happen and I was powerless to stop it. I left my knife and my pistol up on the ledge and I was no match for Albert Magnus Hillis in my current state without a weapon.

"I have adjusted the settings. What is your name?"

"My name was Emile Chirac before my cousin Eliaphas Levi murdered me. Invite me in to your world my friend and we will fulfill the requirement for sacrifice."

I opened my mouth to shout a warning to Magnus, but I could not speak. He was a demon, sure enough, but I believe that the one who spoke to him was worse. But, in act of true cowardice, I did not shout for fear of Magnus using me as his sacrifice instead.

"I, Albert Magnus, invite you, the spirit of Emile Chirac, into this world. Come freely and meet your new master."

Too late.

I crawled back behind the mechanical men, stuffed my journal and pen in my pocket and began to crawl on my hands and knees toward the ledge.

There came a flash of blue-white light so intense I dropped prostrate to the ground in fear and hit my forehead square on the hard rock. I lay unconscious for I cannot say how long.

When I woke, I lay still. Within the cavern time was impossible to know because of the phosphorescent light, so I did not know if I had blacked out for seconds or minutes or even hours. But I heard nothing. After a time, I gathered the courage to get to my knees and, being as careful as a scout, to sneak a glance at the stage where I had last seen Magnus.

And there he was, at the center of the tubule web, his arms cut off at the elbow, and connected at their stumps to the now glowing network of tubes. Blood spread out in a pool beneath him and I saw that his legs, too, were cut off at the knees and each attached to another tubular network.

"Oh, my God," I said softly.

At that moment, Albert Magnus Hillis, his eyes now slits of silver, began to scream incoherently. From the blood on his mouth and the sounds that he made, I knew that whoever cut off his arms and his legs cut out his tongue, too. The sound of his screams sounded somehow insectile to me, and I felt as though my mind could not take much more. What kind of monster had he brought through his ghost box?

I noticed that it was no longer on the platform where Magnus had conducted his experiments. More blood covered the stage. Things were knocked about as though a struggle had occurred. I shuddered to think what had happened.

There was no choice for me now, I realized. Whoever or whatever came through the ghost box had killed Hillis, dismembered him and connected him to the mechanical soldiers, creating an endless loop of ectoplasmic power circulating between the automatons and Hillis's disfigured body.

Whether or not that spirit was in the cavern in human form or had left, my course of action was still the same—I had to get away.

And yet, I knew that I was changing quickly like the other soldiers. I could no longer live among men. In fact, the texture of my own skin made me doubt how much longer I would be human.

I made it back to my ledge without seeing anyone or anything else. The cavern was like a tomb since Magnus quieted. I looked down and saw him, hanging in place in the tubular web like a hungry spider at its center.

These last pages I write to you, my brother. I will walk til I come to your cabin. I may not make it there, but I will try until my last breath to do so. If I can survive that journey, I will place this journal outside your door, then walk away and shoot myself. Then you must, as my last surviving family, do what I could not do. Dynamite the cavern. Bury the monstrous things that reside there under so much earth that they may never rise. Because of my cowardice, you must do what I had neither the courage nor means to do, I beg you.

Do not fault me for not coming to see you, for I believe that I am no longer fit to look upon. I avoid my reflection in streams. If I see my face I shall surely kill myself before bringing you what I have written. Bury that place, don't concern yourself about me. Pass the responsibility down throughout our family if you must. The cave of Albert Magnus Hillis must be forever locked away until you find how to destroy it.

Please forget me. I am metamorphosing; I can feel it. I will not become a silk cocoon, or what it later gives birth to. My pistol and last bullet will save me from that.

God forgive Magnus Hillis for invoking the name of Emile Chirac.

«« — »»

Ian Hunter lay down the journal and looked over at his computer. To his surprise, he saw that it was now October thirtieth—Devil's Night. How appropriate.

His back hurt and his legs were falling asleep. But his mind, his mind was lit with flames of awe and wonder. Bartok was right. If the old man hadn't shown him what was below ground, he would never have believed him.

He stood up slowly and stretched. The journals were spread out over his desk. So much more to read, but he needed to fill Enid on what he'd learned and see how his Uncle Bartok was doing.

He shuddered at the thought of Bartok becoming a cocoon.

Chapter Twenty-One

"Keep her away from me," Wendland said.

He was cowering behind Kenneth for protection, fingers locked in the Kentucky man's red and black checkered sleeves to position him between himself and Ashley Hillis.

"Get out of the way, Kenneth," Ashley said. "He's going to tell me everything he knows or I'll hit him again."

Kenneth spun into Wendland and grabbed the lawyer's ear. He twisted it hard and Wendland screamed.

"Please, no. Enough. Enough."

"Get back in that chair and stay there til I tell you to get up. You got that now? You hear what I'm saying?"

Wendland whimpered and backed into the chair. He sat down hard and the chair creaked under his weight.

With three quick steps, Ashley was in front of him shaking her fists.

"What happened to my husband?" she asked. "What haven't you been telling me?"

Wendland slumped forward and buried his head in his hands. His next words came out in gasping sobs.

"I warned Michael about him. Warned him not to get involved. It was that blackmailer that got us into this, that Josh. I told Michael he was no good. Now that thing that was at the window will never stop until we're all dead."

A soft groan came from behind Ashley, and she turned to look at Granny Hillis, still lying on the floor. The old woman looked like a bundle of discarded clothes.

"She's just healing," Kenneth said. "Let her be."

"But we can't just leave her sleeping on the floor."

"She's a hill woman. She's slept on worse. Let the stone do its work."

Ashley looked unsure.

"You're positive?"

"Mrs. Hillis, that old woman is tougher than you and me put together."

With a still-not-so-sure nod, Ashley turned back to her lawyer.

"Explain yourself. What is this you're saying about Josh? And don't you ever lie to me again or hold anything back or I'll turn you straight over to that Detective Alvarez. And I mean it."

Slowly, Wendland raised his head and straightened his back, as though trying to regain some semblance of his dignity. He straightened his shirt, then reached up and gingerly touched his ear.

"You didn't have to do that," he told Kenneth. "In fact, you can't do that. I won't tolerate it anymore."

"I'll have him do it all over again if you don't start talking," Ashley said. "I have legal redress."

"You don't start talking and I'll rip that ear clean off your head," Kenneth said.

Wendland darted his eyes toward the front door.

"Uh-uh, son. You ain't that fast. Tell the lady what she wants to know."

The room was quiet as Wendland considered his options.

"How you going to look with one ear?" Kenneth asked.

Wendland puffed up his chest, then looked at the two of them and seeing that they were serious, he slumped again and began to talk.

"Michael contacted me to tell me that this reprobate Josh was attempting to soft blackmail him."

"Wait," Ashley said. "What do you mean 'soft blackmail' him?"

"It means he wasn't explicit in his solicitation. He said that he had two manuscripts Michael might be interested in seeing. The first concerned an amazing technology one of his ancestors had created and hidden somewhere beneath the hills in Kentucky. Like those con men who claim to have found the secret diaries of Nikola Tesla. Totally bogus, in my opinion. Area 51 stuff. But you know Michael. The possibility alone was enough to interest him. The second was the real issue."

"And?" Ashley asked. "What was in it?"

For the first time since she they met, Wendland looked her straight in the eye.

"Dark family secrets, I'm afraid."

"Don't you dare try to stall. Just tell me."

The heavy set man looked at her, his eyes round and almost pleading.

"You're not going to like this."

Cold, stony silence.

Wendland sighed.

"It involves my family, too. An ancestor of mine. And an ancestor of Josh's. It's a mess. And then a man contacted Michael about a piece of the technology in the first manuscript. Something called the ghost box. That's how he met Chirac."

"You're not making sense," Ashley said. "Who contacted Michael?"

"A thug named Ricci. And Michael couldn't resist. He was hooked."

"Kenneth, would you please twist Mr. Wendland's other ear?"

Her lawyer threw up his hands and shouted, "Wait, wait I'll talk. I'll tell you what you want to know."

"Then do it."

The story gushed out of him, like pent up water breaking through a dam.

"Corktown. It started in the old section of town called Corktown, where Sharkey's Park is. That's where it all started. It was the poorest section of town. That's where Becker Hillis and my grandfather lived, on a dirt road at the edge the city limits. Josh's grandfather lived there, too.

"Sharkey's Park was owned by old lady Sharkey. Tough old woman with money. She owned the acreage behind her house, including on the far side of the creek where she'd built a park with a dance hall, concession stand, pony's and some rides. The companies, unions and lodges would rent it out for picnics. Kids from the neighborhood would get in by sneaking through the woods. Sometimes the men, too."

Ashley listened to him talk, a rush of emotions flooding through her that was almost too strong to bear. Since that horrible night when Michael disappeared she'd been paralyzed by despair and a feeling that her world had gone crazy. What she'd seen that night just couldn't have happened. Every day she'd questioned her sanity. Worse was the feeling that Michael knew something terrible could happen and had taken her and the others there anyway for some crazy ghost hunt. That he'd kept her in the dark like she was a child.

"There was a lot of drinking when nightfall came. A lot of partying. The neighborhood men were paid to clean the place up when people went home. Some of them, like Becker, snuck in to drink and dance. They looked at it as getting paid to party, I suppose.

"It was a rough neighborhood, but Becker Hillis was the worst of the lot. Michael said he came up from the hills of Kentucky looking for work. I think he was on the run from something. I can't prove it, but that's what I think. By all accounts, he was a charismatic, charming man. A natural born leader. The women in the neighborhood knew he was trouble. In today's terminology, I think he would be categorized as a sociopath.

"One night, he rounded up some of the men, including my grandfather and Josh's and a few others, and led them through the woods to the park. I've looked at photos taken of the park from those days, and at night, colored lights were strung from building to building. Men and women filled it up like it was a concert event. There was even gambling. Strictly illegal, of course, but being so far out of town, the local police turned their heads. I think some of them even participated.

"Becker and the others from the neighborhood did a lot of drinking that night. The journal Josh was offering Michael was written by his grandfather. Kind of a mea culpa, if you can believe that. It says that Becker saw a young girl that he liked. Shall we say, she was mature for her age? That would be the polite way to put it. Becker bought her a soda, and then dosed it with a little whiskey. He took her into the woods when the park closed down. He was going to teach her how to dance, if you can believe that. My grandfather and Josh's grandfather and the others went along for the show. It got ugly after that.

"They raped her, Ashley. Becker was the first. The others, well you can guess what happened. My grandfather, too, God help him."

Wendland stopped and sucked in a deep breath before continuing. Tears formed in the corner of his eyes, and he wiped them away with the back of his hand.

"There was one man there who didn't. His last name was Alvarez, and yes, he was the grandfather of Detective Alvarez. He tried to reason with them, begged them to stop. Becker said they'd kill him if he told anyone. I don't know how to describe this, but they drank even more, the men—except for Alvarez—assaulted her again. She tried to resist and Becker started to hit her.

"The girl blacked out and the men thought she was dead."

For a moment, he couldn't go on. Wendland broke down and began to cry. He covered his face with both hands and began to rock forward and backward in his chair like an overwhelmed child.

"You're lying," Ashley said. "Michael would have told me about this. He wouldn't have kept something like this from me."

But as she said it, she remembered how furious Michael became when she tried to research his family's history. *Oh God*, she thought, *can this be the truth? Did he deliberately try to keep me from finding out?*

"You think you know him," Wendland said. Again he wiped his eyes with the back of his hands. "And there's more."

"Get on with it," Kenneth said.

Wendland nodded.

"After the park closed down, Becker and his boys were supposed to pick up the papers, clean and rake the area. They built a bonfire after every park-party to burn the branches, the discarded wrappers and paper cups and whatever food they found on the ground. Old lady Sharkey was afraid rats, muskrats and foxes would come from the creek and the woods scavenging for scraps. So the men burned the trash in a pit and some fifty five gallon drums they'd cut the top off and put up on bricks.

"Because Becker and the others figured they'd killed her, they needed some place to dump the body. They weren't thinking straight, obviously. Their cognitive functions were so impaired by the drinking and the insanity of what they'd done, they acted mostly on animal instinct.

"Becker made the others gather up the sticks, twigs and trash and whatever else they could burn and got a fire going. Perfectly normal. A good plan actually—except the girl wasn't dead. When they folded her body and stuffed it into a drum full of burning trash, she began to scream."

The study was quiet when Wendland paused to take a tentative breath. Ashley's face was pale.

"It's impossible to accurately surmise the severity of the burns she would have suffered if they'd pulled her out. She might have lived, but the medical facilities back then…"

"You mean they let her burn alive?" Ashley asked. "What kind of men can do something like that?"

Wendland couldn't meet her eyes. After a moment's guilty silence, he continued.

"Later that night, they removed as many of the charred bones as they could find, dug an unmarked grave under some building they were putting up for old lady Sharkey, tossed them in and covered it over. Then they built a new dance floor over it. The horror of that little girl being raped, then burned to death and finally buried under a dance floor will not fit into my head all at once. I can only think of each component separately or I think I will go crazy."

"Michael knew about all of this? Is that what you're telling me? You lie. He would never keep something like this from me. We talked about everything. We trusted each other."

This time Wendland looked up at her.

"I have good memories of my grandfather, dear. When I was just a young boy, I used to sneak up behind his chair and he would reach behind and hand me a stick of gum since my parents wouldn't allow me to have it. Don't you see the horror that man Josh brought us? He was a filthy little blackmailer. If he hadn't jumped off that hospital roof to commit suicide, I believe I would have strangled him myself. All my adult life I believed my grandfather was a wonderfully kind man who by a horribly unfair accident was burned to death in a freak electrical storm. That's what they finally decided was the cause of the first deaths in Sharkey's Park way back when. It gave me the idea to feed the same idea to the police, this time through a consultant to keep them away from what really happened there with you and the others. It cost a lot of money, Ashley, but if wealth can't buy forgiveness it can at least help keep the police off your back."

Kenneth reached over and placed a hand on her shoulder.

"Why don't you go look at Granny's wounds while the lawyer man and me talk?"

"I can take it," Ashley said as she pushed his hand off her shoulder. "Ever since that night I've felt like I was helpless. Something happened to my husband. Is he dead or alive? Was he a victim or did he murder everyone and take off leaving me holding the bag. I'm supposed to write these stories, not be in them. And as for Henry here, I'm not done with him yet."

Kenneth cocked an eyebrow at her, shrugged and said, "Then get to it."

"I'm telling you the truth," Wendland said.

"I'll decide that later," Ashley said. "For now, I just want to see if I have this straight. You're telling me that Josh claimed his grandfather wrote all these events down in a diary and he somehow came across it years later, and then tried to sell it to Michael. He knew that Michael had a lot of money and thought Michael might pay him to keep this whole thing quiet to protect his family name. Is that about it?"

"Yes, there's more, but that's how it all started."

"How much? Ashley asked.

"Pardon?"

"How much money did he ask for?"

"Ah. I see. Five million."

A low whistle from Kenneth.

"My God," he said. "That boy was looking to go from low rent trash to high living trash with one paycheck."

"I told Michael it would be cheaper to have him killed. Wait, Ashley, I didn't mean it literally. It was an extended metaphor. But, as I said, Michael was intrigued by this low life's story. I demanded proof, some kind of evidence that the purported events actually occurred in the way that they were described in the diary. I wasn't about to be deceived by someone who'd spent more time in reform school than I'd spent in college."

"And?" prompted Ashley.

"Josh's grandfather turned out to be the stupidest criminal ever. He'd not only recorded his own and the other's guilt in his diary, he also drew a map of where the burned remains were buried. So Michael bought not only Sharkey's Park, but also the surrounding acreage that which used to be called Corktown. He wanted to locate the grave in secret and dig up the remains to prove it one way or the other. The evidence could then be gotten rid of was his thinking at first. I wanted nothing to do with it.

"But Michael and Josh went to Sharkey's Park and actually found the grave. Can you imagine what that must have felt like to Michael? Maybe to Josh if he actually had any feelings in that crooked little heart of his. But I can only guess what either of them felt. I know that I felt angry. I felt stained. I felt like I wanted to change my name."

Without any warning, Ashley suddenly felt exhausted. The more she heard Wendland talk, the worse she felt. Every new fact seemed to break her trust in Michael even more. Did he actually go to Sharkey's park with Josh and dig up that little girl's grave and not tell her? Worse, why did he take them all back to do a ghost hunt at a site where he'd already been with Josh? Did they see something that night? Did he want to record everything in case he saw it again?

And Wendland was surreptitiously glancing at the door as though waiting for an opportunity to break away. Perhaps he was starting to regret telling her so much. He was such a pompous scumbag that he actually thought he was better than Josh. No matter what Josh did, at least he'd saved her life, and he didn't ask for five hundred dollars an hour like Wendland.

And he'd lied to her and hidden things from her.

"Kenneth," whispered a hoarse voice, "can you help me up, boy?"

Granny Hillis had her eyes open again.

"I'm coming," he answered. "You keep an eye on this big-time lawyer."

"I don't like that man," Wendland said.

"And I don't like you," Ashley said.

Granny Hillis was up on one elbow by the time her great nephew got to her. Color had returned to her face. The cuts on her face and hands from the flying glass shards had quit bleeding. For a woman Ashley thought was dying right on her floor, she had to admit the old woman looked pretty damned good.

"You see okay?" Kenneth asked as he knelt down and looped an arm around her waist to pull her up to a sitting position.

"I see just fine."

"So you don't want these glasses?"

"Don't you sass me, Kenneth."

"Yes ma'am," he said, handing her the wire rimmed spectacles he'd picked up from beside her head.

With the spectacles firmly in place, she blinked furiously for a second at Ashley, and then smiled. When she glanced down at the floor and saw the broken pieces of glass scattered everywhere, she said, "You think you can find a broom and a dustpan to sweep this mess up? I'm too old to be getting glass slivers in my feet."

"Can you watch them both?" Ashley asked Kenneth.

He nodded and began to slowly stand, lifting Granny gently as though she were an injured child so that he could set her down in a chair. For some reason, the bond between the two of them made Ashley want to cry. She moved over to help him, pulling a chair away from the other wall to an area free of glass.

"Don't put her all the way down until I make sure her back is free of glass," she said.

Kenneth agreed and waited for her to give the okay to put her down. But before Ashley could finish, she was stopped by the unexpected sound of heavy footsteps heading toward the front door. Wendland was making a break for it.

"Hold her," Kenneth said to Ashley as he thrust Granny toward her.

"Leave him be, boy," said the old woman. "Haint'll have him before the night's through."

A hard wind blew in through the open front door.

"Close that damned door, Kenneth, or I'll catch a death of cold."

Chapter Twenty-Two

Angry clouds swirled past the moon in a violent rush.

A glossy black Cadillac headed straight toward the security gates.

Wendland tightened his grip on the steering wheel, hunkered forward and pressed his size 14 shoe down on the gas pedal like he was trying to push it through the floorboard.

"I'm going through," he said and held his breath.

A second later he took his foot off the gas and slammed it so hard onto the brake pedal that he almost activated the airbags.

The security gates were opening onto the main road. Moving silently as concealed electric motors swung the thick steel gratings outward. The sharply pointed spikes along the top edge of the gates looked like something that would surround a prison. Or a cemetery. It flashed through his mind as he looked back at the Hillis home half a mile down their private paved driveway.

Why were they opening the gates? Why were they letting him go? He'd been prepared to smash straight through the metal bars if he had to. He had to get away. Had to find someplace to hide. Maybe leave the country.

The haint was coming for them all. One at a time, it would knock them off until every direct descendent of the men who'd raped and killed her were dead. Just like the last time.

Stay or go?

What was wrong with this scenario? Why would they let him go?

"I don't care," he yelled to no one but himself. "I'm doing it."

He floored the gas pedal again, shot through the open gates, and spun out onto the road like a stunt driver who'd been practicing the maneuver for years.

《《—》》

Hallelujah and thank you Lord he was away from Ashley Hillis, Kenneth and that vicious old woman and headed straight for wherever he wanted to go. He wanted as much distance between himself and that man Kenneth as he could possibly get.

A glance in the rearview mirror and he saw the Hillis mansion disappear into the night's blackness and not a car in sight behind him. Wendland expelled a rush of air and loosened his grip on the steering wheel. He was free. The insanity was behind him. Damn Michael Hillis and his obsessions. Damn that son of a bitch, Josh. He got exactly what he deserved. Ten minutes more and he'd be on I-94 east and on his way to Grosse Point.

Every piece of paper that could compromise him was shredded, burned and the ashes tossed in a dumpster far from his office. He'd been around too long to be tripped up by loose ends. Every email between he and Michael was routed through an anonymous server in Sweden, deleted and wiped clean from his computer by a program that didn't leave a trace. There would be cell phone records between himself and Michael, but Michael was, after all, his most important client so it was perfectly normal that they would have talked frequently. And the fact that his ancestor was involved with Becker Hillis and the rape of that little girl would be scandalous, but it wasn't as though he personally had been involved in the crime. He could retire comfortably and drop out of sight. There was no crime or misconduct anyone could charge him with that would stick. The police hadn't asked him what he knew and besides, his conversations with Michael and the details of his activities were covered by confidentiality.

His real worry, the thing that scared him to death, was the haint. If he'd doubted what Michael said about it before, he believed in it now. He looked down at the speedometer and saw that he was doing sixty five miles an hour and slowed down to forty-five. Faint droplets of water splashed against the windshield. The roads must be slick. Got to be safe. Got to stay in control.

Furtive clouds of fog crowded along the road's edge. He hadn't noticed them at first. Too much on his mind. Too many things pressing in on him. The moon disappeared behind billowing black clouds. His headlights were elongated cones of halogen light that revealed tendrils of fog-smoke forming over the black asphalt like a ghostly spider web.

Something shot out from the fog and ran across the road. He slammed on the brakes. The car began to slide sideways and then straightened out.

A deer, a damned deer. Thank God he hadn't hit it. He could have ended up stranded in the middle of nowhere, maybe worse. His palms felt sweaty on the wheel. Heart attack. If he wasn't careful he'd have a heart attack with his weight and all this stress.

He pulled out his cell phone then shoved it back in his pocket. No signal. *Why did Michael have to live out in the middle of nowhere? And where was he now*, he wondered. *Dead or alive and in hiding? Dead. He was probably dead if that thing had gotten hold of him. But if that were true, where was the body?*

Michael had plenty of reason to be on the run. That stupid bitch wife of his had no clue about anything. Up until everything went to hell she'd been living in a dream world. Didn't have any idea that her husband had bilked his investors, bilked the government and was on the edge of being exposed as a complete fraud. Writers. They lived in their own created worlds. She thought Michael was her dream catch. Rich, brilliant and good looking. Guys like him took them in every time. They just saw what they wanted to see.

Wendland squinted at the road ahead.

Where the hell was he? He'd taken a few turns to get to the freeway, but in his hurry to get away he'd lost track of where he was. A deserted barn that tilted ten degrees appeared in a momentary parting of the fog and then disappeared. He didn't recall ever seeing it, but it was hard to remember. Who paid attention to broken down barns?

No time for this, he thought, and pushed the button for his dashboard GPS. Waited. Swore. It didn't turn on. What a time for the damn thing to quit working. He took his cell phone from his pocket. He could use the Google Maps app. But he didn't have a signal. Great. He hated the country. Shit, where was he?

The car began to vibrate and he saw to his horror that he was now on a dirt road. This was bad. He hunkered down over the steering wheel and looked to the right and left for a driveway to turn around in. Who the hell lived out here anyway?

His windshield was fogging over, so he flipped on the wipers and turned on the fog lights. Soft yellow light filled the road ahead of him. He dropped the speed down to twenty five miles per hour. Sooner or later he would find a driveway or an intersection where he could turn around. Acid rose in his throat and he leaned over to take a water bottle from the built-in dashboard cooler. He didn't like this. He didn't like this at all.

Although he loved Michael like a brother, the man got him in the worst shit. They'd raked in millions for research from investors and government energy grants. All Michael had to do was make credible progress. But his stupid catalytic microwave technology never worked, so he and that science bitch he was pounding at the office started faking the results. He'd even lied to him. His lawyer. Why did clients always lie to their lawyers? His job was to protect Michael. How was he supposed to do that when the man lied to him?

Add his insane obsession with the paranormal and Josh showing up with a journal claiming an underground laboratory stocked full of alien energy technology and Michael jumped on it like it was the Holy Grail. A way out. The man was nuts, absolutely nuts. Believed it hook, line and sinker. And when that man Chirac contacted him through his henchman about one of the devices in that journal, well it was all over. Too convenient. Wendland knew it at the time. Chirac knew about the madstone Michael's Granny Hillis gave Becker Hillis. Had to. How had he known about all that? But he really didn't want to know the answer. He didn't want to know anything at all about Mr. Chirac.

The fog was so thick now that it hung in the air like gray cotton. Still no sign of a driveway or a turn around. Maybe he could stop and back up til he was back on a paved street. No. He had to keep going. Backing up would be a sure way to end up in a ditch, stranded in the middle of nowhere. With his weight, he didn't want to think about walking until he found a farmhouse. He slowed to eight miles an hour. Where the hell was he?

There was a break in the fog and he saw a little girl standing in the middle of the road. He slammed on the brakes for the third time that night. Gravel growled beneath the tires as he came to a sudden stop. Fog swirled about her and she vanished in the mist. His chest tightened and he struggled to breathe. Not possible. Not possible at all. Stress was causing his mind to play tricks.

He pulled his cellphone out and again looked for a signal, but there was none. His face felt warm. Sweat collected in the bulging folds of his skin. He set his cellphone down in the armrest tray and unbuttoned his collar so he could breathe.

The fog was disorienting. Bad enough to be lost, but in the swirling gray fog lit pallid yellow by his fog lights, he felt lost at sea like a ship in danger of crashing against dangerous, unseen rocks.

Got to get out of here, he thought.

The Cadillac engine was so quiet he could hardly hear it. He pressed the gas pedal with his right foot while keeping his left on the brake. Heard the engine kick up. Wished he had a muscle car that sounded strong and unafraid.

He reached down and grabbed the shift lever, easing it into reverse, afraid to admit why he did it so quietly. Afraid to admit that when the fog parted again, the little girl would still be standing there. The little girl that Becker Hillis, his own grandfather and the others had raped, beaten and burned to death. It was impossible, but he knew it was true. He'd seen her at the Hillis home. Watched her burst into flames and transform into a hideous demon the old woman called a haint.

Foot easing off the brake, backing up slowly, so very slowly. He could barely breathe and his entire body was now soaked with sweat. Inching back down the dirt road, trying to keep to a straight line so he didn't angle straight into a drainage ditch.

Please, please, please, he thought. *I didn't do it. I didn't do anything. It was Michael and Josh that dug you up and took your madstone. Not me. Really not me. I never, ever hurt you. Maybe my great grandfather did, but I wasn't even born yet when that happened.*

The rearview window was blocked by a dirty gray fog pillow.

Just keep to a straight line. I just have to keep to a straight line.

The fog parted again, opening up like curtains pulled back to reveal to the same little girl center stage, staring directly at him. Walking toward him. Walking quickly toward him.

Wendland panicked and took his foot entirely off the brake. Pushed down hard on the gas and felt the Cadillac fishtail but hang on to the road. Picking up speed. Getting farther away.

The little girl's eyes suddenly flared bright orange, as if on fire.

"Oh shit, oh shit, oh shit," he yelled. "No, no, no."

One hand on the wheel, the other on the passenger side seatback, head turned and trying to see through the volumes of fog covering the back windshield. He risked a quick look at the little girl and saw to his horror that she was flying at him now. Clothes on fire, coming up over the hood of the Cadillac. Melting face pressed against the window as Wendland screamed at the top of his lungs.

"Get away, just stay away from me."

He saw her boney, blackened hands pressed against the glass. Saw her nose drip away and the empty burning eye sockets and then the Cadillac dipped and flipped over and he felt the seatbelt lock into place and the air-bag explode out of the steering wheel and knock him back like he'd been hit with a board.

The car flipped over completely and crashed into the bottom of the ditch. Through a dizzy haze he heard another air bag detonate. He couldn't think straight for a moment, but then realized he must have run off the road at high speed and flipped the car. Blood rushed to his head. The enormous weight of his own body hanging by his seatbelt felt like he was being pinched in two by a giant.

Gasoline vapors filled the car and knew he was in trouble. He must have hit something and ruptured a fuel line.

"Help," he screamed. "Somebody help me."

But he knew he was in the middle of nowhere, knew that no one could hear him.

It was impossible to find his seatbelt release. His girth kept him from reaching back far enough to feel it. The strain was too much. He started to cry. He would die here.

"Fuck that," he wheezed.

He twisted partially sideways with a Herculean effort, got hold of his seatbelt latch but stopped when he smelled smoke. Realizing the danger, he found the release button, felt it disengage and fell into the steering wheel. He was free. He had a chance.

The driver's door was crushed inward, so he turned to see if the passenger door was undamaged.

Instead, from his contorted perch, he saw the little girl sitting with her back to the door. Wendland tried desperately to open the driver's door with his massive weight, but it wouldn't budge. He screamed and pulled as far away from her as he could.

She wore a checkered skirt, a clean white blouse and saddle shoes. Her white socks had a ring of red thread around the top. Her nose was turned up just a little. She had soft brown eyes, big and round. An elf-like chin and yellow-white hair. She looked at him, studying him the way children do.

Her eyes began to burn.

He began to blubber and sob.

She burst into flames and so did he.

Chapter Twenty-Three

"Well?" Enid said. "What'd you find out?"

Bartok still lay wired into place on the guest bed, his skin a sallow blend of light green and yellow. The blindfold was still tied over his eyes. The sight was too much for Ian, who looked away and collapsed into the chair. He'd never felt so tired yet so cranked in his whole life. Since the moment he'd received Bartok's call summoning him to Kentucky, his nervous system had been on overload.

"Did he wake up?" he asked Enid.

"Once. He kept saying something about Michael Hillis and the ghost box. Couldn't make it all out though because he kept sticking in words that weren't words, making noises I didn't know could come out of a human mouth."

"You look like I feel," Ian said.

"Shit, I didn't think I looked that bad. Could use a shave and a piss, though."

"Bathroom is around the corner. I'll watch him."

"Get whatever you like out of the bag," Enid said. "That forty-five Colt in the side pocket is good to go."

"Got my own," Ian said.

"Take the forty-five. Thirty eight's a good pistol, but with what we're looking at right there, you need to go for the stopping power."

Ian was about to object, but changed his mind, got up and grabbed the Colt.

"You like the way it feels?"

"Feels like a hand cannon," Ian said.

"Good. Now flip that safety off and settle back in your chair so I can take a piss before I explode."

"I'll be here when you get back."

"Ian?"

"What?"

"Keep that forty-five ready. Something goes south with Bartok you ain't going to have time to aim."

《《—》》

Enid was back in the other chair, his Bible on his lap, his shotgun across his knees. His gaunt face was haggard, but his dark eyes were alert. Ian had already told him about the contents of Taylor Hunter's journals.

"There's more," Ian said. "But first I'd like to know how you and your brothers fit in."

Enid kept his eyes on Bartok while he spoke.

"That's easy enough. Some of my kin found what was left of old Taylor crawling through the woods. Wasn't much left of him by the time they found him. He was alive all right, but he was changing. Still look mostly human from what I hear passed down. But still looking mighty scary. Thing is, they knew him. He was from around there, and he was a Mason, just like most of the Mozer men have been since way back. Your Uncle Bartok, too, of course."

"Bartok was a Mason? He never said a word about it."

"Is a Mason," corrected Enid. "However much of him is left, that is. He's still fighting the change, I suspect, way he was talking one time a while ago human and the next making them weird sounds. Don't know how much longer he can hold out, but that old boy's tough."

"Always has been."

"Anyway, old Taylor was near dead when they found him, or maybe just getting ready to cocoon like them others you were talking about down below. But he could still talk some."

Ian leaned forward, his hand still wrapped around the Colt, its weight pressed against his leg.

"What did he say?"

Enid didn't answer.

"What did he say?" repeated Ian.

"'Kill me.' That's what he said. He said 'kill me.'"

"From what I read of his journals, I can understand that."

"Yep. He made motions toward his satchel which was wrapped around his neck with a leather strap. One of the boys put a rife against his chest while the others took the satchel off and opened it up. They found the journals you was talking about and a piece of paper he'd writ on said to take everything to his brother who was to keep it secret under the Masonic oath. My kin being Masons, they understood that right enough. Then he kept making noises for them to kill him. Tried to reach up and catch his finger on the trigger the one boy was holding on him."

"What happened?" Ian asked.

"The boy—his name was Wilfred, I think—changed his aim and shot him straight between the eyes. That's what started all this. The Hunters and the Mozers and the Hillis family been tied together ever since. Your kin trying to find a way to end all what's below ground and my kin guarding til the day it's done. Now your turn. Tell me what else you found and what you're thinking."

"Fair enough. I read some of the other journals written by other Hunters, and about their trying to understand what the situation was underground. Didn't take them long to come to understand that the mechanical soldiers were bullet proof, fireproof and what not. Whatever materials that ship created were a long way ahead of what material science could produce in that era. More advanced, according to Bartok's notes, than anything we have today.

"None of the Hunters ever went behind the wall to see the ship except one and he had to be killed because of it. I think Taylor and Magnus Hillis were wrong. That ship's not dead. That's what Bartok thought, too. It went dormant. Hibernating to recharge its power. I have no idea how that's possible, but I'm sure Bartok was right. He and a few other earlier Hunters tested the cavern for radiation and electromagnetism. They couldn't detect radiation, but there was plenty of EMF—that's what it's called."

"I know what it stands for," Enid said.

"They looked for it with EMF meters, like what ghost hunters do when they're investigating haunted houses."

Something seemed to move beneath Bartok's neck, like a small snake slithering beneath the skin. Ian blinked and it was gone.

"Did you see that?"

"What?"

"Never mind. I'm just tired. Anyway, Bartok believed that the alien race ported ectoplasm back and forth between the realm of the dead and the living."

"Uh-huh."

"Yeah, I know. I know how it sounds. You know what ectoplasm is? No? It's the fluid media that spiritualists used to claim was the energy of the astral plane formed to transport energy between worlds. It's bullshit. There's no evidence for such a thing. I've debunked more spirit photos than you can imagine."

"But Bartok believed in it?"

"Bartok believed in all sorts of mystic crap, Enid."

"It ain't crap you seen down below. It ain't crap what's got hold of your uncle lying there all tied up in bed like a wild animal. You're just too damned stubborn to believe your own eyes."

Ian stood up quickly, waved the pistol around in frustration, then stopped mid-gesture and flicked the safety back into position on the Colt.

"Sorry," he said. "This is just the same kind of argument I would have with Bartok. There is no such thing as ectoplasm and there are no such things as spirits. I think what's more likely here is that whatever this thing Taylor Hunter called the ghost box actually is, it transports energy between multiverses. Even the concept of multiverses would have been beyond him when he was spying on Magnus. So he called it what he thought it was. But ghosts don't exist. We die and that's it. Ectoplasm doesn't exist, and even if it did, it couldn't power spaceships across the universe."

"I'll go with what Bartok thought."

"Fine."

"So you got any ideas what we do next?"

Ian slumped back down in the chair. Men like Enid frustrated him.

Why couldn't they go with the facts? Why would any person in their right mind believe in ghosts? Or something as stupid as ectoplasmic energy? For that matter, how could an educated man like Bartok believe in them?

He saw it again. Something was moving beneath the skin of Bartok's throat. Ian felt his stomach lurch.

"What?" asked Enid, his shotgun coming up as he asked the question.

"I think—I think there's something alive inside of him. I saw it wiggling in his throat."

Ian brought the Colt up and aimed it at Bartok.

"Careful," Enid said.

The Kentucky man was up and moving.

"You move to the door. Get up and get to it. We separate. More space between us the better."

No questions. No thinking about it. Ian got up and positioned himself just outside the door, putting the body of the Colt up against the frame, aiming it straight at Bartok's head. The old man said he'd be glad to shoot him when the time came, and the truth was that Ian didn't think of the thing lying on the bed as his uncle anymore.

Enid was to his right, in the corner of the room near the window, his shotgun aimed and ready to fire.

"Body," he told Ian, "aim for the body."

Ian did as he was told.

Bartok began to shake his head from side to side violently. Black fluid shot from his mouth like projectile vomit and sprayed the ceiling.

"Shit," Ian said.

The old man seemed to bulge up in the middle as his shirt and chest ripped apart with a rush of foul smelling gas. His pant legs split up their crease lines and the skin of his legs tore apart. Dark fluid poured out the edges of the wounds. Skin and clothes began to slough away as something began to sit up and the cords ripped loose from the floor. The blindfold frayed and then broke free as Bartok's head swelled to the size of a large melon. Eyes like silver balls lit up with an eerie light as the skin of Bartok's head ripped apart and fell away.

Ian pulled the trigger until there were no bullets left in the Colt and his ears rang like twin gongs. Dark splatters erupted from the creature and dripped down the wall behind it as it was slammed backward then slid down onto the bed leaving a gory black smear on the pastel blue wall.

«« — »»

"Get everything together," Enid said.

He was shouting into Ian's ear.

The room was filled with the smell of gunsmoke and alien death.

Ian could not take his eyes off the carnage on his guest room bed.

"Go. Get those journals; we'll load up the guns."

"We?"

"My brother Rake's here with your car. Don't ask questions. Get moving."

"What are you going to do?"

"We got no time for this. Just load up your car and start driving south on the freeway. Meet you at that Knights Inn down the road. Remember the one, maybe thirty miles back. No matter what happens you be there. When you check in get two rooms for three people. Say you been on your way driving home and was too tired to make it the rest of the way. You got that?"

"I shot my uncle." Enid thrust his index finger against Ian's chest.

"Whatever that thing was, it sure as hell wasn't your uncle. Now quit thinking and get moving. You know where you're going?"

"Yes. Knights Inn. Thirty miles south."

"Good, now get your ass moving."

Ian looked again at what used to be his uncle. For a moment, he couldn't move. Before Enid could tell him to get his ass moving again, Ian looked back him and said, "I'm taking the Colt with me."

Enid shoved a box of bullets into his hand.

"Figured you'd need these."

"Somebody's going to pay for this," Ian said. "Tomorrow I'm going to find Michael Hillis."

"That might be hard to do. Now move."

"What are you going to do?"

Enid was already halfway to the kitchen.

"I'm going to burn this place straight to hell."

And he did. With all the time he served in Iraq and Afghanistan, one thing Enid Mozer knew how to do was set things on fire and not leave much behind.

Chapter Twenty-Four

M r. Chirac arranged the magical instruments along the inside edge of his circle with the same precision that a master chef arranged the presentation of his or her finest food. Everything had to be perfect. He glanced up at his exquisite gold trimmed antique grandfather clock commissioned long ago by the Frenchman Japy Freres.

Two minutes to go.

The spirits came for him every night between three and four in the morning. "The dead," Eliaphas Levi had once told him, "lust after the living." In his case, it was especially true, because he had escaped their pallid world and returned to the rich and sensuous plane of the living. For this reason, their jealously consumed them. For this reason, every night he was forced to create his magical circles to ward off their maniacal obsession with dragging him back to suffer alongside them in their bodiless existence.

He sprinkled crushed salt taken from the Dead Sea as a ward around the perimeter of his circle. As he intoned an ancient banishing ritual, he knelt down and chalked symbols on the floor from John Dee's Enochian language to strengthen the barrier. In the flickering light from four stands of candles taken from a forgotten Indian palace, Chirac's white silk robe appeared golden.

While Ricci slept and Lily paced her cell, Chirac steeled himself for another of the nightly onslaughts that he had endured for over one hundred and fifty years. He had not slept even one night in all that time, nor had he aged more than a day. The reason for his good fortune eluded him, but in time he was confident he would understand.

They came with a whoosh of air that bent back the candle flames. The room filled with pale apparitions, grasping hands extended toward him with insatiable need. Anguished wails and screechings as they surrounded the circle, rebuffed by his wards. He heard his name called over and over as the room filled with the hungry dead.

Chirac sat down in the leather chair he had meticulously placed at the center of the circle, adjusted the cotton in his ears, picked a thin volume of letters written in the script of Proust himself, crossed his legs languidly and then began to read. As the chorus of despair rose around him to a confused wail, he took a moment to consider how satisfied he would be when the madstone was delivered to him. On that momentous day, he would silence the grasping pleadings of these relentless spirits by its power and relegate them forever to eternal inarticulateness.

Tomorrow night, Halloween night, he would meet with Ashley Hillis about the madstone at midnight. If she fulfilled her husband's contractual obligations, he would at last possess the madstone. If not, he would have another female to keep Lily company.

He smiled a thin smile and returned to his reading.

《《—》》

Alvarez got back into his car and lay back against the headrest. His back hurt from sleeping on the couch and nightmares about the little girl with burning eyes gave him fits off and on all night. The towing service had the burned out shell of Wendland's car pulled out of the ditch and up onto the flatbed and were chaining it into place. He'd gotten the call at eight after ten in the morning. After a quick shower, shave and breakfast at a MacDonald's drive through he'd headed toward the scene.

They'd identified the car by the license plate, which had, along with the bumper, blown free in the explosion and was laying thirty feet further down in the ditch. Wendland was reduced to bits and pieces of charcoal. What was left of the car was a melted shell. Since this thing started in Sharkey's Park, he'd seen more burned corpses than he had since he joined the police force. Nothing pretty about a burned body.

Nothing suspicious about the scene to any of the others. Wendland's car ran off the road in the dark and flipped over into a deep drainage ditch. Somehow a fuel line broke or cracked and gasoline came pouring out. Fumes built up to explosive level. Spark ignited the fumes and everything went up in flames. A light but steady rain kept the fields from catching fire and burning out of control. Everyone would buy the accident explanation.

Alvarez might have been okay with the accident theory—assuming the evidence techs didn't find anything to say it wasn't an accident—except for two things. Too many people connected to the Hillis family were dying in fires or lightning bursts or whatever. One more to mark off his mental list. The second thing was the singed doll an accident tech found in the weeds near the car. An old doll. Raggedy Ann style. Like the one he'd seen the little girl in his dreams clinging to while she was being raped. Like the doll he'd seen her clinging to outside of Lincoln Jones's house.

They were wrapping the accident scene up. Doing what they were trained to do.

He tapped his fingers on the steering wheel for a few minutes and then turned the key. The engine caught, he backed up, and started driving back toward Detroit. He had a few things he needed to clear up. Captain might not like the first one, but he could say he was just clearing up loose ends by seeing Dr. Knight again. Mainly, he wanted to ask her to see the microwave generator she'd built. Lincoln Jones was fried one of two ways that he could think of. The first might be far out, but at least it was rational. Maybe it was possible to have done it with a portable microwave generator. Maybe not.

The second was just plain nuts. He was going to find and talk to a ghost hunter named Ian Hunter. Tell him what Ashley Hillis claimed to have seen that night in Sharkey's Park. Then, if Hunter didn't think he was crazy, he'd tell him how Lincoln Jones and Henry Wendland died. If he didn't think that was crazy, then he would tell Hunter what he thought he saw himself.

Alvarez found him on the internet. Hunter had fifteen books on paranormal investigations, mostly debunking them with hard science. YouTube had clips from his television interviews and he seemed as normal as could be expected for someone who made his money investigating everything from haunted cemeteries to Bigfoot sightings. He'd almost landed his own show with the Discovery Channel but was too negative about the possibility of ghosts to yank in the ratings.

Most importantly, Hunter lived in the Detroit area.

Alvarez tracked down his number and called him first thing in the morning but got no answer. So he'd called his publisher, and, hinting that it was for something that might involve a new book, got Hunter's cell phone number. The publisher immediately made the connection to the Sharkey's Park deaths. If Alvarez was anyone than a homicide detective it wouldn't have worked.

As he drove the dirt roads toward the freeway, he dialed Hunter's number. It was answered on the sixth ring.

"Yes?"

"Is this Ian Hunter?"

"Who's calling please?"

"Detective Alvarez with the Milford police department. I have a few questions about a case I'm working on and you seem to be the big paranormal investigator in the area so I thought maybe you could help me."

Silence at the other end.

"Hello?"

"Yes, yes I'm here. I was just, well what is this about? I'm very busy with something just now."

After all the phone calls to so many people of the years, Alvarez picked it up right away. It was the "police problem." Some people were eager to work with the police—usually too eager. Others were naturally suspicious or down and out reluctant to cooperate. This guy was not happy about the call.

"It's about what happened at Sharkey's Park, Mr. Hunter. Specifically about the deaths of the ghost hunters, the disappearance of Michael Hillis and the rather bizarre story his wife told us about what happened that night."

"What?"

The shock in Hunter's voice rattled Alvarez so much he almost missed a turn onto the paved street he'd been looking for.

"Surely you've seen the news reports."

Another silence, then, "Actually I've been out of town on an investigation. This is the first I've heard about this. You're talking about Michael

Hillis? *The* Michael Hillis?"

"Yep," Alvarez said.

"This is terrible."

"It is that, Mr. Hunter. Now will you help me? It will be confidential, of course."

"What do you want me to do?"

"Meet with me tonight. Let me lay out what I need to discuss and you give me your take on it. That's all."

"I'll do it. Where and when?"

They made dinner arrangements and then Alvarez thanked him and clicked off. Time to go visit Dr. Knight again. The Captain might not like it if he found out, but he just had to do it. Had to put his suspicions to bed.

As he entered the entrance to the freeway, he wondered at the palpable fear he'd heard in Ian Hunter's voice.

«« —»»

"Why are you asking this?" demanded Dr. Knight.

She pushed her wire rimmed glasses higher onto the bridge of her nose. *Last time they were tortoise shelled*, though Alvarez. Today she had on wire rimmed glasses colored faint blue. Probably a different pair every day of the week.

"Can we keep walking?" Alvarez asked, "I've got other people to see."

A quick turn and she was walking ahead of him again.

As he hurried to catch up, he said, "And the reason's easy. Forensic people said it looked like the bodies were microwaved except there was nothing there in Sharkey's Park that could do that. Lot of electrical equipment in the vans, though. The guy that might have committed suicide by jumping off the hospital roof where Ashley Hillis was taken was the electrician. He worked for Michael, and who knows? Michael owned this place and you said the new high powered microwave you built is small. So I have to check it out to take it off the table."

Men and women passed by them in the hallway, their eyes darting away when they saw the look on Dr. Knight's face.

She must run a tight ship, thought Alvarez.

They stopped in front of a door with a chrome panel with an inset camera and a keypad. The hallway was clear except for the two of them. She looked at him, gave him the full-powered haughty look she was so good at.

"Do you honestly believe those people were microwaved to death with my invention?"

"Dr. Knight, I'm paid to think, but when it comes to things like this, I have to be shown. So are we going in or what?"

"Fine."

She looked into the camera, waited a moment and then tapped a string of numbers on the keypad so quickly that her fingers seemed to blur. A moment later, the door swung outward. Alvarez stepped to the side quickly to avoid it.

"It's a safety precaution, Detective," she said. "Doors to a hazardous work area open away from that area."

"What's the hazard?"

"Step inside and I'll explain."

The room was large enough to contain a tractor trailer. Conduits thick as his forearms laced the walls. In the middle of the room a four foot by four foot clear plastic square vessel filled with water that seemed to shimmer like suspended fairy dust. A glass panel inside the vessel separated it into two halves. Stainless steel piping ran from the top of the unit and disappeared through a wall. One tube from each side of the internal glass barrier. Built into the far side of the system was what looked like a motor housing.

Four technicians wearing blue lab coats and carrying touch-screen portables walked around the room doing things that Alvarez could only guess at.

"Where's the microwave thing?" he asked.

The look on her face told him it was a good thing he didn't work for her.

"The microwave thing, as you call it, is what you see attached to the back."

"Looks like a motor or a battery pack or something."

"I spent eight years developing the technology, Detective, and I didn't include sufficient visual design elements to make it aesthetically pleasing. How silly of me."

Alvarez ignored her and walked around to the back of the vessel.

"So how about you explain all this to me. What makes the water look like glitter, for starters?"

Dr. Knight reached into her lab coat and pulled out a small amber prescription bottle.

"Anna," she called out across the lab to one of the women in a lab coat. "Get me a cup of water if you please."

"You feeling okay?" asked Alvarez.

"No, Detective. Your ignorance is giving me a migraine."

Chapter Twenty-Five

Alvarez ignored the remark.

After Dr. Knight swallowed three pills chased with a quick gulp of water brought to her by Anna—who looked no less than 140 years old but still had bright red hair—she walked over to place her hand on the clear vessel.

"I will only explain this once for you. You can't hope to comprehend the intricacies of the chemistry so I'll make it simple enough that you may not have to interrupt. Is that satisfactory?"

"Sure."

"And please don't interrupt."

"No problem."

He'd seen the label on her pill bottle before she slid her thumb over it. Xanax. An anti-anxiety medication. Could be the stress of the president of the company disappearing. Add the stress of being the lead scientist on this new energy technology. Chunk in the fact she was talking to a homicide detective. Okay, that could explain it. But he didn't think so. Just a gut call. Not worth anything in court. Not worth anything in front of the Captain, but you didn't get anywhere if you didn't follow your instincts.

"Very good. First, what we have been attempting to do is to efficiently and economically separate water into its two atomic components, which are hydrogen and oxygen. We are doing this primarily to access the hydrogen, which is a clean burning fuel and completely environmentally friendly.

"We are combining two techniques to achieve this goal. The first is our use of predictive catalysis modeling. Before you ask, this means we have developed a mathematical model which tells us what material will be the most likely catalyst to successfully achieve our goals. In this case, our goal is to weaken the polar covalent bond that holds water molecules together. The catalyst will not separate water into its two components of oxygen and hydrogen, but it makes it easier for us to make this happen. Are you following me so far, Detective?"

"Hanging on, Doctor, by a mere intellectual thread."

She grimaced at the metaphor, and he stopped himself from winking. He'd done a lot of research on what Michael Hillis's company was doing and what their new technology breakthrough was about.

"Well, since the bonds are weakened by the catalyst, which is the colloidal suspension that makes the water glitter, as you say, it takes less energy to break the bonds. Because of this, we are able to complete the breakdown of water into hydrogen and oxygen by applying sufficient microwave energy to break its bonds. The key to our microwave technology is that it produces very high output extremely efficiently. It is the combination of catalysis and the efficiency of the microwave generation on which we hope to achieve an economical production of hydrogen as a clean fuel.

"So you see the tubing leading from each side of the polymeric membrane that divides the vessel into its two compartments? One is to carry away the oxygen and the other to carry away the hydrogen.

"This unit you see attached here to the back is the microwave generator. It is part of an integrated dual technology alternative energy system, not a weapon. Are you satisfied?"

Alvarez looked around the room and saw the technical staff filing out another door.

"Am I making everyone nervous?" he asked.

"Hardly. Even scientists get a lunch break, Detective. So I repeat, are you satisfied?"

"Can we grab chairs from that table and sit down for just a few minutes? I can run some things by you and then I'll be out of your hair? Can you do that?"

She sighed, made a big show of adjusting her glasses again and led him over to a bench with two rolling chairs. He sat down and she sat down. She crossed her arms over her chest and he didn't.

"How much has this research cost the government, Dr. Knight? Give or take a few million that is?"

"Accounting is on another floor," she said.

"Well, the grants are public information so I had one of the guys at the station look it up. They have a pretty hefty investment in what you're doing. Michael must have been well connected."

"I don't get involved in finance."

He nodded as though he understood.

"But the thing is, we found somewhere between forty-five and fifty million dollars granted to your work. That's a lot of money."

"Research is quite expensive," she said, "and energy research is especially so."

She leaned back in the chair a little, straightening her shoulders and trying to look professional. Twin Doctorates, impressive academic record and obviously successful as head of MT Quantum Technologies. Alvarez almost felt sorry for what he was about to do. Almost, but not quite.

"Here's one thing I wanted to ask you about, Doctor—did you ever hear of something called Cold Fusion?"

The color drained from her face. His instincts were right.

"Of course," she said.

"Supposed to be a major breakthrough, the guys who claimed it were on the cover of Time magazine and Newsweek."

Good thing she took three Xanax, he thought, *or she'd be up and out of the chair running for the door.*

"And your point?"

Alvarez looked over at the glass apparatus like he was trying to recover his train of thought. Then he turned back and stared straight at her.

"Does this thing work, Doctor?"

She looked back at him, her arms clenched tighter across her chest; her eyes held his for a few seconds, then lost focus when she looked up and to the left. Alvarez could never keep the eye signals straight. Looking up one way meant one thing and looking up the other way meant something different. One of them meant the suspect was getting ready to lie. But he didn't need body cues to tell that she was trying to sort out what to tell him.

"Before you answer me, I have a few things to tell you. The reason I'm going to tell them to you is because by the time I'm done you'll realize how serious I am about the one question I really want you to answer. Can you hear me out?"

Three Xanax tablets was a lot, but Alvarez didn't know the strength of her prescription. But when she nodded her agreement, she looked less panicked than he'd guessed she'd be.

"Okay. First, I'm going to hazard a guess that although everyone in the free world including the government thinks this thing works and it'll be as big a breakthrough as the electric light bulb, I don't think it does. Wait, before you say anything, I want you to know that whether it does or not is really not why I'm here. If Michael was bilking the government, providing fake results, showing receipts for expensive equipment he never bought, et cetera, then he and you have more to worry about than me.

"I don't know if it's the catalyst that doesn't work or your microwave unit that's coming up short. I'm not a scientist, Doctor, I'm a homicide detective.

"And just to make this clear, I really don't think it's a murder weapon. I don't really see anyone carrying it around in the biggest thunderstorm we've had here in fifty years with a big cord dragging behind them. I had to check it out, but the more I think about it, the stupider it sounds. Sure there was a portable generator in the vans, but in that kind of rain, anyone running electrical equipment would probably get electrocuted."

The medication seemed to have taken effect. She opened her mouth in surprise but forgot to close it for a few seconds. Alvarez wondered again why so many smart professional women fell for conmen like Michael Hillis.

"Then I don't understand you. Why are you talking to me if you don't think this equipment was used?"

"Because I'd like some information from you, Doctor. I'm going to make a wild guess that you and Michael Hillis were having an affair."

He held up his hand to quiet her down before he went further. She brushed a strand of hair away from her glasses as though trying to reinforce her dignity and propriety.

"Thing is, I'm just going off cop experience and gut instinct. I don't care, really, except I think it's a hell of a way for the two of you to treat Mrs. Hillis. I have enough grounds to go through records looking for motive, not to mention the issue of possible defrauding federal funds. But I'm not going to go there right now. I'm just going to ask you straight out if you've had any communication of any kind with him since his disappearance. So how about it?"

She looked at him with a combination of nervousness, vacuity and a touch of fear.

"Dr. Knight?"

"No," she said suddenly. "I haven't heard anything from him." Her sense of urgency seemed to grow with each word. "Nothing. Not an email, a phone call and I haven't seen him—physically that is. Last time I talked to him he was asking about the results of an analysis we contracted out for a piece of rock he was all excited about."

"What do you mean, not physically?"

Her eyes darted the room at the equipment as though for reassurance. When she looked back at him, her brown eyes were wide and sad.

"I've had … dreams about him. Terrible, terrible dreams."

"Oh."

"Don't say it like that. I know what you're thinking."

For the briefest of moments, Alvarez recalled Lincoln Jones.

"I'm not crazy," she continued. "They're just stress induced dreams. More like nightmares. I've read the literature about this sort of thing. They're just unexpressed fear and guilt. But they're so damned real."

"Sure."

"I see him trapped, like he's floating in a dark place. He keeps calling to me, trying to tell me that he's not dead. That he's trapped. And these hands, these dark hands are always pulling at him, like they're trying to pull him under water."

Alvarez shook his head. She was sounding more and more like Lincoln Jones.

"Maybe," he said, "maybe it means—"

"It doesn't mean anything, Detective. I think it's real. I think he's alive somewhere, somewhere awful. Some place terrible. Michael's trapped and he can't get out. Don't look at me like that. I keep having the same dream over and over. And I smell smoke. Have you ever smelled anything in a dream? And there's this little girl. I see her face and her eyes are on fire."

Alvarez felt acid rising in his stomach.

Chapter Twenty-Six

The cavern air began to coalesce into an image of phosphorescent red eyes before the suspended figure of Magnus Hillis. Invisible air currents moved them throughout the vaulted cavern, hovering over the mechanical soldiers as though inspecting them, floating over the dry husked remains of the cocooned eggs that a Union deserter had hacked to pieces before running away into the night to deliver his journals to his brother.

The rock wall behind Magnus began to throb and glow red as fresh blood. A pulsation shook the air as luminescent ectoplasm began to surge through the cabling which connected the mechanical soldiers to him. Magnus arched his back, his silver chip eyes flashing with energy.

Light began to radiate from domed crystals fused to the edge of the mechanical warriors. The glassine cabling running through their metal bodies lit up like fluorescent tubing.

As the floating red eyes moved toward Magnus, his body began to shake and he shrieked like a caged animal about to be fed. From behind the flashing blood red wall, the re-awakening ship answered.

«« — »»

"The arson investigators are going to go through my house and they're going to find Bartok's body full of bullets. What am I supposed to tell them, that I shot him because he was turning into an alien? They'll arrest me and throw my ass in jail."

"Now calm down," Enid said. "Me and Rake already took care of that."

They were standing in room one hundred and three at the Knights Inn. Two king sized beds with blankets the color of straw and an internet-enabled television bolted to a maple colored credenza. Enid leaned against the door with his arms folded looking casual as Ian prowled the length of the room between the bathroom and the television, waving his arms around as he paced.

"Yeah, I know, you set my house on fire. Did you ever hear of forensic science? Some fire investigator is going to find some evidence. They'll say like, 'Oh, my. What's this carbonized skeleton doing on the bed?'"

"Lookit. There ain't nothing for them to find. We took out what was there in a plastic tarp and, buddy, there's not enough of what we disposed of to find with a microscope."

Ian stopped and stared at him.

"And how exactly did you do that?"

"None of your damned business. The military trained me to know what I was doing and keep my mouth shut about it after I was done. What you don't know, you can't slip up and tell."

Enid chewed gum. He'd offered Ian a stick, but Ian told him to go to hell.

"I killed my uncle. Don't you understand that?"

"More you say something, the longer it stays in your head. Just forget about it now and tell me about what the policeman said over the phone."

Ian rushed across the room and stopped only inches from Enid. His face was red. He opened his mouth and yelled, "What's the difference? I'm going to jail. And it's all your and Bartok's fault. That crazy old man has ruined my whole life."

The gut punch came without warning. Ian doubled over in pain and fell over, writhing on the floor. Enid stayed where he was, leaning against the door like it hadn't happened. Then he uncoiled, stepped over Ian and sat down on the bed.

"Don't you ever say anything bad about him again," he said. "That old man was better than you and me put together. If there's any chance of stopping what's going on underground, it's because of everything he did to study it and keep it quiet. You're dumber than dog shit, you know that?"

Ian slowly got to his feet, then went over and fell backward into one of the cushioned chairs near the window. He held one hand over his stomach and steadied himself on the chair arm.

"I said, did you know that? I grew up in the military whiles you was running around writing books about there being no ghosts. Well, if there's no such thing as ghosts, what were those faces you saw floating around in them crystal domes on top of them underground robots? And I been in the army, son. What do you think the Department of Defense would do if they found out about them? I know. They'd be weaponizing them. You know what that means."

Ian slowly regained his color, but he kept one hand on his stomach.

"You didn't have to hit me."

"You were losing your nut. I need your brain running on full tilt boogie."

Ian started to laugh. He couldn't stop himself. He laughed so hard his whole body shook.

"You all right there?"

"It's just, what the hell is full tilt boogie?"

Tears were streaming down his face.

"I don't rightly know. Just something we say down south."

All the stress that began with Bartok's phone call left his body the moment he began to cry. He put his hands over his face, folded over and began to sob.

"That's more like it, brother," Enid said softly. "I'm sorry for your loss."

When Ian finally straightened up, he looked at Enid, really looked at him for the first time.

"Who are you?" he said. "Who are you really and why are you here?"

"I told you all that. I suspect what you're really asking me is what we need to do next and will me and the rest of my kin back your play. The answer is we're with you right up until the last bullet's fired. We got to stop that thing down there, Ian. And what we do next is up to you. I say you go meet with that policeman so we can find out what's happened to Michael Hillis. Maybe learn what his wife knows. We got a golden opportunity. Probably you being a ghost-hunting writer's the first big break we got. That'll get you in the door. But you're the only one can figure out how to pull the tarp over that alien stuff. That's what Bartok believed and I trusted that old man completely. You know how much he believed in you?"

Ian shook his head no.

"Well, he broke his Masonic oath for you. Because he believed you were the only one who could get it done, what with him dying and all. Your ancestor wanted that stuff kept secret under Masonic oath. I think he was afraid what would happen if the government—even back then—got hold of it. A Masonic oath ain't a thing you mess with, Ian. He took that seriously. Why do you think he was so upset you was an atheist? Because a man can't be a Mason unless they believe in God. That's what shook him up so. He was praying you'd find God so you could become a Mason and he could tell you everything. That's why he never told you before. He loved you, son, and he was praying for you right to the very day he called you to show you what he was hiding. He made the choice, decided you was the one who could make right what generations of Hunters and Mozers have kept hidden from the world."

"Shit," Ian said.

"Damned straight."

A few minutes of awkward silence followed, and then Enid said, "You learn anything from all that reading can help us shut that thing down for good?"

It was what Ian needed. Something to stop the replays of the terrible images of Bartok's horrible transformation. He needed to do something, to get in gear, and in order to do that, he had to come up with a plan.

"What Bartok thought, at least what he wrote in his notes, was that this thing, this 'ghost box' channeled the energy into the mechanical army, and that if we could find it, then we could use it to de-energize them. He didn't believe that the ship was dead. What he thought was that it went dormant to conserve energy. Like it went into hibernation. Now it seems to be waking up, and energizing that thing, that freak Magnus. So I was thinking we could take Bartok's idea a step further. We could use the ghost box to drain away the energy of the mechanical men, Magnus, and the ship itself."

Enid looked up at the ceiling for a minute, and then looked back at Ian. He nodded his agreement.

"I like that. Bartok was right. You got a good brain in that head of yours."

"Problem is, we have to find the ghost box and take it from whoever's got it."

This time Enid grinned.

"You point me at who's got it, and don't you worry, me and Rake will get it."

"I think when we find Michael Hillis, we'll find the ghost box. Bartok wrote that he got a call from Michael, and that Michael was ecstatic. He told him about having found a hidden technology. Basically, he told him about the ghost box."

"How'd he find out?" wondered Enid.

"Someone gave him part of the journals—some pages that were torn out and it's true, one of the journals we've got had some pages missing."

"Jude Brooks. Never was a Brooks born a man could trust. He was the only one in the party that came on Taylor Hunter that wasn't a Mozer. My kin swore him to secrecy, said they'd blow his head off if any word of what they'd found ever got out. Thieving weasel must have ripped a few pages out and nobody the wiser. Nobody studying them later in your family would have known they was stolen either. One of the Brooks family around today must have found them and tried to sell them to Hillis. Money was all they was ever about."

"That must have been what started this whole thing. But for now we've got to find Michael Hillis. He's the one who will know where the ghost box is."

Enid smiled a broad smile, showing a mouth full of square white teeth.

"Rest easy. Ain't no better trackers than me and Rake. Wherever that boy is, we'll find him."

《《—》》

Granny Hillis slept in one guest room while Kenneth sat in a recliner near her bed and watched over her. He'd closed the curtains to allow her to sleep straight through the afternoon. The madstone had done its work and she was recovering. Kenneth watched a program about hoarders on the room's small television, the volume turned down low. From time to time he shook his head and said, "Don't that beat all."

Ashley slept in the other guest room. She couldn't bear to sleep in her own bed with Michael still missing. The thought of sleep terrified her, but she was too tired to stay awake. Eventually she took one of the sleeping pills prescribed for her, then another to make sure she wouldn't dream.

But she did.

She floated in that other world, vaporous fog swirled around her, covering her with its wet warmth. Michael was hidden in the mist, calling to her, calling for her. She slapped her hands over her ears, but still heard him.

"Where are you?" she cried out desperately.

Still he called her name over and over and over again. The rolling fog concealed everything. There was nothing to see. Only the dense fog.

The other voices came. Pleading. Growling. A mob of spirits gathering round him to take him further into darkness.

A glow ahead. A fiery glow.

A little girl's voice.

Laughing.

Ashley woke up screaming.

«« — »»

Ricci sat on a stool outside of Lily's cell. In the faint red light, his jagged scar was so dark it looked as though it had been branded onto his jaw, as indeed it had been by his own father.

"I told you, first met him, not to swear. He don't like women who swear. I tried to warn you, but there's only so much I could tell you. You don't know him. Aww, maybe you do now."

The big cat growled. Her velvet black fur rippled and she flipped her tail up and down on the straw-covered concrete floor.

"Yeah, I know. I'm sorry, like I said. What do you want from me? There wasn't nothing I could do."

Lily growled another warning.

"Look, I don't know how to make you go back to what you was. I'm just me. Things I know how to do won't do no good for you. And I ain't going to take him on. I think he hears everything I say, did you know that? I don't mean microphones and all that. I mean he hears things we say in his head. Did I tell you I just got another two years on my contract with him? He's always as good as contracts. Thing is, nobody ever gets what they want from them except him."

Lily's yellow eyes fixed on Ricci.

He remembered the first day he met her. A long-legged black woman with hair so long and thick he thought maybe she was a model. An elegant face, like one you'd see on a business magazine. She was dressed like an appliance repairman, and it turned out she worked in a car shop. A beautiful woman who knew cars. What else could a man ask for?

But then he'd made a terrible mistake. He'd told Mr. Chirac about her. He didn't know why. Couldn't understand to this day why, but he had. And Mr. Chirac had asked to meet her.

Lily scratched the concrete with her large, sharp claws.

Ricci winced at the sound.

Chapter Twenty-Seven

Alvarez was seated at the back of the restaurant. He saw the young man looking around, trying to find him. He held up a hand to let him know where he was. Hunter was maybe just under six foot tall. Full head of hair the color of bleached wicker. Solid build, quick eyes that darted about the room nervously.

When he was within six feet of Alvarez, the detective got up and stuck out his hand.

"Detective Alvarez," he said.

Hunter looked down as though he'd never seen a hand before, then reached out, shook hands, and stood there.

"Sorry," Hunter said. "Long day already."

"We might as well sit down," Alvarez said. "Easier on the feet that way."

"Right. Absolutely."

A man came by to ask what Hunter wanted to drink and then took off to get him some beer. Alvarez didn't know what they called them these days. Maybe waitperson. That sounded about right.

"You have a hard time finding the place?"

"GPS found it for me. I hardly know where anything is anymore. I'd be lost within five minutes if the satellites went off the network."

"Ain't that the truth," Alvarez said.

The waitperson returned with Hunter's beer, asked if they wanted to order dinner and Alvarez told him to come back in five minutes.

"I hate this shit anymore," Alvarez said. "You can't sit down and relax. They're always trying to hustle you along. Probably hired marketing consultants who told them to keep the customers moving and the cash register ringing."

"I don't think they ring anymore," Hunter said.

"There's that," Alvarez said.

"So what exactly can I help you with, Detective?"

Alvarez was about to tell him when Hunter held up and hand.

"Sorry," he said and took out his cellphone from his pants pocket. "House caught fire today." Then into the phone. "Oh hello, Rachel. Yes, yes, thank you that would be wonderful. I think I've talked to everyone I'm supposed at the fire department and police department and I'll be glad to talk to your investigator. Insurance is good. No, I don't know what caused it, but

I'm sure glad I've got coverage. No, well, maybe who knows. Could have been vandalism. I was almost back into town. Yes, but I have to go now, I'm talking to someone. Thanks, I'll wait to hear back to you."

Fire. More burning. Before he could stop himself, Alvarez was looking around the room for signs of the little girl.

"Is everything okay, Detective? I'm sorry about the phone call, but I have to talk to them if I want to get a new house. Everything I own was burned to the ground while I was on my way back into town with a couple of my investigators. The only things I have left are the clothes on my back and my car. And a credit card."

"Wow. I'm okay. Better off than you, it sounds like. But today I was at an accident scene. Guy burned to death inside. Homicide before that where the guy burned to death after being nailed to the wall with steak knives."

Hunter looked like he would be sick. "That's awful," he said. "Nobody got hurt when my house burned down. I was on my way back to town. I'd hate to have your job."

"Yeah, well, it's what I get paid for. Anyway, sorry you lost your house. You want to do this later so you can take care of business?"

"No. Right now's good. Besides, here's the waiter. How about if we order? You wouldn't believe how hungry you get standing around doing nothing except telling the same story all afternoon."

They both ordered a burger and fries. The waiter took off to place the order and Hunter took a drink of his beer. They were the only people in the back section. A green shaded lamp shone a cone of light over them. It reminded Alvarez of a high class interrogation light.

"Here's what I was calling you about," he said, and then proceeded to tell Hunter about the incident at Sharkey's Park. "Theory is now everyone got killed by a freak lightning event. Same thing happened a long time ago. Another Hillis involved. Everybody else died the same way, but that Hillis—Becker Hillis was his name—disappeared just like Michael."

"Okay, "Hunter said, "that's pretty strange."

"Yeah, well there's more. But first I have to ask you something. Do you believe in ghosts?"

Hunter took another sip of beer, and then said, "Is that important, Detective?"

"Maybe," grinned Alvarez.

"Well, the answer is that I've disproved a lot of paranormal claims. In fact, every investigation I've ever done that involved ghosts has turned out to be bogus. You ever hear about the Oracle of Delphi?"

"Saw something about it on the History Channel once. Didn't pay much attention to it except I liked looking at the women in white robes."

"I think that's why they included them. But what you maybe missed was that the visions those women received and the spirits they saw turned out to have been induced by exposure to a naturally occurring leak of hydrocarbon gases in the cave."

The waiter came back with their food and for a few minutes neither of them spoke while they finished off their food. Hunter ate like he hadn't seen food in days, and when he'd demolished the last fry, he took a long drink of beer and started talking again.

"I needed that. Now, where was I? I was telling you about the Oracle of Delphi, that's it. Point I was trying to make is that sometimes people see things and they believe they're true just because they saw them. In fact, the Oracles had most of Greece believing in their visions and dreams. All based on an unfortunate exposure to gases leaking upward from underground fissures.

"Ghosts are like that. People see things, so they think they must be true. You might run into the same thing with eyewitness testimony, where the witness's belief in what they think they saw gets in the way of the facts. Me, I've never seen a ghost or found the facts to support the idea that anyone else has seen one either. I'm not ruling out the possibility, just reporting the facts as I find them."

Alvarez held up his cup to signal to the waiter that he'd like more coffee.

"Sure you don't want a beer?" Hunter asked.

"I'd love one, but I think I'll stick to coffee."

The waiter whisked in with a pot, refilled Alvarez's cup and then hurried over to another table.

"So if I told you some of the people associated with the Sharkey's Park murders told me they'd seen the ghost of a little girl, you're saying it might be because they were either predisposed to see her, or they were under a lot of stress or something."

Hunter nodded, looked thoughtful for a moment, and then took another swig of beer.

"That would be my first guess. According to what I read on the internet at the hotel I was at when you called me, the people involved were on a paranormal investigation. So yes, I'd say it was likely they had heard about hauntings in the park. Maybe they were looking for the spirit of Becker Hillis or the other people who died. Was there a little girl killed then, too?"

"No."

"Well, that complicates it a little. Any stories about the ghost of a little girl being seen in the park over the years?"

"No."

"You've researched it?"

"Yep. Had it checked out. How about pyrokinesis? Do you believe in that?"

"What? You mean like yuppies auto-igniting?"

"I'm serious."

"What's this all about, Detective? If you tell me it will make it a lot easier for me to give you a good answer. And before you ask, it stays between us. Nobody will know the contents of this conversation except you and me."

Alvarez thought about this for a minute. How far could he trust Hunter? How far did he have to trust him? What if he spilled it to the press? Alvarez would get busted down to crossing guard, that was what. But he needed to tell someone if he was going to get anywhere. He ran it around his brain a little longer. It would be stupid to tell Hunter everything. What could he possibly hope to get out of it? Answers. He might get answers.

"This is going to sound pretty strange."

"You have no idea the strange things I've seen in my life," Hunter said. "No idea at all."

"See if it tops this," Alvarez said.

He told Hunter everything.

«« — »»

"What do you think?"

"I think it's a least a three-beer story."

"I'm serious. I've got all those people burned to death in Sharkey's Park. I've got Lincoln Jones who sees a ghost in Ashley Hillis's hospital room. I've got Henry Wendland burned to death in a freak car accident. I've got the fact that no one ever knew about the little girl's death until we found her remains had been dug up in the park. And the fact that I've seen her—more than once. And there's the list. All the descendants of the men on that list are now dead except me. And they've all been burned to death, just like the little girl."

Hunter held up his empty bottle, got a replacement from the waiter, and thought about it.

"You're forgetting Michael Hillis," he said after taking a long drink.

"No, I just don't know where the hell he is. See, maybe he planned this whole thing. He and his company are about to be exposed for fraudulent use of government money. A lot of government money. Somehow he finds out the little girl is buried there. In fact, he went around quietly buying up the property the park is on. So he sets up this paranormal investigation, and he plans on mysteriously vanishing during the middle of it."

"Why would he go to all that work? Why not just vanish? And if he's in trouble, I wouldn't think he be hanging around for a paranormal investigation. Don't people still go to jail for fraudulent use of taxpayer dollars? No, something doesn't add up. And I bet you already knew that anyway. What you're worried about, what's got you scared is that there might really be the ghost of a little girl out there getting revenge on the families that raped her and then burned her to death."

Alvarez knew he was right. That was exactly what he was afraid of. Going to the Captain and telling him that he'd solved the Sharkey Park murders. That the killer was the ghost of a little girl bent on revenge. Shit.

"Detective, when you asked me about pyrokinesis, I should have told you that there are one or two convincing cases recorded over the years, but I can't speak to them since I didn't investigate them. There are hauntings that fit this bill, too. The Black Forest Haunting investigated by Dennis Hauck comes to mind, and the case of Anita Hernandez, investigated by Dr. Barry Taff. Again, I didn't investigate them myself, so I can't speak to them. But I have an open mind on the topic. I'm willing to look into your case, completely confidentially and see what we can come up with.

Alvarez felt a wave of cautious relief. Hunter was his first real sense of hope and he seemed genuinely interested.

"Deal," Alvarez said quickly. "What do we do first?"

"The first thing you need to do is introduce me to Ashley Hillis. Let me talk to her in private to see what I can find out. She's the only living witness to what happened that night."

"I was about to suggest that myself," Alvarez said.

《《—》》

Ian could hardly believe it. Everything went just the way Enid said it would. And best of all, Alvarez hadn't arrested him.

He climbed back into his car, started the engine, and then took out his cellphone. Enid answered on the first ring.

"It went just like you said," Ian said. "Tomorrow he and I are going over to meet Ashley Hillis. I asked for some time alone with her to talk about a few things.

"Tell me when you get back. We don't need to talk about this over the phone."

Suddenly the connection filled with static.

"Enid? Are you still there? Can you hear me?"

The line went dead.

Ian wondered if the electric company was working on a substation. He turned around and saw Alvarez's car lights flash as the policeman backed out of his spot and began to pull away.

For nearly a full minute, Ian stared. His mouth was so dry he licked his lips. Slowly, he slid the cover closed on his cell phone. Finally, he blinked.

A little girl was standing beside where Alvarez car was moments ago. He saw the car back right through her. Alvarez drove away, and the little girl with bright blond hair stared after the detective.

Then she turned and stared directly at Ian. When her eyes and hair caught fire, Ian threw the car into reverse, backed up, then jammed it into drive and sped away so fast he drove over the street curb and nearly ran straight into a bus.

157

Chapter Twenty-Eight

Kenneth took her to the guest room where the old woman lay waiting.

"Child, child, tell Granny Hillis about it. Was you having a terrible nightmare?"

Ashley was shaking so hard she didn't answer.

Real, so real. It was so very real.

"Don't just stand there like a lump, Kenneth. Get me my medicine bag."

"Yes, ma'am."

He guided Ashley to the bed and set her down next to Granny, then retrieved the quilted medicine bag from the floor next to the chair he had been sitting on. It had two rosewood handles that made it look like a knitting purse.

"Just lay it next to me, right there," said the old woman. She patted one of Ashley's hands and hummed softly.

Ashley rocked back and forth, crying in tiny, gasping jags. Kenneth stood near them awkwardly, unsure what to do.

"Go fetch me a cup of hot water, and put it right here on the nightstand. Not boiling water, you understand, but hot water."

"Yes, ma'am," Kenneth repeated and headed toward the kitchen.

As he walked down the hallway and then the stairs to the first floor, he wondered how a man like Michael Hillis, who had so much, could just throw it all away. The chandelier hanging in the main entrance probably cost more than Kenneth had in the bank at any one time. The study held more books than the county library down where he was from.

Ashley left all the lights on, even though it was still daytime and Granny told them the haint was through with them for now. Even Kenneth, who trusted every word that came out of the old woman's mouth, felt a tingle of fear as he saw the window he'd closed up after the haint had blown it to pieces.

The kitchen was tiled with pink marble he thought probably came from somewhere over in Europe, like Italy. It had that high-living look to it. Stainless steel and marble just didn't look right to him. With the afternoon sun coming through the orange curtains, it made it seem like the kitchen was on fire.

He found a cabinet full of cups, turned on the water in the sink til it felt hot enough for Granny to make what he thought she was going to make. The way he did it was like she showed him a long time ago. He let it run over his wrist long enough to feel pain. When it was just right, he filled two cups full and took them back upstairs along with a roll of linen-like paper towels he'd found in a cabinet, balancing the whole thing on a velvet covered serving tray he'd found. As he entered the bedroom where the two women sat, he saw himself in the mirror and thought he'd make one ugly waiter.

"See there," said the old woman to Ashley, "here's Kenneth again, just like I told you. Haint won't be coming around here a bit. You trust what Granny tells you and everything will be fine, oh so fine."

Ashley looked up at him twice. Quick little glances like she was afraid he'd disappear. Funny how she was counting on him because he was big and tall. Haints like this one didn't care nothing about how big or strong a person was on the outside. In the car on the way up north, Granny had told him this was one was what was sometimes called a screaming spirit or a wisp of fire. More dangerous than death itself, she'd said. Here was this poor little lady lost a husband to it and shaking and crying and counting on him to protect them, when all along the only prayer they had was this old country woman.

"Now, Kenneth, I declare you be learning. Help me sit up on the bed next to this young woman, then slide the nightstand over and put that tray on it. Just put the lamp on the floor."

As always, he followed her instructions as best he could. She opened her medicine bag when he had her upright, and took out pouches and little bundles of straw. Between her gnarled fingers, she pinched different amounts of dried herbs and put them into one cup, stirring them with her finger.

"Don't you worry about no sanitation, girl. It's the way we done it for as long as there been granny women. The power in a granny woman's finger is more potent than all the herbs in this whole bag, but the magic works together."

Kenneth caught Ashley looking at him for confirmation that the old woman wasn't crazy. He gave her his most solemn nod. The word of a granny woman was tighter than a rope around a hanged man's neck.

"Now you drink this what Granny's made for you and you will sleep again like when you was a baby. The sun ain't come down yet to the edge of the sky, so you'll need your rest for that midnight meeting of yours."

The startled look in Ashley's eyes reminded Kenneth of a doe caught in a flashlight beam.

"How did you know about that?" she asked.

"I dream and I dream and I dream, young woman. Now drink. Drink it all down. Go on. I ain't come all this way to hurt you, but to save you."

After another quick glance at Kenneth, she drank it all. Tentatively at first, then drank it down in one long swallow.

Granny Hillis took out pieces of cloth from her medicine bag and then made two little piles of mixed powders on the cloths. With quick little motions like she was rolling up homemade cigarettes, she made two little pouches. She cupped her hand and scooped water from the other cup of water and dampened the two poultices.

"Now, Kenneth, you help the woman lie back down on the bed next to me, and place a pouch over each eye. Go ahead girl, let the man help you."

Ashley was so worn out she did as she was told. As Kenneth placed the poultices over her eyes, he said, "You rest, Miss Ashley," and felt like he was a soldier in "Gone with the Wind."

He stepped back a few steps. Granny waved him to sit down again in the chair. Then she began to sing, a soft, familiar hymn that went on a long time. But Ashley and he both were asleep after the first refrain.

«« — »»

It was dark for just under an hour when Enid parked his SUV in the weeds by the side of the road.

"I don't like this," Ian said.

"He never likes nothing," Rake said.

"You weren't talking to the cop," Ian said.

"Quiet down, the two of you," Enid said.

"I'm serious," Ian said. "This cop, this Alvarez, he was scared. He actually thinks he saw a ghost and he didn't seem like the type. It might be linked somehow to the ghost box. I just can't figure out how. We're not seeing something. Something important. I can't put my damned finger on it, though."

"It'll come to you," Enid said. "You sure there was nothing when you was re-reading the papers Bartok left you about this Becker Hillis?"

"Nope. Not a thing. Course I'm half blind for lack of sleep, but I couldn't even find the name. But there were those missing pages. Might have to do with that."

"Huh. Well let's keep it on point here. We got to move while the going's the easiest. Staff's still off until Mrs. Hillis calls them back and we need to reconnoiter if we're going to search her house for it. Rake, let's unpack."

Rake was wearing a knit facemask. He and Enid were decked out like something between manic survivalists and rogue terrorists.

The whole thing made him nervous.

"Look," he said, "there's got to be electronic security all over. Hillis has a lot of money invested in this place. Did you see how big it was on Google Maps? He probably has infrared cameras all over the place. And you're like five miles from the property line? I don't see how you're going to even get in."

Rake popped the back hatch and started unloading boxes on the ground. Enid was unpacking their weapons. They had night vision equipment and communications equipment that Rake secured from someone named Roach, which was more than Ian wanted to know.

"You know you're going to look like terrorists if you get caught." Ian said.

"We ain't getting caught," Enid said.

"He ever shut up?" Rake asked.

"He's okay with a pistol when it gets tight," Enid said. "Now, Ian, you take the SUV back to the motel. I call you, you come get us. That's all you got to do. Leave the rest to us."

Ian held up his hands.

"We don't even know if the ghost box is in her house."

"We're about to find out," Enid said.

"All right, all right. Just don't get caught."

"Good night, Alice," Rake said.

Ian was still asking himself what that meant as he drove away.

He looked back in the rearview mirror, but could no longer see either of them. The moon was a pale ghost over the fields.

I don't like this at all, he thought.

《《—》》

"Time to wake, child."

Granny perched on the side of the bed and watched Ashley's eyelids flutter.

"Come back to me, now. Granny done made you some special tea to restore your spirit."

Such a strange sight she was. The simple beauty of a young woman crowned with hair the color of an albino rabbit.

"What, what time is it?"

"Eight thirty at night," Kenneth said. "You been sleeping just fine."

Suddenly Ashley shot bolt upright in bed. "Is it, is it safe?"

"It is indeed, for us," said Granny. "The haint is circling around somewhere close enough. It ain't happy I'm here, but here is where I need to be."

"We've got to get out of here," Ashley said.

"Hush, hush. Listen to what I say. It ain't safe round about tonight, but in here with Granny its safe as can be from that tortured soul. Now drink this. My hands are too old and feeble to be holding on to this cup and saucer all night."

Ashley looked at its peculiar green color and the black sprinkles floating on its surface. She looked up at Kenneth, then down at the cup, and then back again at Granny.

"What's in it?"

"Medicine, child. You wouldn't drink it if I told you what it was, but you'd best heed my leanings and drink it anyways. It's good for you or I wouldn't have made it."

Tentatively Ashley took a sip.

"It tastes like cantaloupe."

"Drink it all down."

When Ashley took the last sip, Kenneth took the cup and saucer from her.

"You've had a hard while, ain't you?" Granny asked.

Tears formed in the corners of Ashley's eyes and her shoulders slumped.

"Now that won't do, child. There'll be time to weep later. Tonight I need you to be strong. Tell Granny about your dreams."

"Can I ask you something first?"

"Go on."

"Do you know what that thing is and why this is happening?"

"I do."

"And do you know where Michael is?"

"I believe I do. Now tell Granny about your dreams."

In between sobs, Ashley told her. It broke the old woman's heart to listen to her. The Hillis women were a put-upon lot and this young thing weren't no different.

"What does it mean?" Ashley asked. "Where is he? What's happened to him?"

Granny chose her words carefully. Out of the corner of her eye she saw Kenneth lean forward. The hallway light was off and only one slender lamp lit the room.

"You know what Granny means when she says the word haint?"

"It's a southern word for ghosts, isn't it?"

"I figured you might know, you being a writer and all."

"I write paranormal romances. I do a lot of research."

"My, my. A haint is a spirit wandering the country what's lost its way, child. Some of them is harmless. Most of them is harmless. Some of them ain't. The haint what came calling last night is what's called by some a screaming haint. A screaming haint is one that died screaming."

She saw Ashley's eyes widen.

"For real?" she asked.

"Oh, it's real enough, child. And it's been let loose again and hungry, horribly hungry for revenge. It once was the spirit of a poor, defenseless little girl."

"Then it's true, what my lawyer told us?"

"About the evil of Becker Hillis and those what was with him? It surely is."

"But it killed all those innocent people in the park that never harmed it. Why would it do that?"

Granny chuckled ruefully.

"It ain't exactly in its right mind, child. Held back for all those years by the power of the madstone what I gave Becker himself to keep that spirit in the ground. He'd been having dreams what frightened him near hanging himself. God help me, I should have tied the knot for it myself. Instead, like a fool, I gave him the most powerful gift the Lord had ever give me to put in that girl's grave. Becker and his boys put it in and all of themselves except Becker died whilst they was doing it. A screaming haint don't go down easy, child.

"So Becker hightailed it back to Kentucky where he lived in an old house we had back in the hills. He eventually did string himself up but didn't die. Not right at all after that, no, not at all. The bad dreams wouldn't let him alone. Set himself on fire one night. Poured the gasoline all over himself. Kin found what was left of him a week later and that should have been the end of it. Would have been if that fool husband of yours hadn't come calling on me."

"Because Josh brought him the diary," Ashley said.

"That's the way it was, I suppose. When your man came asking questions, I acted like an old fool of a woman. Don't know what came over me. I told him the whole story. I told him about the madstone what was holding that haint in the ground."

Granny watched Ashley's face as she took in what she told her. Too much. *It was all too much for her*, she thought. She'd need to be stronger.

"What is this madstone? What's so special about it? Why is it different than other madstones?"

Granny hadn't meant to tell her this part of the story. No, time was precious. But she thought this young woman needed strength to face what was coming at her, so she told her.

"When I was a little girl—yes I was a child myself once—and I was walking through the woods, I came upon a deer. Pure white it was, like nothing I ever seen before or sense. Eyes the color of soft gold."

Kenneth put in, "Not red, not like it was an albino deer like they call them."

"Was you there that day?" Granny asked.

"No, ma'am."

"Well then you'd best let me tell my own story."

"Yes, ma'am."

"Fine. Now it was only a few feet from me. Just standing there, looking like it was waiting for me, like it had something to say. Standing in a little patch of bluebells. I was about to walk up to it, the way that children with no sense do, when my Daddy put a arrow straight through its heart. Don't cry child, most of the Hillis men ain't much to talk about and my Daddy was one of them. Not the worst, but not a kind heart like Kenneth here.

"I went to it. My Daddy was yelling something at me but I couldn't hear what he said. Only thing important to me right then was to lean over that poor thing and pray for God to save it. I prayed and I prayed and I stroked its head til Daddy pushed me aside calling me a crazed little girl. The blood, child, I can still see the red blood on its fur, on my hands, and the smell of death standing right there with us. I cried like a girl hadn't ever cried before.

"But when Daddy took its carcass home, it was God I was most mad at. I was out of my young mind. I loved God, you see, but I didn't know Him. I knew my Daddy and he was what he was. God was supposed to be all good. I kept asking Him how He could let that deer die. I thought He was cruel. I'm ashamed to myself to this day, child, but I was filled with fury for such a little thing. The Lord had a lesson for me, though. Oh yes, he did.

"When Daddy cut it up, it was our way that Momma would search through the innards for a madstone. She was like I come to be. She was a granny woman, and she knew what to look for and she knew this was no ordinary deer. And she found what she was looking for, she found the grace and mercy the Lord had sent that angelic deer to bring. It was the most powerful madstone ever.

"She gave it to me. Said it was God's own gift to me. That's how I came by the most powerful healing stone anybody had ever known. And what did I do with it? Like a damn fool, I gave it up to save my wicked brother's soul. It is that very madstone that held the haint in the grave of that young girl. And to my forever shame I told your husband where it was buried."

"In the little girl's grave in Sharkey's Park," whispered Ashley. "And he dug it up."

"He did. A haint is quick to go down under the power of the madstone, but slow to waken. They get used to being held back. But when they do come to know they is free, they come out with a fury and Lord help anyone it finds."

"It killed Michael, didn't it?"

Granny looked at her a long time before answering.

"No, it didn't. It done worse. It killed all them other people, but Michael, well he is kin to Becker. So it dragged him straight from the land of the living into the dead. Ain't nothing the lost dead hunger for more than a living soul to torment."

"I thought you said it didn't kill him," Ashley said, her voice rising in a panic.

"He ain't dead, child, but he's trapped on the other side and there ain't no way in this life to set him free."

Ashley screamed and began to pull at her hair like a madwoman.

Chapter Twenty-Nine

Ian sat in the Knights Inn with a notepad and pen in front him. All the lights were out in the room except for the single lamp bolted to the corner of the desk. The yellowed journals from Bartok's valise were spread out behind him on the bed. He had his cellphone set to high ring and always vibrate so he wouldn't miss Enid's pick-up call. On the way back from dropping off the twin commandos he'd stopped at a drugstore and picked up a bottle of Nyquil to make sure he went to sleep. The memory of the little girl behind Alvarez's SUV kept coming back. He couldn't possibly have seen the policeman drive through a little girl. He couldn't possibly have seen the little girl catch on fire. He knew that. It was a warning, signaling how much stress he was under. Had to be.

But suppose it wasn't. Suppose there actually were ghosts. Suppose he'd actually seen a ghost? Hypothetically. A scientific hypothesis. What could be the link between Michael Hillis, the ghost box and the little girl's ghost? What was it that tied them all together? He tapped his pen on the notepad impatiently. Nothing. He couldn't see a common denominator. Either his perspective was all wrong or they were missing information.

He got up and began pacing. In the dim light, the carpet reminded him of gray stone covered with patches of dying moss.

The Hillis family was linked to both the events underground and the little girl's spirit. That was easy enough. But how?

Without warning images of Bartok filled his thoughts. The days when they walked together and Bartok revealed to him stories of esoteric orders, ancient legends, hauntings and mysteries of the ancients. Even in those days, Ian struggled with what his uncle told him. His uncle was raised in a different time, with different beliefs. He still believed in the old ways. Bartok was, in a word, superstitious. He talked about ghosts, demons and spells the way people now talked about Google, Facebook, and Twitter.

Ian loved the old man and tried to listen politely, but, in the end, rebelled. The scientific method, he once told Bartok, was invented for a reason. It's here to stay, he'd explained, and maybe the old man should give it a try.

He remembered what happened underground. He could see, vividly see, Magnus Hillis suspended in mid-air, impossibly not dead for over a hundred and fifty years. He saw, in his mind, the cable shoot out and bore into Bartok's neck and he cringed at the memory. The monster dog. Bartok changing. Ian saying he couldn't pull the trigger. Bartok, in the throes of transmutation, telling him that when the time came Ian would be glad to pull the trigger.

He was right.

When he saw the old man's body and that thing discard Bartok's skin and rise up, Ian pulled the trigger immediately and kept on pulling until the gun was empty.

Tears streamed down his face as he realized that he had lost the old man forever. He had never cried since he became an adult, but he wasn't ashamed. There was really no choice, no way to hold it in. He sat down on the bed next to the journals and slumped over. He failed Bartok. Failed to save him. Instead he killed whatever it was Bartok was becoming.

"I'm sorry, Uncle Bartok. I failed you again. God forgive me, I failed you one last time."

After a time, he rose to his feet, wiped his face on his sleeve, got up, and began to pace again.

What would Bartok think about the little girl's ghost? What had Bartok told him about ghosts?

A sudden thought came to him. He walked over, snatched up his cellphone, found Alvarez's business card and dialed his cell number.

One ring, two rings, three rings.

"Hello?"

"Alvarez? It's me, Hunter. I'm sorry to call you so late, but I have to tell you something."

"What time is it?" asked Alvarez.

"I doesn't matter. Listen to me for a minute and tell me if I'm crazy."

"Go on."

Ian told him about seeing the little girl. The detective listened in silence.

"Why didn't you call me when it happened?"

"Because I didn't want to believe what I saw. You drove right through her, Detective."

"I don't like this," Alvarez said.

"I've never seen a ghost before. Ever. I thought it was all hysteria. I debunk them because I've never seen one. Before today. I actually saw her. Really."

"Well, either we're both crazy or there is such a thing as a ghost. I don't feel crazy, do you?"

"No," Ian said.

"Then maybe there really is a ghost."

"Definitely."

If Bartok could hear him now.

"But there's something else, something my uncle told me a long time ago. Don't look in her eyes, Detective, and I don't think she'll harm you. If she looks at you, look away. Look down. Don't look up."

"Can I ask why?"

"I'll tell you later. And if you see her in your dreams, you do the same thing. If you don't, you're going to end up like the others. I'll be doing the same thing. And remember, don't look at her eyes even in your dreams. If you do, I think we'll be scraping your charbroiled body off the floor. That's my hypothesis. No—that's what I really believe. I can't tell you why, but I know it's true."

"Anything else?" asked Alvarez.

"I'm tired so I'm going to bed. I can hardly see straight. I'm living in a Knights Inn until I get a new house. I lost everything today and I'm just beat to hell and back."

"I know what you mean."

"See you tomorrow?"

"I'll meet you at the Hillis front gate at two o'clock."

"Good. Thanks, Hunter. I mean that."

"You won't forget, will you?" Ian asked. "Don't look in her eyes."

"Nope. I'm not ready to die just yet."

After he shoved his cellphone back into its holster, Ian studied himself in the mirror. He looked different than the night he left for Kentucky. He looked ready for a fight. He felt different inside, too; he now believed in ghosts and had asked God's forgiveness for what he'd done to Bartok.

"Old man," he said, "if you could see me now."

《《 — 》》

"Let her go, Kenneth," Granny Hillis said.

Kenneth, who rushed over and pinned Ashley's arms to her sides, gradually loosened his grip. Because she seemed to have herself more under control, he stepped away from the bed.

"Sit down, go ahead, boy. She's stronger than she seems."

Ashley looked up at Granny. Her eyes wide and moist, like a little girl done crying, but ready to do it again at a moment's notice. *When young women grieve*, thought Granny, *they cry like they did when they were little girls.*

"He's alive," Ashley said.

"Yes."

"But we can't get him back."

"And you wouldn't want him back. When the living is pulled across to the other side, it's too much for their minds to take. They ain't supposed to see what they see there. They go crazy. It's hard for you to hear this I know, but your husband ain't what he used to be. It happened differently to that little girl, but those that die in wretched agony lose their minds. They're crazy mad and you don't need me to tell you why they call them screaming spirits."

Granny watched her carefully for signs. This one, this young woman, had an anger streak in her. She saw her look down at her hands. *The young and the old alike did that*, she thought. When they were beat down and wanted to rise up, they looked down at their hands for strength. *Lord help me*, she thought, *if I ever look to my hands for strength. Every time I look at a piece of my skin I see another age spot.*

"Now let's talk about where you're off to tonight. The hour's coming closer. Tell me the story."

Ashley repeated everything Wendland had told her about the ghost box, the deal for the madstone, and the little she knew about Emile Chirac.

"I don't even know how Mr. Chirac knew about the madstone," Ashley said. "Unless Josh told him about that like he did the ghost box. I don't know what was in those papers Josh sold to him."

"Granny," Kenneth said, "this ain't a good night for her to be out and about. Maybe we should go with her."

"I can take care of myself," Ashley said.

"What Kenneth is trying to tell you is that it's a special night tonight. It's Halloween night, when the things of the dark is strong. They is strongest just at the touch of midnight, and that's when he asked you to come calling."

"Halloween's just another holiday," Ashley said. "I know the superstitions, but there's no such thing as Freddy Kruger or Jason."

Granny wrinkled her chin. Her memory was bad going to worse, but she had no idea of what the girl was saying. She turned to Kenneth for help.

"They's movie characters, ma'am," he explained. "In monster movies. You wouldn't like them at all."

"You'd be surprised, boy. I was around when the movies first was going. But I didn't come all this way to talk about movies. I came to get my madstone back and see to it returned to where it should be. Give that girl's crazy spirit peace. She's suffered more than any child should suffer."

Kenneth got up from his chair and rubbed his hands together.

"So we's going with her?"

"Sit down, boy. Looking up at you gives me a neck ache. And ain't nobody going with her. She got to do it all alone. Ain't that right, young lady?"

Granny saw the flash in the girl's eyes. She'd been right. Simmering right below the girls tears was a fire.

"I can take care of myself. I'm going to find out what this Chirac knows about the madstone and whatever contract Michael signed. This man's a business man. When I find out what I want to know, I'll tell him my husband is presumed dead and his contract isn't worth the paper it's written on. If he doesn't like it he can sue me. I'm tired of doing nothing while everyone else tells me what to do. It's time to take charge of this whole mess."

Granny stared at her, not saying a word. After a few moments, the young woman began to look less sure of herself. When she looked toward the curtains covering the window, the color drained from her face.

"That's right," Granny said. "The haint's still out there. You still so full of yourself? But I can help you with that. That's the easy part."

From out of her medicine bag, Granny withdrew a small bundle of sticks twined together to look like a little man. It hung on a length of cord like a necklace.

"What is that?" Ashley asked nervously.

"Don't matter what you call it. You just slide this over your neck and wear it wherever you go and you'll be safe from the haint tonight. Like I said, that's the easy part. You got to be stronger than you think. Before you go, you listen to what I'm going to tell you now and you'll know why."

Ashley looked over to Kenneth, who nodded reassuringly.

"Tell me," she said.

"Many years ago down in the hills, there was a man who came calling on all the granny women, one at a time. They called him the dark man. He was looking for a madstone, a very special madstone from a white deer and had hard cash to buy it. Now you don't know nothing about the ways of the granny women, young Mrs. Hillis, in fact not many do. That's because there ain't many left. In fact, far as I know, I'm the only one. But the fact is, no granny woman would ever sell any madstone. It's an evil thing to do, and would bring evil on the head of the woman who did such a thing.

"But this man, the dark man, he kept pushing. When they told him there wasn't such a thing as a madstone from a white deer, he would go away hotter than a coal pulled from a burning stove. Couple days later, the granny woman he left would be found dead. Every one of them."

Granny took a deep breath before she continued. She felt the room's dim light flicker and fade but knew it was in her mind. At that moment, she was back there again, a young girl who had just been given the madstone taken from the intestines of the white deer.

"There never was many granny women, you understand. The hills are lonely and the kind of doctoring you have nowadays wasn't nowhere to be found. Wasn't many towns to speak of in the hills. You could go a long time without seeing anybody except kin. Something bad happened like the murder of old healing women, though, the word would spread in its own way.

"One day, after my Daddy had been dead six or eight months, the dark man came to see my Momma. Boys out working the field and it was just me and my Momma in the house. When he came walking into the yard, she told me to run out the backdoor and hide under the porch so he wouldn't see me. I was scared, but I didn't ask no questions and I didn't sass her. She made me take the madstone with me and told me when I was under the porch to keep my eyes closed and never open them til she came for me."

The old woman's eyes clouded over. She felt, for the first time in a long stretch of years, her own urge to cry.

"What happened?" Ashley said.

"I kept my eyes closed like she told me until she came for me. She wouldn't tell me nothing at all except it was time for me to go stay with kin. Had my oldest brother take me away to my aunt and uncle's house. It won't help you if it I tell you how hard I cried. But that's what I did. I took what little things belonged to me and we was on our way. Me and my brother. I knew I'd never see my Momma again. I already had the sight, you see, and the madstone from that white deer."

"He killed her?" Ashley asked.

Granny swallowed slowly, like her throat was parched.

"Thirteen granny women dead that year," she said. "My Momma was one of them."

"I'm so sorry," Ashley said.

"He wasn't looking for just any madstone, child. He was looking for my madstone. He was asking everybody if they had the madstone from the white deer. We never heard another word about him. Never heard tell of him again. But the thing to figure is how he knew about my madstone. He was going to see granny women 'cause he thought they was all old. He wasn't looking for a young girl like me. Otherwise I'd be dead, too."

"Oh my God. How did he know about your madstone and who was he?"

Granny shook her head.

"I don't know how to answer that for you. But no one else has ever known about the white deer's madstone. Even when Becker came asking for help, he didn't know about the madstone from the white deer. One madstone was the same as any other to that boy. And I've had my share of madstones. They's part of a granny woman's medicines. And I never told nobody about it after my Momma give it to me because she made me promise on her life that I wouldn't. And now you done told me this man you're going to see was asking your husband—a man from the Hillis bloodline—can he get him the madstone from the white deer. Tell me again, child so full of herself, who is it you think you going to see?"

Chapter Thirty

Ashley felt the hair on the back of her neck pimple. She was suddenly filled with dread. Was it possible, was it really possible? Was the man she was going to see at midnight the same man who had killed Granny's mother and all those other old women? Suddenly her desire to leave the safety of the house vanished.

"You think it's the same man?"

"That's the question, ain't it?"

Ashley looked at Kenneth, who had been quiet through most of this.

"He'd be older than Granny—no offense, Granny. It ain't likely he's still around."

"I think this man collects antiques is all," Ashley said, trying to seem more confident than she was. "He's just a business man looking to turn a profit."

"How much closer can you get to the devil than a businessman?" Granny asked.

Ashley couldn't think of anything else to say.

"Granny," Kenneth said, "let me go with her."

"No," Ashley said.

"I've got a bad feeling about this," Kenneth said.

"No, I'm not having you go in with me like I can't take care of myself."

"I told you, Kenneth, she's going to do it herself."

"I could go with her and stay in the car," Kenneth said.

"And leave Granny here by herself? No. I'll do this myself, but I will take the stick thing, if that's okay."

Granny handed it over to her, and Ashley stared at it. It felt rough as wicker in her hands. How could something as small and simple as this protect her from the haint?

"How does it work?" she asked Granny.

"Never you mind. You pay attention to me now. When you meet this man at his house you remember three things for this old granny woman. You don't eat nothing while you there, you don't drink nothing while you there and you don't take anything he offers you. I mean anything. If you do that, you'll come home safe tonight. Now put that little man around your neck."

Ashley didn't argue with her. She slipped it around her neck.

"Now hide it beneath your shirt. We don't want this man to see it. And don't forget that you don't eat nothing, drink nothing or take anything he gives you."

"I won't forget."

"Good girl. Now give Granny a hug, get yourself ready and let Kenneth walk you out to your car. You taking one of those cellphone things with you?"

"Yes."

"Kenneth, you give her your number. Hurry it up. I got praying to do and I want to get to it."

Ashley made it to the bedroom door when she stopped, turned and walked right back to the old woman.

"Could your madstone bring Michael back?"

"If God don't bring a body back, they should stay dead. And you remember, child. That madstone is all there is to give that little girl's spirit peace."

«« — »»

Enid moved cautiously through the cool, wet weeds. The smell of long wheat grass filled his senses. The wind was resting and the Halloween moon lit the night with a pale gray light.

Rake was quicker, he knew. He'd be there to the edge of the Hillis property long before him. Been that way since he was a boy. He was fifteen years younger than Enid and better at this game. Like he was born to infiltrate. Smooth as silk and moved twice as soft. Enid was good, but he had to work hard at it. Nothing natural about what he did. He moved through the grass on his belly, crawling slowly and zigzagging as much as he could to avoid anyone spotting movement in a straight line.

He stopped often to scan the area with his sensors. In some ways, he wished he had Rake's natural approach. Looking for EMF and thermal variations wasn't as clear cut and sophisticated as it sounded. Once a man in his unit was shot through the neck while scanning an area with a thermal imaging device. Enid caught the blood spray. The lesson stayed with him. Don't get killed trying to be safe.

He did it the old way. All his equipment taped into place to keep the noise down. Never take your equipment off unless you were going to use it and tape it right back into place when you were through. Sleep with it if you had to. He wasn't obsessive, just careful. It was how he stayed alive all those years ago in Viet Nam.

But the field surrounding the Hillis property wasn't a war zone. Enid was just trying to find out what kind of security there was. It was important he do it in person, to look to see if there was something special. If Michael Hillis had the ghost box, no telling what he'd lined up to protect it.

The hooded digital readout on his EMF meter read normal. He scanned the area with thermal imaging, but saw nothing unusual. He sniffed the air. Nothing but the smell of dirt, wet weeds and the sweet smell of pine.

Not too much farther, he thought.

There were trees a quarter of a mile ahead that would give him a place to stand up and get the stiffness out of his joints. He was eighteen when he'd joined the army and got shipped to Viet Nam. He was a lot older than that now.

He remembered one of his instructors from Recondo telling him how you see better at night lying on your belly, looking close to the ground like it was a big secret. Enid grew up in the dark woods of Kentucky. He knew all about sneaking around in the dark. He didn't need anyone to tell him about how far scent carried. Deer spooked a hell of a lot quicker than the Viet Cong and they could pick up scents no hunter or soldier would even know was there.

Keep your mind on the job, Enid thought.

He was about to tape his equipment back into place when the reading on his EMF meter pegged, stayed that way for a few seconds, then returned to normal.

What the hell was that? Sensor sweep coming back at him?

Not good, whatever it was.

"You catch that?" he whispered into his lapel microphone.

"Quiet like death here," answered Rake into his earbud.

"You pick up any random sweeps?"

"Nope, just waiting for you to get here."

"There was something. Quick reading on the EMF, then it was over. Place may have some fancy new stuff we ain't seen before. You be careful, brother."

Some kind of pulse detection technology? Shit they came out with so much new stuff now days, there wasn't any way to keep up with it unless you had a team of technical experts keeping you informed. Like Michael Hillis maybe. Enid had mostly been worried about trained dogs. A pair of Dobermans was a recon man's worst nightmare. But Hillis owned a technology company with a bunch of scientists working for him. Defense contractor, too. Probably had access to all sorts of stuff Enid never heard of. Viet Nam was a long time ago. Things had changed since then.

No sense over-thinking it, though. Only question was whether to call Rake back or join him.

He started crawling forward.

The Hillis fence was not far beyond the stand of trees. A heavy-duty metal thing with spear shaft points rowed along the top, like they did in some cemeteries. The main gate was a couple hundred yards to the north of where he and Rake were planning on setting up surveillance.

Had to keep going, had to do this. He hadn't told Ian about the call he'd gotten from the boys back in Kentucky. Strange sounds coming from below ground. Like giant machinery moving around. Something happening down there. He wished Bartok were still alive.

He was ten feet from the trees when he heard Rake's voice in his ear.

"How far you away?"

"Just coming up to the trees," he whispered back.

"Well you ain't going to believe this, but I just saw two people come out of the house. One was a woman. She got in a car and drove away. The other was a man who walked her out and turned around and went back in."

"Could you make out the man? Was he armed?"

"Not armed. And I could see him plain under the porch light. It was Kenneth Hillis."

Enid stopped mid-crawl.

"Who?"

"You heard me. I'd know that boy anywhere. Almost tore my arm off once over a damned pig."

"What in the hell is he doing here?"

"Don't know, Enid, but where he is, Granny Hillis can't be too far away. They's joined at the hip."

"Son of a bitch. I'll be there 'fore too long."

This thing just couldn't stay still. Hunter figured it right. There was something they was missing or that old woman and Kenneth wouldn't be here.

He made it to the trees and was about to get to his feet when Rake came back at him.

"Enid?"

"I'm here."

"There's a little girl standing right in front of me. Came from nowhere."

Enid felt a coldness settle over his heart. He remembered what Ian had seen in the parking lot.

"You get out of there, Rake. Just get out of there as fast as you can."

"What you doing out by yourself, honey," Rake said. "You shouldn't be out here alone."

"Run for it, Rake."

"Where do you live? Does your mommy and daddy know you're out here all by yourself?"

Before Enid could voice another warning, he heard Rake screaming.

««—»»

Enid was on his feet, running through the trees as fast as he could.

"Rake? Rake? Can you hear me, boy?"

Nothing but static so loud he tore the earbud from his ear as he ran. He pumped his arms hard. Fear gripped like he'd never felt before. He gulped in the cool night air til his lungs hurt. Up ahead, near the Hillis fence line, he saw a fire burning.

"Rake," he yelled.

He had his pistol out and the safety off. Running harder than he knew he could at his age.

When he got to the smoldering remains of his brother, Enid dropped to his knees. Too late. He was too late. Rake was dead, The skin had melted right off his face and left behind only a blackened skull. They should have listened to Hunter. This would never have happened if they'd listened to Hunter.

Behind him, he heard a little girl's hesitant laughter. He brought his pistol up, thought better of it and ran straight toward the fence. Grabbed the metal and pulled himself up. Heard a shriek from behind him and worked harder, trying to get traction with the edges of his boots to help him get to the top.

He slipped, but pulled himself up again. Looking straight at the porch light as he got to the top and heaved himself over. A spike tip cut into his bicep and he felt the flesh rip. No time. His pant leg caught on another spike and he heard the fabric tear as the sharp point cut through the skin on his shin. Felt it scrape against the bone as he went over.

He landed on the ground hard, knocking the wind out of him, but he rolled forward and up to his feet. His leg screamed with pain but he kept moving. He made it inside the cone of porch light and up onto the porch before he looked back. He saw the little girl standing beyond the black metal fence.

He raised his hand to pound on the door, but it opened at that exact moment.

Kenneth Hillis stood just inside the door.

Before Enid could say a word, Kenneth barreled into him, knocking him down onto the bricks. He was on him, pinning his arms down with his knees. Enid felt the pain flash through his wounded bicep. His vision blurred from the impact of being thrown down onto the porch.

Kenneth's arm cranked back to hit him in the face.

"For God's sake, Kenneth," he yelled, "it's me, Enid Mozer. There's something coming fast behind me and we need to get inside."

A confused Kenneth Hillis lowered his arm.

"Take that mask off," he said, "so I can make sure."

"I could do that," Enid said, "if you'd get off my damn arms. And we got to get inside quick."

A look of grim amazement stole across Kenneth's face.

"She ain't coming past the property fence. Granny done seen to that."

Chapter Thirty-One

Ashley pressed the button inset into the richly decorated brass plaque and waited. Unconsciously she reached up, touched her shirt and felt the reassuring presence of the bundle of twined twigs that hung around her neck.

On the drive through the city, she'd passed groups of trick-or-treaters going from house to house. The youngest were dressed in movie-themed monster costumes and walking with their parents. The older they got, the less they dressed up. Teenagers were on the streets carrying bags, like bank robbers without masks. Lights were out on a lot of the houses. Seniors huddled inside, hiding in the suffocating dark, waiting for the hour to pass.

But Mr. Chirac's neighborhood was different. There were no innocent children on the streets, no threatening mobs of teenagers; in fact, she had seen no one at all in this well-tended neighborhood. A vacant silence seemed to thin the air. There were no cars on the street and no litter. The lamps that lined the side street that led to his home looked to be lit by real gas flames that danced bright yellow-white inside etched crystal globes.

She was glad the man named Ricci had given her directions over the phone when she first called for Mr. Chirac. 1412 Blood Road wasn't listed on Mapquest and her GPS had never heard of it. But she made it on time. A few minutes early, in fact. Even after missing the side road twice.

Kind of creepy, she thought, *to live on Blood Road.*

But with all that had happened since the night in Sharkey's Park, she wondered if being creeped out would become a permanent condition. Her dreams about Michael were so vivid, so terrifying that she thought she would never get a good night sleep again until they stopped. And standing alone on the stoop, she worried that his great grandmother Granny Hillis had fallen over the edge of eccentric and landed in the canyon of crazy.

The nights had moved so quickly that Ashley hadn't kept on her anti-anxiety medication or her antidepressants. Her nerves were so overloaded she could feel them burning beneath her skin. In the morning she would call Dr. Geitner and ask him again for the name of the therapist he gave her while she was in the hospital. People under stress imagined things or, saying it right out straight with no Oprah elements, maybe even hallucinated. No, not people. Maybe she, Ashley Hillis, was going out of her mind. It was okay to write paranormal romance novels. There was a big market for it and she was starting to get a following. But haints?

The door opened and she stepped back.

In the opening, against the soft yellow backlight of an elegantly appointed vestibule, she saw the outline a bulky man with shoulders nearly as wide as the doorframe. Without thinking, she took a step back.

"Mr. Chirac?" she asked.

"No."

As the man moved aside, she caught a glimpse of a zigzag scar that cut from his cheekbone to his chin. His bald head glistened in the vestibule light as though oiled. Even when he turned completely sideways, there was hardly room for her to pass. His light brown jacket was stretched tight across a weightlifters chest. The single button that held the two sides of the jacket together seemed in danger of snapping loose at any moment.

"Are you Ricci?"

"Yes."

"I'm here to see Mr. Chirac."

"You got to come inside if you want to do that. He's expecting you."

Ashley took a tentative step forward and then stopped.

Realizing that his bulk so close to the doorway made her uncomfortable, he turned and moved to let her in.

"Thank you," she said.

"Take off your shoes and close the door," he replied.

She pushed it closed. He was already walking down the hallway.

"Follow me," he said over his shoulder.

As she followed Ricci's bulging shoulders down the champagne carpeted hallway, she could not help but glance up occasionally at the chandelier-like light fixtures that had the delicate look of suspended ice crystals arranged in a circular halo of soft pink light. In the center of a spacious living room that opened off to one side of the hallway, Ashley saw a glossy black piano so polished she could see a curved image of herself move across its side as she went by.

"I can't hear myself walk," she said.

"It's quality carpet," said Ricci without looking over his shoulder.

"What a wonderful art collection," Ashley said as they passed gild framed paintings along the wall. It was like walking through a museum after closing hours.

"Yeah," said Ricci.

Two large dark wooden doors bracketed by a frame of rose-colored marble stood like the doors to a French monarch's palace at the end of the hallway. Ricci turned to face her.

"He's in here," he said.

Ashley was so close behind him that she stopped only six inches from his chest.

"What's he like?" she asked nervously.

"Don't swear around him."

"Pardon?"

Ricci looked at his watch.

"He don't like women that swear," he said. "And quit chewing your lip."

"Why?" Ashley asked.

"I don't like him seeing blood," said Ricci.

«« — »»

"Come in" Mr. Chirac stood and motioned her into the room with a graceful arc of his left hand.

Ashley took three steps forward, but when she saw Mr. Chirac she stopped.

"Please come in," urged Mr. Chirac. He smiled a thin but warm little smile and continued, "Forgive me that I still wear formal clothing, dear lady, but there was a private exhibit of Titanic relics that I simply could not miss. But it is you that are important. I must say, Ricci, that your friend is the most beautiful woman ever to grace my home with her presence."

Ashley reached up to the button between her breasts and made sure that it was fastened. Ricci moved to stand by the wall next to the door, like a soldier guarding the entrance.

"I apologize for staring, but I thought you were much… older."

He reminded her of Errol Flynn.

"I take no offense. I have been anxious to meet you. When my friend Ricci said you had called I was immediately anxious to be of service. He implied that you wished to discuss your husband's arrangement with me," and here he waved his hand in a mysterious sigil, "and please accept my sincere sympathies for your situation."

Mr. Chirac seemed to study her. Ashley followed his appraising stare as he took in her white hair. His dark, attentive eyes followed the fine lines of her neck. She stiffened when he noted the way that her breasts pulled tight the fabric of her shirt. He nodded approval as he discreetly followed the inward curve of her waist, the outward flare of her hips, and then looked down to stare at her feet.

He did not look up for what seemed like a decidedly long moment.

"Ricci asked me to take off my shoes," she said self-consciously.

"Then I shall, too," Mr. Chirac offered with a smile, and he did it right then, sliding his stocking feet out of a pair of patent leather so lustrous that Ashley could see the vague outline of her face in them.

Despite the mild temperature, Ashley felt herself beginning to feel uncomfortably warm.

"You have a beautiful home," she said.

He stepped across the room to stand directly in front of her. He smelled of crushed chamomile. Even with his shoes off, he was a half a foot taller than her. With him standing so close, she had to look up to see his eyes, which were as shiny as fresh paint.

"You grace it with your beauty," he said in a voice low and menacing and so seductive she felt slightly dizzy.

"May I sit down?" Ashley asked. "It's been difficult since my husband went missing and I tire easily."

"Come with me," said Mr. Chirac as he slid his hand behind her and held it against the small of her back.

He walked her to a couch draped in green and gold imbued with such vibrant depth of color that Ashley thought no one had ever before sat on it.

"Sit, please" Mr. Chirac said.

"Thank you," she said, but did not move.

"I am so pleased that you have come," he said, and moved forward so close to her she almost fell back onto the couch cushions.

"I'll sit now," she said in a strangled voice.

"Would you like some wine?" Mr. Chirac asked as he moved away toward a brass and burgundy leather bar.

"No thank you. I'm on medication."

Mr. Chirac poured himself a glass of wine from a bottle made of amber colored glass. With a graceful flourish, he held the wine glass just under his nose, grasping it by the stem so as not to affect the temperature of the remarkable vintage, and sniffed it as though it were the heart of beautiful but fragile flower.

Ashley watched the process play out as though she were watching an old movie. A wealthy man, attired in a tuxedo that had been tailored just for his slim physique, stands in the study of his mansion and sips expensive wine before turning to aid the beautiful young woman who has come to him for assistance. It really did seem very much like a movie.

"In the evening, I find that it relaxes me," Mr. Chirac said. "A relaxed man is a man who does not make awkward judgments. So, one glass of wine each evening—never two.

"However," he said with a nod in her direction as he walked over and sat in a leather chair opposite her, "to your situation. Tell me please what it is you wish to know."

Ashley crossed her hands in her lap just as Mr. Chirac was languidly crossing his legs. She felt unbalanced, disconnected. Listening to Granny Hillis had disoriented her. This Mr. Chirac was nothing more than a wealthy businessman. That much was clear from his home. There was nothing for her to be afraid of, so she took a deep breath and began.

"Our lawyer, Mr. Henry Wendland told me that you and Michael had a contract regarding an exchange."

"Ah yes," said Mr. Chirac and shook his head slightly. "Such a tragedy."

"I'm sorry?"

"His death. He confided in me that a heart attack was his greatest fear. When Ricci informed that he died a short while ago when his auto ran off the road, upended into a ravine and burst into flames, I was appalled."

Ashley felt shock as she remembered Granny Hillis telling her that the haint would deal with Wendland. But it was hard to believe. Alive and then dead.

"I hadn't heard," she said.

"He's dead," Ricci confirmed.

"Are you sure you wouldn't like some wine?" murmured Chirac.

"I—no. No, thank you."

"Perhaps something to eat to settle your nerves?"

"No. Thanks. I'm fine. I'm just having a hard time with so much unexpected death."

"So, just so. May I return to your question, then? Good. I am a dealer in rare artifacts, in particular those having to deal with … mystical attributes or legends. I apologize for the unintentional vagary, Mrs. Hillis, but English is not my first language. There are times when I struggle to convey my meaning properly. If you will allow, I can perhaps show you more easily than explain my profession."

He rose from the chair easily, then walked toward a glossy black credenza. Over his shoulder, he said to Ricci, "Please bring Lily to join us."

"I'd rather this be private," Ashley said.

"Lily was a witness to the agreement between your husband and I."

Before Ashley could object further, Ricci left the room, leaving the door slightly ajar.

She looked back at Mr. Chirac and saw him advancing toward her, carrying by its handles what looked to be an ornate brass serving tray the size and shape of a dinner plate. From beneath it extended a tiered stem base. Tiny gold bells were suspended from around the edges of the tray by strips of black velvet. Theytintinnabulated as though to warn of the man's approach.

"This," said Mr. Chirac as he set the object in the middle of the coffee table that stood between them, "is a Laotian phaa khwan."

"I'm sorry, what did you call it?"

"A phaa khwan. For many centuries," said Mr. Chirac, "this phaa khwan never left what is now known as Laos. The personal servants of the Laotian high priest guarded it because it was the only phaa khwan ever formed by the hands of a spirit. Khwan means spirit, and phaa means 'you see again.' Phaa khwan may therefore be translated as 'with this spirit you will see again.'"

Feeling drawn to inquire, Ashley asked, "What was it for?"

"When," he said, "a priest was possessed by a khwan, he became that spirit. Do you comprehend this, my dear? A priest taken over by a spirit made this phaa khwan. Hence the legend that it was 'formed by the hands of a spirit' is quite literally true."

From the breast pocket of his suit jacket, Mr. Chirac withdrew a folded piece of parchment paper that he laid on the phaa khwan. It unfolded partially, exposing gold writing in an elegant scrawl.

"But you asked, did you not, what it is for. Are you familiar with the kuji-kiri employed by certain Japanese cults?"

"No," Ashley said.

"The kuji-kiri," Mr. Chirac said, "is the mystical art of writing an intention on parchment, then disposing of that document in a way that brings that intention forth into reality. Sometimes it is floated down a stream that flows through a place of power. The Laotian priests burned it in a phaa khwan."

He reached down, and from somewhere beneath the table conjured a gold lighter. A cast-silver wolf's head on its front was set in relief against a circle of black opal. With a flick of his thumb, a yellow-blue flame jumped to life. His eyes locked on hers, and he spoke with a mesmerizing intensity.

"You see, do you not, the writing on this piece of parchment? Ancient legends have it that whatever it is I have written will come to be if I light it and allow its ashes to burn in the phaa khwan."

Despite herself, Ashley gulped.

"Such things are rarely revealed in a public school education, but in the esoteric mysteries, this knowledge is highly prized."

He closed the lighter, picked up the phaa kwan gently and returned it to the black credenza. When he had done so, he returned to his divan, but did not sit.

"Most would ask what was written on the parchment," he observed. "Yet you did not. The quality of reserve is much to be admired in a woman. Forgive my impudent question, but why did you not inquire?"

"Honestly, I was afraid. I don't know why. The stress of so much happening so quickly."

"So, just so," Mr. Chirac said.

Chirac was nothing like she expected. She wasn't prepared for this. Damn Granny Hillis and her superstitions. A glass of wine really would calm her nerves. She needed that. But she could not get the old woman's warning out of her mind.

"Mr. Wendland Michael said wanted something from you called a ghost box. Can you explain to me what that is? Is it another of your magical antiques?"

Mr. Chirac smiled, revealing a row of small white teeth.

"Magical antiques? What a lovely phrasing, Mrs. Hillis. Lovely indeed. It does, however, in certain respects fall short in describing the ghost box. The device itself is reported to be a fusion of different world views. It unites superstition and technology by means which, it is said by some, none shall ever understand. It is this concept which I believe fascinated your husband almost to the point of obsession. The very idea that a machine could link the world of the living with that of the dead ignited his imaginative faculties."

Ashley was about to ask another question, when, from behind her, she heard a low growl. Slowly, carefully, she turned to see a massive black panther held back only by Ricci, a thick metal cable, and silver rod structure caged around its neck. Its ears lay back as it snarled. The sight of its terrible teeth terrified her. Its yellow eyes were pools of animal hatred.

She screamed, leapt off the couch and ran straight into Mr. Chirac, who grabbed her firmly by the shoulders and said, "There's nothing to be afraid of, my dear. Lily is quite harmless to those who please me."

181

Chapter Thirty-Two

His face was so close to hers she could hardly breathe. Her body trembled and without his powerful hands holding her up by the shoulders, she would have collapsed to the floor.

"I am a man who keeps his agreements," said Chirac. "Your husband had an agreement with me and, since he has disappeared, that agreement, that contract, falls to you. In your heart you know where your husband is—suspended between life and death. Trapped for eternity at the mercy of spirits whose hunger may never be satiated. With the ghost box, you can bring him back. Save him from eternal torment. Only you can do that, Mrs. Hillis, only you. I desire the madstone for private reasons, and if you deliver it to me, then I will give you the ghost box and you may save your husband's very life with it and return him to yourself unharmed."

Ashley struggled to get away. He laughed at her efforts and then released her without explanation.

"You—you're crazy," she said. "I'll get a lawyer, I'll go to the police. You can't get away with this."

Ricci had chained Lily to the rose colored obelisk and freed her from the mechanical structure that prevented her from turning on him. Chirac gestured toward the sleek black cat.

"Are you listening, Lily? Should I be afraid of the civilized restraints of a courtroom or its enforcement personnel?"

In that moment Ashley realized that it was Mr. Chirac who was the focus of the panther's anger. She felt sick with fear and wanted to bolt from the room as quickly as she could. The sense of impending doom pressed down on her like a heavy weight.

"This is crazy," she said. "I don't know where your madstone is."

Mr. Chirac held up three fingers on his right hand, but her attention was drawn to the ring on that hand with a jewel the color of thin blood.

"Three days, my dear. You have three days to deliver to me the madstone. Do you not miss your dear husband? Would you not like to hold him in your arms again? To caress his cheek and kiss him deeply?"

"Stop it, stop it," Ashley cried.

"All this can be yours for a simple stone. A rock wrapped in superstition that is of no use to you. What I offer in return will restore Michael's life to your bosom."

"You can't promise that," she said, backing up toward the door.

"Oh, but I can," Mr. Chirac said. "I have personal experience with this device. But it is aged and has only enough power to perform one more miracle before it is completely drained. It will then be of no more use to your lost husband than a grandfather clock. But you have three days before I sell it to another client who is already quite interested and then you will lose your chance forever."

"You wouldn't do that."

The tremor in her voice betrayed her anguish.

"But I would. And at that point, I would with no regrets, assume ownership of what your husband so nobly pledged as his guarantee. You seem surprised my dear, but should you be? Your husband had a rather feckless reputation, so I stipulated that he turn over his most important asset to me should he fail."

Ashley took another step backward toward the door.

"I'm not bound by that. I've never even seen the document."

"Oh, but you are," said Mr. Chirac.

"I told you, I don't know where this … this madstone is."

"Then find it," he said, "while there is still time to save your husband. Ricci will now follow you out. Time is precious, Mrs. Hillis, and once gone it may never be reclaimed."

Before she could answer, Ricci's bulk was at her side, edging her out of the room. Still in shock, she allowed herself to be moved along. But at the door, she suddenly whirled and faced Mr. Chirac, who sat casually on the edge of his divan.

"And you're not getting our house. I don't care what you signed. Or his company."

As Ricci crowded her into the hallway, she heard Mr. Chirac call out, "It wasn't your house or his company that he pledged, my dear. It was you."

The horror of his last words stole her voice. She watched mute while the door closed as though pushed shut by an invisible hand.

"Time to go," Ricci said.

«« — »»

She couldn't remember getting in the car, but she was driving with her hands gripping the steering wheel so hard they hurt. She couldn't loosen her grip.

"I'm not property," she cried. "I'm not property."

He was the most evil man she had ever met in her life. After the first three blocks she had to get control of herself before she ran off the road and into a tree. She was taking the corners too fast, cutting the wheel too hard, trying to put as much distance between Mr. Chirac and herself as she could. Within ten minutes she was so lost she had to get out her GPS and have it direct her home.

A thin drizzle of rain was coming down. The roads were slick and shiny as freshly poured tar. The buildings she passed were indistinct. All she could concentrate on were Chirac's words.

It wasn't your house or his company that he pledged, my dear. It was you.

It couldn't be true. Michael would never have signed such a document. Never. He loved her. She loved him.

How could this all have happened? She'd asked herself this question over and over again since that night in Sharkey's Park. Everything was perfect. Their life was perfect together. Then this. Damn Michael and his ghosts. But it was how they'd met. She remembered his face that night at the Ghost Hunting 101 meeting they'd both attended. He was the most handsome man she'd ever seen up close. They were married within a month and she was never so happy in her whole life. She stayed home and wrote. He went to work on his inventions, doing wonderful, interesting things. When they were together, they told each other everything they'd been working on, how much they missed each other, how one day they would travel the world after Michael's technology and his company were bought out. They would visit far away fascinating places, follow the trail of the Templar mystery and visit Stonehenge. All her dreams gone that one terrifying night.

How could Michael do business with a man like Mr. Chirac? And why didn't he tell her? They had an open, honest relationship. At least that was what she thought.

The GPS guided her onto the freeway entrance ramp. She eased into traffic, terrified of the oncoming cars whose coned white headlamps came at her like interrogators shining the lights on her guilt.

Could what Granny Hillis told her be true? Did she really not know what type of man her own husband was?

«« — »»

Enid took the call on his cell while Granny Hillis finished bandaging his wounded arm. The smell of her poultice was like the stale earth beneath a freshly turned log. Kenneth leaned back on the chair across from at the kitchen table, balanced on two legs and watching the proceedings carefully.

"Watch what you say," he warned Enid.

"It's Tyree," he said.

Then, into the phone, "What's up, brother?"

"We got problems here," Tyree said.

"Talk to me."

"We got some kind of glowing green gas came out of the ground after all them noises we heard. Killed all the plants and trees for about fifty feet. Me and Johnny cleared out when we saw it coming out. It's mostly disappeared now, but we ain't going any closer. Them electronic ears and detectors Mr. Bartok had us install a couple of years back ain't working worth a shit now. All we can hear is bullshit static."

"Don't listen to it," Enid said. "We don't know what that kind of noise can do to you. Just keep recording it so we can look at it on the computer without listening to it."

Silence on the other end of the line for a moment.

"Never thought of that. Shit. Wish you was here, brother."

"Me, too."

"How's you and Rake making out?"

Enid looked at Granny, who'd finished dressing his wound and was sitting to his right at the table looking at him with eyes like a bird looking at a worm.

"Rake's dead, Tyree."

"Can't be true."

"It is."

"How'd it happen?"

"Got blindsided, brother."

"That Hunter do it?"

"Nope. He's with us."

"Bartok?"

"Bartok's dead, too."

"Shit. What's going on up there?"

"A lot."

"What do I tell his wife and kids? This is going to kill them."

Enid looked down at the surface of the glass table. He could see his haggard reflection staring back at him. Felt the eyes of Granny and Kenneth on him. An awful grief welled up inside him like black water rising in a well.

"I'll tell her when I get back. She'll want to know what happened and I need to tell her face to face. Ain't nothing I'd rather not do."

"Enid?"

"Yeah?"

"What if you don't come back?"

《《—》》

"Who the hell is he?" demanded Ashley.

She'd come back home in a trance, exhausted and cried out to find Granny Hillis, Kenneth and a strange man with a bloody bandage taped to his upper arm sitting at her kitchen table.

"He's a friend, come to help," said Granny. "Isn't that right?"

The man nodded.

"Yes, ma'am. Name's Enid. Enid Mozer. From Kentucky."

"You look terrible, Mrs. Hillis," Kenneth said. "Are you all right?"

"No, I'm not all right," she snapped. "Granny was right. He was a horrible man. That Ricci looked like a big convict and he brought a panther into the room. A panther, a real panther. He said it was a witness to the agreement between Michael and him. I feel like I'm losing my mind. Granny, you've got to help me. He said if I don't get the madstone to him in three days he'll sell the ghost box to another client and he'll claim me as his property." She waved her hands wildly as she spoke. Her hair was wet and hung limp. Red flushed her cheeks and she started crying again.

"He said you'd be his property?" Kenneth said, getting out of the chair.

"Wait a minute," Enid said. "Did you say ghost box?"

"That's what I said. Don't ask me what it is, but he says it can bring Michael back unharmed."

"You're sure he said ghost box."

"How many times do I have to repeat myself?"

"I'll break his neck," Kenneth said.

"Thank you, Kenneth," she said. "Granny, you've got to help me sleep. I need sleep. I can't function like this. I've always been on a schedule. Always. I can't have those dreams again. I can't. I just can't. And that terrible policeman and an idiot ghost hunter are coming to question me tomorrow. I'll take my pills so I can sleep, but you have to save me from my dreams."

Granny stood up and went to her.

Ashley wrapped her arms around the little woman and held her close, sobbing.

"There, there, child. Granny will keep those dreams away and Kenneth and Enid will keep you safe. Don't you worry about that policeman and the other. The boys will send them on their way."

"Uh, Granny," Enid said.

"What is it?" she said impatiently.

"That idiot ghost hunter is a friend, too."

Chapter Thirty-Three

At six thirty in the morning, Ian got a call from Enid. He was fully dressed lying underneath the blankets, with the cell phone only inches from his face.

"Hello?" he said. His words were thick as sludge.

"Get the shit out of your mouth and wake up."

"You want me to come get you?"

"Not exactly."

"Is everything all right?"

"Not exactly. Rake's dead and I'm inside the Hunter house with Michael's wife, his great grandmother, and Kenneth Hillis."

Ian sat straight up in bed.

"What the hell happened?"

"The haint got Rake and it was after me, too, so I hightailed it to the Hillis house."

"The haint?"

"That little girl's ghost. Burned him alive. Ain't seen nothing like it since Vietnam."

"I'm so sorry, Enid."

"Me too."

Ian rubbed his eyes, threw the covers off and got out of bed. Flipping through the pile of clothes on the dresser until he found what he needed in the way of clean ones.

"Tell me what to do."

"Just come on over with that policeman like you were planning to do anyways. We got some problems I can't see my way through, and I need that brain of yours. We got friends here, but they got serious issues tied in with yours. So you need to hear it straight from them."

"I should ditch the policeman," he said.

"No. Granny says bring him along and she'll say what we tell him."

"We're going to leave this up to someone named Granny?"

"She's got the sight, Ian. She can see a man's soul like we see their face."

"I'm going to shower and drink coffee. This is too weird for my head without caffeine."

Bartok was dead. Rake was dead. Everything was out of control. He had to do something. So far he'd only reacted. He was going to have to change that.

«« — »»

Alvarez was already over the line and he knew it.

He'd been taking personal time to dig into the Hillis case. Running it close, using the databases and some tech time, but nothing that would hang him. Today was different. Today he was taking Ian Hunter, Michigan's own paranormal investigator in to talk to Ashley Hillis. He'd pressured her into it. He hadn't told her about Wendland's death and she hadn't asked. That would provide him a little cover with the Captain, but not much.

And he could try to say that he was baiting her with the paranormal investigator, trying one last time to get something out of her she might have forgotten because Wendland burning to death in a car accident was just too coincidental for him. But the Captain wouldn't buy it. The potential Wendland connection maybe, but not the paranormal investigator.

He should be digging up leads on the Lincoln Jones case, but he already knew who'd killed Jones. And Wendland, too, for that matter. And maybe all those people in Sharkey's Park. But he was keeping that to himself. If he told anyone in the department that he thought the murderer was a little girl's ghost, well, it would be all over for him. He wouldn't blame them, either.

The thing he couldn't figure out was, what the hell happened to Michael Hillis. And for that matter, Becker Hillis the last time the murders occurred in Sharkey's Park. The little girl was the link, but he couldn't understand why, for example, Michael Hillis would buy Sharkey's Park and the surrounding property then dig the little girl's bones up. What the hell did that accomplish? Probably started the whole mess all over again. And if he was supposed to be mister amateur ghost hunter, shouldn't he have known that?

More questions to ask and not answer, but he pressed his foot on the brake pedal as he came up to the black iron gates of the Hillis property. The gates were wide open. He looked for Hunter's car, thought he saw it parked in front of the Hillis house so he drove through the opening and down the long concrete driveway leading to the house. The spiked fence reminded him of an urban prison.

The fact that Hunter didn't follow through and wait for him at the gate pissed him off. They were supposed to go in together. In fact, he wanted to do it that way specifically to control the spin. Things could be out of control already.

By the time he parked his car and knocked on the door, he was borderline furious. Amateurs were like that, though. You couldn't count on them to follow the plan. They liked to make things up as they went alone. On the other hand, Hunter was right on the money about what to do if he saw the little girl in his dreams. No excuse for going in without him, but at least Alvarez got his first good night's sleep since the whole thing started.

A hard looking man with sunken eyes opened the door. Thick gray-black hair cut military style. Wearing a black t-shirt. Bandage wrapped around one bicep.

"Come on in," he said. "We're all in the living room."

"What happened to your arm?"

"Jumped the wrong fence," the man said with a southern accent as strong as white lightning.

"Uh-huh," Alvarez said. "How many is we?"

"Count 'em yourself," the man said.

"I asked you a question."

"I'm too damned tired to be impressed."

"And I'm a homicide detective. Answer the question."

"I know who you are. I just lost my brother last night, Detective. I'm going into the living room to sit down. So if you're done acting like a hardass, just follow me and we can all talk together."

Without another word, the man walked down the hallway.

《《—》》

"Hunter, what the hell is going on here?"

He'd followed the big country man into the living room where Hunter, Ashley and another big man wearing faded jeans and a black and green flannel shirt were standing. Hunter was looking a little the worse for wear, like he was running on too little sleep. Ashley Hillis had the same look, and the skin around her eyes was puffy and red from crying.

"Not what you're thinking, Detective."

"You don't know what the hell I'm thinking. So I repeat—what the hell is going on here? We were supposed to meet out front at the gate, and then come in together. When we have a plan, I'd like to know that you can stick to it. Am I clear on this? I didn't plan on having two total strangers in our conversations."

Hunter looked at the others, then back at Alvarez.

"There wasn't time," he said.

Before Alvarez could straighten him out on how easy it was to pick up a phone, a tiny older woman with thin gray hair tied behind her in a braid came into the room. She wore a blue flowered dress and although she looked just south of one hundred, her back was straight and she held her head high.

"Okay," he said, "this is too much. Hunter, I want to talk to you outside."

"You must be the detective," the old woman said.

"Yes, ma'am, I am, but—"

"I was wondering if you would have tea with me in the kitchen before you talked with everyone."

"Not just now," Alvarez said, trying to keep his anger in check. "I'm going to talk with Mr. Hunter first."

But Hunter didn't move. Instead, he looked to the old woman for reassurance.

"Hunter, are you coming?"

"You really should sit down with me first in the kitchen," the old woman said. "I have things to tell you before you talk to these young people."

Alvarez couldn't take it any longer.

"Ma'am, this is a homicide investigation and I'll decide who I talk to and when."

"My name is Granny Hillis, and I'm afraid I'm the one that started this all."

Her eyes were gray-blue and slightly cloudy. She spoke with a tobacco-roughed voice. Alvarez wondered for a moment if she was crazy.

"Okay. You win" he said finally. "I'll talk to you first. The rest of you, don't leave this room until I tell you to."

«« — »»

"So what's this all about, ma'am?"

Granny arranged two silver trimmed cups and saucers carefully in front of her after sitting down on one side of a small wooden table. She lifted a small teapot from a ceramic square, then filled each cup in turn with a dark red liquid that filled the air with the scent of peppermint.

"It's good for your digestion," she said. "Go on, go on, sit down. It's poor manners to stand when an old woman invites you to sit down."

Alvarez reluctantly pulled out a chair and sat across from her.

"I'd like to have tea with you, ma'am, but the rule is we don't drink anything offered at the homes of people we're investigating."

She lifted her cup and inhaled the aroma.

"You got to do more than drink a tea," she said. "You got to let it fill the room around you so you can breathe it in."

"I didn't know that, ma'am."

"You may call me Granny. What do I call you?"

"Detective Alvarez."

"All right, well will you tell this old woman why you won't drink tea at the home of a person you're looking to investigate?"

Alvarez looked embarrassed.

"Because they might add something to it. Not like you people, you understand, it's just some of the hard cases don't have much class. Like once a partner of mine, he had a suspect urinate in his coffee before he gave it to him. You should have seen his face when my partner switched cups on him. Things like that is what I'm talking about, ma'am. So we don't drink things at people's places. If you see what I mean."

"Do you want to switch cups, Detective Alvarez?"

"No, ma'am. I guess I can have tea with you. I'm just kind of unhappy that Mr. Hunter changed plans on me, that's all. I don't like surprises."

He stared at her hands as she slowly pushed the other cup and saucer to him. The knuckles were thick and shiny. Age spots covered her hand like dark, ugly freckles.

"I got the arthritis," she said. "Sister told me it's calcium like they got in milk building up and getting real hard like rock. You imagine that? Milk's supposed to build our bones, not ruin them."

"I'm sorry to hear that. I have an aunt who's got it bad, too."

In all his years in police work, Alvarez had never drank anything, not even water, at a suspect's house. But there was something about the old woman that caused him to trust her.

"Before I tell you the reason I asked you to sit with me and talk, may I look at your hand?"

"I'm sorry?"

"Give me your hand, Detective."

Without knowing quite why he did it, Alvarez extended his right hand to her, palm up.

"The left, if you please."

When she had hold of his left hand, she leaned forward and peered at it closely. He felt ridiculous, and looked around at the kitchen cabinet in embarrassment.

"You trying to read my future?"

She looked at him curiously and said, "What a peculiar idea. Truth is, I'm a very old woman and I don't get to hold hands with enough younger men."

After a moment's shocked silence, Alvarez began to laugh.

"That's the reason I invited you to tea with me, Detective—to hear you laugh."

The old woman released his hand slowly, and then took a sip of tea. Alvarez could not figure her out. She was a few cents short of a bank loan, but, so far, he liked her.

"You see," she said, "I believe that after I tell you what's happened, today will be the last day of your life that you ever laugh."

Alvarez looked down at his tea with an uneasy feeling.

"There ain't nothing there but fine quality tea. Hill people call it sun tea. I been making it and drinking it since I was a little girl and it's done right by me. No, I ain't poisoned you. What I am trying to tell you in my own fool way is that soon you'll be in the arms of your dear wife again. It's important you know that."

His field of vision narrowed and all he could see was the old woman's face. As though he were lying in his coffin and she'd leaned over to say her regrets.

"Ma'am, my wife's been dead a lot of years now."

A sad, wistful look came across her face. She reached across and took his hand again and held it while she spoke.

"I know that, Detective. I am so very sorry to tell you that you will not live through this coming night and neither will I."

Alvarez felt himself go cold.

Chapter Thirty-Four

"You can't know that," Alvarez said. "Nobody knows things like that."

"I know what the good Lord gives me to know. It ain't easy telling you this. If there was any other way I wouldn't tell you what's coming. But you're the only one can save that little girl before she kills anyone else."

He'd been just on the verge of getting out of his chair and telling her it was time to go back to the living room with the others.

"Don't tell me you don't know who I'm talking about," she continued. "She killed Enid's brother just last night. Burned him into nothing. You got to help me put her back in the ground."

This was not turning out the way he'd planned. He and Hunter were going to come and see Ashley Hillis. Hunter would ask her about the events in Sharkey's Park.

"While you're sitting there thinking I'm a crazy old fool, Detective, I'm going to tell you what happened the night she died at the hands of Becker Hillis and his friends and what happened to Becker afterward."

"You know that?"

Instead of answering yes or no, she told him the story. She explained to him the mystery that tormented him for so many years. When she got to the madstone, Alvarez's mouth opened and closed like he forgot what to say.

"So this stone, this madstone," he said, "it held her ghost in the ground all these years?"

"Your tea will go cold."

He drank it in one quick gulp.

"If it did, why would you give it to a son of a bitch like Becker Hillis?"

"I've asked myself that question over and again," she answered. "Look out this big old glass sliding door. See that sun shining through them clouds look like dirty cotton? It's past noon heading toward dusk in a few hours. I'd like my last day on earth to be clear as a crystal spring. But that ain't going to happen and I believe that's because of what I done. I gave the most precious gift God ever gave me to the worst man I knew just because he was family and because I was filled with pride. A proud woman is as easy to deceive as a proud man, Detective. And having so much power like a granny woman does blinded me to my own weakness."

"And Ashley's husband started it all over again when he dug up that girl's grave with Josh."

"Yes, sir. That's what happened. He came to see me. Old women like me don't get a lot of family visitors, and even with the best of intentions, my thankfulness was once again blinded by a lack of common sense."

And she told him of Michael's visit, and how she once again made a terrible mistake by telling him about the madstone. As she told the story, Alvarez felt the power of truth behind her words. He felt as though he were a witness to the events she was describing. The mystery and horror of what happened at Sharkey's Park became not only understandable, but real.

"My grandfather was one of those men with Becker Hillis when they killed the little girl," he said when she was done speaking.

"I know that," she said quietly. "The problem with having the sight is you see the bad and the good."

"He didn't participate, but he didn't stop it, either."

"What I'm looking for is whether or not you're ready to do the hard things we got to do to make it right. Can you do that?"

Something in the way she said it gave him pause.

"I'll do anything legal," he said.

"That ain't good enough."

"What is it you have in mind?"

She waved a bony hand toward the living room

"First you got to find the madstone and you got to find it tonight. We got to put that stone in with that girl's bones in her grave."

Alvarez scratched the stubble on his chin.

"That's going to be hard to do, ma'am. Her bones are in evidence lock-up. And there was no stone like you described in the girl's grave. You say Michael took it, but we don't know where, and I don't know where to start. Is that it, or was there more?"

Her eyes softened.

"First you find it, you see her bones are put back in the ground and the stone placed in with them."

Alvarez shot to his feet.

"How exactly am I supposed to find this stone? You said I'm going to die. Is that right? Isn't that what you said? How do I find it?"

But then he remembered what Dr. Knight had told him. He took out his cellphone and dialed. The old woman watched him, a satisfied glint in her eye.

When Dr. Knight answered, he told her what he needed. While he waited, he looked out the window at the carefully manicured lawn. He took out his notepad and pen and wrote what she told him.

"Okay," he said. "Lucky shot, but I know who's got it."

"The Lord is with you. There's hope yet."

"Now we just have to figure out a way to get her bones and re-bury her."

"One more thing, Detective."

"What's that?" he asked.

"I know in my heart neither one of us is going to make it through the night, but I don't know more than that. So if you see the Lord before me, I want you to tell him I'm sorry for what I've done."

«« — »»

Ian could see the change in Alvarez's face. The lines on the policeman's face looked deeper. His eyes were filled with things he didn't want to know. Granny told him about the madstone; she'd told Enid and Ian about it earlier. He felt sorry for Alvarez. Since everything started, Hunter had been exposed to more than he wanted to know. Things beyond the realm of his comprehension. Problems with no solutions.

Welcome to the club, he thought.

Alvarez walked Granny over to a free chair and then addressed the group. "I want to apologize for my earlier behavior. This is a stressful situation. Sorry, Hunter. But you still should have waited for me."

"Sorry," Ian said.

But he wasn't. He had other things on his mind. Enid had found out where the ghost box was from Ashley and Granny Hillis. He'd nearly died on the spot when Ashley told him about Mr. Chirac. It was impossible, of course, that it was the same Emile Chirac that had duped Magnus Hillis into bringing him back from the other side. Utterly impossible. That would make him over a hundred and fifty years old. But when Granny had told them about the man killing granny women for the madstone and why, he'd felt cold dread fill his heart.

"Granny told me that in order to put this … ghost to rest, we have to find the madstone and bury it with her bones."

"But we don't know where it is," Ashley said.

"We do now. I've written the name and address of the company your husband sent it to test it and someone has to go get it."

"Why don't you go get it?" Kenneth asked. "You're the police."

"Can't do that. I've got to go get her bones out of the evidence locker."

"And how are you going to do that?" Ian asked. "They're evidence, aren't they? You can't just walk out with them."

"That's my problem. Mrs. Hillis, since you're Michael's widow, you'll have to be the one that goes and picks it up."

"Don't worry, I'll get it," Ashley said. "Michael started all this and I'm going to finish it."

She's tougher than she looks, thought Ian.

"I'll go with her," Kenneth said.

"I'll go, too," Enid said. "We got maybe five hours til dark and I want the thing that killed my brother back in the ground."

Ian couldn't believe what he was hearing. They knew who had the ghost box. He caught Enid's attention, but the look in the Kentuckian's eyes told him he was going and to stay out of it.

"Let's do it, then," Alvarez said. "Mrs. Hillis, I put my cellphone number on that piece of paper. Hunter, you stay here with Mrs. Hillis. And this time do what I tell you."

"I—"

"Just do it."

Five minutes later, everyone cleared out and Ian was left alone with Granny Hillis.

"Young man," she said, "it's about time you and me had a talk. You hiding secrets I believe I need to hear."

Chapter Thirty-Five

A coupling connecting a mechanical soldier to Magnus Hillis fell free from the first mechanical soldier. The fluorescent light housed beneath its crystal dome ignited with pulsating purple-green fireworks. Three more couplings for three more mechanical soldiers fell away over the next ten minutes, each landing on the floor with a hard metallic clink. The others stood in silent rows, waiting for the ship to rebuild enough power to activate them.

With a fluidity that defied over one hundred and fifty years of silent standing, the four de-coupled automatons began to walk toward the suspended figure of Albert Magnus Hillis. Each advancing footstep tremored the ground like a wrecking ball. When they were assembled below him four across, Magnus emitted a terrible scream so loud the luminescent air rushed away from him in pressure waves.

One by one, the four mechanical soldiers marched behind the rock wall that concealed the ship.

《《—》》

"She called again, Doctor. That's three times in the last hour."

"Jesus, I hate that woman. I mean I'm sorry she's out of her gourd, but we've got to wipe this place clean and get out of here before the landlord shows up and seizes all this equipment with a court order. I need to focus. I can't focus with her calling me all the time. And here's how much time we have to get out of here." He held his right thumb and forefinger only a half an inch apart. "Where are those movers?"

"You want me to give her your cellphone number?"

Dr. Robert Garrison hit himself on the forehead.

"Et tu, Jean?"

"She's on her way up, I think."

"What?"

"I think she was calling from the parking lot and on her way up."

"Now you tell me. Is the door locked?"

Jean Shesso looked over at the door and then back at Dr. Garrison.

"I don't think so."

"Then go lock it so we can be sure."

"Maybe you should talk to her. She just wants that sample."

"Like I know where the hell it is? Everything is boxed up and I don't have time for this. Now go lock the door and turn out the lights."

Dr. Garrison extended his right index toward the door and like a laser pointer.

"Now."

Jean was twenty-three and oh, could she walk. Any other day he'd asked her to take her time. But today he wanted speed.

"Hurry," he urged.

Too late.

The door opened wide, and in came Ashley Hillis. She looked just like her picture in the newspapers. Nicely shaped and attractive, except for the gray-white hair. He didn't know what to make of that. Or the white eyebrows.

She looked around at all the boxes.

"Are you planning on moving?" she asked.

"Mrs. Hillis, I'm so sorry. I would have taken your calls, but as you can see we are, in fact, moving. I have to be out today and the movers are on the way. So can we talk about this next week?"

He walked toward the door, beaming his best smile, hoping to walk her outside and shut the door behind her. Jean perched herself on a nearby desk.

Two rough looking men suddenly appeared at the door.

"Ah, you see," he said, "they're here now. It's been nice meeting you, Mrs. Hillis, but as you can tell I'm very busy. Call Jean next week, no the week after that and make an appointment."

One of the men, who was nearly six foot six with the arms of a gorilla, took a step toward him and said, "Her appointment is right now, buddy. You got something she wants and if me and Enid here have to take apart every box in this place we're going to do it. So why don't you just go get it before we start tearing things apart?"

Dr. Garrison took a nervous step back.

"You're not the movers?"

"They're definitely not the movers," Ashley said.

"Then I have to ask you all to leave. Don't make me call the police."

The man named Enid said to Jean, "Excuse me, ma'am, but would you like to escape before I lock the door and we have a talk with your boss?"

Jean swung her legs back and forth for a moment and then said, "No, I think I'd like to stay and watch."

«« — »»

Alvarez got out of his car carrying the largest briefcase he'd been able to find. It was scuffed brown leather and looked like something traveling salesmen carried back in the nineteen fifties. He'd stuffed it a quarter full of old newspapers about the Sharkey's Park murders so it would have a little weight.

Neither of us will live to see the morning, the old woman said.

Every time he thought about it, it gave him the chills. She'd said it like he would say it looked like it was going to rain. Like she knew, like she really knew. In all his years as a policeman, he'd never met anyone like her. The years he'd tried to solve the mystery of how and why his grandfather died in Sharkey's Park. Trying to locate Becker Hillis but finding nothing. In one hour, she'd given him the explanation he hadn't been able to find by himself. Now, here he was, a police detective going in to steal evidence from an evidence locker so he could give a little girl's ghost peace before anyone else was hurt.

If he died before morning like Granny said, at least he wouldn't find himself in an interrogation room trying to explain why he stole case evidence.

Death.

He'd thought of dying, especially after his wife died. Nothing else to live for, he remembered thinking. But he did what the living always did. Kept on living like it could never happen to them. He'd gone to church for a while, trying to understand, but in the end all he could understand was his job. Things like life and death were too big for him to get a grip on. Instead, he investigated other people's deaths and tried to make sense of them. Came home to an empty apartment. Went to work the next day and that bleak rhythm was what he came to understand as living.

If I die before I wake, he thought, *I pray the Lord my soul to take.*

"Too much thinking," he said to himself, "and not enough action."

With that, he walked toward the building.

Twenty-five minutes later, he returned to his car with a briefcase full of bones.

«« — »»

"I knowed your uncle," Granny Hillis said. "Enid told me about his passing."

Ian panicked.

"He did? What did he say? I mean, did he say how he died?"

"Young man, Mr. Bartok said you was smart, but he was right about you and card playing."

"Pardon me?"

The old woman laughed and said, "He told me, Lord help him if he tries to make his living playing poker."

"That sounds like Uncle Bartok. But I'm confused. How did you know him? He never mentioned you to me."

"Couple of my crazy kin wasn't happy the grave of old Albert Magnus was buried on Hunter property. Seems a long time ago your people bought the land thereabouts in a right mysterious way. So some years back, my kin asked me to speak to him about it. They tried, but your uncle and the Mozers ran them off. They thought he might go easier on an old woman. And yes, I was old even back then."

"What happened?"

"I liked your uncle soon as I met him. Nice looking and smart to boot. He told me it wouldn't be right to desecrate the graves of Albert and his wife. I asked what he was hiding and he said I was too nice a woman to know. Some things, he said, are best left undisturbed. But by the look on your face since you been here, and with what's going on, I think that something has been disturbed. Am I right? And look me in the eyes when you're talking so I'll know if you been telling the truth."

"I can't."

"You want me to hex you and your family for the next seven generations?"

"I don't believe in hexes," Ian said nervously.

"You believe in the ghost of a little dead girl but you don't believe in hexes? Come have tea with this old woman and tell her your story."

Over the same table that she had sat with Alvarez, he finally told her everything, including the name of the man who came through the ghost box. She never took her eyes off him while he spoke.

"That is the damnedest story I've ever heard," she said. "And that's something, me being what I am. Your damned fool of an uncle should have told me. The man had too many secrets for his own good. They killed him in the end. A man can't hold something like that inside."

"It wasn't the secret that killed him, it was me. And he was right; when the time came I was glad to pull the trigger. You can't imagine what that thing that took over his body looked like. It was terrible. And I was supposed to save him. I always let him down. Always. And now, if you have the others put that madstone in with that girl's bones, Enid and I will have to risk stealing the ghost box. I have to have it to stop whatever's going on in that cavern. Uncle Bartok thought the ship was powering up again, stronger than ever before. I have to stop it. I can't let him down."

"Be quiet," said Granny suddenly.

"What?"

"Ain't you got no ears? Hush up and let me think."

Hunter was about to ask her what she was thinking about, but thought better of it. As he watched, she closed her eyes and began to hum softly to herself. She went still and stayed that way for so long he worried she'd gone to sleep. He leaned over to touch her hand, but before he could touch her, her eyes popped open and he pulled back in shock.

"That's why he wants it," she hissed.

"I don't understand."

"Then be quiet and listen. That man, that wicked man Chirac, wants my madstone to keep away the spirits of the dead that always be calling to him. Don't you see? That damn fool Albert Magnus called him back from the dead to the land of the living. The spirits won't let him be. They want him back. It ain't natural what happened. The dead is supposed to stay dead. But he got brought back to life and the others are pulling at him, tugging at him to drag him back. My madstone can keep them away. But he'll never get it. Never, as long as I've got breath in my body."

"But I need that ghost box. It's the only way to take those mechanical soldier's power and send it back to the other side."

She held her finger up and shook it at him like a school-teacher.

"You can't have it. And don't you worry none, Kenneth and Enid will go with you to get that ghost box back."

"Granny, I don't think you're remembering one important thing here."

When she focused her eyes on him, really focused her eyes on him in that moment, Hunter could feel the force of her personality. The hair on his arms felt prickly, as though he were standing too close to an electrical substation.

"And what is that?" she asked.

"Emile Chirac was the man that cut off his arms and legs and hooked him to those metal monstrosities. The man whom Ashley met has the same name, but if he's the same man, then he's over one hundred fifty years old."

Chapter Thirty-Six

"Don't drop that," Dr. Garrison shouted. "It's a sensitive piece of analytical equipment. It cost me nearly fifty thousand dollars."

"He hasn't actually paid for it yet," Jean said from her perch on the secretarial desk near the front door. "I ought to know. They call all the time asking for their money."

"Open it and dump it," Ashley said. "We need that stone."

They'd broken open thirty seven boxes and piled the contents on the floor. Nearly an hour and a half had passed. Jean watched and chewed gum while Dr. Garrison glared at her. Ashley supervised Kenneth and Enid. Green and white packing popcorn covered the floor.

"We ain't found it yet," Kenneth said, "and we still got another roomful of boxes."

"I'm tired of this shit," Enid said. "You open the window and I'll hang him over the edge, and if he don't tell us what box it's in, I'll drop him."

"We're only on the second floor," Jean said. "You should take him up to the roof."

"I like you," Enid said. "You got any ideas?"

"About time you asked," she grinned.

"You mean you know where it is?" Dr. Garrison asked. "They've destroyed nearly a million dollars' worth of analytical equipment and you knew where it was the whole time? You're fired."

"You haven't paid me in two months," she shot back.

Ashley walked over to the girl and pleaded with her.

"Jean, I'll hire you. You want to work for a real company with a real paycheck and work for someone who doesn't stare at your rear end all day? I'll hire you starting right now. Your first job is to find me that stone. Please. It's more important than you realize."

Jean thought about it for a second or two.

"You going to get rid of me after I show you where it's at?"

"He would," Ashley said, pointing at Dr. Garrison.

"I resent that," he said.

"But I wouldn't," Ashley finished. "Help us. Please."

"It'd save a lot of wasted time," Enid said.

"Okay. I packed most of this stuff."

She hopped off the desk, went around to the other side and pulled out a drawer. From inside the drawer, she retrieved a clipboard and began running her fingernail down it.

"Got it," she said. "MV Quantum Technologies. Box 42-C. It's in the other room. I'll go get it."

On the way there, she grabbed Kenneth's box cutter.

"She sure can walk, can't she?" Dr. Garrison said to Kenneth.

"You open that mouth of yours again and I'm going to have these two men take you up to the roof and drop you," Ashley warned.

«« — »»

"We got it," Enid said into his cellphone. "If it wasn't for the office manager, we would have never found it in time."

He looked in the rearview mirror and saw her smile.

"How far are you out?" Alvarez asked him.

"Maybe half an hour."

"Swing by my apartment and pick me up. Pull in the back parking lot. I'll come out when I see you."

Alvarez told Enid his address while Kenneth wrote it on the back of a MacDonald's bag.

"Why we doing this? It'll take extra time."

"Because I'm leaving my car here. Something happens to me I don't want my car over at your place."

"We're on our way."

Enid and Kenneth sat in the front; Ashley and Jean sat in the back.

"Do I want to know what's going on?" Jean asked.

"No," Ashley said.

"It's not illegal, is it?"

"No. We're dropping you at your place first, and then we have some things to take care of. I've got your number and I'll call you in a few days to tell you where to show up and what you'll be doing. Thank you, Jean, for what you did back there."

"He's not a bad guy," said Jean. "He's just an idiot."

"Young lady," Enid said over his shoulder, "when you're in a tight spot and you need to count on somebody, there ain't much difference."

«« — »»

"Logically," Ian said, "I know that it can't be the same person, but that's what worries me. Nothing in this whole mess has been remotely logical."

Granny bent over, picked up her quilted bag and rested it on her lap. Without a word she took out a bundle of straw-like twigs, a bundle of red yarn strips and a pair of scissors. After separating the yarn into three piles, she picked up several thin twigs and began twisting them together.

"What are you doing?" Ian asked.

"Making little men to keep Mrs. Hillis and the rest of you safe tonight. You'll be doing dangerous work. The haint's getting stronger. I don't know how much help these will be, but it might be enough."

"Are they charms? Like magical wards?"

Her fingers wove the twigs together in slow, methodical threadings. Before long, they looked like little stick people.

"Explaining things hides the truth. You talk the words, but don't know what they mean. All you need to know is you wear this around your neck, and you'll be a tiny little bit safer. The more you think about these little men I'm making, the less they'll work for you."

She tied each figure with tight little yanks on the twine, and then took out long strips of leather. When she threaded the leather through the small bundles, they became necklaces.

"What else you know about the dark man calls himself Mr. Chirac? Time's coming up quick when you and your friends have to act and all this talking will be done."

Ian thought a moment.

"Almost nothing. He told Magnus Hillis that he was murdered by the French occultist Eliaphas Levi."

"Do tell."

"I looked them both up on the internet. There's no mention of Emile Chirac anywhere. There's a lot about Levi, but no hint that he ever knew a man named Chirac, much less murdered him."

"Internet knows all, don't it?"

"Look," Ian said defensively, "I haven't had a lot of time to do anything else. All I really know is what I read in Taylor Hunter's journals and I think he was out of his mind when he wrote them. Uncle Bartok believed him. That's all I really have to go on. But he hasn't been wrong yet, and I'm not saying that because he's my uncle."

Ian corrected himself.

"Was my uncle. Right up until the night I killed him."

When she'd finished her fifth little man necklace, granny laid them out on the table in a row, like cut-out dolls.

"Put this one around your neck," she said.

Ian did as he was told.

"Now I'm going to tell you something you keep to yourself. Can you do that?"

"I can—I mean, I will."

She nodded as she put her scissors back in her bag, which she then laid on the floor.

"There be things that look like people walking all over this world. Some of them three or four hundred years old. Ain't spoken to no one who knows how long they stay the way they is. You look at them real close, stare at them like. They won't like it and will try to get you to look away. But if you do it long enough you'll see they don't look real. They'll waiver every now and then like they part smoke, part man or woman."

"What are they?"

"Ain't no one knows. All we do know is they's evil. Closest word I can come up with is demon."

"You think this Chirac is the same one that came through the ghost box? Do you believe he's that old, that he's a demon? Isn't it more likely he's a descendent?"

Granny stared out the window for a while, lost in her own thoughts. When she looked back at him, he could see the worry in her face.

"No. And hear me clear. You thinking about breaking in to his house like burglars to steal what you want. Leave that idea be. You and Enid go into that house, I don't believe either of you'll come out alive, and that'll be the least of your worries."

"Then what do I do? We have to have that ghost box. I told you Hillis's plan. Those things were made to march to Washington D.C. and destroy it. And neither Hillis nor his robot soldiers know or care that the Civil War is over. Uncle Bartok said in his notes they're made of some metal and dense energy complex. He didn't think anything the military has got will stop them."

"You saying the army and the Air Force can't blow them up into little pieces?"

"I don't know. But they're made with a technology beyond anything we have."

Granny slapped the table so hard the teacups rattled. Her mouth set in a thin, tight line.

"Then you got yourself a terrible problem, young man. Cause that dark man ain't getting my madstone."

Like a man leaving a poker table after a losing hand, Ian pushed back his chair and stood up. He began to pace the kitchen. Finally he stopped and held his hands up toward her in frustration.

"I have to stop those things. I don't know what's going on below there, but Enid told me his brothers have been hearing strange sounds from below ground. A toxic cloud escaped and killed everything it touched. I'm terrified, Granny. You've never seen those things. If we can't trade that madstone for the ghost box, what am I supposed to do? You say we can't break into Chirac's house and steal it. But we might be able to drain both Magnus Hillis and his automaton's of their power using the ghost box. I don't know if it will work, but we've got to try."

"Find another way," she snapped.

"Listen, you want to put the girl's bones back in the ground and bury the madstone with them. That will stop the haint. Well, what if someone digs them up again? What if the police go looking for them when they find out they're gone and then dig them up again and the madstone falls out? What happens then?"

"Lord help whoever does that," she said. "The haint will come screaming out and kill anyone it sees. Look what happened to them poor souls at Sharkey's Park."

"And?"

"I'm gonna it anyway. Only way to stop a haint. We can't be guessing what's going to happen later."

"And if the mechanical soldiers get enough power to come to life? What then?"

"Find another way. You're supposed to be real smart. Enid says Bartok believed in you. So you find another way. And don't you even try to cross me. I'll cast a spell on you, you'll wish you hadn't been born."

"I already wish I wasn't born. I can't solve this problem. You're making it impossible. You say we have to put the madstone in the little girl's grave. Chirac has the ghost box and he won't give it up without the madstone. And if anyone takes the madstone out of the little girl's grave, they won't know what's going to happen to them and the haint will kill them. If we try to take the madstone from Chirac, he'll kill us, we can't stop the mechanical soldiers. I—" He stopped mid-sentence and stared off into space with his mouth still open. He looked down at the floor then out the kitchen window.

"I think I know how to do both," he said slowly. He nodded his head and said, "I just need a swathe of cloth maybe four feet by four feet. Say we cut a piece from a sheet. That would do it."

"Are you clean out of your mind," Granny asked.

"No. I think I just found it again. And it will work. It's the elegant solution. Wait, I see one problem."

"What in the good Lord's name are you going on about?"

Suddenly Ian snapped his fingers so loud it startled Granny.

"Can you cast spells? Like when you said you could hex me? I'm serious. I need to know. Everything depends on it."

"Who are you wanting me to cast a spell on?"

"On Chirac."

"Lordy be," she said. "What is in that fool mind of yours?"

He told her.

When she smiled up at him, he wished Uncle Bartok was there to see it.

Chapter Thirty-Seven

They loaded the back of Ashley's SUV with flashlights, fire extinguishers, shovels and the piece of cloth that Granny cut for them. It was thirty minutes til dusk and a fine November rain misted the air. The drive to Sharkey's Park would take over an hour. Kenneth wasn't happy that Granny was staying behind by herself.

"I got something to ready that can't be denied," she told him. "But don't you worry none, that haint won't dare to come at me again. No, she'll be coming for the five of you."

Kenneth eyed her suspiciously.

"What is it you got to do?"

"Don't you question me, Kenneth Hillis. Just do as I say."

A few seconds passed before he said, "Yes, ma'am."

The car was parked outside the front door, with the engine running. Ashley in the driver's seat, Alvarez next to her with the big briefcase on the floor between his feet, and the others piled into the back. Granny went around to the passenger side window and knocked on it. Alvarez turned to look at the same moment the automatic lighting system revealed her in a cone of light, staring at him through tinted glass. He thumbed the switch and the window lowered.

"Yes?" he said.

With the lights behind her, her face was hidden in the shadows. She was as insubstantial as a spirit. Dusk was upon him.

"The Lord be with you, Detective," she said. "You're a good man."

Alvarez couldn't think of what to say.

"Let an old woman kiss you on the cheek before you go."

"Okay."

As she drew close to his cheek, he felt an unreasoning desire to pull away and scream. He closed his mouth and sat rigid as her wrinkled-wax lips pressed against his cheek.

"Don't be afraid," she said. "Do what's got to be done and remember your promise."

Granny stepped back from the vehicle.

"We'll get it done and be home soon," Kenneth said over Alvarez's shoulder.

"You better," said Granny.

Before Alvarez's window closed all the way, Granny stepped toward it and yelled, "Girl, you be strong" to Ashley.

The window closed and Ashley pushed the gas pedal.

"We didn't get a good-bye," Ian told Enid.

"Just shut up," Enid said.

They drove down the same road that Henry Wendland had on his last night on earth.

«« — »»

Puffs of smoky fog drifted through the headlight beams, forcing Ashley to reduce her speed. She set the wipers to a low setting to clear the windshield.

"We're about halfway, right?" Alvarez asked.

"I think so," Ashley said.

Alvarez took the briefcase from between his legs and passed it back to Ian. "You keep this. Ashley, stop here, get out and change sides with me."

"Why?"

"Because I know where the grave is."

She slowed to a stop, unbuckled her seatbelt and got out. Alvarez was already at her door by the time her feet touched the ground.

"Hurry," he said.

As she opened the passenger door to get in, Ashley froze. Up ahead on the road, she saw the faint outline of a little girl.

"Get in," Alvarez shouted.

Ashley climbed into the seat as fast as she could.

"Don't look at her," Ian said. "Close your eyes."

Ashley clamped her eyelids together as hard as she could. The sight of the little girl terrified her. But her mind captured the image like an old time photograph. A little girl like any other little girl, except that this little girl was dead.

The car lurched forward and Ashley's eyes popped open. Alvarez had the gas pedal pressed to the floorboard.

"No," Ashley screamed when the little girl was only six feet away.

Curly golden hair began to smoke. The little girl's eyes turned angry orange-red just as they drove through her. Ashley twisted in her seat to look out the back window, but there was nothing there except the glow of their taillights reflected back from the fog.

"Son of a bitch," Enid said.

"Yeah," Alvarez said. "That's what I was thinking."

He backed off the gas pedal.

"She knows where's we're going," Ian said. "She'll be waiting for us at the park."

"What do we do?" Kenneth asked.

"We're going to do it like this," Alvarez said. "You guys ever watch SWAT teams on TV? That's how we're going to do this. I'm going to park twenty feet short of the grave."

"Closer'd be better," Kenneth said.

"He's right," Enid said. "We need to be as close as we can."

"You didn't see Wendland's car. She sets this thing on fire; we don't want to be near that explosion. So we do it my way. Soon as I stop, everybody out. Ashley, you've got the madstone. Enid and Kenneth will go around to the back and I'll have the hatch already popped. Get the shovels and I'll grab the extinguishers. Hunter, you carry the bones and that EMF detector in case it gives us a warning she's near. We move, and we move quick to the grave. I'll lead the way and everyone stay close behind me and I mean real close. Nobody splits off on their own. Everybody tell me yes so I know you're listening."

"What about the flashlights?" Ashley asked.

"Good point. First, we have the headband camping headlights that Enid and Kenneth picked up. Slide those over your forehead now and make sure you know how to turn them on and off. It's easy. You just twist the light and it will come on. I want to hear yeses now and then you all put the head-lamps on and test them."

When everyone had said yes and tested the lights, he continued.

"We have three big flashlights. Ashley carries one in her coat, I do the same and Hunter, too. When we hit the grave, Ashley, you lay yours on the ground pointing toward the grave. Hunter you do the same. I'll keep mine to watch for her.

"Kenneth and Enid, you two dig like sons of bitches until your two or three feet down. Hunter, you throw in the cloth and then pour the bones in after it. When he's done that, Ashley you put the madstone in with them and Kenneth and Enid, you start shoveling dirt over everything."

"What do we do if she shows up?" Ian said.

"If she starts to burn, I'll spray her with the fire extinguisher."

"You think that'll work?" Ian said.

"Don't know, but if you got any better ideas now's the time to speak up."

Enid's cellphone rang. He went through two pockets before he found it.
"Got to take this," he said. "Hello."

Whoever was on the other end, Enid listened for a full two minutes before answering. Ian watched him nervously.

Finally, Enid spoke.

"There ain't nothing else to do," he said. "Get the cement mixer. Then dig it up all the way to the door and then start pouring. When the concrete dries, pile some dirt on it. We're working on it at this end. I told you we're working on it. Text me when you're done. Call me, too. If I don't answer, I'll call back when I can. I said we're working on it. Now get it done."

When he'd put away his phone, Alvarez asked him, "What's all that? Anything I need to know about?"

"Nope. Trouble at home."

"How bad?" Ian asked.

"Worse," Enid said.

"Holy Jesus," Ian said.

«« — »»

The cold night air filled with the rolling, grinding noise of the diesel cement mixer. The sky was clear and filled with tiny points of light which were lost in the glare of the portable halogen lights the two men had set up. Tyree and Johnny shoveled furiously to uncover the protective door beneath the mock graves of Albert Magnus Hillis and his wife Emma. They piled dirt on the longest sides, careful to keep the way clear to seal the hole with concrete when they reached the barrier.

"What do you think is going on down there?" Johnny asked.

"I don't know and I don't want to find out so shut up and keep shoveling."

Beneath them, the sounds grew louder and more frequent. With each tremor, dirt slid back into the hole. Tyree wiped sweat from his forehead with the back of his hand and got back to shoveling.

"It's like tanks moving around down there," Johnny said.

Tyree said nothing, but his thoughts were running wild.

A sharp clanking sound as Tyree hit metal.

"You start cleaning off the dirt while I check the mixer so we can start pouring," he said.

"Do it," Johnny said.

Tyree scrambled up the side nearest the mixer, slid back once, and then pulled himself up and over the lip. He lost a shoe right at the edge and it fell back in. The sound of gears turning stopped him where he stood.

"What's that?" he called down.

He could hear the terror in Johnny's voice as he called up, "The door, it's opening all by itself."

"Well, fuck it," Tyree said. "Get the hell out of there."

An eerie mix of purple-green light began to shine up from the opening, and Tyree stood transfixed. All these years watching and now this.

"Help me up," Johnny called.

Tyree leaned forward and extended his hand. He saw Johnny's face but could hardly recognize him. Terror twisted his features into a frightening mask.

Suddenly a light filled glassine tentacle snaked up from the ever widening opening and cinched around Johnny's neck like a noose.

"No," Tyree screamed.

With a quick yank, Johnny's neck snapped and the tentacle heaved his body backward and pulled him back through the opening. He disappeared into the twisting spectral light.

The ancient gears continued to turn and the door continued to open. Tyree was about to run for his shotgun when he remembered the cement mixer. He turned and grabbed hold of the dump lever and pulled forward as hard as he could. Wet cement poured out over the graves lip and into the opening.

He'd taken two quick steps toward the truck to get his shotgun when another tentacle shot up through the wet cement and wrapped around his waist. He screamed and tried to untwist it but he couldn't get it loose. His unshod foot raked over stones as he was dragged backward into the pit, still screaming as it pulled him through the wet cement.

Chapter Thirty-Eight

Alvarez drove straight through the wooden gate that blocked traffic from entering Corktown. It broke apart with a gunshot crack. He slowed as they drove onto the gravel road, past the boarded up houses that looked like cheap tombstones.

"Two blocks down and the entrance road to Sharkey's Park cuts off to the left," Ashley said.

"I been here before, remember?" Alvarez said.

"I forgot."

"This whole neighborhood's abandoned," Ian said.

Alvarez looked briefly into the review mirror and caught his eyes.

"Corktown. That's what they used to call it. Like in Detroit. Immigrant neighborhood. Poor people lived here. My grandfather was one of them. And Michael's, too. Rough place, frustrated people. Cheap houses."

"They should fix the streetlights," Kenneth said. "It's too dark here."

"Nobody lives here anymore," Alvarez said.

"I was just whistling in the graveyard," Kenneth said.

"Is that the turn off?" Enid said.

A metal sign with faded red letters read "Welcome to Sharkey's Park. Picnic Grounds for Rent" on two wooden posts. Cyclone fencing blocked the entrance and yellow crime scene tape stretched across the road just inside. Alvarez stopped and revved the engine. He was about to drive through a crime scene tape. When had he quit thinking of himself as a policeman?

"What is it?" Ashley said.

"Something. I don't know."

"I feel it, too," Ian said, "it's like standing in front of a big microwave."

Alvarez pressed the accelerator pedal down and they shot forward. Just before they broke through the gate, the headlights dimmed by half and then they were through onto another dirt road. A deeper darkness descended on them as they drove slowly forward. With the headlights so weak Alvarez had to lean forward to make sure he missed the broken branches from the earlier storms and didn't go too fast over the decline that led down to the bridge.

"I've heard of this happening," Ian said. "Lights dimming when you enter a haunted area. Never believed it. Never thought I'd see it."

A dark mass crouched ahead. Threatening. Ominous. In the weak light thrown forward by the headlamps, it finally resolved into a stand of trees.

"That's where we waited," Ashley said. "When Michael and Josh went down to check the bridge."

This is where we found the bodies, Alvarez thought.

"I can't see the creek," Hunter said.

"Is the bridge safe?" Ashley asked.

"I don't think anything here about is safe, Mrs. Hillis," Kenneth said.

"Bridge is okay," Alvarez said. "We checked it out before we drove across it when we were called in. Swings a little, but it held up. Cross your fingers."

As they went over the edge and down on the road to the bridge, Alvarez cast a quick glance over at Ashley to see how she was holding up.

"I'm okay," she said.

"Sorry about before," he said.

"What?"

"Grilling you at the hospital. I didn't know about all this then."

"I see the bridge," Ian said.

"Here we go," Alvarez said. "Headband lights on everybody. We make it over the bridge and we got maybe a hundred feet til I put the brakes on and we roll into action. Anything on the EMF, Hunter?"

"Low level, but something's going on."

Alvarez slowed down a little more as he pulled onto the bridge. He noticed the moss on the wooden side rails and heard the planks clankety-clanking beneath the tires. He didn't look to the right or left because he was afraid of what he might see.

I'm getting through this night alive, he thought. *After that, it's one day at a time. I'm not going to die here.*

"I can feel the madstone," Ashley said. "It feels warmer."

"Let me see it," Ian said.

"No time," Alvarez said.

They were across the bridge. The dancehall/bandstand building loomed up ahead. A ticket box and what was left of a ruined merry-go-round and a concession stand.

Harder on the gas pedal. Up the incline.

Alvarez felt the night press in on him. Twenty feet more and he'd put on the brake. The car would stop and they would have to open the door and step into the night.

"EMF reading?" he called over his shoulder to Ian.

"Same."

He put on the brakes and the car came to a stop near a wide swathe of grass.

"Let's do it," he said.

He left the engine running and the headlights on.

«« — »»

Enid and Kenneth were out of the backseat before Ian could clip the EMF detector to his coat. He clutched the big briefcase close to his chest as he slid toward the driver's side and hopped out. The grass was slick and he slipped but caught himself on the door before he could go down.

The headband lamp spread a circle of blue white. Bright enough to five or six feet ahead of him but not much more beyond that.

"Get a move on it," Alvarez shouted.

The grave was defined by four white stakes painted red on top. A sheet of plastic covered it. The corners were held down with rocks. Enid and Kenneth made short work of those, removed the plastic and started digging. Alvarez flicked on a bright flashlight that looked big enough to light a runway.

"Put the case down, open it up and get out your flashlight. We have to move it."

Ian did as he was told, and Ashley covered her eyes to protect them from the sudden light. She stood clutching the little sample box they'd picked up at Dr. Garrison's lab. Enid and Kenneth made short work of digging through the soft dirt that police evidence technicians had already dug through once, but Ian grew increasingly nervous.

"EMF is rising," he told Alvarez.

"Shit. Deep enough," he told Enid and Kenneth. "Get out so Hunter can put the bones in."

Something tugged at the edge of Ian's fears. Something. Forgetting something. The EMF began to beep as he leaned over to get the bones.

"Wait," he said. "Where's the cloth?"

"Didn't you bring it?" Alvarez asked.

"It won't work if we don't put the cloth down first," Ian said.

He looked back toward the SUV.

"Got to get it," he said, and took off running.

"No," Ashley shouted, but he was already running through the wet grass.

Ian felt his heart pumping in his chest as he ran. So close, so close and then this. The EMF meter began to beep louder. He reached up without thinking to touch the twig man on his necklace and found to his horror that it wasn't there. Panicked, he ran faster, swinging his arms back and forth. His chest felt tight and part of his mind thought he was having a heart attack.

«« — »»

"Do something," Ashley shouted.

She trained her flashlight on Ian's back as he got closer to the SUV, but Enid knocked it away.

"Keep that light off of him," he said. "I'll go get him."

But Alvarez was already in motion.

"I've got the fire extinguisher," he yelled back over his shoulder.

Stupid son of a bitch, he thought as he ran.

Ian had the cloth out of the vehicle and was turning around to come back. Alvarez saw the little girl appear at the right driver's side wheel well. He pulled the pin on the fire extinguisher and kept on running.

She hadn't moved by the time he caught up with Hunter.

"Stay still," he said.

"What? We've got to get back."

"We have company," Alvarez said quietly.

Alvarez saw the look of horror when Hunter saw her.

"I've lost my stick man," he whispered to Alvarez.

"Never mind. Start walking slowly and keep me between you and her."

Alvarez forgot to look away from the girl. His mind struggled to process what he was seeing. She looked like any other girl in the backlight of the weak headlights. He could actually see the curls in her hair, see the dress she wore, her skinny legs and the saddle shoes.

"Slowly," he said.

They were ten steps away when her eyes began to glow orange-yellow, like tiny burning coals. By the time they were fifteen steps away, her hair began to smolder and then it burst into flames. The night air was filled with the smell of burnt flesh. Alvarez pulled the fire extinguisher trigger and sent a stream of milky-white fluid at her. The flames crackled and popped but didn't go out. He dropped the empty fire extinguisher can and began to back away.

The wind kicked up, blowing a stream of sparks at him. He took another step backward and looked for Hunter. Gone. A glance toward the grave showed that he'd covered half the distance, moving at a fast clip now trying to get the cloth to the gravesite.

Burning, she stood there burning. No little girl anymore, but a blackened, twisted shape within the flames. Alvarez felt paralyzed. She began to float toward him. He reached up for the leather string around his neck and yanked the stick figure free. He trust it up and in front of her like a cross to keep away vampires.

She stopped. He felt the hatred coming at him like acid waves. He knew he couldn't stand there forever. He remembered Granny telling him neither one of them would make it through the night.

He looked back at Hunter. Two thirds of the way there. When he turned his head back, he saw the haint was looking in the same direction. Hunter lost his stick figure. Hunter was unprotected.

The little girl began to lift up in the air, a burning pillar of hatred, burning eyes fixed on Hunter.

"My grandfather stood by while you were raped," Alvarez said in a voice that shook so bad he could barely understand himself.

"He got branches for the fire that burned you," he continued. "He thought you were dead. You don't want that guy over there, you want me."

The haint rose another foot in the air, and he could feel it focus on him.

"You don't like this, do you?"

He held up the stick figure.

"You can't come any closer, can you?"

Angry flames shot out in all directions from the haint. Alvarez covered his eyes with his forearm.

"Well, come get me," he said, and threw the stick figure toward Hunter's retreating form.

Then he ran for the creek.

«« — »»

"Help him," Ashley said.

"Nothing we can do," Kenneth said.

"Yes there is," Ian said.

He lay the cloth down into the freshly dug grave and he and Enid began putting the bones on top of it.

"Some dirt," he told Kenneth.

Kenneth took a spade of earth and threw it on them.

"Ashley, the stone. Press the stone down in the dirt between the bones."

He looked back down the hill with fear building in him so quickly he thought he'd explode.

"He's almost to the creek," Kenneth said.

And he was. Ian saw Alvarez lit by the flamed spirit flying through the air after him. Burning arms outstretched, reaching for him.

"Come on, come on," he said.

He turned and saw the madstone slip from Ashley's trembling hands and fall into the grave.

"It has to be pushed in between the bones," he yelled.

Ashley jumped in the pit and groped for the madstone.

"Light, shine some light down there for her," Ian said, but Kenneth had already picked up a flashlight and aimed it where Ashley was looking.

In a moment that would stay with him for the rest of his life, he saw Alvarez reach the edge of the creek and leap out over it. He understood what the detective was up to. If he made it to the water, the haint couldn't burn him.

The twisting flames caught him mid-jump.

Ian heard Alvarez's scream as though he were standing next to him. He watched as the detective burst into flames. Wrapped in an embrace of fiery death twisting and shrieking in agony. It went on and on and Ian could not take his eyes away from the hideous sight. Tears filled his eyes and he grew angry. When the haint finally released what was left of Alvarez, Ian saw his body drop but didn't hear the splash.

"We're putting you down," he said, looking right at the burning apparition.

It flared and started flying at them.

"Ashley, have you found it yet," he yelled.

"Give me a second," she said. "It's here somewhere."

"Hurry up, for God's sake. The haint is coming for us now."

He saw Ashley look up, drop back down.

"Turn off the flashlight, Enid and let her find it by touch," Kenneth said urgently.

Enid turned off the light.

"These will hold her off," he said, holding up his twisted-stick figure the way Alvarez had.

"I don't think so," Ian said. "Not this time. She's pissed."

Screams filled the darkness and Ian knew he was hearing what happened the night the little girl was raped and burned. They were urgent, desperate, begging for mercy screams. Ian couldn't bear listening to them and put his hands over his ears. But he could still hear them. The haint was almost on them and it was burning so brightly it was like looking at a flare.

Kenneth and Enid stood in front of Ian to protect him and Ashley. Ian could feel the heat coming straight at them and the haint was less than twenty feet away.

"Find the madstone," he shouted.

The hot air blasted them and all three men were knocked off their feet and blown over to the far side of the grave.

Ian hit the ground as his shirt burst into flames and he rolled over and over in the wet grass screaming. When the flames finally went out, he sat up and looked around. The haint was gone.

"Thank you, Miss Ashley," Kenneth said. "That was the closest I've ever been to being burned alive by a dead person."

«« — »»

They each took a corner of the cloth and lifted it out of the grave. Before lifting it, they'd put in extra dirt to make sure that the madstone didn't roll out from among the bones. Careful as if they were handling unstable explosives, they put the cloth in Alvarez's big briefcase and folded the extra cloth over top of it, then forced the lid closed.

"You two take that to the car while Kenneth and me clean up here," Enid said.

Ian and Ashley walked toward the SUV in silence. He was mindful that with each step they took, they were closer to Alvarez's body lying in the creek.

When they arrived at the vehicle, Ashley said, "I wonder how he knew to leave his car back at his apartment. Do you think he knew he wouldn't be coming back with us?"

Ian considered the question for a moment.

"I honestly don't know. I've seen so much I wouldn't have believed could happen before this all started that I can't give you an answer."

"It's my fault," Ashley said. "None of this would have happened if I hadn't married Michael. I feel like I was married to a total stranger."

"Maybe you married someone from one of your books," Ian said. "Sorry. I didn't mean that badly, I just meant, well, I don't know."

He put the briefcase on the passenger side floorboard. The thought of Alvarez's blackened body lying in the creek made him shudder.

"It's okay," Ashley said. "I think maybe you're right. I think I've been too wrapped up in my own stories. It's just… it's just, there've been so many deaths."

Ian thought about Bartok. Wished he had been there with them. Maybe he could have saved Alvarez.

"Ashley, I don't think any of this was your fault. If you'd never married Michael, he would have done what he did anyway. The Hillis family has a long history of bad men."

He remembered Albert Magnus Hillis hanging like an insane spider above the cavern floor. Remembered the journals of Bradley Hunter. Remembered the glassine tentacle burrowing into Bartok's neck.

Enid and Kenneth came up to the car.

"I think we're done here," Enid said.

"Maybe," Ian said, "but we're not done for the night. Did you hear back from down south?"

"Nothing. No texts. I called while we was walking back. No answer. I don't like it."

Kenneth asked, "What in the world is it with you two? You got more trouble?"

"Serious trouble," Ian said. "We'll tell you on the way to pick up Granny."

Ashley drove while Ian talked. Enid tried objecting to him telling them about it, but Ian told him to shut up. They needed all the help they could get.

Chapter Thirty-Nine

Ricci opened the door to something he'd never seen before.

Ashley Hillis had called ahead, demanding to see Mr. Chirac, telling him she had the madstone. Ricci relayed the message to Mr. Chirac, who agreed to see her. At midnight. She was carrying a big briefcase, and she wasn't alone.

Five people were standing in front of him. An old woman standing next to Ashley. Two tall rangy looking men carry shotguns stood behind her and next to them stood another man holding a pistol.

"You sure want to do this?" Ricci asked.

"The men will be waiting in the car. If I'm not out in a half an hour, they're coming in."

"Suit yourself," Ricci said. "What about the old lady?"

"I'll be going in with her," the old woman said. "You can call me Granny."

Ricci considered this for a moment and then shook his head.

"Mr. Chirac only said she can come. He never mentioned you. And people Mr. Chirac don't mention can't come in."

"I'd rethink that," Enid said.

"Nothing to rethink. Mr. Chirac's rules are Mr. Chirac's rules."

"Hush, Enid. I thank you kindly, but I'll do the talking to this man. What's your name?"

"Ricci."

"Now, that's an unusual name. May I see your hand? Your left hand?"

"You should wait in the car, ma'am," Ricci said.

Enid racked a round in.

Ricci stared at him. He didn't blink, he didn't flinch.

"Please," Granny asked.

Ricci stared at her for a moment, sighed, and then extended his hand. She took it and turned his palm up.

"My, my," she said.

She let go of his hand and he let it fall at his side.

"So is that about it? You ready to wait in the car?"

"He doesn't know your sister is still alive, does he? You let him think she's dead and he believed you."

This time, Ricci flinched. Who was this old woman? He didn't like what she said. Didn't like it at all. The scar that ran from his cheek to his chin felt hot.

"Don't say that again," he said.

"Should I ask Ashley to tell him?" the old woman asked.

"Why do you want to go in?"

"To make sure he keeps his agreement."

"He always keeps his agreements," Ricci said.

"Does he now? Did you know he came to my house years ago?"

"Ma'am?" Ricci said nervously.

"Yes, sir, he did. A long time ago. To see my mother. He was looking for my madstone even back then."

"Your madstone?"

"Yes, sir. My madstone. It's only right I be the one to give it to him."

"About my sister. If I let you come in, you won't say anything, will you? Either one of you?"

"You have my word," Granny said.

"Mine, too," Ashley said.

"He's going to ask why I let you in," he told Granny.

"No, he won't," the old woman said. "You tell him it's my madstone and he won't hurt you."

Ricci rubbed his chin with the back of his hand, sized up his situation and then stepped aside.

《《—》》

"Mrs. Hillis, such a pleasure to see you again. I must say I'm surprised that you were able to fulfill your husband's contract earlier than the expiration date, but am quite pleased nonetheless."

He wore a black velvet jacket and an open necked white shirt. His hair was perfectly combed and he stood behind a French colonial desk. Ashley saw, to her horror, that the black panther lay on the floor. The metal collar and chain looked inadequate to hold it back

Ashley felt sick to her stomach.

"What's this, Ricci? I see we have another guest. Perhaps you will explain this situation to me."

Granny Hillis stepped in behind Ashley and Ricci followed.

"She says it's her madstone and she wants to be the one to give it to you."

Mr. Chirac's eyes narrowed. He looked the old woman over carefully.

"She also says you came to see her mother about it a long time ago."

From the corner of her eye, Ashley saw the black panther rise up and sit back on its haunches. There was such an intensity about the animal, Ashley thought it was actually following the conversation.

"Fine animal you got there," Granny said.

But Mr. Chirac was staring at Granny, not the panther.

"You say I visited your mother. Have you and I perhaps met? Forgive me, but might I ask the occasion? But first, I beg your pardon. Please, Ricci, bring another chair before my desk. Lack of consideration is an embarrassment to a host."

Ricci set a chair next to the one Ashley took and they sat facing Mr. Chirac, who also sat down, but only after the two of them were seated. Ricci then went to stand at a safe distance from the panther.

"May I provide you with something to drink? Some tea perhaps?"

"No, thank you," Ashley said.

"It was down in the Kentucky hollers." Granny spoke as though she hadn't heard him. "You came asking about my special stone my mother took from the innards of a white deer."

Mr. Chirac steepled his fingers and his face took on a faraway look. The stone set in his ring flashed like a pale red stop light.

"I do not remember you. Perhaps you are mistaken."

"You never saw me. My mother made me hide under the back porch when you came calling. Told me to close my eyes and not open them 'til she came and got me."

When she saw a thin, momentary smile cross Mr. Chirac's face, she felt faint. It was true. Every bit of it. He was the dark man.

"She died two days after."

"I am so sorry to hear that. But, *la mort n'a peut-être pas plus de secrets a nous révéler que la vie*? Forgive me; it is a saying from my home country and translates poorly. My condolences for the untimely death of your beautiful mother."

"We have sayings in the hollers, too," Granny said. "My favorite is that the devil who never lies is hardest to catch."

Mr. Chirac nodded his agreement with a deprecatory smile.

"So, just so. And you say that the madstone you have brought me this fine November evening was yours all along? Were you aware of this fact, Mrs. Hillis?"

"Just recently," Ashley said.

"May I ask where you found it?"

"My husband had given it to a laboratory to analyze."

Chirac sat bolt upright. His nostrils flared slightly as he slapped his palms hard on the desk.

"Was it in any way damaged?"

"No," she said. "It was never touched at all. The laboratory was going out of business. They put it in a sample box and didn't do anything to it."

The furious tension in Mr. Chirac's face relaxed. He settled back into his chair and steepled his fingers again.

"Excellent," he said, "then we may proceed with our transaction. I will retrieve the ghost box and then return."

When he'd left the room, Ashley looked at Granny for reassurance. The old woman gave a slight nod. Her posture was straight, unbowed and determined. Ashley wished she felt the same way.

It was difficult for her to ignore the frightening presence of Ricci and the panther.

The room itself was intimidating. There was a sense of decadent luxuriousness about it that was somehow unsettling. The bookshelves behind Mr. Chirac's desk were lined with old volumes. Titles engraved along their spines with gold ink calligraphy. One nearly two inches thick in the middle of the shelf bound with a thin, creamy white leather the color of a young child's neck. Overcome by a sense of morbid horror, Ashley rose to take a closer look.

"You should sit down," Ricci said. "He likes it when he comes back to a room and everything is the way he left it."

"I just want to see the titles on the books," she said, pointing to the shelves.

"Not a good idea."

Ashley sat down again. She wondered what power Mr. Chirac held over this brutish man.

"Thanks for not saying nothing about what the old woman said," he added. "I owe you one."

«« — »»

When he returned, Mr. Chirac carried a wood and glass box inlaid with brass knobs and needle gauges that looked like they were taken from a Civil War submarine. It was three feet high and though it must have been heavy, he carried it effortlessly across the thick champagne colored carpet. Ashley saw that Mr. Chirac's feet left no impression. How could Michael have dealt with this man?

Granny never took her eyes off Mr. Chirac. She seemed to have no interest in the ghost box itself.

Ashley risked a glance toward Ricci and saw that he hadn't moved. Hands folded in front of him because his power lifter's physique made it impossible for him to fold them behind his back. What had he done? How did he come to be manservant to this dark man called Mr. Chirac?

The panther lay down again. It was staring at her, head resting on its paws. Yellow-green eyes fixed on her. Its sleek fur rippled with an involuntary muscle spasm. Ashley watched as the big cat licked a front paw, and then extended its claws. She had never seen a panther's claws, but her breath hitched when she considered what they could do to a human being.

"How unfortunate that your fear of Lily distracts you from this magnificent piece," Mr. Chirac said as he set down the ghost box on one end of the long desk. "Yet she so longs for the comforts of human conversation that I could not deny her. Your husband fell under her spell. He was a man who understood neither beauty nor danger, but was drawn imprudently to the precipice of both. But now, to the conclusion of our agreement. I have displayed this ghost box before you, now show me the madstone."

Ashley stared at the ghost box. The reality of what it was eluded her. Could it really bring back the dead?

Granny nudged her.

Could it really bring back Michael? She couldn't stop a sudden flashback to the dream-visions of her husband drifting, through darkness, pleading for help, screaming to be saved.

"Child?" prompted Granny. "This man would like to see the madstone."

"Yes, yes of course."

Ian and Granny had coached her many times on this, the crucible moment. But that moment was now, and it was everything she could do to keep her hands from shaking as she picked up Alvarez's briefcase and laid it on its side at the other end of Chirac's desk.

"It's inside," she said and sat back down, holding her breath for fear she would lose control.

"Open it if you please," said Mr. Chirac. "I do not open that which I have not closed."

Ashley got up again and unsnapped the lashes on the briefcase. Both Ian and Granny had instructed her not to go around to Mr. Chirac's side of the desk when she did it. She took a deep breath, and then lifted the lid open on its hinges.

As she sat down again, Mr. Chirac said, "Please do not provoke me, Mrs. Hillis. Unfold the cloth so that I may see the contents. Pray that I am not displeased."

This time, Ashley, unfolded the cloth, revealing the dirt within. She looked at the dirt, was about to sit down, keeping her eyes downcast as Ian had told her to do, when she lifted her head to stare directly into Mr. Chirac's eyes

"It's there, in the dirt where it belongs. We're done now. I'm leaving with the ghost box. That was the agreement you made with my husband and if it's binding on me, it's binding on you."

Granny grabbed her hand and squeezed.

"Reach your fingers into this dirt and take it out for me to affirm," said Mr. Chirac, his face purpling with rage.

Granny interrupted.

"You have to do that yourself," she said without rising. "She's brought it to you, it's yours now. But I wouldn't advise digging it out."

Mr. Chirac strode over to within a foot of where Granny stood. Ashley moved over to stand closer to the old woman. She felt the raw fury building inside the man and was afraid they would never leave his house.

Granny stood, opened her collar and took out her necklace with its row of five tiny twisted stick men. She fingered them as she spoke.

"Cause my madstone is pressed in between the bones of a little girl been dead a long time. We put it there to hold down her haint, what some call a screaming spirit. If some fool were to remove that stone, why the screaming spirit would burn them alive. This old woman knows the dead real well and the good Lord help whoever would set that haint free."

Mr. Chirac's face purpled with rage.

"You dare mock me in my home? Do you not know who I am?"

"Oh but I do. I know the dead real well, and I can hear them calling for you. They knows they own and they won't ever rest 'til they bring them back home."

Mr. Chirac's face began to change. Ashley saw it but couldn't believe it. Something beneath the surface of his skin with hot red eyes burning with a rage as hot as the haint's.

Chapter Forty

"How long they been in there?" Kenneth asked.

Ian checked his cell phone.

"Twenty five minutes."

"I wish Enid would get back. Waiting out here gives me the creeps. Ain't right Granny being in there without me. Her and Ashley all alone in the house with two strange men and a tiger. It ain't right."

"Panther," Ian said.

"It don't make no difference. They're in danger is all I'm saying."

"Yeah, I know."

Sitting in the car and doing nothing was wearing on him. The tension made it impossible to think. His mind kept looking through negative scenarios. He couldn't seem to shut it off.

The night was cold and silent. No wind, no driving rain, no portents of disaster. That was the worst. The storms were contained within his mind.

Enid was out scouting the perimeter, looking for a way into a house. Shotgun and night vision goggles, a grim look on his face. He disappeared within moments of leaving the car and hadn't come back.

The colt pistol felt heavy on his lap. How did he get here? Sitting outside of a house on Blood Road in the middle of nowhere somewhere past midnight with a loaded gun. Kenneth and Enid ready to bust down the front door and start shooting.

The back door of the vehicle opened and the interior light came on. Enid slid in and closed the door. After a few seconds, the light faded and then disappeared.

"What'd you find?" Kenneth asked.

"I don't exactly know," Enid said.

Ian turned to look at him. In the gray light that filtered through the film covered windows, his face was drawn with frustration.

"What's that mean?" Kenneth asked.

"It means I don't know. This whole building is like Fort Knox. There ain't no way in, brother. No windows, no doors except this one here in front. It's like a prison. And I been thinking about it. I don't think we can get through that front door unless it's open. It's like this whole damned place was made to keep everybody out except who they let in."

"What we going to do?" Kenneth asked.

"We wait," Ian said.

"That front door is big enough," Enid said. "If it don't open on time, we drive through the fucking thing."

«« — »»

"You have to honor your agreements," Ashley shouted. "You are bound to honor your agreements."

Granny had said as much to her on the way over. He had to. He had to. Everything depended on that one fact.

Within seconds, Mr. Chirac brought himself under control. The hideous visage was gone. There was no sign of the rage Ashley had seen moments before. It was as though it had never happened.

"Girl's right," Granny said.

Mr. Chirac walked over to where Ricci stood, glanced down at the panther, who barred its teeth and then returned to his desk but did not sit down.

"So clever, so very clever," he mused.

With his left hand, he opened the desk drawer, withdrew a piece of paper, stared at it a moment, then methodically tore it into tiny pieces which he pushed into a pile.

"Your obligation to me is complete," he said to Ashley. "You have indeed delivered the madstone. But I will not give you the ghost box."

"Not quite done," Granny said. Her fingers wove complex patterns as she spoke. "You are now bound to tell anyone else who you trick into taking the madstone out of that little girl's remains what will happen to them if they do."

Ashley felt disoriented, disconnected from herself. The room seemed to flicker as Granny spoke. She looked at the old woman's fingers moving in and out, intertwining with each other. One over the other, another over another. Mr. Chirac stared at Granny, his eyes unfocused as though dazed.

"So you are bound now and forever," Granny said softly, then dropped her hands to her sides.

Mr. Chirac seemed to be in a trance; he began to fall forward but then caught himself.

"What have you done?" he said. "Tell me what you have done. Tell me this minute."

"I have bound you," Granny smiled innocently.

"You cannot, you have not the power. Do you think you can provoke me without consequence? Go now. Leave empty handed before it is too late."

"But you have to keep your agreement," Ashley insisted. "You have to."

He smiled at her, and then laughed at her like she was a foolish child.

"I will do nothing of the kind. Leave now. Ricci will escort you to the door."

Ashley couldn't believe what she was hearing. She had to have the ghost box. Had to. She couldn't leave without it or everything was lost, but what could they do? Everything for nothing.

"You have to keep the agreement," Ricci said.

Ashley, Granny, and Mr. Chirac turned at the unexpected voice. Ricci stood where he was, his face void of feeling.

"I got two years left on our agreement, and if you don't keep your agreement with her, how do I know you'll keep the agreement you have with me?"

Ashley suddenly felt the menace emanating from the far side of the room. The chained panther was suddenly up on all fours and snarling. Ricci's implied challenge. The tension in the room was palpable. She looked at Granny, but could not read her face.

"Our agreement is separate from mine with these people," Mr. Chirac said.

There was an edge to his voice that terrified Ashley.

"You break one, you can break another," Ricci said.

"Do you see what you have done?" Mr. Chirac hissed at Ashley. "Now you involve my servant. I will not tolerate this. I will not yield to you. The ghost box is mine. I will not be provoked or questioned. Ricci, escort them to the door, and then you and I will discuss again the nature of your obligation to me."

"Not without what they came for," Ricci said.

Mr. Chirac withdrew a gold letter opener from the desk drawer and ran its blade across the back of his hand. Without looking up, he asked, "And how do you propose to persuade me to do as you ask? What is your offer?"

He waited, head inclined, staring at the blade. Interested now in what Ricci would offer. Ashley wondered what he was thinking. Confident, he was always confident.

She heard a metallic sound, and turned her head. Mr. Chirac looked up and stared, confused fear in his eyes.

Ricci now stood next to the panther holding a key ring, swinging it back and forth. The panther was on all fours, looking directly at Mr. Chirac. Ricci selected one particular key and then went down on one knee as he stroked the animal's neck.

Without looking up at Mr. Chirac, he said, "Deal?"

When Mr. Chirac didn't respond, Ricci inserted the key in the panther's shiny metal collar. The animal began to growl, a low threatening sound. It pawed the floor in anticipation.

"Wait," Mr. Chirac said. "We have an agreement."

《《—》》

Ian took the ghost box covered in a black cloth and put it behind the backseat, securing it with elastic straps. He held onto the edge to keep it steady during the drive. Enid slid in next to him and Kenneth took the wheel. Granny would sit between them and Ashley would ride up front.

The two women stood outside the car talking to the big, bulky man who had let them in. Ian rolled the window down an inch to hear what they were saying.

"Will you be all right?" Ashley asked the man. "What will he do to you? Why don't you come with us? Please. That was so brave what you did."

"I been in prison, I live in Hell," he said. "Go home. Take that thing with you and make it mean something."

"But you can't go back in there."

"Lady, did it ever occur to you I deserve to be in there?"

Before she could respond, he turned and walked away.

"Get in the car," Granny said, "we ain't done tonight."

"But—"

"Hurry," Ian said. "We have to hurry."

Chapter Forty-One

Enid put the ghost box on the cherry wood dining room table. He carried it like a priceless antique vase, although it felt like it weighed nearly a hundred pounds. The walk from Ashley's SUV felt like the longest walk in a long lifetime of too-long journeys. But they'd done it. They'd got the one thing in the world that might shut down Magnus Hillis and his underground army.

He remembered Bartok, and thought, *Old friend if only you were here to see this. That nephew of yours done you proud tonight.*

"Lock the doors," he heard Ian say. "Granny showed me the security door you used when the haint fire-balled the glass. Every one of those you have, Ashley, bolt them up."

"What are you thinking?" Kenneth asked.

"He's thinking we might be getting a visit from that Chirac. Ain't that right, Ian?"

"Yes. And I don't know who or what he is, but we'd better barricade ourselves in fast as we can, and turn this thing on in case he comes after us."

"We'll take care of it," Kenneth said. "Granny, you stay here with Ian and Enid if you would. Ashley, lead on and let's get it done."

When they were gone, Enid looked at Ian and asked, "You're sure you know how to work this thing?"

Ian had Bartok's journals spread next to the device on the table, comparing diagrams and checking the knobs. He looked up at Enid's question and said, "No. I'm trying to figure that out now from Uncle Bartok's notes and Taylor Hunter's journals. But Enid, you and I have come through hell in the last few days, and you know damn well I'm going to be making this up as I go along so give me a break, will you?"

Enid rubbed his jaw. He knew Ian didn't know shit, but the young man had done all right so far. Bartok was right. He was smart. Maybe he had enough IQ points left to finish the job.

"How about if I make us some coffee while you try to figure this thing out in peace and quiet?"

"That won't work," Granny said. "We got to be on the lookout in case that dark man comes calling tonight. You're a better shot than this old woman. I'll make the coffee and prowl around and make sure we're safe."

"How much you afraid of this man, Granny?" Enid asked.

"I ain't afraid at all for myself. I'm afraid for you and the others."

Enid considered what she said. He'd never understood the old woman. Never knew really what a granny woman was. Never wondered about it. There weren't hardly any doctors in the hollers where he grew up. They didn't like riding the hills, and Enid couldn't really blame them. He'd just known there wasn't anyone else to go to when sickness came except the granny women and their herbs and charms. Besides, hill people didn't much trust outsiders. But he'd never been to one himself except once when he was stricken with a high fever. His parents were afraid he was dying and they'd bundled him off to an old woman that to this day he couldn't remember.

"You want a gun or knife?" he asked.

"Child, I don't need nothing like that, but you ought never to be without a weapon. You sleep with it under your pillow or next to your bed, Enid Mozer, because you ain't never going to be safe another day in your life until that dark man is put down. Same with the others. You remember what old Granny says. Now I'll go brew some of that coffee. I ain't got much rest lately and I'm too old for this. Go on. Get going."

"Yes ma'am," he said.

He wandered the halls, checking doors and windows. Thinking about what Granny had said. Neither her or Ashley had said much on the way home. Nothing that made a lick's worth of sense. Crying over that big hulk of a man that let them through the front door like they was losing a brother or something. The man looked like a convict. One of those scary people they had on TV sometimes on America's Most Wanted til they closed that down.

Kenneth showed up ten minutes into Enid's search with coffee. One cup for Enid, another for himself.

"How you holding up, brother?" Kenneth asked.

"Hanging in," Enid replied. "Lay-down dog tired, but that's about normal these days."

"Me, I can't quit thinking about that policeman hanging in the dark, burning like he was soaked with gasoline and lit on fire."

"Yeah, ain't seen nothing like that before. Thanks for the coffee. I need to stay awake tonight if I ever needed to in my life. Hey, can we set the alarms for an intrusion trip?"

They were headed for the connecting door between the garage and the breezeway leading to the house to check it again.

"Ain't happening, Enid. Haint blew out that one window frame and fried the alarm system. Best I could do was lock them metal security doors over the opening and sweep up the glass."

The door to the breezeway was locked and bolted. Metal security doors were slid into place and secured. Enid thought it was time to go back and check on the others.

"Granny told me something I didn't like," Kenneth said as they headed back. "She said whatever happened to her tonight, I wasn't to pay it no mind."

"Say what?"

"You heard me. Said I was to stay here and look after Ashley. She wouldn't answer no questions either. Just told me to keep out of it, no matter what happened."

"Damn," Enid said.

Understanding that old woman was like trying to hang on to a wet catfish with your bare hands.

"Sorry about Bartok and Rake," Kenneth said.

"That haint killed my brother and that thing down in the caves killed Bartok. Haints back in the ground and tonight we going to turn that old box on and drain that thing underground until it bleeds to death."

"We all in this together," Kenneth said. "I knowed you since you was eight years old and I ain't going to let you down. We was raised the same year in the Lodge, brother. We hill people and Lodge brothers. So I got your back. You remember that tonight."

As they walked into the living room, Enid Mozer, who had secrets to hide more than most, thought what a strange man Kenneth Hillis was.

«« — »»

Ian saw them return. Two mountain men carrying shotguns with a grim set to their jaws. Two weeks ago if someone would have told him what he'd being doing tonight and who he would be doing it with, he would have thought they were crazy.

"We all locked down?" he asked Enid.

"Tight as we can be. You ready to do it?"

"Best I can be," Ian said.

Ashley and Granny Hillis were sitting at two chairs on the far end of the table. Ashley's hands were clasped together on the table and she looked worried. Ian stood in front of the ghost box and felt the same way. Granny reached over and patted Ashley's hands.

"I checked for text messages," Enid said. "Nothing. Tried calling again, but got the damned voice mail. I'd say we got trouble. So let's get going."

"Ashley says that Mr. Chirac told her the machine is only good for one more try. I don't know if that's the truth or not, but when Magnus Hillis first used the machine, according to Taylor Hunter's journal, it took him a long time to make contact with someone on the other side to facilitate the transfer of ectoplasmic energy to our world."

"What did he just say?" Kenneth asked Enid.

Ian answered before Enid could respond.

"I don't know if anyone will ever understand this thing exactly, but the best I can come up with is that it transfers energy from one dimension or plane of existence to another. The crashed ship was like an advance guard for the aliens. Bartok as much as said they went from one galaxy to the next to tap into the energy of the dead in that system. Think of it this way. We each have a certain life energy. When we die, that energy, maybe our soul maybe our energetic patterns, moves to another dimension—what we call the afterlife. Energy is never created or destroyed; it just changes back and forth from matter, that's what scientists have thought for quite a while. But what if when we die our life energy is able to move through a sort of inter-dimensional barrier to reappear on the other side? All the energy of all the dead would be there. That's what the aliens were harvesting. They used the energy of the dead as a source of power."

"Uh-huh," Kenneth said.

"We do the same, in a way," Ian said. "We take coal and we burn it. It's dead, but we use its energy as power. We take that from the means of its external form. But there's an internal energetic pattern within every living creature. What if, instead of simply dissipating after death, it goes to an-other dimension? That dimension would be filled with energy. Every living thing dies, Kenneth, and if I'm right, all that energy can be tapped. With this device, with this ghost box, it can be channeled through to our own dimension. The ghost box is a miniature of the alien technology that drove their ship. Do you see what I'm saying?"

Kenneth looked extremely uncomfortable. "I guess so," he said finally. "But I was never good in things like science."

"Ashley? Enid? Granny?"

"Let's just do it," Enid said. "We can catch up with the understanding later. We're in deep shit here and I don't think we got much time to stop it from getting a hell of a lot deeper."

"I guess you're right. I'm about at the limits of my thoughts on the mat-ter anyway."

He turned a page in Taylor Hunter's journal, looked at the settings and reached for the first knob.

"Wait," Ashley said, "I won't let you do this. It's my ghost box and if it's only got one use left I want you to use it to save my husband."

Chapter Forty-Two

"We don't have time for this, damn it," Enid said.

Ashley was on her feet, moving over to confront Ian.

"You're worried about saving the world, but what about Michael? He's trapped on the other side being torn apart by the dead. I hear him screaming for help in my dreams. We've got to save him."

Ian didn't know what to do.

"Ashley," he said finally, "I'm sorry about your husband, but I don't think we have a choice here. If those things get loose, thousands of people could be hurt or killed. Maybe more. You've never seen them, I have. You never saw what they did to Enid's dog or to my uncle Bartok, but believe me, if you'd seen even a glimpse of what I've seen, you would agree with me. We have to stop those things."

"No. I will not let you leave my husband in that other world. You don't even know what's going on down there. So Enid has lost contact. Maybe there's something wrong with the cell towers. Maybe there was a solar flare. I don't know and you don't know. But you can't use my machine unless you're trying to save my husband."

"Please, Ashley."

"No. Save my husband. My whole life's been torn from me. You've seen some of what I've been through since you got here. But you weren't there that first night with me at Sharkey's Park. The death. The horror. I can't live with this anymore. I need my husband back."

He looked to Granny for help, but she gave him no answers. Just looked at him expectantly. But before he could come up with a solution, the situation changed. Enid raised his shotgun and pointed it at them.

"We're going to settle this right now," he said. "Ian you do what we set out to do. Ashley you go sit down. Go on. This here's loaded with double ought buck and it ain't pretty what it can do."

He waved it at Ashley, motioning her to go back to her chair.

"Put that thing down," Ian said.

"No, sir. Bartok and my brother didn't die for nothing."

"This isn't the way," Ian tried.

"It's the only way I know," Enid said.

But when Kenneth slipped his knife under Enid's chin and held it to his throat, the situation changed again.

"Careful, brother," Kenneth said. "You just put that thing down. Nobody has to get hurt. We all under a lot of stress here, but we got to think clear thinking."

"This is the second damned time in less than a week I had somebody sneak up and stick a knife to my throat. I'm getting damned tired of it. This time I ain't backing down."

In a voice so low Ian could barely hear it, Kenneth said, "Ain't you learned nothing from them years you spent in Viet Nam? Ain't you learned yet there's other ways than the barrel of a gun?"

But Enid's shotgun didn't waiver.

"What's every Mason looking for in their life, brother? More light. Not more dark."

Ashley stepped toward them and said to Enid, "What would you do if it was your wife?"

"Ain't married."

"What would you do if it was one of your brothers?"

"Don't know. All I do know is my kin been protecting everybody for all these years and when it finally comes time to finish the job, I ain't letting it slip away. So you best go sit down."

"You done swore a Masonic oath, brother," Kenneth said, the knife still hard against Enid's throat. "And here you is waving a shotgun and another Mason's kin? This ain't what you signed up for."

Enid closed his eyes.

"Now I'm going to take this knife away, and go set it on the chair behind us. Then you show me how a Mason does his business."

Slowly, Kenneth pulled the knife away and put it on the chair. Enid opened his eyes and lowered the shotgun.

"You a fine man," Granny told him.

"We got to do something," Enid said. "Tyree and Johnny ain't checked in, Granny. I'm thinking they're dead."

"They is," she said. "I can feel it, too. The evil done rose up and took them into the earth."

Granny turned to Ashley.

"Now child, it's time for you to clean out what's between your ears. You say you want that worthless husband of yours back, but you know better. You heard what that big man Ricci said when we was leaving that awful place tonight? He said he deserved to be where he was. Where do you think in your heart Michael deserves to be? I told you before and I ain't ever lied to you. Michael's gone. When the living is pulled through to the dead, they mind is gone. They ain't right anymore. You try to bring your man back and what you'll get will be a monster. Where do you want that monster to be?"

Ashley broke down and began to sob.

"I need him, Granny. I need him. My life is so empty now. I can't go on like this."

"Child, you write all them books, don't you? Think why you do that. You surround yourself with people that ain't there. You make them talk, you make them answer. But they ain't there. Tell me the truth, child, didn't you spend so much time with them imaginary people you didn't know who you was married to? You knew how bad he was, didn't you?"

"I don't know. I can't think. You want me to give away the only part of my life that ever made sense and I can't do it."

Time slipped away as Ashley stood trying to decide. Ian felt they were balanced on the edge of a dangerous precipice.

"She's too much like her husband," Enid said. "We're done."

"What did you say?" Ashley demanded.

"I said you're like Michael. All hell can break loose as long as you're getting what you want. And if you bring him back through that thing, Granny says you'll be getting a monster. But you can't let it go. You're like him."

The comparison horrified Ashley.

"No, I'm not."

"Then show us you mean what you say."

She searched their faces. The last one of them she looked at was Kenneth.

"What would you do?" she asked. "I trust you. What would you do?"

Kenneth scratched the top of his head.

"It ain't much of a choice is what I think. Save a monster or save the world."

She thought about it. Ricci's words came back to her.

"Do it," she said. "Save the world."

«« — »»

When he'd adjusted the knobs to the positions in Taylor Hunter's journal, Ian stepped back. The ghost box began to hum. He heard static. The scratchy sound of white noise filled the room. The tiny mirrors within the casing lit with an unearthly light.

Like a psychomanteum, Ian thought. Endless reflections bouncing back and forth where the light folded in upon itself. Enid had turned the dimmer switch down to lower the lights in the room. Shadows gathered in the corner to observe.

The others stood around the table, their attention riveted upon the apparatus. Granny alone seemed disinterested.

"Is it working?" Enid asked.

Ian held up Taylor Hunter's journal. It was this next part that made him nervous.

"I've got to say the words that Magnus Hillis did. But I don't know if that will make it do what we want it to do. The enchantment that he spoke was to draw the energy of the dead to our side of the dimension. We want to do the reverse."

"Do you know how to do it?" Ashley asked.

"I have a theory. It's a common practice with incantational magic. You say the words forward and one thing happens. If you say them in reverse and you get the opposite effect. But I don't know for sure if it works that way. I just don't know."

"What if something terrible happens?"

"We have to try anyway," he said. "Enid was right. Too many people have died trying to stop what's happening back in Kentucky. We have to try."

That was when the lights within the ghost box dimmed. Only a softly emanative glow remained, like the last coal of a dying fire.

"What happened?" Kenneth asked.

"It only had a little power left," Ashley said. "That's what Mr. Chirac said. This is terrible. He's going to win and everyone else will lose."

Not knowing what else to do, Ian tapped the sides with the palm of his right hand. Nothing happened. The light within the ghost box's psychomanteum structure was dim.

"Hit it again," Enid said.

"I think maybe I need to shut it down before we lose whatever power it's got so I can take it apart and see how to boost it maybe with an additional power source."

"You think that will work?"

"Enid, I don't even know the operational principal for this thing. It's alien technology mixed with nineteenth century tools. I don't know what's going to be inside. Wires? Who knows? They didn't have circuit boards back then so I really don't know until I open it up."

"We're dead."

"No, we're not. I know a little about technology so let's see what I can come up with? What else can we do?"

They were all quiet. Ian felt a sense of dread creeping in. Who was he kidding? He might know something about computers and electrical equipment, but he hadn't gotten his degree in alien technology. It was Granny who finally broke the silence as he was reaching for the knobs to shut it down.

"Don't do that," she said. "Listen to me instead."

He pulled his hand back.

"I'm willing to try anything to stop those things underground from breaking out," he said.

She got up and walked over to him.

"You seen a lot in a little while, ain't you?"

"I have, Granny."

"You believe in ghosts now?"

"I do."

"Why is that? Tell this old woman why."

"Because ... because I've seen one."

"You believe in aliens now?"

"Yes, I've seen the evidence for that, too."

She lay her hand on his shoulder affectionately and patted him like she would a child.

"Now I'm going to ask you to believe in something you ain't seen. I'm going to ask you to do something on faith. Do you trust me, young man?"

"I do."

"That's a start. A little trust in another person, can lead someday to bigger faith. So you close your eyes. I'm going to lay my hand on your forehead. Go ahead, do what I say."

"What's this got to do with—"

"Answer me."

"Okay, yes I trust you, but I don't see how it's going to help."

"That's fine. Now close your eyes."

He felt her hand on his forehead. It was a dry touch of a woman who'd outlived most. Cool. Calming.

"Now," she said, "you think of what you saw in that cave. Remember it; remember every little thing about it you can. It will link you to that place."

The image of Albert Magnus Hillis came to him with shocking clarity. He could see the wild, silvered eyes, the straggly black hair that hung down over his shoulders and the severed arms and legs plugged in to the glassine tubes of pulsing light. And he was shocked to feel that Magnus Hillis knew he was seeing him. Ian widened his mental view and Magnus grew smaller. He could now see the rows of mechanical soldiers, but in his vision, they were moving now. Organizing. Building something he couldn't make out. Something that hurt him to see, something so alien he had to turn his mental eye away from it or he thought he would lose his mind. The cavern air was truly alive with tiny palls of light that lit the rock walls and the terrifying things within. It was as though millions of fireflies had filled the cabin.

A soft melody filled his mind, and he realized that in stark contrast to his nightmare vision, Granny was humming.

Brass-hued mechanical soldiers gathered around the suspended Magnus Hillis, and Ian was drawn to the sight. As he grew closer, he saw that they carried mechanical arms and legs.

Magnus stared directly at him and Ian saw the beginnings of an insane smile.

"They're going to take him down," he shouted.

He opened his eyes to free himself from the vision.

"You done good," Granny said. "Bartok would be proud."

"You don't understand. The mechanical men are going to—"

"Hush," she said, then turned to Kenneth. "Goodbye, Kenneth. You remember what I told you."

She placed her hands on the ghost box and began to pray.

The room plunged into total darkness.

A moment later, it was filled with a soft white light. Granny Hillis's entire body glowed and the ghost box's psychomanteum interior burst into brilliant colors. The air thickened. Granny became an oval of white. Ian and the others stepped back, moved to the edges of the room filled with terrified awe. A molten cloud of red and yellow light appeared on the ceiling above her and they heard the sound of turbulent water rushing through the room. From within the cloud, as though birthed, the head of a spectral face came through. Distorted, anguished mouth and vacant eyes the color of pale mushrooms. Stretched thin like ghostly smoke.

It flew towards the oval light and passed through it and into the ghost box. Another spirit appeared, and then another from within the cloud. One after the other they were drawn toward the light and into the ghost box. Ian watched in disbelief as a milky white fluid fell toward the floor and disappeared before striking it. On and on they came. He would never know how many spirits came through that night, but each of them were pulled through the light and into the ghost box to disappear. The ectoplasmic energy that would have powered Magnus Hillis's automatonic army disappeared with them.

Ian looked toward the others and saw their shock and amazement.

When it was finally finished, the cloud disappeared and so did Granny Hillis. They were left standing dumfounded and alone.

Epilogue

"I got something to give you," Enid said.

He took one hand off the steering wheel and handed Ian a folded up letter that he took from his back pocket.

"It's from Bartok," he explained.

They were on the way to the Knights Inn to pick up their belongings and figure out what to do next. Enid had to go back to Kentucky to, as he said, set things right and Ian wasn't sure what to do yet. First on his list was finding a new place to live. He couldn't stay in the Knights Inn forever.

It was one o'clock in the afternoon on a cold bright day. The worn-out freeway stretched ahead of them like it would never end.

He took the letter and stared at it a moment before ripping the envelope open. It was two pages long. They drove in silence as he read it.

"You think they'll be okay?" Enid asked.

"What?"

"Ashley and Kenneth. You think they'll be okay what with that Mr. Chirac still mad at them. They got to be careful."

"I hope so. Kenneth's a hard guy to read, but he can take care of himself and he won't let anything happen to Ashley."

"It won't look good," Enid said, "what with them both being widowed and living together."

Ian couldn't help but smile.

"They'll take care of each other."

"You going to tell me what it said in the letter?"

"Uncle Bartok said it isn't over. There's more to do."

"Huh."

"He said we need to go to Atlanta to find a woman named Hathaway. He gave us her address. He said if I'm up to it, she'll explain the rest of it. Said he was sorry, too, about pushing me away."

"That it?"

"He said it was wrong and he hoped I'd forgive him. He said he'd probably be dead when I read this."

"And?"

"And he said he was proud of me and sorry he took so long to say it."

"Huh. What's this about what he wants you to do?"

They came to their exit. Enid flipped the turn signal and started to turn. Hotel and motel signs lined the road up ahead.

"He says there's another ship."

"Damn his hide. I knew it."

Ian grinned and said, "You up for a trip to Atlanta?"

««—»»

Pitch black.

The vast emptiness of the cavern was encased in silence. Nothing moved. The rows of mechanical soldiers were invisible. The stagnant air no longer fluoresced. It was now cold and dead. The plated door hung shriveled like shed snakeskin. The back wall that blocked in the alien ship no longer pulsed with alien light.

In that sterile blackness the body of Magnus Hillis hung like a dead spider in a world of eternal darkness.

The months passed like a silent pronouncement of judgment.

But one black December night, his eyelids lifted and the bright metal orbs of his eyes sparked a sudden silver and glowed like an alien jack-o-lantern.

He hung there, screaming.

Forever alone.

Forever insane.

About The Author

Ferrel Moore is a Michigan writer specializing in dark fiction. His stories have appeared over the years in anthologies from Elder Signs Press and Sams Dot Publishing. A lifelong passion for the martial arts and esoteric pursuits frequently find their way into his writing.

He is the Author of *Tainted Blood*, published by White Cat Publications, LLC. Currently, he is working on the sequel to *Tainted Blood*, which is tentatively titled *The White Death*.

You can contact him via his blog at:
http://thewriterandthewhitecat.blogspot.com